Dry Run, Oklahoma
a novel

Lucinda Stein

First Edition

Printed in Charleston, SC

ISBN-13: 978-1546704553 ISBN-10:
1546704558

Other Books by the Author

Minnie's Antique & Curiosity Shoppe

Jadeite's Journey
a young adult novel by Inkspell Publishing

Sanctuary: Family, Friends, & Strangers
a 2015 Colorado Book Award finalist

Spiral of Darkness

Tattered Covers

Three Threads Woven
a 2010 WILLA finalist

Maggie's Way: The Story of a Defiant Pioneer Woman
Western Reflections Publishing

To Rob,

who loved his Comanche grandmother.

Introduction

My husband's beloved Comanche grandmother, Osie Tahsuda Carney, inspired this story. The tale of Belle Tahsuda in my story is not a retelling of Osie Tahsuda's life. Rather, I wanted to write about Oklahoma during the time period in which she lived, the struggle of being Indian in the first half of the twentieth century, and life during the Depression. The effects of the Dust Bowl were most severe in the Oklahoma Panhandle, but the drought years definitely affected the rest of the state as portrayed in Dry Run, Oklahoma.

After a brief trip to Oklahoma in 2012, my husband and I visited with his second cousin, Ray Tahsuda, and his wife, Dorothy, in Anadarko. We took an extra day out of our schedule and traveled to his grandmother's home place, which still stands near Quinton. My husband recalls many pleasant memories spent with his grandparents during the hot Oklahoma summers. To this day, he misses his grandmother.

After we returned to Colorado, the idea for this story slowly began to percolate. Through research, I became better acquainted with the Oklahoma of the 1920s and 30s. A few scenes in the book come from family stories. My husband's great-great-grandmother did dress her son as a girl before entering Fort Sill. The story of the Comanche woman slashing the bear's paws was handed down from Osie Tahsuda, as was her insistence of blood connection to the infamous Quanah Parker. I hope Osie would be pleased with my humble effort to portray this time period and the proud people who call themselves Comanche.

Belle

TO HER CHAGRIN, BELLE STILWELL was known as the Scorned Wasápe—the Comanche word for bear—the widow whose husband died chasing another woman. Despite the decades that had passed since that unforgettable event. Despite the fact she remarried and had lived among the gossipers for years.

People have long memories. But she had to admit, it was more likely the label just stuck. Only those closest to her knew Belle had chased her husband until she nearly died herself. But before she ever chased, she ran…

Chapter 1

-1923-

THE AFTERNOON SUN BLAZED OVERHEAD as eight-year-old Belle Tahsuda raced down the dirt road, dust spinning at her feet. An owl shrieked, and Belle's black braids swung as she turned to the eerie sound. Her dark arms pumped as humidity pressed against her chest like wooden clamps on Grandfather's workbench. The orange-peel scent of a crushed hedge apple lifted on the breeze. Another screech pierced the air in an odd, high-pitched whinny. Her grandfather hated screech owls. He always looked over his shoulder when the birds were around, swore they were a bad omen.

She ran to meet her father, who would be coming soon with the horse and wagon. He always brought her something from town. A piece of hard candy. A red ribbon for her hair. She'd wait for him at the bridge where the late September day resembled summer more than autumn.

Belle lived with her father, grandmother, and Grandfather Tahsuda on their allotment of 180 acres in south-central Oklahoma.

Her Comanche grandmother shook her head at Belle's constant running. Belle would smile and tell her, "Every day is a good day when you run."

"Careful, now." The beginning of a smile betrayed her grandmother's admonishment. "Don't wear those skinny legs to a point."

Belle loved running. She could run in any direction, fast or slow, uphill or across ditches. Whatever she chose. She'd fight the wind or turn and let the wind give her wings. Alert to the passing scenery, she watched for rabbits, birds, and sometimes deer. Let others slog through life, not Belle.

Overhead, robin's-egg blue stretched forever, and a few lone clouds strayed to the north. The thud of footfalls rang as her shoes slapped the dirt. What she loved most was the power of her legs, limited only by the strength of her lungs.

Water rushed down the creek that wove through the brambles. She panted. Her leg muscles contracted. Lost in thought, it took a moment for Belle to remember that the slow, meandering creek was usually silent. She hugged the curve in the road and sped to where the water emerged from the trees. The growing burn in her lungs came as a welcome challenge to the practiced little runner, but the reddish-brown water brought her to a dead stop. That and the churning moan of the creek. The tranquil stream with its soft whisper of water had shape-shifted into a whirling wild beast. The rising water threatened to break over the bank.

She stood panting. Logs bobbed in the silty syrup of water and sank again. Planed wood plunged violently below the surface and pitched back into the air. The sharp bite of teeth against her bottom lip prodded her into action, and she raced ahead. She spotted a misshapen form, dark and wet, that blasted down the swollen creek. Her mind lagged until she made sense of it. Then her stomach sank like the helpless wood in the water. The black creature coursed down the surging creek, the dead horse swept away.

Belle forced her legs to pump faster and catch up with her rapid breath. Arms swung at her sides and propelled her up the road. She raced a quarter of a mile to where the wooden bridge crossed the water. The familiar point of the creek came into view. She tripped. On her knees, Belle stared at the spot where the bridge should have been.

The next morning, her grandparents ate their breakfast in silence. Grandfather finished his last cup of coffee—his favorite, Hills Brothers Coffee with a tablespoon of sugar. Grandmother cleared the table.

"Do you think the flood kept Father in town?" Belle studied the familiar corners of her grandmother's mouth, the creases between her eyebrows, and the cloaked eyelids. "He might be helping people upstream. Isn't that right?"

"Time will tell, Arabella." Grandmother Tahsuda stared out the window.

Belle followed her glance but saw only trees across the road. Her grandmother's wrinkled brow frightened her. "Maybe he has to take a long way home because of the flood." She fidgeted in her chair. "Couldn't that be?"

"Time will tell, child," she repeated. "Do your chores."

From the porch, Belle gazed at the empty road. She shuffled into the barn, hoping her father would appear from behind a stack of hay in his overalls and straw hat. Belle mucked the stalls, one of her morning chores. Dust motes swirled in the weak light as she shoveled manure. With the pitchfork, she tossed fresh hay for the milk cow. Outside, she flung chicken seed over the dirt. The familiar bok bok bok of the multicolored fowl rose as the flock rushed forward and pecked the earth.

She finished her tasks and headed for the smokehouse. The hardwood building, the size of three outhouses, had been built without windows or chimney. Despite the lack of smoke oozing from the door, she imagined her father placing chunks of beef into brine-filled wooden barrels. The smell of smoked meat permeated the shed's exterior. She opened the door.

Her heart leapt at the shadowy figure in the center of the building. Her eyes adjusted to the dark, and her shoulders slumped. It was a ham hanging from the rafter—a ham the size of a man's head. She shut the door and kicked the ground. She needed to run.

Belle flew down the road. Her father might be driving home this morning, the dappled gray horse, Charlie, trotting in high steps. He'd pull the gelding to a stop upon seeing her, leap from the saddle, and take her into his arms with a deep laugh. She couldn't wait to hug his neck.

Gray mist swirled through trees along the creek and snaked above the elevated water. She was careful to avoid the side of the road where the creek ran. The words her grandfather spoke the night before rang in her ears.

"It's an evil spirit that makes a creek flood under a blue sky." Grandfather Tahsuda's braids hung at the sides of his sullen face and fell to his chest. His lips drooped at the corners.

Uncle Jay called it a flash flood.

She glanced at the fog hovering above the creek and watched the mist float like a specter. Belle ran faster. At the bridgeless crossing, the water remained too high to traverse safely. She sought fresh wagon tracks on the other side but saw none. She turned and raced home through a bank of trees opposite the sinister creek. Belle skirted a barricade of bodark trees and cut through switchgrass that rose above her knees. She pumped her arms. Trees blurred, her nose dripped, and still she ran. She sped on, moving faster, swifter until a flaming sensation swept over her legs. A thousand blazes of heat. Had the evil spirit caught her?

Hot prickles ran up and down her legs, and the burning increased. She raced to bare ground and pulled her dress above her knees. Ticks sprinkled her legs like pepper. Belle screamed and ran back to the farmhouse.

Grandmother Tahsuda sat in her rocker on the porch, fanning herself.

"Grandma, help me!" Belle bounded up the steps.

"What's the problem, child?" Grandmother's round face remained calm.

Belle shook the hem of her dress and twirled in a circle.

"Stop now and tell me what the trouble is."

Rivulets of warm water ran down her cheeks. Belle lifted her dress.

"Ah, seed ticks. What have I told you about running through the brambles?" Grandma rose from her rocker. "I'll get the vinegar." With her back turned, she said, "Slip the dress to your feet and remove your drawers." The screen door slammed.

Grandma returned with a bottle and a rag. She dabbed vinegar over the ticks until the insects pulled out. "Wait here."

Her grandmother reappeared with a bucket of warm, sudsy water. Belle leaned over the bucket, and Grandma washed behind her ears and sudsed her hair. Grandma laughed as Belle stood dripping wet and naked. Her grandmother kissed her cheek and nudged her shoulder. "Put on some fresh clothes."

Belle dressed in the bedroom she shared with her father. The low cot where she slept sat across from her father's iron bed. She climbed onto her father's high mattress. Grandma entered the room and motioned her to the other side of the bed. Her grandmother curled next to her. The night before, Belle had slept fitfully. Several times she awakened to vague sounds or bad dreams. Warm and secure, she fell asleep midday.

Belle woke to the sound of wailing. She bolted upright. Light from a kerosene lantern seeped into the bedroom. The high-pitched keening from the parlor chilled her to her toes.

Her bare feet pressed against the cool wooden planks. Concealed in shadow, she watched the women from the doorway. Belle recognized the death wail though she had been only four when her mother died from Spanish influenza. That sound was the only thing she recalled from the death of her mother.

She crept along the wall, her back sliding against the logs, at times splinters catching her dress. Another Comanche woman, a neighbor from two miles away, wailed with Grandma. Her grandmother's face was unrecognizable. She looked like another person, not the calm woman Belle loved. Even stranger, Grandmother's slashed hair fell ragged at her chin, her shorn braids limp over her lap. Worse was the knife the elderly woman clutched in her hand. Thin, red gashes lined her grandmother's forearms while blood trickled down and streaked her hands.

Father was dead.

Beads of sweat formed above her lip. Before she realized it, Belle was running out the front door. No one shouted for her to stop. The sun sank below the horizon. The remaining light washed everything a smoky blue with trees in dark silhouette against the sky. The world looked so peaceful, a lie brewed up from the evil spirit. She ran down the road, the only sound the slap of her bare feet. Cool air swept across her face. She'd run clear out of Oklahoma, run to the Comancheria—the land west of Oklahoma her grandfather told stories about, land that the strong Comanche warriors had ruled for years. She would run to the land of their ancestors.

She reached the gap in the road where the bridge once stood. A shrill sound rose in the midst of silence. A coyote? The scream of a cougar? The keening stretched across the night, loud and lasting, until she recognized her own mourning cry.

At sunrise, Belle woke to the renewed sound of wailing. The piercing cry of mourning confirmed the previous day had been more than a bad dream. Her father's body had been found a mile downstream slung over the bank.

Slowly, she dressed for the journey her family would undertake that morning. She rubbed her eyes and ambled to the wagon already hitched to a team of horses. Her grandfather nudged her toward the wagon bed.

Her father lay on a blanket in his best clothes—the dark suit and hat he wore to the mission church. Red paint covered his face, and his eyes were pasted shut. Even lying in the wagon, her father looked like a fierce warrior. Belle glanced at his eyes again. Red clay packed the hollows of his eye sockets. The earth over his eyes declared the truth of his death more than his

Sunday clothes, his prone position in the wagon, or the terrible stillness of his body.

Her grandfather motioned for Belle to climb onto the wagon seat beside her grandmother. Astride his gelding, Uncle Jay followed behind the wagon. Grandfather made a clucking sound and shook the reins.

They rode for a long time with the creak of the wagon, the thud of horse hooves, and the sound of her grandmother's wailing. The horses' flanks jogged back and forth. Their ears twitched at unseen sounds in the brush. The pungent smell of horseflesh drifted back, along with the wavering scent of the evil creek that took her father's life.

Belle folded her hands over her lap and stared at the road. It was hard to believe her father was dead, and the family was traveling to his gravesite. Last week, he told her tales from when he was a boy. Only a few days ago, he'd picked her up in his arms.

Grandfather's voice shook her from her trance. "We're moving west, the direction of the setting sun." He looked at her for a moment. "Do you know why?" His eyes were soft, but they looked hollow and distant.

She shook her head.

"The setting sun will escort Joseph's spirit to the world beyond."

"Is it a good world, Grandfather?"

"The Old Ones are there. All the People gather in the spirit world."

She nodded. That made sense. Indian people loved any reason to come together.

Grandmother's wailing commenced. Yesterday, the sound had frightened her. Belle wanted the noise to stop forever. But in the light of dawn, the mourning rite was fitting. Someone must cry for her father. The horrible journey of his passing must be acknowledged. Belle reached for her grandmother's hand, but the woman shook it off. Grandma's glazed eyes stared at something Belle could not see.

The horses plodded down the road on the long slow journey to the mountains. The day warmed as the sun rose higher. Heat and humidity coiled around Belle's neck. The jagged peaks of the Wichita Mountains came into view. Scrub oak covered the lower slopes in a dense green shawl. Grandmother reached for Belle's hand and patted it. The road was bumpy. The wheels rolled over stones and rocked the wagon. They rode for another hour, ascended the hills, and moved deeper into red cedar, the road narrowing into two ruts.

Jay's horse sprinted alongside the wagon seat, and her uncle pointed at the rocky crags. Grandfather pulled the team of horses off the road. He helped Grandmother climb into the back of the wagon, and Belle's uncle hitched a leg over the railing and joined her. Belle gasped as they bent Father's knees upon his chest and tied cords around his flexed legs. A canvas tarp was wrapped around his body and corded again. Curled like a round ball, the body no longer looked human.

Uncle rode his pony to the rocky hill. After a few minutes, he returned and dismounted. The men hoisted the bound corpse onto the saddle. Each walked on opposite sides of the horse and braced the body in position. Belle's grandmother took her hand, and they followed the men uphill. Needles crushed beneath their feet, and the piney scent rose in the air. The procession stopped at a crevice in the rocks. Belle looked into the space a yardstick wide and as deep as her grandmother was tall. The men lowered her father's body into the crevice.

Her uncle opened a buckskin pouch and sprinkled tobacco into the cavity. Her grandmother spread a blanket that usually lay at the foot of her grandparents' bed. Her grandfather drew arrows from a quiver slung over his shoulder. She recognized her father's arrows. With loud snaps, the old man broke three arrows in half and tossed them over the wedged body. A slow, deep voice chanted a song. Belle looked up to see Grandfather Tahsuda singing a sad melody. She recognized a few Comanche words—students were forbidden to speak their native language at the mission school— something about the sun, sky, and the Great Spirit. The heartbreaking song pulled at her chest.

Everyone, including Belle, laid sticks across the crevice. Branches cracked as the adults ripped them from nearby bushes. These were placed on top of the sticks until the crevice was filled. Flat rocks were set on top. Grandmother tugged on Belle's hand, and they walked down the hill toward the empty wagon. Belle glanced back at the gray outcrop of rock where her father disappeared into the earth. She wanted to go with him. A hard yank propelled Belle forward and out from the Wichita Mountains.

Chapter 2

BEHIND THE BARN, A GOLDFINCH landed in a tree and gazed down on Belle from beneath its ebony forehead. Black wings edged in white contrasted with a bright lemon chest. Its song, per-chic-o-ree, rang sweet and clear over the air. She would have preferred a gray bird, something with dull feathers and a glum song, a bird that didn't celebrate life so boldly.

Her grandmother continued to grieve at sunrise and sunset in the tradition of the Old Ones. Belle continued to run. If she ran like a whitetail deer—faster than she had ever run—she could forget her father for a moment.

The days moved slowly. Some things stayed the same. Belle was expected to do her daily chores. But one morning, her grandmother added an additional task to her list. "Gather some Osage oranges," she said, "and place them around the foundation of the house."

"What for?" Belle envisioned the tree's thorns ripping her skin.

"They keep—" Her grandmother coughed for a spell and cleared her throat. "They ward off cockroaches and spiders."

Belle headed for the bodark trees behind the barn. Her grandfather said the name came from the French who called the tree Bois d' Arc, meaning wood of the bow. He claimed the trees made a fence as secure as barbwire. She agreed. With relief, she found the fruit had fallen at the base of the dark trunks. Her arms wouldn't get slashed plucking them from the sharp branches. The grapefruit-sized fruit were lime green, and the knobby balls resembled brains more than fruit. No one ate them, though Grandmother claimed the seeds were edible. Belle filled the basket. On the warm September breeze, the tart smell of orange peel lifted from her hands.

She made several trips to the house and lined the foundation every few feet with the fruit. Raspy coughing erupted from inside. Grandmother had a terrible cold. Maybe it was too much sadness that made her ill. Belle understood. Some nights her stomach ached when she thought of how much she missed her father.

After bordering the house with the Osage oranges— some called them hedge apples—she checked on Grandmother. She wasn't in the kitchen. Her rocker sat empty in the front room. Belle's stomach knotted upon finding her in the bedroom. She had never once seen her grandmother in bed in the middle of the day.

She stroked her grandmother's forehead, warm like hot baked bread under her fingers. "Grandma, can I bring you a glass of water?"

The elderly woman nodded and coughed again. "Cover me with another blanket. I'm chilled."

Belle unfolded the extra blanket at the foot of the bed. She hurried to the cistern at the side of the porch, drew a dipper of cold water, and rushed back.

"Drink, Grandmother."

She took a sip and rolled over on her side.

Belle raced towards the barn. Grandfather Tahsuda sat outside on a stump with a rag in hand, a can of oil at his feet.

"Grandmother's terribly sick." Belle's words rushed out. "She's in bed. And she has a fever."

Grandfather closed his eyes. The next moment, he stared at Belle. "Make her drink often even if you have to wake her." He resumed oiling the horse harness.

In the following days, Grandmother's fever came and went. Sometimes, she shook with chills. Other times, she kicked off the comforter. By the fifth day, her cold worsened, and she coughed up green phlegm. Belle's grandfather paced across the front room, a watery gaze in his eyes. Late at night, Belle lay in bed and listened to the persistent coughing. She wondered if her grandmother would die. Many of their neighbors had relatives who had died of pneumonia.

Belle stiffened. Her stomach cramped. Maybe she'd get sick, too. Maybe they would both die. As much as she wanted to join her father on the Other Side, she didn't welcome death.

The next day, Grandfather had Uncle Jay hitch up the wagon and fetch a Native midwife. People relied on the midwife to treat illnesses along with birthing their babies. Belle was relieved when the woman arrived, though a stern look etched the midwife's face. She threw Belle a wary look as she passed on the porch. Belle wondered if the woman's tight face was from watching too many babies die under her care. Belle shadowed Grandfather as he escorted the midwife to the bedroom. She watched from a respectful distance.

The midwife studied her grandmother for a few moments and shuffled to the kitchen. The woman minced several cloves of garlic and added them to a steaming cup of hot water. The penetrating smell pervaded the entire house. The woman propped Grandmother against the headboard rails. "Uh nuh h h h," Grandma moaned. Belle understood the Comanche expression for pain.

The midwife made her drink. Belle squinched her nose as she imagined the taste of the hot elixir. Grandmother grimaced, and she waved the cup away. The midwife said something sharp in Comanche, and Grandmother did as she was told.

In the kitchen, the woman gestured them over and gave instructions. She heated oil over the stove, and soaked a cloth in the warm liquid. Several minutes later, the midwife placed the soft linseed poultice across Grandmother's chest and bound it with long strips of cloth. She raised three fingers and spoke sharply in Comanche.

"Three times." Grandfather turned to Belle. "Apply a fresh poultice three times a day."

Belle nodded. She wished Uncle Jay's wife hadn't died in childbirth two years ago. Ruth Ann would have remained by Grandmother's side until she was well again. It seemed the Tahsuda family kept losing its women.

Three days passed and still there was no change in her grandmother. The medicine man's appearance on the fourth day brought fresh fear to Belle. The midwife's remedies hadn't worked. The medicine man was their last resort.

Belle backed against the wall at the sight of the healer. The old man wore a beaded cap with two prominent buffalo horns, and his face was the color of tobacco, much darker than her grandfather's skin. As he passed, she caught a whiff of sage, fried meat, and wood smoke. Wrinkles creased his eyes and mouth like furrows in a plowed field. Though the man stood only a head taller than Belle, his eyes were fierce—black and cold.

With tongs, the medicine man took two coals from the woodstove and set them in a tin pan. He withdrew cedar sticks from his leather bag and placed them on top until they began to smoke. The medicine man chanted as he fanned the smoke with an eagle feather. The writhing smoke slid into every corner of the room.

He approached Grandmother's still form on the bed and smudged smoke over her body from head to toe. He chanted and danced around the room, the bell on his cap keeping time with the beat of his moccasins.
Grandfather watched from the doorway, his shoulders stooped.

Two more days passed, and Grandmother had not improved. In the early morning, Belle's grandfather called her into the front room. He sat in the shadows, rocking. Grandfather Tahsuda stared at the flames in the stone fireplace, the chair creaking with each backward motion.

"Your grandmother is ill," he whispered.

Didn't they all know that? Belle sat at his feet and waited.

"She may not get better." His words vibrated strangely and then quit. "We have no other women to take care of you."

"But Grandfather, I don't need—" "Be
still." He glared, eyes narrowed.

The stern expression on his face scared her.

"You must go to the Indian Boarding School," he said. "They'll tend to you, and you can continue your studies there."

"But I want to take care of Grandma," she blurted, "and you."

"You're too young. Pack your clothes." He gave a single piercing glance and stood.

At the risk of provoking his wrath, Belle protested. "But I can help—"

He thrust his hand horizontally through the air. "This is how it must be." Her grandfather stomped outside.

Belle pounded the floor and wept. Sunlight seeped through the east window. At last, she stood. She had a plan. She'd run away from the Lawton boarding school and come straight home. Once her grandfather saw how much help she could be, he'd change his mind. He'd realize they'd never be able to keep her at school. She was too fast. Too clever. Her resolve kept her strong as she packed. For good luck, she added the hair ribbons her father had given her.

Late afternoon, a horse-drawn buggy pulled in at the road that led to the house. Belle watched from the porch. Clad in a black wool coat with a beaver collar, a man stepped down. A black band encircled his gray bowler hat. Belle recognized the reverend from the mission school. His cheeks sank into his gaunt face. The thin man nodded in her direction.

Grandfather Tahsuda nudged Belle forward and followed. She plodded down the dirt lane as if her shoes held rocks and paused at the buggy. Reverend Lake stretched out his hand for her satchel. Belle turned to her grandfather, who gazed into the distance. She whirled and wrapped her arms around his waist, but Grandfather Tahsuda remained still. His hand twitched at his side. She spoke to him without words. I'll be back to take care of you and Grandmother.

Belle boarded the buggy. The man reeked of cigar smoke. A quarter of a mile down the road, Reverend Lake spoke in a low drawl. "Bea-u-ti-ful weather this fall."

She wouldn't speak any useless white talk. Belle clutched the edge of the seat.

He glanced over and tried again. "You've grown taller over the summer."

She stared ahead. "Humph."

"There's no lack of good food at the boarding school. You'll never go hungry." The horse nickered as a rider passed. A white stranger tipped his hat.

She didn't look at the reverend. Their food would never be as good as Grandmother's. Belle folded her arms and set her jaw.

As they approached the town of Lawton, Belle wondered if she would run away on the first day of school. It might be wiser to learn the school's routine before deciding the best time to escape. She was so intent on her plans that several minutes passed before she realized they had skirted the town.

"You missed Lawton, Reverend." Was the man feeble?

He clucked his tongue at the horse and snapped the reins. The mare's trot quickened.

"Reverend, the town?"

Reverend Lake pressed the horse into a slow gallop.

15

"Reverend," she shouted. "You missed the town." Was the man deaf?

"Not headed there." The man's skin stretched over his bony face like a drum. "You will attend Chilocco Indian Agricultural School."

"Where's that?"

"Top of Oklahoma near the Kansas border."

"That's too far from my family," Belle said. "They won't be able to visit me."

"Your grandfather worried you'd run away from the Lawton boarding school."

She lied. "Why would I do that?"

The Reverend tossed her a hard look. He must have remembered her first morning at Sunday school. She ran away during the opening prayer.

She pouted. Several minutes passed before the horse slowed to a trot. An hour. Another hour. The sun slowly sank to the earth. Belle studied the horse's hooves as they bound over the ground, and she glanced at the side of the road. She'd jump. The frail Reverend would never catch her. She'd head for the nearby brambles and escape into the blackjack oak. Her right foot slid to the side. With her face aimed forward, she edged her foot closer, and readied herself for the next curve in the road. She slipped both feet to the side of the buggy.

A burning grasp on her arm constrained her. Like the jaws of a bear trap, the reverend's bony fingers dug into her skin. They approached a farmhouse where a white farmer raised a hand in greeting as the reverend drew the horse to a stop.

"Afternoon, Reverend." The man bestowed a toothy grin.

A globe of brass light perched on the horizon as the sun set. The horse's shadow stretched across the bar ditch and fled the road.

"Might I have some assistance, sir?" The reverend jutted his sharp jaw toward Belle. "I'm taking the girl to Chilocco Indian School, but I'm afraid she's trying to run off. Would you have a short rope to confine the little savage?"

Savage! If Grandfather had heard that, he might have changed his mind about sending her away. Belle's face grew hot. She gritted her teeth and struggled as the farmer went for a piece of rope. Despite his frail appearance, the reverend's grip held fast. She glanced at her brown arm where pink skin ringed his fingertips.

The farmer restrained her as Reverend Lake tied Belle to the buggy seat. Not just her arm. The scratchy rope bound her entire chest. Hot tears of rage streamed down her cheeks. She kicked at the buggy. That proved to be the wrong thing to do. Reverend Lake proceeded to tie her legs together. The gold ball of sun disappeared.

"Eschiti! Eschiti!" She shouted the only curse she knew in Comanche. Her father once laughed about a disgraced medicine man's name. The word meant "coyote rectum."

The reverend gave a puzzled expression, and the farmer shrugged. They talked for a few more minutes. The men shook hands. Reverend Lake slapped the reins against the horse's rump and drove down the road.

"Such a scowl on a little brown face." Shadow from the brim of his hat concealed the reverend's eyes. He laughed. It was an evil sound.

The mare's hooves clobbered in the eerie twilight as Reverend Lake lashed the horse and drove deeper into the night.

Chapter 3

PATCHES OF KEROSENE LIGHT MARKED a row of houses. The clopping of horse hooves dwindled as the animal slowed its gait. On the outskirts of town, Belle barely made out the sign that read Elgin, Oklahoma. Reverend Lake drove down a lane bordered with cottages. He pulled the horse to a stop in front of a dark-paned church, its steeple in sharp silhouette against a sliver of moon. He tied the mare to a hitching post. The reverend strode to the rectory alongside the church and rapped on the door. After a moment, a blaze of light struck the ground, and he was ushered inside.

Belle shivered in the cold, her arms throbbing where the reverend had bound her with rope. In the distance, a dog barked. A man's voice shouted a few words, and the barking stopped. A choir of crickets taunted her with their familiar song of home. She couldn't believe her grandfather allowed this man to take her away. Why did Grandfather Tahsuda force her to leave? Belle was no longer a beloved daughter or a cherished granddaughter. She had become the night itself—dark, cold, and nameless.

A door slammed. Boot steps rang out as Reverend Lake approached. She avoided eye contact and remained silent as he untied the ropes. He pinched her forearm with his long-fingered grip.

"We'll stay here for the night." He pushed her toward the rectory. "Behave yourself and you might get something to eat."

A stout woman in an apron escorted them to the back kitchen. A white cap draped over her gray hair like a mushroom. Onion and black pepper lifted on the warm air. Two bowls of soup steamed on the small table designed for one person—the resident cook. Belle was not introduced. A low stool was set before her, and a bowl placed at her feet.

"Chilly night ain't it, Reverend?" the dour-faced housekeeper said.

"Rather be in my warm bed." Reverend Lake tucked a napkin at his neck. "But the Lord's work is not always easy. We must do our duty."

"Aye, the Good Book says so."

"When will Reverend Jamison return from his trip?"

"Tomorrow night." She gave a sad look. "Afraid, you missed him, sir."

"Give him my best when you see him."

"Aye." The housekeeper nudged the breadbasket toward the reverend. She tossed a hard heel in Belle's direction. The bread skittered across the floor.

Belle hadn't touched her soup.

"Eat!"

Belle jumped at the Reverend's sharp voice.

"Eat or you'll go to bed hungry." The housekeeper glared.

All eyes were on her. Belle stared at the soup and lifted a spoonful of broth to her lips. The housekeeper and Reverend Lake returned to their bland conversation about the weather. She stifled a grimace upon tasting the salty soup. Three lumps of potato and a few carrot slices floated in the watery broth. A single piece of meat or chicken was not to be found. Belle laid down the spoon. She had no appetite.

The cook cleared the table. "You may retire in the Reverend Jamison's bedroom tonight, sir." The housekeeper curtsied. "Down the hall to the left."

A cold wave ran through Belle and sank to her stomach at the thought of sleeping in the same room as her captor. Reverend Lake looked back at Belle with dark eyes. Nauseated, she didn't budge. Belle stared at the crazy pattern in the floor's woodgrain.

"Night ma'am." He stomped down the hall.

Belle sighed, grateful she wasn't ordered to follow him.

The housekeeper stacked dirty dishes in a tin basin. Ten minutes later Belle was shown to the housekeeper's bedroom. A blanket was tossed to the floor, and the old woman gestured at Belle's sleeping arrangement. Starlight trickled through a high window under the eaves. The door closed, and a metal latch snapped. The housekeeper undressed in the dark.

"Don't you try nothin'," her sour voice came from the shadows. "I have the key around my neck, so it won't do no good to get any ideas."

The bedsprings squeaked as the heavy woman crawled into bed. In a few minutes, loud snoring erupted in the pantry-sized room. The thin blanket did little to ward off the chill that slithered across the wooden floor. Belle struggled against tears. Why cry, she told herself, there's no one left in the world to care. It was as if her life at the farm with its sunshine, animals, her loving father, and gentle grandmother had never existed. If not for the bitter cold, she might have doubted her own existence.

Weak light from the kitchen window threw a stripe across the unvarnished floor. Like the soup served the previous night, the pasty oatmeal was flavorless. Belle ate slowly and stretched out each spoonful. She welcomed the lumpy mess. It afforded her time to soak in the warm heat of the wood-burning stove. The discomfort of sleeping on a hard floor with a thin blanket had kept her awake most of the night.

"Humph." The housekeeper wagged her head toward Belle.

"Looks like," Reverend Lake said, "she's learned to eat when food's put before her."

Belle stared at the bowl and stirred the oatmeal as if she hadn't heard. It was best to remain invisible.

"Might I bother you to accompany us to the train this morning?" the reverend asked.

"Certainly, Reverend," the housekeeper said. "It would be my Christian duty."

He was putting Belle on a train.

Minutes later, they rode to the Elgin Depot. Belle sat wedged between the reverend and the plump housekeeper on the narrow buggy seat. Belle was sure the old woman's Christian duty included her tight grip of Belle's wrist. In the distance, two grain elevators rose above a row of houses. "What's the population of Elgin now, my fair lady?" Belle muffled a laugh with a forced cough.

"It's over 200 souls." The housekeeper flashed a look at Belle. "The town is growing steadily."

At the station, each took an arm and dragged her in their talons. Belle was escorted to the ticket agent as if she were a criminal. Reverend Lake purchased a one-way ticket to Ponca City. The unlikely threesome waited on the platform for the next scheduled train. The reek of a lit cigar drifted across Belle's face, and she spotted the source of the offensive smoke. To their right, a well-dressed gentleman puckered his lips over a fat cob of tobacco. After a few minutes, a long whistle blew from down the tracks. Another train whistle sounded, and the steam locomotive rolled into sight.

The locomotive drew to a stop with the sharp squeal of steel upon the rails. Steam shot into the air. Belle had never stood so close to a train. For a moment, she forgot her anxiety about boarding school and took in details of the engine and its long chain of cars.

Reverend Lake tipped his hat and bid the housekeeper goodbye. He shoved Belle up the steps to a passenger car, his grip burning her upper arm. On board, he spoke to the conductor, whose hat just cleared the car's plank ceiling.

"Sir, could I ask you to stand by this child until the train picks up speed and is well on its way?"

"Must be a runaway." Two rows of brass buttons shone on the man's double-breasted suit.

"Without your help, I'm afraid so." The reverend frowned and shook his head.

The train whistle shrieked and a voice outside shouted. "All-a-board!"

"Don't worry, Reverend," the conductor said. "I'll ensure her passage."

Reverend Lake nodded as the conductor grasped Belle's arm. The clergyman leered at Belle and stepped off the train.

"Might as well enjoy the trip." The conductor narrowed his eyes at Belle. "Many a hobo has fallen to his death jumping trains, men far stronger than you, little girl."

Belle bit her lip and stared out the window, watching as the scenery passed. The engine picked up speed, and the train rumbled louder. She was moving further away from her family's peaceful little farm. Her destination might as well be the end of the earth.

Curled in the seat, the warmth of the train car made her drowsy. She yawned. Belle soon fell asleep. She woke at the next stop and found the diligent conductor standing over her. The train regained its speed, and the rhythmic motion lulled her back to sleep.

Upon arrival at Ponca City, the conductor personally led her from the train. Clouds clotted the sky except for a blue ribbon to the east. Belle longed to return to the sleepy warmth of the passenger car. The conductor walked her to the platform where a man in a black fedora held a sign that read: Chilocco Indian School.

"Reverend Lake tells me she's a live one," the conductor said.

The black-hatted man ignored the conductor and looked at Belle kindly. "You'll like Chilocco. You'll make lots of friends and learn new skills. We have a beautiful campus. You'll see."

The friendly man extended his hand, and the frowning conductor was forced to release Belle.

"I'm Mr. Haywood." He sat on his heels. "And whom might you be?"

"Belle Tahsuda," she whispered.

"Let's get started." He gestured toward a team of horses hitched to an open wagon.

Haywood didn't grab her arm but allowed her to walk independently. A warm breeze brushed her face and then shifted to a cool current of air. Belle observed five students in the wagon bed who sat with wide eyes and somber faces. Three boys and two girls. Belle made the third girl. Two boys looked the same age as Belle, one boy appeared much younger, and the two older girls might be fifteen or sixteen.

Mr. Haywood outstretched his hand and assisted Belle into the wagon. He handed out shiny red apples to each student. One of the older girls smiled at Belle. The thin little boy glanced over and looked back at his hands.

"Here we go, everyone." Mr. Haywood flapped the reins, and the horses walked toward the main road. The wagon headed north.

"Are you an orphan?" the pretty girl asked.

Belle hadn't thought of herself as an orphan up to now. She nodded.

"All the littler ones are," she said. "You won't be alone." The girl patted her hand. "It's gonna be okay. We, Natives, stick together, even if we're from other tribes."

"What are you?" one of the boys asked. "Comanche."

Belle sat straighter.

"Me, too." He gave a smile with one side of his mouth dipping lower.

"I'm Choctaw," the girl said. She nodded towards the bigger girl. "She's Apache."

"I'm Ponca," another boy said, puffing out his chest. He gestured toward the scared little guy. "We think he's Cheyenne."

She wasn't alone in this strange business of boarding school. Still nervous, Belle breathed deeper. As she glanced at the other faces in the wagon, some of the fear oozed out. Gray clouds covered the sky and hovered low. She avoided thoughts of running through her familiar farm fields, her sick grandmother lying in bed, her strong father wedged in the rock crevice, and Grandfather Tahsuda afraid to hug her goodbye. She tried with all her might but failed.

A screech tore through the air. Belle searched the empty sky and scanned the faces of the other students for a sign of recognition, but they remained oblivious. Was it her imagination or had the ominous cry split the wide Oklahoma sky?

Chapter 4

FOG HUGGED THE GROUND, AND the world disappeared. Harnesses jingled, the wagon creaked, and invisible draft horses plodded down the road.

"Whoa, there." Haywood drew the team of horses to a halt and pointed as the arched entryway to Chilocco emerged from the fog. He glanced over his shoulder.

"Since ancient times, the arch has symbolized entrance to civilization."

The students listened with blank faces. One of the horses snorted, and the smell of warm horseflesh drifted back.

"You've heard of the Greeks and Romans. No?" A grin formed on his face. "You'll learn. I teach history, along with mathematics."

The older girls glanced at each other, careful to keep straight faces.

"See the swastika at the top of the arch?"

Brown eyes stared at the four bent arms of metal.

"The Navajo, Apache, and Hopi tribes use that symbol to represent friendship."

"I saw that design on beadwork," the younger boy said.

"So have I, Jonathan." Haywood's face lit up. "Let's move on." He slapped the reins against the horses' rumps, and they traveled down a road as straight as a metal rod. Fog danced over the wagon and shrouded the teacher.

The girl with a single, thick braid spoke beneath the rumble of wagon wheels. "My sister went to school here." She cupped her hand to her mouth. "Watch your step. Most teachers aren't friendly like Mr. Haywood."

The teacher looked back. "There's a beautiful lake on each side of the road."

The fog thinned for a moment, and what looked to be an endless lake appeared. In sunshine, it might be pretty, but in the vapor, it was frightening. The gray expanse could swallow a person whole.

The fog lifted, and the campus came into view. Stone buildings jutted like forbidden fortresses and rose above the prairie in grave judgment.

"Pretty impressive, isn't it?" Mr. Haywood said. "When the first building was constructed years ago, it was called Prairie Light. Do you know why?"

The same boy as before shook his head, his mouth gaping.

"Because its light shone like a beacon across the prairie." Haywood winked.

To Belle, they looked like buildings where giants and ogres might live. She counted three stories as they approached the first structure.

"The buildings are built with native limestone blocks quarried from the reservation."

Chill from the leaden sky rolled over Belle's skin. She scanned the other students' faces. All but the two older girls wore worried expressions.

"Is this a prison?" Belle whispered to the girls.

"Naw," the girl who patted her hand earlier said. "But it might as well be." The older girls giggled.

Their laughter did little to reassure her. Belle bit her bottom lip and fought back tears, not wanting the girls to think she was a baby.

The horses clobbered down an oval lane where a fountain rose in the center. Like soldiers at attention, an army of imposing structures ringed the plaza, which appeared to be the hub of the campus.

Mr. Haywood leaned back and pulled the reins. He applied the brake and dismounted from the wagon. A man and two stoic women emerged from the rolling fog. "The dormitory staff will show you to your accommodations. Welcome to Chilocco." Haywood strode toward the center building where a sign announced: Superintendent's Office. A few feet from the door, the fog engulfed the driver, and he slid into oblivion.

A heavy man escorted the boys away. One woman led the older girls in the opposite direction. Belle stepped in line with the departing group, but a hand held her back.

"Home Three is the dormitory for the younger girls." A thin-lipped woman shepherded Belle toward another building. The matron held open the heavy door and waved her inside.

Belle peered down the long hall, gazed at the high ceiling, and shifted her eyes to where the wood floor shimmered. She could see her reflection in the shine. The matron passed her with quick strides.

"Miss McCarthy will go over the rules with the new arrivals this evening," the matron said without looking back. "First things first."

She led Belle past dorm rooms filled with rows of bunks—hordes of girls sharing the same room. How unlike the cozy bedroom she had shared with her father.

"How many kids live here?" Belle's shaky voice fell flat in the corridor. She wasn't sure if the matron heard.

"I believe," the woman said after a moment, "the last count was around 700 students."

The matron led her to the basement where the air smelled musty. Belle was assigned a small chest and ordered to empty the meager belongings from her satchel.

"This is where you'll put your traveling clothes after you change into your school uniform."

They moved to another room that reeked of antiseptic solution. Two solemn young girls stood in line. The matron folded her hands.

"The nurse will check you for lice."

Belle leaned to the side and watched the nurse fine comb a girl's hair. The woman inspected the girl's scalp as if she might find gold there. The nurse lifted her head and said, "Next."

It was Belle's turn. "I don't have any bugs. My grandma keeps me clean."

The nurse narrowed her eyes.

What did she say wrong?

"We check all the students. You wouldn't want to get lice from other girls, would you?"

Belle shook her head. The nurse raked her scalp with the metal comb. The comb's teeth were small and fine. The scratch of the comb made her back shiver. She was relieved when the nurse said next and nudged her away.

The matron walked Belle to a nearby office with a desk that filled half the room. She shoved a piece of paper at Belle.

"This is your schedule." The matron's eyebrows squinched together. "Don't lose it. Otherwise, you won't know where to go."

Belle rolled her lips, almost afraid to ask. "What's a schedule?"

"It tells you where you should be at any given time of the day."

Belle had never needed a schedule back home. Their chores started at sunrise, and all work ended at sunset. Belle noticed that a black-rimmed clock hung on the wall of each room. At home they didn't have one clock on their wall. Grandfather Tahsuda owned a gold pocket watch, a present from his oldest sister. He rarely looked at it, and when he did, it was only to admire the etched design in the shiny metal.

A girl stood at the end of the hall.

"Ah, Flora. There you are." The matron turned to Belle. "We have a new student. Belle arrived this afternoon, and I would like you to accompany her to dinner tonight."

The dark-skinned girl nodded. She didn't look at Belle. "And I would like you to escort her to all her classes tomorrow." The girl's eyebrows rose.

"Of course that requires that you miss your classes. I'll make sure your instructors excuse you."

"Ma'am."

The matron hurried upstairs to the main floor, her thick shoes slapping the tile with each step.

"I'm Flora," the girl said as if they hadn't been introduced. Her skin was darker than Belle's. "I'm a group leader, so I know the ropes around here pretty good." The girl glanced at the package in Belle's hand. "I see you have your uniform."

Belle nodded. She decided the girl was at least four years older.

They stepped into one of the empty dorm rooms. Flora watched people walk past the window while Belle changed clothes in the corner. Encumbered with thick black cotton stockings and heavy bloomers, Belle wanted to spit.

"Nobody likes the uniform," Flora said, "but we're required to wear them. We're all in the same shabby boat."

Belle stared down at the heavy high-top boots. In those clunkers, she'd never be able to run.

"Everybody hates those bullhides," Flora said. "They're at least a decade behind in fashion." She took Belle's hand, and they walked to the stairway. "It's pretty scary when you first get here. It gets better. Kind of depends on your attitude." Belle liked Flora.

They climbed the wide stairway. "Some kids love it here. Some never get used to it. We have runaways all the time, mostly in September and October."

Others had done it! And they probably weren't as good at running as Belle. Hope bloomed in her heart.

Flora paused near the door to the outside. "Give it some time before you decide about Chilocco, kid." She opened the door halfway. Outside, a trumpet blared. "That's our signal for dinner." Flora winked and led her down the walkway. "Get used to that sound. There's twenty-two bugle calls a day. It announces everything we do."

She laughed and Belle laughed along with her. What a strange place. She remembered Grandfather Tahsuda saying his father hated the sound of bugles at Fort Sill.

Flora pointed to a building at the end of the lane. "That's Leupp Hall where we eat. The girl's cooking classes are held there in between meals. Watch me and follow."

The girl swung her arms and stepped briskly. Her voice drifted back, "We march to everything at Chilocco. We march to breakfast. We march to classes. We march to church. Everywhere." She giggled.

Like soldiers Belle had seen at Fort Sill, long rows of students marched in formation into the dining room, girls in separate lines from boys. Like drab paper dolls, all the girls wore the same government-issue blue chambray dresses. Most of the students were older, eleven years and more. Boys stood at long tables on one side of the dining room and girls at the other side. In the middle of the room, matrons perched on stools at high desks. Like great-horned owls, they monitored the students.

Students bowed their heads and recited a prayer, a sing-song chant, and when they sat in unison, a rumble resounded throughout the dining hall. A bell rang and everyone began eating. Belle saw ham and beans on the table. She had trouble finding the ham.

Flora leaned over and whispered, "We eat lots of beans here." She made a face, and Belle laughed. "Sometimes stew, soup, or hash."

Belle missed Grandmother's cooking already. She remembered her weak, pale face and wondered if she was okay. Was she still alive? Belle would have to talk to Flora about writing a letter home.

A bell rang from the high desks. Belle reached for another bite of biscuit. Flora shook her head and lowered Belle's hand.

"When the bell rings, you have to stop eating," she said, "whether there's food on your plate or not." Flora shrugged.

Grandmother would have protested the wasted food, but then the food here wasn't that good anyway. The boys were dismissed first and marched from the dining room in orderly lines.

A matron's sharp voice rang out. "All new girls will remain for orientation with Miss McCarthy."

With hand to her mouth, Flora whispered, "We call her the Broom."

In a tight line, the girls marched out. The Broom? Belle had visions of students bending over for a hard swat. She'd never seen such a crazy place.

A tall matron took centerstage, the woman bony and thin with hair swept up in a bun above her narrow face. She inspected the group of girls.

An elbow jabbed Belle's side. Flora gestured below the tabletop with one fist above the other. She made a sweeping motion and nodded toward the matron. Flora mouthed the words: the Broom.

"Welcome to Chilocco. I'm Miss McCarthy, Head Matron." The woman scanned the newcomers, but a smile never crossed her face.

"We are here to ensure you get a decent education. The lessons you learn will help you throughout your adult life." The matron slipped on a pair of wire-rim spectacles. She glanced down and shuffled papers. Her nose was long and thin like the rest of her. "We have specific rules at Chilocco. These will be enforced, and disobedience will result in demerits. Too many demerits will earn you extra chores. This is done for your own good and the good of all at Chilocco Agricultural Indian School." She cleared her throat and looked out over the new students, scrutinizing them one by one.

"First of all, there is no moving between the boys and girls dormitories. Imagine, if you will, an invisible line between Home Three and Home Four. Do not cross that line." She stared at them over glasses riding low on her nose. "You will march in orderly form to classes and the dining room." She consulted the paper in her hand. "You must follow orders given by all staff and student leaders on campus. As you know by now, students must wear the required school attire." She glanced up. "For you young ones, that means clothing.

"Specific chores are required of all students. These tasks include cleaning the dormitories and assisting in the kitchen or laundry. Older boys will have agricultural jobs that will help them as future farmers. Girls will learn housekeeping skills: cooking, cleaning, and sewing.

"Your morning will start with reveille. Room inspections occur every day, so keep your room shiny or, as I like to say…" Miss McCarthy looked out over the students and her face contorted, "…spic and span."

It took a moment to realize Miss McCarthy was attempting a smile.

"You must rely on your schedule because you will have a very busy day. When lights go out in the evening, you will be expected to be quiet and go to sleep. Remember, your day starts early and you will need your rest." The matron pursed her lips and paused. "Are there any questions?"

If any girl had a question, Belle doubted she'd ask. Miss McCarthy wasn't the kind of person anyone would go to with a concern. The woman was scary.

"You are dismissed to your dormitories. Again, welcome to Chilocco." The head matron exited through a side door, and the other matrons ordered the girls to line up according to their assigned dorms.

At Home Three, Flora waved and headed down the walkway. "See you tomorrow. Don't worry, I'll help you find all your classes."

Belle stepped inside, but her feet refused to move any further as tears leaked down her cheeks. She brushed them away and at last, trudged to her assigned dorm room. Flora had told Belle it was one of the biggest dorm rooms on campus. The students referred to it as "The Barn". Forty beds filled the room in precise rows. In contrast to the first time she'd seen it, the room now teemed with girls. A buzz of conversation and activity surrounded her. Chubby girls, slim girls, tall girls. Belle felt more alone than she had all day.
She located her assigned bed—number twenty-seven. On the cot next to hers, a younger girl slumped on her bed.

"Where are you from?" Belle didn't feel like talking, but she felt sorry for the forlorn little thing. The girl glanced at her for a moment and turned away. At least Belle had tried to be friendly. Oh, this was a horrible place that took kids away from their families.

Later after the lights went out, a few whispers could be heard, but after a while, the room quieted. Belle lay in bed, staring at the dark walls. Her stomach ached. The sound of breathing and twisting bedcovers came from all around. Convinced she couldn't sleep in the strange place, the restless night at the rectory won over, and she slipped into dreams where mothers and fathers lived to be old, people didn't get sick, and kids were never torn from their homes.

Chapter 5

AT 5:30 AM, REVEILLE BLASTED, and a bustle of activity erupted around Belle. She rubbed her eyes and watched the younger girls strip their beds. The older girls flipped their mattresses.

"Better get moving," a skinny girl whispered. "They'll be here for inspection in a few minutes."

Belle jerked the sheets off her bed, puzzled why they made the bed completely over. At home, they only stripped the bed when it was wash day.

Heads lifted as student officers strode into the dormitory room. Two teenage officers marched between rows and examined the beds. One officer tossed a quarter on a mattress.

"Make it again, slacker."

Belle whispered to the girl who had given her the heads up. "What did she do?"

The girl whispered back without turning her head. "They throw a quarter down to see if it bounces. If it does, the bed is made tight."

Belle glanced at her covers, doubting a quarter would bounce on her bed. The student officer was three beds away. She closed her eyes. When she opened them, the officer stood over her.

The chubby girl studied her bed and looked back at Belle. "You're new, aren't you?"

Belle gulped and nodded.

"I'll give you a break this time, but that bed better be tight tomorrow morning or you'll get your first demerit. Got it?"

She nodded again. The officer moved down the row. Finally, inspections were completed and the officers left. Belle dropped to her bed.

"Don't do that!"

Belle jumped to her feet.

Flora laughed as she smoothed the covers. Another bugle punctuated the air. "Time for breakfast." The girls lined up, and the student officers waiting in the hall led them to Leupp Hall.

During breakfast, Belle learned that half her day would be classes and the other half work.

"They use the students to keep this place running." Flora reached for a biscuit. "How do you think they keep this place so clean?" Belle recalled the shiny halls.

"Not just cleaning. Cooking, mending, and laundry. We do it all."

Belle hated cooking and cleaning. That's why she had been given so many outdoor chores at home.

The infamous bell chimed, and Flora placed a half-eaten biscuit on her plate. As the boys marched from the dining room, Flora studied Belle's schedule.

"Sorry, Belle. Your schedule states your work detail starts this morning." Flora looked up from the paper. "Because you're young, you're considered prevocational."

"What does that mean?" It sounded like a birth defect, like a calf born with a crippled leg.

Flora grinned. "Basically, you're a worker bee. You're assigned to the kitchen and dining room." Another student leader plopped two metal trays before the girls. "Thanks," Flora said. "Let's clear the tables."

Belle stacked dirty dishes on the tray and strained to lift the heavy load. She followed Flora to the kitchen where they emptied dishes onto a wide wooden table.

"Now, we do it all over again." Flora headed back to the dining hall.

Belle scanned the room with its row upon row of tables, enough to feed 700 students. All she wanted to do was run—run from this military life and its stiff rules and constant supervision. The room wavered under her teary eyes. She missed the farm with its fresh air and animals. Missed running free through the countryside.

Flora nudged her and whispered. "Hurry up, the matron's watching."

Belle glanced back just as the matron turned her head in Belle's direction. Belle hurried and slammed the heavy plates onto her tray.

After all the tables were cleared, some students were sent to the kitchen to wash and dry dishes. Flora and Belle were given the task of washing tables with buckets of soapy water and rags.

The next hour was spent sweeping the floor. Would the morning ever end? Half your day will be work detail. She was a slave to these cold-eyed matrons. Grandfather Tahsuda had talked about the Comanche keeping slaves in the old days—captive Indians from other tribes and black people, former slaves to the whites. Is this what they felt like? A life with neverending toil? Even at eight, Belle knew they had it far worse, but she couldn't help feeling sorry for herself. Chilocco was more prison than school.

After a few hours, the students were allowed a short break for restroom visits and a snack of hardtack. The dining room crew spent the rest of the morning wiping down chairs and setting tables for the noon meal.

Belle sighed. She glanced at Flora, who stuck out her tongue. Had she done something to offend her? Maybe she was doing something wrong. Flora winked, and Belle realized she was teasing, probably trying to lighten her mood. Belle smiled and stuck out her tongue in return.

"After lunch, you'll go to classes," Flora said. "Then you can decide, which you like better." She laughed.

On the way to writing class, Belle studied the students they passed in the hall. There were older students—older than Flora, who was thirteen. The students in Belle's dorm ranged from six to ten. Skin color varied, too. There were students who were dark skinned, dark as the bodark trunk, some who were the same color as Belle, and others much lighter.

"What tribes go to school here?" she asked.

"We have everything from Apache to Ponca, Cherokee to Pawnee, Kickapoo to Wichita," Flora said. "Full-bloods to mixed bloods. Baptists to stomp dancers. Methodists to peyote eaters." She pointed to the door. "Here's your class. One teacher said we have forty different tribes."

They sat in the middle row towards the back. The teacher turned from the blackboard and noticed Belle immediately. The short woman retrieved a tablet from the end of her desk and approached them, her thick shoes broadcasting each step.

"A new girl, I see," she said. "And who is my new student?"

"Belle, ma'am. Belle Tahsuda."

"Welcome, Belle. I'm Miss Potter."

Belle looked down. White people always seemed to stare at people's eyes.

"Here's a tablet for you." The woman handed her the paper. Her hand had strange spots where pigment was missing from her skin.

Was it another of the white man's illnesses? She gingerly reached for the far end of the tablet. Whites were known for carrying horrible diseases. Years ago, her grandfather told her many Indians died from sickness that whites spread to the People. That was probably why the school gave those horrible shots in students' arms.

"Since you weren't here at the beginning of the semester, I want you to copy the alphabet chart on the wall. You can begin now."

The teacher took roll, and each student stood when her name was called. The class was entirely female students.

Miss Potter instructed them on the writing lesson for the day. "Copy the words that I've written on the board. When you're done, we'll pronounce them and discuss the various terms."

Belle noticed the words all had something in common. The kitchen. The list of words written in chalk included: milk, butter, bread, baking soda, baking powder, flour, sugar, and milk. She turned toward Flora, who looked bored.

"Do they think," Belle whispered, "girls can only cook and clean?"

"Miss Tahsuda," the teacher's voice boomed. "We do not talk during class unless the teacher has spoken to you."

Twenty heads turned to stare at the transgressor. Belle lowered her head.

"I realize you're new to Chilocco," Miss Potter continued, "so I will not give you a demerit this time. But next time will be different. Is that understood?"

Belle nodded but avoided eye contact.

The teacher banged her ruler on the desk. "Look. At. Me!"

Belle lifted her head, her face warm, and stared into the teacher's livid expression.

"Do you understand?"

"Yes, ma'am." That time, Belle held her gaze though it took all her courage to not look away.

"Let's move on. Students, I'll give you five more minutes to copy your terms for the day." With her hands clasped behind her back, Miss Potter strode up and down each row of desks. At times, she stopped to correct a girl's penmanship or tell a student to sit straighter in her chair.

Belle didn't like it here. She hated the school. The only good thing was Flora, and after today, she wouldn't even have her.

The next class, mathematics, followed the same format as the writing class. According to this teacher, the whole purpose of math was for use in the kitchen or at the general store. The lessons that day dealt with fractions for measuring recipe ingredients and counting change back from a storekeeper. If it wouldn't warrant a demerit, Belle would have slumped in her desk.

After dinner that evening, Flora walked Belle back to her dorm.

"Well, this is it, I guess," Flora said. "Remember to check your schedule each day, and you'll do fine, Belle."

"Thanks for helping me." On such a large campus, she'd never see Flora again.

"Don't look so sad," Flora said. "You'll make friends with the young girls in your dormitory."

Belle nodded out of politeness—not from belief.

"Take care." Flora hugged her quickly and spun around. "See you in the halls," she said, with her back to Belle.

Belle trudged down the hall to her dormitory and fought tears that threatened to make her the object of ridicule. Flora had warned against appearing weak to either staff or students.

That night her stomach ached again. It was a long way to the restroom. She tried lying on her side, her back, and once on her stomach in an effort to ease the pain. Under the cloak of darkness, she allowed the tears to come and stifled her sobs with the down-filled pillow.

At breakfast, Belle played with her scrambled eggs. She wasn't hungry but worried that the matrons might notice, forced herself to swallow a few forkfuls. Her stomach churned. She sipped at the water. Her stomach cramped and gurgled. She took another sip of water. That was when she knew. She was going to be sick.

Dread of vomiting in the dining hall overcame her. The matrons would give her demerits. Even worse, would be the ridicule from the other students. She wouldn't be able to live with the embarrassment. Belle did something she hadn't done for days. She ran.

Heads turned at the sound of her footsteps on the hard dining room floor.

"No running!" came from the matron assigned that morning. "Get back here."

There was no time. Belle sped up and, unsure of the location of the nearest bathroom, fled outside where she vomited over the groomed lawn. She retched over and over. Had to be the meals from the day before. She wiped her mouth on her sleeve when a door slammed.

The matron stopped short of the puke in the grass. "Oh, heavens. You're sick." The woman's face crinkled up in disgust. "Follow me to the dispensary."

Belle wondered how many demerits she had earned. One for running. One for not stopping when the matron yelled. One for soiling the lawn.

Inside, she shadowed the heavyset matron down the hall. At an open door, the matron pointed to a bench where five other students waited. The air was stuffy and warm. The scent of antiseptic pierced her nostrils. Belle hoped she wouldn't get sick again. She sat next to a husky boy who hung his head between his legs. A young girl on the other side looked flushed. None of the students talked, though a girl at the far end of the bench moaned occasionally. Minutes passed before the moaner was escorted into the inner office. Belle studied the lines in her palm and grew drowsy in the heat.

"You're next," a voice shouted.

Belle opened her eyes and focused on the group leader's scowl. The older girl grabbed her arm and pushed her into the nurse's office.

Head down, the nurse shuffled paperwork. "Sit down, please."

Belle sat in the empty wooden chair facing the colossal desk. The horsefaced nurse lifted her head and stared at Belle.

"What's your ailment?" The nurse joined her index fingers together and formed a teepee shape.

"My stomach," Belle whispered. Did students get demerits for being sick, too?

"Be more specific."

Belle shifted in her chair, unsure what the nurse was asking.

The nurse sighed. "Tell me how you feel."

"My stomach aches. I threw up after breakfast."

The nurse walked around the desk and placed a thermometer in Belle's mouth. "Don't talk and don't touch it." After a minute, she withdrew the glass stick and studied the alignment of mercury. "You don't have a fever. How long has your stomach hurt?"

"Ever since I got here. Especially at night. It really hurts at night."

The nurse peeled an eyelid up and looked in at her. "Open your mouth and stick out your tongue." Belle complied.

"It's just a case of homesickness. You miss your family, right?" Belle nodded vigorously, hoping they'd send her home.

"You'll get over it in a few days, once you get used to being here." The nurse motioned for Belle to stand. She scribbled something on a small piece of paper and handed it to her. "Here's your pass to your next class. Don't dawdle. I wrote the time on it, and your teacher will know if you take a detour."

Belle plodded through the rest of her classes and the dreaded dining room tasks. Each day her schedule reversed, one day kitchen chores in the morning, the next in the afternoon. She considered what the nurse had said. If being away from home could make her sick, it made sense she needed to run away as soon as possible.

Chapter 6

BELLE SAW HER OPENING. After the evening meal, students were allowed to play outdoors for an hour in the designated playground. She studied the buildings and shifted toward the rear of the crowd. When the matron on duty turned her back, Belle ran.

She wove between the three-story dorm and the laundry building to the east, expecting the matron's shout or the squeals of students eager to tattle. The distant laughter of children rose as she skirted the gym and raced past the water tower. Directly behind the tower were employee living quarters, and just then, a teacher appeared in one of the doorways. Belle ducked behind the tower and considered her next move. She ran across the road that separated the shop buildings from the dairy barn. The sour odor of manure brought memories of home.

From behind the barn, she sprinted across the field, ecstatic to be outdoors and away from the regimented life within the oppressive buildings. A ribbon of willows revealed the curl of Chilocco Creek. She hid behind brush that grew along the water and removed her shoes. Belle waded across the creek. The distant lowing of cattle sounded from the far pasture. She scrambled up the bank and gasped.

The bronze prairie stretched for miles. Her arms fell limp, and her shoes landed on the muddy bank. Belle recalled the long wagon trip from Ponca City and the endless train ride from the Elgin Depot. Thoughts of a getaway plummeted. She trampled through high grass and crossed the creek. Belle tugged socks over her wet feet and laced her heavy shoes. Reluctantly, she trudged back to Chilocco.

She peered around the corner of the dormitory—not one student in sight. Silence pronounced her judgment. She slid through the gap of the partially open door, careful to close the door quietly. Belle removed her shoes and tiptoed down the hall. Outside the door to her sleeping room, the matron called student names in alphabetical order.

"Mary Wild Dog."

"Here."

She'd missed roll call.

Her heart raced as she struggled for a way out of her dilemma—take her place at her bed with forty heads turned in her direction or hide in the lavatory and sneak back under the cover of darkness. She shook her head. By that time, the troops would be called out. She could claim she'd fallen asleep outside, but the matron on duty would have seen her. Perhaps, she should run away tonight. That was her plan, wasn't it? But she couldn't imagine navigating the dark amid snakes, badgers, and packs of coyotes.

Decision making halted when a matron materialized at the end of the hallway. Belle froze. The matron bore down on her and yanked her collar.

"You missed roll call." The woman cast a withering look. Without waiting for an answer, she shoved Belle into the room. "Is this one of your students, Miss Dawson?"

"She certainly is, and that's five demerits." The matron nudged her glasses to the bridge of her nose. "Take your place."

"Her shoes are caked with mud."

"That's another matter." The matron glared at Belle. "This will require a visit to Miss McCarthy first thing in the morning."

The Broom. Belle would face the most dreaded matron on campus.

At nine o'clock sharp, lights were extinguished and the room plunged into darkness. Whispers rose and circled around her.

"Where'd you go?"

"Were you trying to run away?" came another voice.

"Aren't you afraid of the Broom?" a voice further away whispered.

"We're all prisoners here," Belle said at last. "Don't you see that?"

"Who's talking in there?" The matron's silhouette appeared in the doorway. "No more talking or you'll all polish floors until midnight."

The questions ceased, and Belle was left to consider her sentencing.

At sunrise, she was summoned into the Broom's office. The matron turned her attention from a pile of paperwork as Belle stood before her desk. The woman's gray eyes matched the hair pulled back from her thin face and knotted in a high bun.

The matron's knobby fingers braided over the center of the desk. "What do you have to say for yourself?"

Her heart pounded. Belle searched for the right words, but all she could manage was a shake of her head.

"That's not an answer." The Broom flashed a disappointed look from below furrowed brows. The head matron shuffled papers and tapped her finger on the top sheet. "Your room matron reports you were late for roll call and that your shoes were packed with mud." She narrowed her eyes. "Is this correct?"

Belle was surprised the matron asked for confirmation. She expected immediate judgment. She nodded, but on second thought, answered, "Yes, ma'am." Her stomach twisted, and Belle examined the swirls on the wooden desk.

The Broom lifted another piece of paper. "I see you were also sent to the nurse. Her report says you're having trouble adjusting to boarding school." She studied Belle's face. "I've talked to the group leader who accompanied you on your first day at school." Would she punish Flora, too?

"You're homesick, aren't you, Belle?"

She nodded, unable to stop the tears trickling down her cheeks. One drop hit her nose.

"I have decided on a rather unconventional arrangement."

Belle took a step back from the desk. In the military-run boarding school, they probably forced errant students into stockades.

"Flora is a very responsible young lady. She talked highly of you." The Broom cleared her throat. "I have decided to allow you to room with Flora."

Belle's gaze shifted from the desk to the Broom.

"Now, Miss Tahsuda, you must understand that I'm going out on a limb for you. If you do not conform with our rules here at Chilocco, not only will there be severe consequences, but it will also affect Flora and her standing as a group leader."

Belle shifted her feet. She didn't want to hurt the only girl who had befriended her at Chilocco.

"Do you understand what I'm saying?"

Belle recalled the teacher yelling at her for not making eye contact. She forced herself to look into the Broom's eyes. Fine creases etched into the woman's skin.

"Yes, ma'am. I do. Flora's been kind to me."

"Then we understand each other?"

Belle nodded. The slight movement at the corners of the matron's lips reminded her of her grandmother.

"That's all for now. I'm afraid you've missed breakfast, but that seems only appropriate given the circumstances. Head off to your duties." The head matron picked up a stack of papers and resumed reading.

In the hall, Belle leaned against the wall and sighed. She not only dodged a severe punishment but had been given a wonderful gift—she'd be rooming with Flora. That morning, she fairly skipped through her task of clearing the breakfast dishes. Of course, actual skipping was not allowed at Chilocco.

Belle glanced at the clock. Her duties in the dining room were almost finished. Lunch would soon commence, and she had no idea which group was Flora's. If she didn't find the right group, Belle might be sent back to her original room. The idea of approaching the Broom again was unthinkable.

Lines of students entered the room. Where was she supposed to sit? Panic set in. Belle spotted the girls from her original room as they paused at the dining room door. Not knowing what else to do, she left to join them. A finger poked her back. Was she too late?

Belle turned and saw Flora's smiling face.

"Hi, roomie. This way. You'll eat with me from now on."

Belle followed, the cramps in her stomach diminishing. Everyone stood and lowered their heads as the common prayer echoed across the dining hall. Once lunch was underway, Belle leaned toward Flora. "The Broom—why did you stand up for me?"

"I like you, Belle," Flora whispered. Her bright eyes danced.

After one day of escorting her across campus—after a single day— Flora had become her friend. Belle recalled the mission-church stories of the angel announcing the birth of baby Jesus to the shepherds. Flora was her angel.

After dinner, Flora led Belle to her new accommodations. To her surprise, there were only three beds in the room.

"Group leaders sometimes get private rooms," Flora said. "Lana transferred to another school this week, and that's why there's room for you."

The cozy space was so much better than sharing a room with forty girls, more like a bedroom than a dormitory.

Flora flopped onto her bed. "That one's yours." She pointed to the middle bed. "So you're Comanche. I'm Choctaw. This year there's mostly Cherokee, Choctaw, and Creek students at school."

"So why did you come here?" Belle swung her feet over the side of the bed. The mattress was even firmer than her former one. It didn't sink when she sat on the bed.

"After my father died, my ma couldn't feed all of us. She sent me here for an education, knowing I'd get fed."

"How many brothers and sisters do you have?"

"I have two younger brothers back in McAlester. What about you?"

Belle wiggled her feet. "My father died when the creek flooded, and then my grandmother got pneumonia. My grandfather sent me here." She stared at her feet. "I don't even know if she got better."

"What about your mother?"

"Died when I was four." Belle shrugged.

Flora bolted upright. "I'll help you write a letter. I know a matron who'll give me a stamp." She retrieved a tablet of paper from a low desk in the corner. "I write my ma once a month." Flora waved an envelope in the air. "Tell me what to write." She sat on the bed, pencil poised over the paper.

"Dear Grandfather Tahsuda…" Belle didn't want him to worry. "I'm doing well." She paused. "I have dining room duty every day. The school helps girls learn how to cook and clean." If her grandfather realized she could be of help around the house, he might want her to return. "I have a new friend named Flora. She's really nice." At this Flora looked up, and Belle grinned. "Please tell me about Grandmother. I'm very worried about her. Please write me back or have the mission preacher write for you." She paused again. "I miss you and Grandmother. Love, Belle Tahsuda."

Flora's hand spun across the paper. She dotted the last period and raised her head. "That was nice, Belle." She shuffled through the desk and waved an envelope in the air. "What's your address?" Silence.

"Belle?" Flora glanced over. "Don't you know your address? Please, don't cry." She moved to Belle's bed. "I'll ask for your address in the administration office. It's on file there. It's one of the advantages of being a group leader."

With Flora's arms wrapped around her, Belle knew what it was like to have an older sister.

Chapter 7

BELLE INSERTED HER PENCIL INTO the sharpener bolted to the wall and cranked the handle. She examined the point and reinserted it. Satisfied with the sharpness, she lifted the pencil to her nose, the smell of wood and graphite a small pleasure in the midst of another dull day. Her life had become one rigid routine after another.

She returned to her desk and glanced at the blonde to her right. Unlike the matrons and teachers who loved to stare at students, she tried to be polite. At home, Indian children were taught to avert their eyes, especially with authority figures. Belle took another quick peek.

"What are you looking at?" the pale girl said.

"Nothin'."

Miss Hillrose stepped into the hall and visited with another teacher.

"You are, too." The girl wouldn't let it go.

Belle's grandmother had taught her to be honest with people. She took a deep breath. "I was wondering why they made you come here. You know, to this Indian school."

"Ha! I knew it." The girl narrowed her eyes.

The teacher entered the room and stomped to the chalkboard. The blonde faced straight ahead.

"I'm Cherokee," the girl whispered. "I'm as Indian as you." That explained the many white kids on campus.

After class was dismissed, Belle apologized to the girl. "Sorry about before. I'm Belle."

The girl gave a doubtful look. "Kids don't like us Cherokee 'cause we're pale skinned. It's worse if you have hair like mine."

"I don't mind. I like you."

"You like me?" With pursed lips, the girl gathered her books. "You don't even know me."

"You stand up for yourself," Belle said. "I like that."

The girl glanced over. "I'm Laura."

The two walked down the hall side by side.

After lights out that night, Flora pushed her bed next to Belle's. Mary, the third roommate, joined them.

"We're going to tell ghost stories," Flora said.

"But we have to be quiet," Mary warned. "If you squeal at the scary parts, we'll all be scooting down the halls, waxing those famous Chilocco floors."

"Yeah, we'd be slaving all day Saturday." After a pause, Flora whispered, "I'll start. This is a real story. Listen carefully." Belle's hands grew clammy. She was scared already.

"Dead Woman's Crossing," Flora said in an ominous voice, "happened on July 7, 1905 in Oklahoma. A woman named Katy DeWitt James and her baby boarded a train to visit a cousin. The day before, she had filed for divorce. Katy's husband was cruel, and she knew she had to get away from him.

"Well," Flora gave a dramatic pause, "her father received several letters from Katy, but when the letters stopped and she never arrived at her cousin's home, he hired a private detective to find his daughter.

"The detective found that a lady who fit Katy's description had stayed with a woman she met while traveling on the train. Get this—the woman was a prostitute."

"Ooh," Mary whispered. "A lady of the night."

"That lady of the night's name," Flora continued, "was Fannie Norton from Clinton. They stayed with Fannie's brother-in-law. The next day the two women and baby were seen leaving in a buggy.

"The detective found witnesses who saw a buggy with two women and a child disappear into a field near Deer Creek."

In the dark, a soft hand reached for Belle's arm, and she flinched.

"Forty-five minutes later, Fannie appeared in the buggy—alone—with the child. She drove to a nearby farm and left the baby with a young boy. She told him to watch the baby until she returned. The baby's dress was stained with blood. The stunned boy watched as the woman tossed something from the buggy several yards down the road. Later, his father retrieved a bundle of baby clothes the woman had thrown into the bar ditch. The boy remembered seeing blood dripping from a buggy tire.

"When the detective caught up with Fannie, she claimed Katy had met a man on the buggy ride and left with him. The detective didn't believe her and went to the local authorities. Fannie denied she had murdered Katy, even weeping uncontrollably. Later that night as the detective talked to a reporter in the hall, Fannie vomited and died.

"Turns out she'd taken poison. In August of that same year, a man from Weatherford found a body while fishing and get this—he found only the skeleton. A gold ring on the skeleton's hand and some fragments of clothing were identified as belonging to Katy.

"The coroner reported a bullet hole in the skull. Katy's cruel husband was called in, but it was determined that Fannie had murdered the woman. They concluded her motive was robbery, since it was known Katy was traveling with a fair amount of money." At that point, Flora lowered her voice to a slow drawl. "To this day, if you stand at the crossing near that field, it's said you can hear a woman calling for her baby.

"And if you stand under the bridge, you'll hear a buggy squeak. If you listen real close, you can hear Katy softly calling, F-a-n-n-i-e. Fannie's... going... to... get you!"

Mary squealed and slapped her hand to her mouth. Flora giggled. Belle kept quiet as promised but dreaded moving the beds apart and lying in the dark. But Flora had more on the night's agenda. "Mary, it's your turn."

On Saturday, Flora informed Belle that they had to clean their room from top to bottom. "The matrons do a white-glove inspection every Sunday," she said.

They dusted the tops of doorframes and swept dust bunnies from beneath their beds. The girls even dusted the springs under the mattresses. They lined the hangers so they all faced the same direction and folded their clothes neatly in the drawers.

The next morning the girls left their drawers and closet doors open for inspection. Even their shoes were lined up beneath their beds. As Flora warned, the matron entered wearing white gloves. Her index finger traced the top of the doorframe and poked beneath the bed. Drawers were inspected for precisely folded garments.

"Good job, girls," Matron Hailey said. "No less than what I expect from group leaders." She left the room.

Without sound, the girls waved their arms in the air and did a silent dance of victory.

Two weeks later, Flora delivered a letter from Belle's grandfather.
Dear Belle,

I was glad to receive your letter. I hear from Reverend Lake that you   are doing well. Your grandmother is improving, but she is still very   weak. We want you to continue your studies at Chilocco and grow   into a capable young woman.

                                        Grandfather Tahsuda

Belle looked up from the stationary and stared at the blank wall.

"Your grandmother," Flora whispered. "Is she…"

"She's alive."

Flora remained silent.

Belle slumped forward and covered her eyes. "They don't want me to come home."

"Oh, Belle." Flora sat beside her on the bed. "You know they love you."

"But I could help Grandmother around the house. I've learned that much here."

"That's Chilocco for sure." Flora smiled. "Your grandparents are doing what they think is best."

But it wasn't best for her grandmother who needed her help. And it certainly wasn't best for Belle.

An air of unrest filled the dining hall. It could have been the boring sermon given earlier that Sunday morning. Chilocco brought in clergy from various denominations. Reverend Hoffmann from a German Lutheran congregation gave a droll sermon about sin and repentance. His monotone voice lulled some students to sleep and others to fits of twitching and leg bouncing.

Perhaps it was the hash and hardtack served for the noon meal. Flora said soldiers called the hard biscuits "teeth-dullers" because they were so hard. "I call them 'teeth-grinders'," she said. "I worked in the kitchen last year, and we found bugs in the hardtack. Shows you how long they sit around the government storehouses."

Belle set the hardtack on her plate.

Whether it was the yawn-producing sermon or the tasteless meal, the students were restless. A few rows away, several boys shoved each other beneath the table. Girls giggled. A sharp whistle trilled across the dining hall.

"Everyone stand!" The matron propped hands at her hips. "Because of today's inexcusable behavior, everyone will stand for an hour. No talking. Keep your face forward!"

A hush fell over the mess hall. The still, straight lines of students reminded Belle of pictures of unearthed Chinese statues, rows upon rows of life-sized soldiers. No one moved, not even a twitch. After several minutes, she fought a desire to yawn. From the corner of her eye, she saw Flora remained somber.

Belle guessed that thirty minutes had passed. Since they couldn't move their heads, she could only see what was straight ahead—rows of tables, backs of students, and the far wall of the dining room. To the side, something slammed to the floor. She flinched at a hard thump behind her. Still no one moved. The matrons scurried behind Belle. Another thud and a thin girl two tables ahead collapsed to the floor. Belle knew then. The students fainted from standing so long in the heat.

Still the command to stand remained in effect. Ten minutes later, the girl who had fainted ahead of Belle was brought back to participate in the mass punishment for a few disorderly students.

A matron broke the silence. "Keep your eyes straight ahead or we'll increase the required time," she barked.

No one wanted to stand a minute longer than an hour. After an eternity of standing, the students were dismissed. They filed from the dining room without as much as a whisper. There wasn't one student who wanted the abuse to continue.

Welcome relief came when Flora and Belle stretched out on their beds. "That was horrible," Belle said.

"I hate it when kids faint," Flora said. "I always worry someone will hit their head on the table and die."

"At first, I thought the matrons were angry and dropping things on purpose."

"Yeah, who knows what they might do." Flora produced a deck of cards, and they played crazy eights for the next hour.

"So what do the boys do at Chilocco?" Belle asked.

"You've seen the cattle, right?"

Belle nodded. The day she stole back from the creek she'd walked straight through the herd.

"Chilocco's famous for their Hereford cattle. The boys also raise feed crops, cultivate the vegetable garden, and prune the orchards."

Belle laid down an eight of hearts. "Clubs," she announced.

"The older boys are pretty daring. You know those Virginia creepers that cover the dorms?"

"Some of those vines are as big as your arm."

"They climb down two or three stories to escape at night. They sneak around the campus, doing who knows what, and climb back to their room before dawn."

Belle filed the information away. Along with running, she was good at climbing.

Changes in seasons no longer marked Belle's life as it had on the farm. Except for occasional trips to Chilocco Creek, brick walls, wood floors, and tin ceilings had become her world. Winter then spring passed uneventfully, but her friendship with Flora made up for everything she had lost.

Flora liked a Cheyenne boy in Home Two. Albert was tall with a good sense of humor. Sometimes they snuck out on summer nights just to talk, something which wasn't allowed except at dances. One night, Flora invited Belle along. Outside the barn, they approached the pasture where several horses lifted their heads and snorted. The army had sent saddle horses to Indian schools since animals were being replaced with trucks. Several boys jumped the fence and approached the horses with ropes in hand.

"There's Albert." Flora pointed. Belle watched him loop a rope around a dark horse. Another boy opened the gate.

The boys jumped on the horses and rode bareback. One of the geldings was used to leading, and when Albert passed that horse, the animal took off. The boy riding the dominant horse couldn't control the gelding though he yanked the reins with all his might. All at once, the entire herd of horses was running out of control. The horses crossed the dam over the lake and raced past the gymnasium.

"Those crazy guys." Flora placed her hands at her hips.

Belle thought of Comanche braves, racing across the plains. In the dark, it was easy to imagine warriors in buckskin and war paint.

Staff housing was situated behind the gym. On that warm summer night, Mr. James, the agricultural teacher, held a lawn party behind his house. Several tables spread across the lawn heaped with food. Japanesestyle lanterns hung overhead. A small group of staff mingled on the lawn as the rogue horses stampeded through the yard.

"It must have seemed like the old days," Albert later recounted. "By the looks on all those pale faces, you'd think we were a war party come to scalp them."

Albert's friend tried to turn the lead horse from the coming disaster, but the frenzied gelding galloped straight through the yard. The rest of the young riders followed close behind.

"These were Cavalry horses, remember," Albert reminded her. "Jumping was nothing to these horses."

Although they'd seen it firsthand, Flora and Belle enjoyed replaying the event. "It was like a fancy rodeo," Flora said, "watching all those horses leap over the tables. I laughed so hard, I peed my pants."

The Cavalry lead horse had caught the cable of lanterns and dragged it behind like he was leading a parade. The horses turned back through the campus buildings and when they slowed to round the corner, the boys piled off.

"Best performance on horseback I ever saw," Belle said.

Under the cover of dark, the staff didn't recognize the boys. They suspected certain students but didn't have any proof. They called in several boys the next day, but nothing came of it. No one caved. The boys would rather be beat than rat on one of their own. It was an unspoken creed.

After that adventure, Flora fondly called her boyfriend Scout. The escapade became one of the most famous tales told on campus.

Chapter 8

-1927-

BELLE WOULD NEVER HAVE SURVIVED four years at Chilocco, if
it wasn't for running. Afraid to jeopardize the privilege of rooming with Flora,
she was ever wary. She knew exactly how much time it took to sneak to
Chilocco Creek and return in time for roll call. Mallards and Canadian geese
flew in low and settled near the bank. If she remained still, a coyote or deer
might approach for a drink of water. Once she saw a red fox chase a quail
through the prairie grass. For a few precious minutes, Belle left behind clocks
and schedules, lines marched in precision, and hard-eyed matrons.

Flora would graduate that spring. Belle would have been devastated
except for the fact that her friend had been offered a job at Chilocco upon
graduation. Flora was highly respected by the matrons, but there was another
side to Flora. She loved a practical joke, what the students commonly referred
to as "trixing." One night the three roommates snuck out of the dormitory. The
dark windows of the three-story fortresses glared down on them, Chilocco
even more intimidating in the dark. With buckets in hand, they crossed the
lawn and tiptoed behind the employees' housing quarters.

Mary giggled.

"Quiet or we'll end up in the lock-up." Flora crept from the safety of one
shadow to another. Belle and Mary followed as willing co-conspirators.
Behind the staff building, the girls stole honey from the employees' beehives,
filling their buckets to the brim. But it wasn't enough to steal their honey.

"Belle, you're the most artistic," Flora whispered and handed her a
paintbrush. "You're in charge of drawing."

Belle painted paw prints on top of the hive. Under the full moon, it was easy to see what she was doing.

"They're so real they look frightening," Mary said.

Belle stood back and admired her work. In the dark, the prints appeared authentic.

They left their "signature" behind not only for the fun of it but also to outfox the staff. Strict military life on campus begged for student retribution. Often, it was the bolder boys who performed pranks, but Flora insisted the girls not be outdone by the boys.

That spring, the school had a matron recognition day. The older girls in Belle's dorm were commissioned to bake a dessert for the planned tea. Flora allowed Belle to help them in the kitchen. With an index finger to her lips, she brought Belle into the conspiracy. She and another girl measured salt instead of the sugar called for in the recipe.

Later as the girls scrubbed the dormitory halls for an entire Saturday, they giggled and agreed the punishment was worth the trixing. The girls had covered for Flora, insisting she knew nothing about it.

"Flora would have busted our butts if she'd known our true intentions," Meredith told the infuriated matron. "She doesn't like us anyway. She knows we're usually up to no good." Meredith's lower lip quivered and tears leaked from her brown eyes.

Belle stared. If she hadn't known better, she would have believed the girl's lies. Meredith had a natural calling to be an actress.

The matron glared at Belle. "You will no longer work on projects with older girls." She turned to Meredith. "Won't have you corrupting the young."

There were many advantages to having a group leader sympathetic to her peers. Flora was well liked, because she never ratted on other students though she would sometimes have a talk with them about their behavior. Though not required to polish the halls that day, Flora goodheartedly pitched in and helped. Belle followed suit.

Belle was moved from prevocational to vocational status. She spent half her day darning socks over light bulbs, cutting fabric with patterns, and operating the sewing machine. They initially taught the girls to patch worn clothing. The next projects included making hot pads, then aprons, and by the end of the year, they were sewing dresses for Sunday services.

"Patch, sew, and darn," she complained to Flora. "That's all we do."

"Don't you know by now? Most of what they teach us keeps this place running. We help cook, clean, mend, and do the laundry," Flora said. "Besides, the school figures since you're a woman, you're going to be a wife."

"Yeah? I got news for them."

"Belle, you're a regular spitfire."

Little did the administration know that their newly hired employee had mischievous leanings. Even after becoming an official part of the school staff, Flora came up with new pranks.

"We have a special mission tonight," Flora announced one evening.

"Tell us." Mary bounced on the bed.

"You'll have to wait and see." Flora gave an enigmatic smile. "Thirty minutes after lights out, we'll begin our secret operation."

Under a sliver of moon, they hid in shadows outside the dorm. They trailed Flora to the back door of the bakery where Flora dug into her pocket and withdrew a skeleton key. After an unsuccessful try, she twisted the key again and the door opened.

"Quick," she whispered and the three of them slipped inside.

"Light the kerosene lamp," Mary said. "I can't see a thing."

"Do you want the staff to catch us? Give me a minute. I brought a candle."

The flickering light formed reverse shadows up Flora's face. She looked spooky. Flora opened the pantry doors and drew a glass bottle from the shelf. "Find some measuring cups, girls." She dipped the candle until a small amount of wax dripped on the table. Flora held the lit candle until the wax cooled and fastened the stick.

Belle was the first to locate tin cups. "Found 'em!" She placed them on the table.

"What are we doing?" Mary asked.

"Having a party," Flora said, "in celebration of my upcoming graduation."

"And your new job." Flora wasn't leaving Chilocco upon graduation, and for Belle, that was the best part. The label on the glass bottle read Sail On Vanilla Extract.

Flora twisted the cork and poured a generous amount into each measuring tin. "Ah, doesn't that smell good."

Belle had never sniffed anything so wonderful.

"Let's toast," Flora said. "Raise your glasses." "To

the best group leader ever," Mary said.

"To my best friend ever." The sweet scent of vanilla filled Belle's nostrils.

They clinked their tin cups together.

Belle sipped the flavoring and choked.

Flora and Mary exchanged looks and burst into laughter.

"What's in this?" Belle asked.

"Just a little alcohol." Mary giggled.

Flora held the bottle to the candlelight. "85% alcohol to be exact." She laughed. "Bottoms up."

Belle tried it again, and heat radiated down her chest as she swallowed. The girls' giggling magnified with each sip.

"This is excellent vanilla." Flora held her pinkie finger in the air.

"Better than in those hard old cookies they make." Mary poured everyone a refill.

Belle never laughed so much in her life.

An hour and a half later, the girls staggered home. They weren't halfway back to the dorm when Belle leaned over and vomited.

"Eww!" Mary backed away.

Flora patted Belle's back. "You okay?"

"The buildings are spinning."

"Let's get you to bed."

"I can't move." Belle held out her hand. "I have to sit."

"We can't get caught out here." Mary gazed up and down around the campus.

"Go ahead. I'll wait with her."

Flora took her arm and coaxed her a few feet to the laundry building. "Let's scoot against the foundation, so we're out of sight." The girls sat on the cool earth under deep shadow.

"Oooh, I'm so sick," Belle wailed.

"Shh. Be quiet. Breathe deep."

With eyes closed, chin on her knees, Belle made herself breathe. The cool night air helped until another wave of nausea swept over her.

The yip of a coyote sounded from across the prairie. "Do you think you can walk now?" Flora said.

"No, please, no. If I move, everything starts to spin again."

Flora sighed and leaned against her. Belle drifted off for a while. She woke later with Flora's head on her shoulder. More yipping rippled on the night air. Flora was asleep. It sounded like a pack of coyotes roaming the plains, but they didn't scare her. The coyotes howled again, their prairie song comforting, something familiar from home. She adjusted her back, and the spinning started again. To the tune of Flora's snoring, Belle told herself she'd never, ever get drunk again.

After class one afternoon, Flora skipped into the room waving envelopes in the air. "Mail delivery. One for you, Belle, and one for me." She threw a letter on Belle's bed.

Letters from home were rare. Belle received letters at Christmas and on her birthday, but this was unexpected. Had something happened to her grandmother? She tore the envelope open.

Dear Belle,

Hope this finds you well. Your uncle planted corn for us last week. Your grandfather's rheumatism makes it hard for him to do much farm work anymore. I think of you when I take a loaf of bread from the oven. I remember how much you loved warm bread with butter and cane sugar. By now, I imagine you've learned how to make bread at school. I wish we could visit you, but it is such a long trip and we're both getting up there in age.

With love,

Grandma Tahsuda

Belle still burned at Reverend Lake's decision to send her to the far reaches of Oklahoma. There were other boarding schools he might have chosen and made it easier for her grandparents to visit. She sighed and refolded the letter. Belle glanced over at her friend.

Flora's eyes locked in a trance. Her characteristic smile had disappeared, and her shoulders hunched forward.

"Flora, what's wrong?" Belle asked.

"Momma's sick."

Visions of burials flashed through her mind.

"She wants me to come home and take care of the boys."

"But your job—doesn't she know about your new job?" Her chest tightened. Panic swept over her.

"She knows." Flora met Belle's eyes. "Family comes first."

Belle froze. Flora was right, but she couldn't bear school if Flora left.

"Maybe I'll come back after she's better."

Somehow, Belle knew that once Flora left she'd never return. Despite how quickly her mother might improve. If she improved. She moved to Flora's bed and sat beside her. Flora held her hand.

"I'll sure miss my little sister." Flora smiled down on her.

It took everything inside Belle to smile back. The last thing Flora needed was Belle's heartbreak, and she loved her friend too much to add to her burden. Flora gave Belle her home address so they could write each other. Though they could correspond, she knew deep inside she'd never see her friend again. That evening was the worst night since she'd slept on the floor near the crotchety housekeeper in Elgin. That had been the first time she realized that those she loved would be a world away.

Chapter 9

THE TEN DAYS SINCE HER friend's departure might as well have been ten years. Without Flora, Belle was inconsolable. She talked only when spoken to and withdrew to her room during free time. That year Belle worked in the laundry. The student crew washed, folded, and mended the school uniforms for Chilocco. Belle folded a boy's shirt and pants, clean home clothes from a recent arrival. After the matron stepped from the room, Belle stuffed the clothes in her book bag.

Her mind worked overtime. Fresh apples from lunch, a rarity at Chilocco, were added to her bag. She managed to hoard two and smuggled hardtack and a cornmeal muffin. That afternoon Belle planned her break. On occasion, students were allowed a trip to town where they could draw on their funds for a little spending money. Town Day would be her Independence Day. She was going home, at last.

On the wagon ride to Ponca City, black oil derricks dotted the prairie like strange mechanical trees.

"That millionaire, Marland, owns all those," an older boy said. "He leased land from a Ponca Indian named Willie-Cries and struck oil. Now he's got a refinery and warehouses. My uncle said he can load 100 rail cars a day with oil."

Once in town. Belle drifted away from the other students, glad none of her school acquaintances came on the trip. A Tin Lizzie rumbled over the cobblestone street. The dark blue vehicle was an older Model T like the one

Chilocco's superintendent drove. According to the boys at school, the newer models were painted black. Belle imagined the skinny tires driving through mud over roads designed for horse travel. She shook her head.

She strolled through town, vigilant to remain inconspicuous. Citizens and law enforcement officials were routinely on the lookout for runaways from Chilocco. The school offered a five dollar reward for a student's return to the institution. The first thing Belle purchased in town was a newsboy hat. She ducked behind a building and dressed in the boy's clothes nabbed from the laundry, the baggy shirt hiding her budding breasts. With scissors she'd absconded from sewing class, she chopped off her two dark braids and snipped at uneven places. She checked her work in the dirty glass of an alley window and shrugged. It was the best she could do. Belle donned her new cap and examined her reflection, the image startling. A young boy stared back.

She had to be especially careful as she walked to the train depot. A fidgety kid would be suspicious. Belle passed a service station where a black Model T honked and pulled into the station expecting immediate service. A red sign in the shape of a triangle read Marland Oils. The quaint building resembled pictures she'd seen of English cottages. And like a cottage, delicate bushes and blooming flowers had been planted around the building. The service station came as a welcome relief to Chilocco's formidable buildings.

The Chicago, Rock Island, and Pacific Railroad station at Third and Otoe came into view. Decorative brackets braced the deep overhang of the depot roof. She was in luck. Passengers detrained and milled over the platform, allowing her to slip through the crowd and into the depot. She flicked her eyes like an owl, watching for any sharp-eyed glances from authority figures as she searched for a railroad timetable. Belle snatched one from the counter and slipped into a corner. Skimming the fine print, she found the train would depart in less than ten minutes. Headed south. The meager spending money allowed by the school wouldn't buy half a ticket. She had to find another way. Belle slipped outside where the crowd had thinned, though several people remained on the platform greeting family or enjoying fresh air before their journey continued.

She skirted the platform and avoided eye contact, which came naturally for her. With her bag slung over one shoulder, she walked parallel to the train, at what she hoped would be a less conspicuous distance. A uniformed employee wheeled a wooden cart piled with luggage and paused at the car located behind the engine. Porters would not be requesting tickets in the baggage car. But the car sat in front of the platform where porters and other train employees shuffled back and forth. If she was caught trying to hide in the baggage car, she'd be duly taken into the custody of a police officer.

Belle waited until passengers flooded the platform again and slipped between a heavy woman with three drippy-nosed children and two men in suits. A railroad employee had unloaded the baggage cart, and several feet away, another man donning a dark-blue trainman hat wielded a loaded cart. There was no time left. She cut through the crowd and dashed into the baggage car. Searching about the open car, she scooted behind the highest stack of luggage, moving one case aside to hide behind a steel trunk.

Baggage slammed onto the floor of the car. Footfalls. Belle squeezed low and held her breath. A loud thud, probably another heavy trunk, hit the wooden floor.

"Any more baggage, Henry?"

"That's it for this trip."

"Good to hear," the first man's voice came, "my back's been acting up today."

The baggage door rolled shut with a sharp bang. The bright sunshine turned to blackness and chill. Having been on a train only once before, she prayed air remained in the dark cavern of the baggage car. In case there was less oxygen, she slowed her breathing and thought of the peaceful sunrises back home. When the train whistle blared, she clapped hands over her ears.

"All aboard," a man cried. The metallic slide of doors came from distant cars. Two short toots sounded from the rear of the train as it slowly rolled forward. They were on their way. The clackety-clack of wheels over the track boomed in the baggage car, much louder than in the insulated passenger cars. Without a seat to stabilize her, Belle tossed back and forth as the train gained speed. After four long years, she was headed home.

But she wasn't free yet. She could be easily detected when the men retrieved the luggage at the next stop. Chilocco administration threatened severe consequences to runaways. Students could be expelled. At that, Belle smiled. But with her luck, she'd be kept at school to face a dire penalty. By that evening, she would be officially labeled as AWOL. It would have been a delightful thought except fumes from burning coal leaked into the car. Dizzy and nauseated, she hung her head.

Hours later, the train slowed and lurched to a stop. Her heart raced when the heavy doors rumbled open, and luggage was tossed around. She peered over a trunk as the baggage man tossed satchels and pokes onto a half-filled cart. The man turned his back as he tossed another bag on the cart. It was now or never. With her vision dazed by the bright sunshine, Belle sailed over the luggage straight into the man's thick arms.

Chapter 10

"HOLD ON THERE, BOY," THE baggage handler shouted. "Dirty little stowaway."

Belle struggled against his tight grip to no avail. Dirty was a clear reference to her dark skin. She tossed a look over the man's shoulder and in the deepest voice she could muster, shouted, "Knife him, chief."

The man's eyes grew wide, and he swung toward the crowded station. In doing so, his grip loosened, and Belle flew into the crowd. She ran behind the depot, crouched between two parked automobiles, and caught her breath. A slow smile formed. She'd used the man's prejudice against him. Whites feared Indian men, especially if they were drinking. They knew many Natives carried knives. Most whites believed the Indian people were still savages.

Male voices swept around the corner of the depot.

"You look that way. I'll check over here."

Through the bottom of the car window, she saw a railroad man at each side of the parking area. They'd soon be upon her. She had no choice but to run in full view between them.

"There he is," one of the men yelled.

She ran as fast as possible and heavy boot steps gave chase. Out of practice, her lungs protested. Headed toward the residential area behind the depot, she raced past hedges, slipped between houses, jumped picket fences, and hopped chicken-wired gardens. The perfume of lilacs drifted in the air. In an alleyway, a garage door was left ajar. Belle spent the next half hour crouched in the dim interior until she was sure the men had given up and gone back to the depot. They couldn't spend all afternoon chasing a young boy, could they?

Belle headed back in the same direction but at an angle to avoid the depot. She came out in the business district where she strolled up the street and peered at window displays of fine china. Other store windows touted men's suits on wooden hangers and women's garments fitted on dress forms. Her stomach rumbled, and she darted into the alley. Sitting on a discarded wooden box, she pulled out an apple. A door swung open and a black man appeared carrying a long case and a satchel. He strode towards a black automobile across from where Belle sat.

"Hey there, boy," the man said. "Having a little lunch?"

Belle nodded like a boy might and ate with her mouth open. "What kind of car is that?"

"A Model T Tudor, my boy." The man smiled and reentered the building. After a few minutes, he returned with a shirt on a hanger and another case. He tossed the shirt in the middle of the back seat.

"Need some help, sir?" Belle asked.

The man peered at her. "Like to earn a few pennies, I reckon."

Belle nodded, knowing she'd need to buy food on her long journey. She felt like a panhandler. Difference was, she was willing to work for the money.

"Come on, then." The man waved her over to the running board. "Place this case in the luggage rack and meet me inside."

Belle fit the case next to one standing long side up in the accordianstyle rack. Would the rack retain the luggage over bumpy roads? In long strides as she imagined a boy might take, she strode to the back door. Inside, her eyes slowly adjusted to the dim light of a narrow hall. The corridor opened up to a room where a row of stools hemmed a wooden counter against one wall. A variety of bottles lined shelves surrounding an ornate mirror. Oddly, there were no windows in the room.

"Keep coming." The man opened a door at the far side of the room.

The adjoining room held street-side windows covered by drapery. Wooden planks covered the floor, nicked and scratched from heavy use. A stage rose along the back wall, and stacked metal chairs lined another wall. The smell of stale smoke oozed from the room. Belle realized this room served as a false front. Flora had told her about such places—the back room was a speakeasy!

"Hey, boy." The man gestured to the stage. "All these instruments have to be placed in cases and carried to the car."

Belle judged which case best fit each instrument: trombone, trumpet, and saxophone. The man leaned against the bar and propped his heels on another stool.

"Now, ain't this the life." He laughed deeply.

She snapped two cases shut and carried them outside. Halfway to the car, the man joined her. "There's another rack on the other running board. Not a lot of luggage room on these Tin Lizzie's. Smaller cases will have to go on the backseat floor."

Like a puzzle, Belle fitted the larger cases in the rack. She saw a flyer on the front seat that read: Oklahoma Blue Devils. She'd heard of territory bands that traveled across states to play their music.

"Well, now. I guess that earned you about five cents."

It was more than she expected. "Thank you, sir."

"Sir," he mimicked. "Now, ain't that nice."

"Where ya headed for next?" She tried not to stare at his dark skin, much darker than hers, dark as a moonless night. She shifted her eyes to his face. The man had friendly eyes.

"Texas." He tilted his head. "You ever hear of Texas?"

"'Course."

"Well, that's our next gig."

"Think I could trade this five cents for a ride?" Her grandmother would have a heart attack at the idea of Belle riding with strangers—men, no less. Even Flora would have been shocked. But she was a boy, wasn't she?

"You're not a runaway, are you?" The musician scrutinized her.

"No, sir. Been at school, but I have to get home to take care of my sick grandmother." Her words rolled a little too fast.

"What's your name, boy?"

She couldn't hesitate. "Joseph. Joe Tahsuda, sir."

"I like you, Joe Tahsuda. Think you'd mind being squeezed between two big men in the backseat?"

Her throat grew thick, but she managed to answer. "No, sir." What a mess she'd gotten herself into.

"Snoring don't bother you?"

"No, sir."

"Or farting?"

"No, sir." She hated it when boys farted.

"Then you keep your money and the ride's on me. I have an old grandmammy, too." The large man stretched his lower back. "I'm Walter. We leave within an hour." "Thank you, sir."

"I love that, a little Indian boy calling me sir. Aren't you the polite gentleman?" A low, deep laugh erupted from the man.

Belle smiled, but not too wide. She smiled cockeyed like a boy.

It turned out, she didn't have to be squished between two huge men in the backseat. One of the band member's girlfriend had surprised him by driving her daddy's car up to meet him. Walter announced little Joe would ride shotgun up front. Belle's first ride in an automobile, and she got to ride up front. She couldn't believe her luck. And as if that wasn't enough, Walter offered her a piece of cold fried chicken from a paper sack.

"You gobbled that up like you haven't eaten in weeks," Walter said.

"Boarding school food stinks."

"That so?" With his left arm out the open window, he raised his hand straight up and signaled for a right turn.

"That food should be thrown to the hogs."

"Bet you can't wait for your Grandma's cooking."

She shook her head. "No, sir. I can hardly stand the wait."

The man called Hot Lips sang from the backseat, and after a moment, the other man joined in. Belle listened to their beautiful, deep voices sing "Bye Bye Blackbird." If the men played their instruments as well as they sang, they must be fine musicians.

The song made her ache for home and a good night's sleep in her old bed. The men were all shades of color, not unlike Indian people, only darker. Belle found it fascinating. She felt more comfortable around black men than she'd ever been with the male teachers at Chilocco. After much deliberation, she decided it was the band members' attitude. They didn't treat her as strange or inferior, just different. Different in a good way.

Within minutes after the singing ceased, the men in the backseat were snoring.

"I warned you about that, didn't I?" Walter said. "You'd never know it, but when they're not exhausted, they're full of energy."

She grinned and looked back at the road. An automobile was an unbelievable way to travel. The miles vanished as if the car were a soaring eagle.

They drove through the night. After a while, Walter quit talking, and she must have fallen asleep. She woke to the gray light of dawn and glanced at the driver's side. A strange man was driving. Caught in a foggy dream, more like a nightmare where she was trapped, Belle peered in the backseat. Walter slept with his mouth open. Slowly, things made sense. Hot Lips must have traded off driving with Walter sometime during the night. She'd slept through the whole thing.

"You must have been dead tired." Hot Lips glanced over the seat. "You never woke up once."

"Guess I was," she said. Belle rubbed her eyes and studied the landscape. Flat farmland stretched for miles. In the distance, a stroke of pale light played over the rolling hills. "Where are we?"

"I reckon we're about an hour from Lawton," Hot Lips said. "Walter said that's where you get off."

"My grandparents live there." She reconsidered her words. "They're expecting me." This close to making it home, she wouldn't jeopardize her long awaited return. "You're a good singer."

"Why thank you, Joe." He winked. "They say I'm even better on the trumpet."

"What's your real name?" Grandmother always said she was awful curious about things.

"Oran," he said, "Oran is my given name."

"That's a nice name." She sounded like a girl. "I mean, Oran's a good name for a guy."

Oran smiled. "My mammy would agree with you."

It was twenty miles to home from Lawton. She'd walked ten miles in one day before, but twenty? Didn't matter. She'd made it this far. The night before she left Chilocco, she prayed. Not to the God who stayed in church buildings with statues and crosses, but to the Jesus they said walked among the people. From the stories she'd heard so far, He liked to be around real people not just sit in some hard pew. He healed the sick, talked to the poor, who everyone knew were dirty and ragged, and He treated women like they were valuable. He had protected her throughout her journey and kept her safe. She had a newfound respect for Him this bright promising morning.

On the outskirts of Lawton, Walter woke and stretched his arms overhead. "Where should we drop you off?"

She scanned the landscape and spotted a grain elevator near the railroad tracks. "The feed store. They'll meet me at the feed store."

Oran made a left and crossed the tracks. As she hoped, a feed store sat across from the elevator.

"This is good," she said.

Walter got out of the car and said goodbye. Belle felt like hugging the kind man but stuck out her hand instead. He shook it and laughed.

"It was nice to meet you, Joe," he said.

"I'll never forget you, sir." Tears sprang in her eyes. Her grandmother always said the kindness of a stranger is often the best kind. In church, they talked about angels unaware. Was Walter her angel?

Walter slapped her on the back. "There, there. You're almost home."

She nodded. "Thank you for everything."

"God bless you, Joe." Walter climbed into the passenger side.

Hot Lips aka Oran leaned out the window and waved. "Nice knowing ya."

She slung her bag over her shoulder. As they drove away, Belle waved. She had a feeling the last twenty miles were going to be the longest.

She passed the feed store and strolled aimlessly for ten minutes until she neared the business area. Belle knew one thing. She was hungry. Without enough money to eat at a café, she entered a brick grocery store. She strolled through the aisles, the food displays only making her stomach ache worse knowing she couldn't afford them. She picked up a five cent bottle of milk from the cooler and headed for the cash register. At the end of the aisle, she spotted a display of candy. Hershey bars were five cents each. She rooted in her pocket for change.

"What's going on there?"

The back of her shirt collar was yanked. A tall man scowled down at her, his wrinkles etched deep into his pale face. White streaks of hair sprung like eagle feathers at his temples.

Belle struggled against his hold.

"Where do you think you're going?" the familiar voice bellowed. Reverend Lake's sour breath blew like a gathering funnel cloud.

Chapter 11

THE BURNING GRASP ON HER upper arm prevented Belle from running. She was so close to home, but he'd send her back in a hot Oklahoma minute.

"You, Injuns." His black eyes squinted. "Always stealing things."

An older boy approached. "Is there a problem, Father?" The Native teen glanced at Belle and back at the reverend.

"This boy stole a candy bar." Reverend Lake avoided eye contact with the older boy.

With broad shoulders and thick arms, the teenager stood even with the man of the cloth. The reverend hadn't recognized Belle dressed as a boy, but stealing was a serious charge, especially when an Indian was accused. "I have the money to pay," she blurted. She dug into her pocket. In her outstretched palm, an Indian-head nickel and five red wheat pennies glimmered.

"Seems you were mistaken, Reverend." The boy stepped in front of Belle and stood with hands at his waist, elbows jutting like barricades.

"Not what it looked like to me." Reverend Lake tossed a steely glare before he stomped away, grumbling.

"They always suspect us skins." The boy extended his hand. "I'm Chase."

His Comanche accent was soothing to her ears. "Bel—Billy, I'm Joe Billy." Belle shook his hand. "Sure scared me."

"Reverend Lake is famous for his harsh ways."

"Like a snake."

Chase laughed. "You a drifter?" Belle saw his eyes assess the bag over her shoulder.

"Going home. My grandparents have a farm south of here." She headed towards the cash register, the clerk backlit by sunlight streaming through the storefront window.

"How far?" Chase squinted against the glare of light.

"Twenty miles." She handed coins to the clerk.

"That's a far journey. You walking?"

She nodded. "But I'm strong. Used to be a runner."

Chase laughed again. "Happens my father and I are headed out to buy a bull. Could get you as far as fifteen miles south."

She closed her eyes and offered a silent prayer of gratitude.

"You okay?"

"When do we leave?"

"As soon as you pay for your goods. My father's waiting outside."

At the register, Chase purchased chewing tobacco, and Belle followed him outdoors. He motioned across the street where a team of horses were hitched to a wagon with wooden railings. "Mind riding in the wagon?" They crossed the street together.

"Beats blisters on my feet," she said.

"Father, this is Joe. He needs a ride to his grandparents." Chase turned to Belle. "This is my father, Tosaguara, White Bear." Chase handed the tin of tobacco to his father.

The older man gave a nod. A long braid fell down his back in the old style.

Chase opened the back gate, and she climbed onto the wagon bed. The smell of manure lifted from the swept floorboards, but to Belle it was a welcome scent, reminding her of the barn back home. Once they reached the outskirts of town, Tosaguara urged the team of horses into a trot. Jostled back and forth, Belle contrasted her luxurious ride in the Model T with the rough ride in the wagon. Might as well get used to it. Grandfather certainly didn't have Ford's automobile.

She had time to think about her unexpected family reunion. Would Grandfather be angry she'd left school? What would her grandmother think of her shorn hair and boy's clothing? No doubt about it, she wasn't the same little girl who'd known only the world within a five mile radius. For four years, she had dreamt of running away from Chilocco, but was she prepared to go back? Her heart still ached for her friend, Flora. Confused by conflicting loyalties, she focused on her empty stomach.

She unwrapped the Hershey bar, closed her eyes, and inhaled the delicious scent of chocolate. Hunger quickly trumped her intention to relish the candy bar, and she devoured it in a few bites. Belle chugged the last swig of milk. Her stomach churned at the sweet, sloshy meal and worries of her coming reception.

The sun hung high overhead when she parted ways with Chase and his father. At the dusty crossroad, the air stirred hot and sticky. She had five miles to home. Between the heat and lack of a solid meal, she forewent running. Five miles wasn't that far to walk. Her slow but deliberate progress spooked a jackrabbit at the shoulder of the road. As she continued, she spotted several more that scurried from the bar ditch into the trees.

During the heat of the day, freshly plowed fields were abandoned. The earthy scent of turned soil smelled of home. Farmhouses along the road made her homesick and excited at the same time. Alongside a faded barn, chickens pecked in the dirt. A mile farther, she passed an older couple catching the breeze on their porch. The woman waved. Though Belle didn't know the farmwife, she waved back enthusiastically.

From behind came the clop of hooves. She glanced back. At the sight of the black buggy, she plunged into the bar ditch and fled into the thick blackjacks above the road. Her heart raced as the buggy passed, but the driver turned out to be a young man. The memory of the day she left home still haunted her.

Her heart lifted as she passed neighbors who had helped her family over the years. Dark hands shot up in greeting, though surely they didn't recognize her with shorn braids and pants. The landscape became more wooded as the road followed the creek. Unfurled leaves and green grass swirled in a fragrant elixir. Horses in pastures stood head to tail and swished flies from each other.

Despite the heat, Belle ran the last mile, slowing to a walk only when her empty stomach turned in on itself. The road curved and the home place came into sight, the most beautiful scene she'd seen in four years. She strolled up the lane to the farmhouse and wondered how she might look. Wrinkled clothing. Disheveled hair. She wiped her mouth with the back of her hand in case any chocolate lingered. Grandfather Tahsuda stood on the porch, one arm hooked around a post.

"Greetings there, young man," he said. "Need a drink of water?" She stopped a few feet from the porch, unable to speak.

Grandfather narrowed his eyes and frowned. He stepped from the porch. "Is that you, Belle?"

She nodded, tears building.

He spread his arms, and she ran to him. His chest vibrated in a strange way as she drank in the familiar smell of his skin and the vestige of tobacco smoke on his shirt. He pulled away to get a better look, his eyes like still pools of dark water threatening to spill over.

"What have they done to you?" He inspected her from head to foot.

"I cut my hair, Grandfather." She looked down at her clothes. "It was easier to…to leave dressed like a boy." She held her breath, waiting for his objection.

He held her by the shoulders and stared for a good long time. His eyes closed for a moment. "I'm happy you're home."

She hugged him, burying her face in his rough canvas overalls. Unlike his usual reserved demeanor, he stood still and accepted her long embrace. He rested his chin on top of her head, and his strong hands pulled her close.

A screen door slammed. Behind them, Grandmother dropped to her faithful rocker. Belle ran up and hugged her. Her grandmother smiled. Deep wrinkles around the woman's eyes and lips had formed in the past four years. "Why are you here?"

Belle's shoulders drooped. It had been Grandfather's reaction she dreaded.

Her grandmother smiled and plucked an apple from a basket next to her chair. She pulled a paring knife from her apron pocket and began peeling.

Belle found her voice at last. "I'm back, Grandma." She squared her shoulders. "I'm home to stay."

Belle woke in her father's bed, sun streaming through the window. Without a bugle's harsh announcement of morning, she'd overslept. She hurried to the kitchen. They'd already eaten. Grandmother poured hot water into the basin and stirred soap flakes with a wooden spoon. A box of Lux soap sat on the counter.

"Morning, Grandmother."

Her grandmother swung around and nearly dropped the spoon on the floor. "You're still here?"

Belle's blood drained to her feet. Her grandmother turned back and dropped silverware into the basin.

"I'm home for good, Grandmother." Wasn't she wanted here? Her grandfather seemed happy to see her.

Belle grabbed a dishtowel and waited for the final rinse.

"Thank you, young man, but this is women's work."

"Grandma, it's me, Belle."

"Whose boy are you?" Her old dark eyes peered into Belle's.

"I'm Belle. Joseph's daughter."

"Joseph didn't have a boy. I would have known."

The clean white dishtowel dropped to the floor. The door slammed behind Belle. She raced into the barn where the dusty smell of hay spun in the shadowy interior. In a corner of an empty stall, she slid to the floor.

Hooves clobbered in the center aisle, and the stall door swung open.

"What are you doing, child?" The gray gelding poked its nose over Grandfather's shoulder and inspected the intruder.

She stood and sniffled as she wiped at her tears.

After putting the horse in its stall, Grandfather joined her outside the barn.

"She didn't remember you, did she?"

She shook her head. A sad, lonely look seized his face.

"Your grandmother has the old-people disease. Half the time, she doesn't know who I am."

Belle didn't know what to say. She dreamed of coming home for four years, but she never envisioned this situation.

"We'll have to be patient," Grandfather Tahsuda said. "Don't argue about what's right. She'll only get angry."

She nodded.

"I'm glad you're back. You can be a lot of help to us now."

In the midst of heartache, a warm, sweet feeling filled her chest. This was her chance to help, regardless of whether her grandmother knew her or not. The pain in her grandfather's eyes broke her heart. But one thing was certain, he needed her help more than he had ever needed it before.

When Belle wasn't helping around the house, she roamed the farm. Every day brought something new as she tromped through the woods. She surprised a deer with twin fawns, watched fish jump in the creek, and spotted a hawk with a mouse in its talons. She practiced her slingshot on water moccasins—good riddance—and an occasional rabbit for the stew pot.

In the early evening, she loved to run. After a few weeks, her physical stamina returned. She felt fully alive with the wind against her face and her lungs expanding with fresh air.

Surprisingly, the regimented life of Chilocco wasn't easily left behind. The morning no longer started with a bugle blast. Sometimes she'd find herself in the middle of a room feeling lost, like a soldier with no war to fight. Her grandparents didn't shout orders every minute of the day. Her grandmother's chores didn't keep her as busy as school duties and classes. Though she hated the noise on campus, her ears nearly rang with the stillness of rural life. She was happy to be home, but it was like adjusting to a new country.

The following week, Belle rode with her grandparents to Uncle Jay's farm a few miles to the west. Grandmother sat in between them, saying little on the trip.

"We're going to pick up a side of beef." Grandfather Tahsuda shook the reins, and the horse's gait quickened. "It's in trade for the hay I gave Jay this winter."

"He's raising cattle?"

"Crop prices aren't so good," he said. "Most farmers are just getting by. Good thing we can grow most of our own food."

They pulled up to a house smaller than her grandparents'. The structure's raw wood had been left unpainted. A little boy played in the dirt, his face smeared with dust. A woman appeared in the doorway, a younger child on her hip. Grandfather assisted her grandmother from the wagon. He hadn't told her Jay's new wife was white.

"Mary Lou," Grandfather tipped the brim of his hat.

"John," the woman said. "Jay's in the back shed."

The woman never smiled. Mary Lou flashed her eyes at Belle and turned toward the house. Grandfather had already walked away. Belle knelt next to the young boy.

"What's your name?" The boy glanced at her and returned his attention to the wooden truck.

"His name is Matthew." The screen door framed Mary Lou's silhouette. "Come inside if you want tea."

Belle slid her arm around Grandmother's elbow and escorted her into the house. Old newspapers upholstered half of the tattered sofa. Children's clothing littered the floor next to a wicker basket. She couldn't tell whether they were clean or dirty. Through a doorway, a table could be seen heaped with dirty dishes that flooded over onto one of the chairs. The smell of soiled diapers drifted from somewhere in the house as they followed Jay's wife into the kitchen.

"Sit down," Mary Lou said. Her stomach protruded from the dingy housedress.

Belle directed her grandmother to a chair at the end of the table and removed a pair of toddler's pants from another. She was startled by her uncle's wife, who was only a few years older than Belle. Uncle Jay had been busy in her absence, married with two young children and another on the way.

With her bulging abdomen preceding her, Mary Lou brought two steaming cups to the table and plopped in the chair opposite Belle. "Abe's down for a nap, thank goodness." Mary Lou motioned toward Grandmother. "How's the old woman?"

"Some days are better than others," Belle whispered. "We make do." Her grandmother was putting teaspoon after teaspoon of sugar into her cup. Worried she'd empty the entire sugar bowl, Belle nudged it from her reach.

"So, I heard you were at Chilocco," her young aunt said. "How bad was it?"

"It's a different world that's for sure." She blew at the hot tea. "We marched everywhere. Didn't have a spare moment until late in the evening. It's like being in the army."

"Try waking up every few hours to nurse a baby." An indignant look flicked Belle's way. "Try cooking and cleaning and watching kids until you drop into bed at night." A wail came from outside, but Mary Lou didn't budge.

From what she'd seen, the woman didn't do much cleaning or watching kids, for that matter.

"I'm sure being a mother is a lot of work," she said to be polite.

"Just you wait." Mary Lou's eyes narrowed in warning. "Just you wait."

"So how's Uncle Jay?"

"He's a man, ain't he?" Her mouth pursed in a grimace. "He's always off somewhere doin' somethin'."

Uncle Jay, what have you gotten yourself into? She gave a weak smile and wished she'd followed her grandfather to the shed.

After forty unbearable minutes with Mary Lou, Grandfather appeared in the doorway.

"We're leaving."

Belle couldn't wait to get home.

Outside, she greeted Uncle Jay, whose face had grown creases around his eyes.

"You've grown, Belle," he said. "You look like your mother."

"Good to see you again, Uncle Jay." A few photographs of her mother lay buried at the bottom of a trunk. She quit asking her father to bring them out when she saw how sad the pictures made him. After he died, Belle often studied them when no one was around. The photographs revealed a beautiful woman with high cheekbones and wide brown eyes. Her uncle thought she looked like her mother?

A quarter mile down the road, Grandpa snorted. "His wife didn't even offer us lunch. Your grandmother always fed anyone who came to the house, especially near meal time."

She glanced up at her grandfather. "Would you really want to eat in that mess?"

"You've got a point there, girl." He shook his head.

"That woman," Grandmother said, "needs someone to teach her how to clean."

Belle and her grandfather broke out laughing.

Grandmother looked puzzled. "Don't you think so?"

"You're so right, Huutsi." Belle used the Comanche term for grandmother. "You're absolutely right."

Belle poured water into the basin and sprinkled soap flakes over the steaming water. She stirred the dishwater with a wooden spoon. Once the soap was dissolved, she added enough cold water to keep from burning her hands. A spring breeze carried the song of meadowlarks through the open window.

A year had passed since she walked up the lane and greeted her grandfather. She gazed at her grandmother asleep in the chair. That was how her grandmother spent most of her days. Belle almost preferred it to the way the old woman would stare out the window for long periods without speaking. Belle did all the cooking and cleaning, but she didn't resent it. Grandfather could never get by without her help.

Outside the window, Grandfather Tahsuda and another man strode to the barn. She leaned toward the glass. It was Otis Harwood. She couldn't believe the tall young man with broad shoulders was the same neighbor boy she used to play with—a skinny, scrawny youth with his hair always tangled. Otis caught her looking and grinned. She pulled back from the window, her face warm from more than dishwater.

Grandfather had asked her to cook extra for the farmhand he hired for spring planting. She had no idea it was Otis until then. In a few minutes, she'd pluck the chickens Grandfather had killed that morning. She dipped one of the fowl in a pot of boiling water, which helped loosen the feathers. A pail of potatoes from the root cellar awaited washing and peeling. Otis Harwood. The silly boy didn't look so awkward anymore. His mama was Comanche, his father white. Otis was a fine looking mix of the two races.

In the front yard, she rang the bucket-sized dinner bell, hurried inside, and checked her appearance in the mirror. Wisps of hair poked around her face, those stray pieces that never seemed to stay in place when her hair was pulled back in a braid. She glanced at the tidy place settings on the oak table and was reminded of her classes at Chilocco. Government boarding school had groomed the boys to be farmers and the girls to be wives or domestic help. Belle had other plans. She wanted to help run the farm with Grandfather, but so far she hadn't made much progress. In the meantime, it was more important that she continue her household chores.

Boots stomped on the front porch. She spun around and added a serving spoon to a pan of mashed potatoes.

"Sure smells good," her grandfather said. "Look who's here, Belle."

She turned around and tried to smile naturally. "Otis, I'd know you anywhere. How are you?"

"You sure have changed," Otis said.

Her grandfather helped move Grandmother to the table. "We're going to eat now, Ma."

Otis's eyes rolled over her. Belle pretended she hadn't noticed and transferred the chicken to a platter. "How are your folks?" Up close, he was even better looking.

"Ma's fine. Pa's had some trouble with his back."

"Sit down, boy," Grandfather Tahsuda said. "Belle's fixin' to serve a mighty good meal."

Once everyone was seated, Grandfather offered a brief blessing. Belle passed the platter to the men, then the mashed potatoes, and finally a plate of cornbread.

"Otis here is a good helper."

Belle passed the butter dish. "I'd like to help, too."

"Aw, this is good chicken," Otis said. "Too good to waste your time in the field."

"I can learn." She sat taller.

"These good vittles are worth an acre of land," Grandfather said.

Otis mumbled with full cheeks. "Sure are."

She slumped and settled on eating. Men. They could be so stubborn.

"My son, Jay, is so busy farming his place and feeding those children of his, I decided it best to pay someone to help me this year." Grandfather gently nudged Grandma. "Try to eat a little bit, Cora."

Her grandmother took a half-hearted bite of chicken.

"So, Otis, how are your brothers doing?" She deflected the conversation away from her grandmother. "Are they still around these parts?"

Otis wiped his mouth with the side of his hand. "Albert moved to the Panhandle to ranch. Jess married a gal in Texas and works at her father's general store. George and I are the only ones left on the homeplace.

"I'm sure your mother's happy about that." She didn't like the way he stuffed his mouth with food. Couldn't he slow down and chew? "There's a lot more food where that came from."

"That's good, 'cause I sure am hungry."

She didn't mean to feel superior, but she wondered if Otis had ever been more than ten miles from home. Bet he'd never driven with a traveling band. Or been a stowaway on a train. Even Chilocco was an experience she was beginning to realize had some good points. She'd been around a bit. Though

Otis was good to set the eyes on, he probably couldn't carry on a conversation further than the world of sowing and threshing.

"That was mighty fine, Belle." Grandfather pulled his chair away from the table. "Time to get back to work, boy." "Yes, sir."

Grandfather escorted Grandma to the bedroom for her afternoon nap. Otis remained in the kitchen. "Care to go horseback riding some evening?"

"We'll see," she said as she scraped the plates. "Sometime, maybe."

"Well, then. Sometime. Thank you for the mighty good meal, ma'am."

She wheeled around. How dare he call her ma'am like she was some old maid. But Otis was out the door, striding to catch up with her grandfather. She was almost thirteen, tall, and wearing a brassiere beneath her dress, but ma'am?

With the house to herself, Belle pulled out her letter from Flora and reread it for the tenth time. She had written to Flora and told her how she ran away from Chilocco. It took three weeks to receive a letter back. Flora said she was busy taking care of her ill mother. She'd laughed at Belle's daring escape. Belle refolded the paper and started a new letter to her friend. We have something in common. My grandmother isn't well, and I've taken over the cooking and cleaning...

In the middle of the afternoon, she carried a jug of cold lemonade to the field. The day was warm, and the men would be thirsty. But she had an alternative motive. She wanted to learn the business of farming. How hard could it be?

A shortcut through blackjack oak brought her into an open cornfield where a fire was burning. Otis tossed cornstalks into the flames, and Grandfather Tahsuda poked the fire to its best advantage. They were clearing the field for that year's crop of alfalfa.

"Tell me that's some cold, sweet lemonade." Otis pulled a bandana from his overall pocket and swept his forehead.

"Thought you might be thirsty." She headed to the side of the field, and they all sat under the shade of a towering oak.

"This sure hits the spot," her grandfather said. Thirsty gulps soon made an end of the lemonade. "Thank you, Belle. Guess it's time we got back to work."

"Can I help?" she asked.

Grandfather narrowed his eyes. "It's hard work, and that sun's mighty hot."

"I'm willing." Out of the corner of her eye, she saw Otis shake his head in derision.

"Give it a try, then." Grandfather headed for the middle of the field where last year's cornstalks crackled in the breeze. "Now, watch." He squatted and grabbed a few stalks. He hooked a curved cutting blade at the base of the stalks and with one swift movement sliced the cornstalks and tossed them to the side. He handed her the corn knife. "Every so often, carry a pile of stalks to the fire."

The sun glinted off the 12-inch blade. She stared at the sharp knife but wasn't about to be shown up. Her first try was dismal, but she learned to put more muscle behind her swing. She found relief by carrying armloads of stalks to the fire. Sweating, she found it much harder than she'd imagined. Otis glanced over as she went back to cutting. The sun beat down on her head. She berated herself for thinking she was up to hard manual labor, but her pride compelled her to continue for an hour and a half.

"Grandfather, I forgot my straw hat," she said. "I'll bring some more lemonade."

"Hurry back," he said.

She couldn't decide if her grandfather was serious or holding back a smile. She marched past Otis. "Forgot my hat."

He grinned but didn't say a word. She wanted to wipe the cocky expression right off his face.

A few minutes later, she stepped into the soothing coolness of the house. A short afternoon nap was worth a blow to her pride. She passed through the sitting room and peered into the kitchen. Grandma must be napping. Belle cracked the door to her grandparents' room. The bed was empty.

Chapter 12

"GRANDMA?" BELLE RETURNED TO THE front room where her grandmother often sat in the dim corner, staring straight ahead. But the room was vacant.

She took one last futile look in the kitchen and raced outside. Behind the house stood a stack of firewood and a dishtowel flapping on the clothesline. Belle checked the barn and searched every dark stall. The tart lemonade rumbled in her stomach. It was her fault. She shouldn't have left her grandmother alone for so long. The thought of telling Grandfather brought hot chills down her neck.

She raced to the north, expecting to see Grandmother shuffling down the road, but there was no sign of her on the half mile to the Black Bear family farm.

On her front porch, Agnes watered tomato seedlings growing in a tin bucket.

"Mrs. Black Bear, have you seen my grandmother?" Belle knew by the puzzled look on the woman's face her grandmother had not made it that far. "We'll head north and look." Agnes wiped her hands on her apron. "You head back, she might have returned home by now."

Belle averted her eyes. "Thank you." Everyone knew her grandmother's condition. It was Belle's duty to take care of her. She ran, her mouth dry as dirt. Her shame threatened to crush her to the ground. Back home, her stomach sank at the sight of the empty chair on the porch, one of Grandma's favorite places to sit after her nap. Belle undertook another quick sweep of the house to no avail. She returned to the road and ran south. Please, God, don't let anything happen to Grandmother. I beg you. Punish me instead.

Seventy-five degrees was stifling in the humidity. A mile down the road, she came to Otis's house. He would justifiably consider her a foolish girl, wanting to help the men in the field instead of fulfilling her obligations. She rapped on the screen door. Footsteps came from the distant reaches of the house. Mrs. Harwood opened the door, her dark hair swept up in a red scarf, a paring knife in hand.

"Belle, how good to see you. Come in."

"Have you seen my grandmother? Has she been here?"

"No, dear. I doubt she'd walk this far. Are you sure she's not somewhere around the house?"

"I'll check again. Thank you, Mrs. Harwood." She flew off the porch steps and raced home, dreading Grandfather Tahsuda's response. Her heart sank at the mental image of his frightened face. The roadside scenery blurred in salty tears as she ran back. She wiped her eyes and glanced up to find Otis sitting on the porch next to Grandmother, who was laughing at something he said.

"Where—" Her breathing was labored. "Where was she?"

"I was headed home through the trees and found her sitting on a stump, singing."

"Does Grandfather know?"

"He stayed behind to make sure the fire went out."

"I should have stayed at the house. Please don't tell Grandfather." What right did she have to ask him to keep a confidence?

Otis guided her to an empty chair. "Everything's okay, Belle. Your grandmother's fine."

"But it's my fault—"

"It's hard when they get like this. Don't blame yourself." He removed the bandana around his neck and wiped her wet cheeks. "No harm's been done. I won't say anything."

"Your mother knows. I checked at your place."

"I'll explain it to her. She'll understand. She went through the same thing with her father."

Her grandmother hummed and traced the flower print on her dress.

"Go inside and fetch us some of your good lemonade." Otis tilted his head and smiled. "It'll help you compose yourself before your grandfather comes back."

Belle imagined her red eyes, swollen nose, and tear-stained face. She had to look a mess. She glanced down at her dirt-filmed hands and back at the young man standing before her. Otis's eyes were intelligent, despite the fact he'd never seen much of the world. His face held so much compassion and grace that her tears threatened to surface again. She rushed toward the door before that could happen.

In the kitchen, a bowl of lemons filled a yellow-ware bowl. She cut the fruit and placed half in the cast-iron lemon squeezer. The tart citrus scent filled the room. She squeezed more lemons and added a scoopful of sugar to the pitcher of cold water. Otis made the sour day turn sweet like lemonade, and she had found a friend where she least expected one.

Grandfather Tahsuda never knew about his lost wife. Otis was true to his word. Ironically, after that time she grew closer to her grandfather. One evening, Belle escaped the warm kitchen and caught a breeze on the front porch. Near the barn, a corral enclosed a patch of red earth, the clearing free of dry grass that might catch fire. She asked permission to build a bonfire.

She dragged a stump for a seat and made several trips carrying firewood. At dusk she lit kindling, and by the time the fire blazed, the sky was black, and stars salted the night sky. As the fire snapped and spit, she gazed at the constellations. The Seven Stars of the Great Bear was the only constellation she recognized. Whites called it the Big Dipper, but Indians considered the handle to be the bear's tail. The campfire crackled, and flames leapt in the dark as if trying to catch the stars. A twig broke somewhere in the dark. She spun around. A large form approached in the gloom.

"It's only me, Belle." Grandfather Tahsuda placed his hand on her shoulder.

"Good night for a campfire. Take my seat, Grandfather." She grabbed a long stick. "I need to stir the fire." To her surprise, he accepted her offer. She often sat on the porch with her grandmother, but rarely did he join them. At dinner, conversation was sparse and when he did talk, the subject was usually about farm chores.

"Ah, the Milky Way." He pointed. "Do you know how it came about?"

"Tell me, Grandfather." She smiled in the dark.

"Long ago, a grizzly bear climbed up a mountain to go hunting. But this was not an ordinary hunt, he wanted to hunt in the sky. The higher he climbed into the heavens, the colder it became. Snow and ice clung to his fur. The grizzly crossed the sky, hunting for game. Ice crystals trailed behind him. Today, we call the trail of ice crystals the Milky Way."

"I'll share that story with my children someday," she said. "I'll tell them their great-grandfather told me the story by a campfire one night."

In the firelight, a slow smile formed on his face. "The People used to live under the stars." He stared into the campfire. "Your people, Belle. When the Comanche people were asked about their numbers, they claimed they were as numerous as the stars.

"They lived closer to the earth than we do now." Firelight played over his high cheekbones. "They drank from streams so clear the water sparkled. Children played in the long grass while their fathers roamed the prairie hunting for buffalo. They only took what they needed to live and never wasted anything." He stared at the campfire for a moment. "How often the People must have studied the stars on a night like this. Can you imagine smoke rising in the twilight from a hundred campfires?"

"I can see it, Grandfather." She imagined teepees lining the Red River like trees.

"The first generation on the reservation couldn't comprehend the concept of private property." Grandfather's low voice rolled over the night air. "They never claimed to own land, only the right to hunt and live on it. The People respected the earth and its creatures. The whites thought they were doing us a favor by allotting land to each family. But they had taken away our freedom to roam the plains and move from site to site. The whites knew by allowing the slaughter of vast herds of buffalo they were destroying our way of life. It was easier to move us on the reservation after our main source of food disappeared."

She'd never heard her grandfather speak about the time before the Comanche were forced to live in Indian Territory. With her father gone and her uncle busy with his family, Grandfather had few opportunities to talk about the past.

Grandfather Tahsuda tossed another log on the fire and hobbled to the stump.

Belle figured his rheumatism must be acting up again.

His voice turned solemn. "When soldiers drove my father's family to Fort Sill, my mother was afraid. She'd heard stories of warriors sequestered in a roofless building, guards standing outside and tossing raw meat over the wall. They treated the men like wild animals.

"Worse yet, some of the warriors were shot and killed for no other reason than the soldiers were afraid of them, afraid of the fierce warriors who had been brought so low they stooped to live on the reservation. Sometimes it was pure hate that made the soldiers do it.

"My oldest brother was probably fourteen or fifteen at the time. Our mother was worried for his safety, so she dressed him in women's clothing. Remember that all the men had long hair back then, and it was easy to fool the whites. Years later, my brother insisted Mother saved his life."

She thought back to Chilocco and how the government-run school tried to press the students into a white mold. It appeared the government had tried to strangle the Indian out of their dark skins for a long time.

"I'll also tell my sons that story, Grandfather."

He nodded. "It's good they'll know their heritage." They sat without speaking as the fire died down.

"Go inside and check on your Grandmother," he said. "I'll watch the fire burn out."

Belle leaned over and kissed his cheek. "Thank you for sharing your stories."

With one palm, he warmed her face for a moment.

"Good night, Grandfather." She was halfway to the house when she paused and looked back. The smell of smoke drifted on the air. It was hard to tell in the flickering light, but for a moment, it appeared he was dancing.

Belle was about to serve the evening meal when a wagon rattled up the lane. Grandfather Tahsuda looked out the screen door. "It's Jay and his whole family."

Surely, they didn't expect to be fed? Grandfather walked back to the kitchen.

"Hold on, Belle," he said. "I'll find out if they're eating with us."

"But we don't have enough food." There wasn't but one piece of chicken each if Uncle Jay joined them. The potatoes wouldn't go far enough. "Grandfather, remember how Mary Lou didn't even—"

Her grandfather held up a hand. "We'll make do with that fresh loaf of bread you made this morning."

Belle followed him to the doorway.

"Just about to sit down and eat," Grandfather said. "Care to join us?" "I am mighty hungry." Jay looked back at his wife.

"Thought you'd never ask," Mary Lou added. She held the latest addition to their family, another boy.

Belle slumped and returned to the kitchen. She sliced more bread and pulled four plates from the cupboard. "Grandmother, can you add four more settings of silverware? We have company."

Grandmother shuffled to the cupboard. "Who are they?"

"Uncle Jay, Mary Lou, and their kids."

"Mary who?"

Belle withdrew four more glasses.

Jay's family arrived in the kitchen like a sudden thunderstorm. Matthew pulled the two-and-a half year-old's hair, and Abe screamed. Even the baby was crying, but Mary Lou seemed oblivious to all the commotion. "Somebody take care of that baby," Grandmother grumbled.

Mary Lou tossed her a hard look.

"Sit down everyone and I'll set the food out." Belle pulled the roasting pan from the oven. The squalling baby was a good excuse, she supposed, for Mary Lou to avoid helping. She glanced over, surprised that it was Uncle Jay who jostled the baby in his arms while Mary Lou sat at the table and buttered a piece of bread without waiting for Grandfather's blessing.

At last, the food was on the table, and Grandfather offered a prayer. "Thank you, Great Creator, from whom all this bounty comes. Bless it to our good health. Amen."

Mary Lou wiped crumbs from her lips. When the platter of chicken came to Belle, she chose a wing and spooned only a dollop of mashed potatoes, so the men would have at least one decent serving. Belle looked over to see Mary Lou had taken the chicken breast and helped herself to two servings of mashed potatoes. Grandfather wanted her to be hospitable, but it was becoming harder by the minute.

Four-year-old Matthew tossed his bread to the floor. Mary Lou didn't appear to notice.

"No, Matthew," Belle said. "We don't throw good food away."

Mary Lou reached over and gave the boy another piece. Matthew caught Belle's eye and flung the bread over the table where it landed on the floor again.

"No!" Belle reached for the bread plate. "No more bread for you."

"He's just a little boy," Mary Lou said. "Haven't you been around children before?"

Not like your spoiled kids, she thought but held her tongue. Once more, Matthew tugged at Abe's hair. Despite the fact that Abe sat on his mother's lap, Mary Lou did nothing to correct the boy.

"Hush now, child," Mary Lou said. "Pass the chicken, Belle."

The platter was empty. "I'm afraid, we weren't expecting company. May I butter you a piece of bread?"

"If you're going to be a wife someday, Belle, you'll have to learn to cook larger amounts of food."

"I don't plan on getting married, thank you."

"You'll never get married?" Mary Lou looked astounded. "Don't you like men?"

"I like them just fine, Mary Lou." Belle glared at her aunt.

"She's an odd one, huh," Mary Lou said to her husband, without much effort to lower her voice.

Matthew pinched his little brother, and the child wailed again.

"I need to feed the chickens." Belle marched from the room, but instead of heading to the chicken coop with its well-fed fowl, she ran through blackjack oak and into the clearing where Grandfather had burned cornstalks. At the edge of the clearing, she picked up rocks from piles that had been cleared from the field. With all her strength, she pitched fist-sized rocks, one at a time, deeper into the woods. With each throw, she pictured the self-absorbed face of Mary Lou. After twenty rocks and a stiff shoulder, she could breathe again. She waited forty minutes before she returned home. As she'd hoped, Uncle Jay's wagon was gone. In the bedroom, Grandfather settled

Grandmother down for the night. A cluttered table and a host of dirty dishes awaited in the kitchen. Food splattered across the floor, heaviest beneath Matthew's chair. She started the burner under the kettle of water and scraped leftovers into the slop bucket.

Belle finished cleaning the kitchen and headed for the porch. She sighed and relished the quiet evening. To the west, light clung to the horizon, maintaining its final hold on the day before darkness swept it away.

The screen door opened.

"Thank you, Belle," Grandfather said. "I appreciate it." Nothing more was said about the affair. He joined her on the porch and sat in the rocking chair. The sky turned red-orange at the horizon. "I never grow tired of watching a sunset."

"That's the good thing about living in the country," she said. At Chilocco, a rare glimpse of sunset might occur on the way back from kitchen duty. She had to admit even run-ins with Mary Lou were better than being at boarding school.

Grandfather talked about the planted alfalfa and the east pasture turning green. She inserted an occasional question. The sky had turned dark when she realized he was talking to her like one of the men. It was a good feeling to be included on what went on around the farm.

After a while, they sat in silence. A coyote yipped in the distance. Grandfather leaned forward in his chair, and a moment later, a trill of yips came in return. Haunting yet beautiful, the feral song drew shivers down Belle's back.

"The song-dogs are at it again." He stood and arched his back. "Think I'll make a cup of tea," he paused, "Should I make two?"

She didn't like the flavor of tea, but it was a rare occurrence for her grandfather to offer anything from the kitchen. Was he pacifying her after the tense dinner?

"Sounds good, Grandfather."

Several minutes later, he returned with two china cups. She sipped the hot tea, and the flavor of honey and peppermint skipped over her tongue. "This is good."

A full moon rose above the barn, flushing light across the yard.

"Good night for a pack of coyotes to hunt," he said. "We may hear them again." He blew on his tea. "It's a Comanche Moon."

"Why do they call it that?"

"Our people were noted horsemen. Except for maybe the Apache, no other tribe could outride or outshoot a Comanche on horseback. Even the women were good riders. My grandmother talked about her mother lassoing an antelope on the prairie when she was a young woman."

She marveled at the idea of a woman who accomplished more than being a wife and mother. Pride blossomed in her chest.

"The Quahadis were the fiercest band of all the Comanche. They were the last tribe to come into Indian Territory. Before they finally surrendered, the Quahadis raided remote settlements across the Texas Territory. During the spring and summer, they made so many attacks under the light of a full moon that terrified settlers referred to those nights as a Comanche Moon." A series of howls rang out, followed by sharp yips.

"That's a sound I never tire of hearing," Grandfather said.

"Me, neither." And she never would.

Otis appeared at their door early one evening. Behind him, two horses were tied to a tree.

"How about that ride, Belle?" he said.

She looked back at Grandfather. He nodded, a smile nudging his mouth.

"Thank you, sir." Otis held the door open for her.

The big draft horses were made for farming. She refrained from smiling. It was going to be a dull, plodding ride.

"They're slow," Otis said, "but we'll see the world from a different perspective." He cupped his hands together at the horse's side.

She slipped her foot into the makeshift stirrup and hopped aboard the horse's bare back. "What's his name?"

"That freckled guy is Fred," he said. "This big gal is Fanny."

"Fred and Fanny," she said. "Good names for a pair of plow horses."

"Don't let them hear you," Otis said. "They think they're thoroughbreds."

Otis was right, riding atop the tall horses gave her a fresh view of familiar scenery. She could see higher in the trees and further in the distance over open fields.

At the new bridge, they dismounted, tied the horses to a tree, and headed down to the creek. They sat on the bank without talking and watched the current run between boulders.

"What's the matter, Belle?"

"The creek brings back memories." She brushed a hand across her eyes. "I miss my father."

"I'm sorry. We shouldn't have come here."

"Nonsense," she said. "It's just that I don't have anyone to talk to about it. I can't trouble my grandparents, and I just miss him sometimes."

"Of course, you do. I have a good buddy who died in a hunting accident." Otis nudged a rock with a twig. "It always comes back to you when you aren't expecting it."

They watched the current for a while. All of her senses drank in the boy sitting beside her, his long fingers, his quiet breathing, even the smell of his clean shirt. She glanced at him, and he slowly leaned towards her. Mary Lou's disheveled hair came to mind, the squalling babies, and her taunt, "Just you wait."

She stood and dusted off her pants. "Let's go back, and I'll serve you some apple crisp with whipped cream."

"Why, sure." Otis turned his flushed face and followed her to the road.

Later that night, she lay in bed and wondered what Otis Harwood's kiss would have felt like.

Hardly a week went by that Otis didn't come calling at the Tahsuda farm. Sometimes he asked her along on an errand to town. Sometimes they'd go fishing in the creek and catch more flies than fish. Once he strolled up to the house and delivered a bouquet—a fistful of purple locoweed, goldenrod, and the delicate white blossoms of pale smartweed. It was on another picnic that she discovered Otis had a hidden sense of adventure.

She set two tin plates on the blanket and unwrapped her warm fried chicken. The creek gurgled below them.

"That smells mighty fine," Otis said. "A guy could get used to your cooking."

She smiled, ignoring the innuendo.

After Otis had finished all of her potato salad and chicken, he retrieved something from the saddlebag.

"Do you like Stevenson?" he asked, flipping through the book.

"Who?"

"As in Robert Louis." He raised one eyebrow. "You're the one that went to the fancy school."

"Of course, I've heard of Robert Louis Stevenson." It was a book that boys preferred.

"Mind if I read you some?"

"Go ahead." She lay back on the blanket, her hands behind her head.

"...that filthy, heavy," he read, "bleared scarecrow of a pirate of ours, sitting, far gone with rum," Otis looked over and winked.

She liked the sound of his voice and smiled at how Otis manipulated his tone depending on the verse. Her farm boy was more literate than she expected. He set down the book and sang the famous pirate song about a bottle of rum.

"Do you know how a pirate kisses?" He leaned in.

"With a breath of rum, no doubt." She jumped to her feet, packed the dishes into the canvas bag, and pulled the drawstring closed.

"What?" He stood with hands at his waist. "No dessert?"

"I didn't think you cared for cherry pie." She laughed and withdrew two carefully wrapped objects from the bag. Belle untied the twine wound around each slice.

"If it wasn't for the fragile delicacy in your hands, I'd paddle you, girl."

"Like to see you try."

"Don't tempt me, and hand over the pie."

He bit into his slice, closed his eyes, and moaned in delight. Otis was a kind person. He stroked his horse's neck and never used a harsh tone with the animal even when it preferred to plod along. She'd seen him stop to move an injured sparrow from the road. She'd never heard him say a bad word about anyone. But it took only a visit from Mary Lou and Uncle Jay and her sniffling brats to convince Belle that Otis was best saved for a friend.

Chapter 13

BELLE ROSE ONE LATE-NOVEMBER morning and found her grandfather motionless in the kitchen. An unlit lantern rested on the table. He usually checked on the animals while she ground beans and made coffee. Slumped in the kitchen chair, he sat with his eyes closed. Her heart skipped a beat.

She pulled a chair close and waited silently. His chest rose almost imperceptibly. A stroke? She'd heard that that was a common occurrence with the elderly.

She took a deep breath and whispered, "Grandfather." One eyelid quivered. "Grandfather, are you all right?"

A lone tear coursed down his dark cheek. His eyes opened. "She's gone, Belle. Cora's gone."

She wrapped her arms around her grandfather, and his chest shuddered.

"Go tell Jay." He rose and shuffled into the bedroom.

Through clouded eyes, she saddled the old gelding and managed to get him bridled. The horse clopped down the road in the low light of dawn. Her grandfather's grief broke her heart. Before Belle left, she had caught the form of her grandmother curled under the comforter, peaceful as if she were sleeping. From the doorway, Belle watched Grandfather Tahsuda crawl under the covers beside his wife of sixty-one years.

Later that evening, Belle slipped through the mourners gathered in the kitchen and parlor—friends and neighbors who had come from miles away. Her stroll down the road in the pitch-black night didn't bring apprehension.

Every bend and curve was familiar. Away from platitudes and offers of sympathy, her tears flowed freely. That was when she heard the haunting call of the screech owl, its cry piercing the darkness and tearing her heart.

Though in spirit, her grandmother had been gone for a long time, Belle still found it difficult to accept her death. Grandma had been a constant in her life since she was a little girl, and it felt like the sun no longer rose. But for her grandfather, the loss was even more tragic. The morning after the funeral, Belle entered the kitchen to make coffee as usual. Her stomach twisted at the sight of Grandfather's field coat on the entry hook. She tiptoed to his bedroom. In the dark, his body curled over the bed. Had he died from grief? Her eyes dilated. Still of this world, his chest rose and fell.

That was the start of a new routine. Always an early riser, her grandfather now woke two hours later than usual. Several mornings, she had to keep his breakfast warm in the oven. He cared little about the operation of the farm, so Belle helped more outside, and Uncle Jay assisted with the planting and harvesting. Her grandfather was never the same after they laid Grandma's body to rest.

Belle talked about cheerful things, but her grandfather didn't respond. She finally gave up trying to engage him in conversation. It was like talking to a stranger. So busy with running the household along with helping around the farm, she had little time to think of anything else. Belle welcomed Otis's visits, which gave her someone to talk to and helped her remember she was only fourteen.

July of 1929 sizzled with heat. A year and eight months had passed since her grandmother's death. With beads of sweat rolling down her forehead, Belle dunked her feet in the slow moving creek, the afternoon muggy and miserable. She dipped her hand in the cool water and splashed her face. Lying on the bank, she listened to the creek gurgle and the flutelike melody of a meadowlark. A soft rustle in the brush suggested a squirrel or rabbit. Slowly the babbling water lulled her to sleep.

Something had changed. Her eyes flew open. The bees stopped buzzing. All birdsong ceased. The creek gurgled on, the only remaining sound under the hot sun. Not a hint of a breeze stirred, making the humidity unbearable.

She was disturbed not by a sound but by something more sinister—a blanket of silence.

She sat upright and a moment later, a monstrous roar surrounded her, the rumble of a great freight train rushing full speed ahead. She ran to the road and darted for home. Dirt swirled in the air, making it difficult to see. At the side of the road, a thick limb slammed against a tree trunk with a loud crack. Rocks flew inches from her head, and a branch whizzed past her ear. She jumped into the ditch and crawled inside a galvanized steel culvert. A battleground clamored around her. Soil whipped up into a fog as rocks, leaves, and branches spun in all directions. Unrelenting snaps and thuds filled the air. In the middle of the tornado, she clapped hands over her ears. Her eyes remained open as if her life depended on it until dirt stung her eyes. In the uproar that whirled overhead, her cries went unheard.

The pandemonium continued until she thought she'd go crazy. Her heart pounded out of control. When the storm finally passed over, silence rang in her ears. She huddled in the culvert until the dust settled.

Belle wiped grit from her eyes and squeezed from the culvert. Heavy limbs blocked the road. Leaves were scattered everywhere like autumn but they were green and it was the wrong season. She headed in the direction of home and found boulders pitted in the center of the road. Overhead, the afternoon sun hid behind a sky heavy with dirt.

A quarter of a mile farther, she passed an unfamiliar clearing. Dazed, she kept walking. She was disoriented, and everything around her looked foreign. Her stomach lurched. She wondered if she'd been dropped by the tornado in the next county like in the book, The Wizard of Oz. She stopped and turned around, scanning the alien landscape in desperation. The cupola from their barn rose above the trees, and a shriek of happiness escaped.

She ran back the way she'd come. The clearing she'd passed moments ago held a narrow outhouse that jutted from the earth at a strange angle. The outhouse should be hidden from the road by her grandparents' farmhouse. In the distance, the barn stood intact, straight and shingled as always. But the farmhouse had vanished.

A few feet away, she spotted strange lumps on the ground. Upon closer inspection, she discovered three dead chickens, one with blood running from its beak. All three birds were plucked clean.

A black-faced cow moseyed through the tangled grass. A starling chirped. Wood creaked, and a slab of wood opened like the cover of a book. A phantom emerged from the storm cellar and hesitated, its gray face searching for its next haunt

"Grandfather?"

He stared, unhearing.

She rushed to Grandfather Tahsuda and urged him to a nearby stump. "Sit here." His shaking arm felt frail, so unlike her strong, stalwart grandfather. She sat cross-legged on the ground and reached for an Osage orange. The rough bumps rolled across her fingertips as she revolved the sphere around and around. They sat without speaking as starlings swept overhead, eager to continue their day.

Grandfather Tahsuda grew more feeble by the day. The death of his wife had hit hard, but having the family home ripped from the foundation— the house he had built and lived in for years—completely broke him. Homeless, they stayed at Uncle Jay's. Nineteen twenty-nine was a desperate year and not just due to poor crop prices and bank closings. Belle had laughed when Otis told her he first thought the Stock Market collapse was a disaster at a local cattle auction.

Living around Mary Lou and her renegade children became unbearable. Belle would have escaped the din and dirt of the household and stayed in the barn, but she worried Mary Lou would neglect her grandfather as she did her own children. Belle was miserable.

At the dinner table, she had to coax her grandfather to eat, but he swatted her hand away after a few forkfuls. After a week, he refused to eat altogether and even Uncle Jay's exhortations had little success. She fled the table, unable to watch any longer.

Belle leaned against the porch pillar. The screen door slammed, and her uncle's hand rested on her shoulder.

She looked up through tears at Uncle Jay. "He's got to eat."

"Afraid he's lost the will to live," he said softly. "This last year's been too much for the old man." A glaze shone in Uncle Jay's eyes.

In the background, a child screamed and another laughed wickedly. Mary Lou shouted. Crying erupted in the house. Belle closed her eyes. "Nothin' we can do, now." Uncle Jay's boots hit the wooden steps, and he ambled in the direction of the outbuilding.

She took off in the opposite direction and ran down the road until she couldn't breathe, couldn't think, and most of all, could no longer feel.

A month later, they laid Grandfather to rest in the grove behind the plot that once held the farmhouse. Once again her grandparents slept together.

Family and neighbors gathered at Uncle Jay's farm. Many good things were credited to Grandfather Tahsuda, and people still talked about her grandmother, as if a person couldn't discuss one without the other. Otis and his family arrived. She was grateful when Otis suggested a walk. He held her hand, and she relished his warm, steady grasp.

"You've had a bad year, girl," he said. "First your grandmother, now your grandfather. And that tornado. Those darn storms are completely unpredictable. Couldn't believe the storm destroyed your house and left the barn intact like nothing happened. Doesn't make sense."

"A lot of things don't make sense," she mumbled. She hadn't eaten much for two days and was bone tired.

"I know it's hard." He stopped on the dirt road and cupped her face in his hands. "I'm so sorry, Belle."

For a moment, she thought he might kiss her. She wouldn't have cared one way or another. When he removed his hands, she missed their warmth and comfort. They continued to walk hand in hand.

"I'm going to Texas," he announced.

"Texas. What for?"

"I'm gonna work for my brother. Remember I told you he works in his father-in-law's store?"

She found it hard to breathe. She couldn't imagine Otis gone. "But why all the way there?"

"I want to see more of the world than just these few acres, I guess." He dug the toe of his boot in the gravel.

She remembered when she thought he didn't have an ounce of adventure in him.

"Ain't like we're a regular couple, now is it?" He lifted his chin, and his eyes held questions.

She didn't answer. It was like her tongue wouldn't work. Aware she could say something that would change his mind, the opportunity hovered like the still air before the tornado hit. But images of Mary Lou's unkept house and the squalling, undisciplined children spun through her head. What if she did get together with Otis? He was a kind man, gentle, and not hard to look at. But she didn't see herself becoming a mother so soon. And then what? She'd be stuck with babies and cleaning and forsaking all chance for anything else in life. The pressure of his hand continued as they strolled down the road. The moment vanished, and she didn't have the presence of mind to know if that was good or bad.

"I'm leaving Monday," he said in a low voice. They walked back to the house. The hum of voices rose as people offered condolences and visited with neighbors. His parents were ready to leave.

"Guess this is goodbye." He kissed her on the cheek and walked away.

With shoulders slumped, arms at her sides, she let him leave. Tears streamed down her cheeks as she waited for his friendly wave. Waited for his crooked smile. Otis never looked back.

The days passed slowly, her grief punctured only by the chaos in her uncle's household. Bawling, screaming children filled each day. Her help with meals soon became expected. Most days Mary Lou reclined on the sofa, the baby in her arms an excuse to avoid cooking and cleaning. At first, Belle refused to clean the filthy house until she couldn't stand living in such squalor. She held her breath and scraped the soiled diapers out back of the house. Soaked the fabric in bleach and water on the back porch. And still Mary Lou was not happy.

"Wash me some clean clothes, Belle." Mary Lou whined. "I need fresh clothes to wear to town tomorrow. And start those beans or they'll never be ready by dinner."

Belle stood with arms akimbo and frowned.

"Don't look at me that way," Mary Lou said. "You're gettin' free room and board here, ain't ya?"

The toddler stared up at her. Belle didn't have the heart to fight in front of the children. She headed for the kitchen and simmered the soaked beans on the stove, setting the pot on the back burner out of reach from tiny hands.

She slipped through the backdoor, saddled the horse, and rode ten miles that day.

The following morning, she took her uncle aside. She insisted that she farm the old home place. She'd live in the barn.

"Girl, you can't farm alone." Uncle Jay shook his head. "Plowing, cultivating, harvesting—you know you can't. I need to lease that land out." He held up open hands. "Besides, Mary Lou needs your help at the house."

She didn't acknowledge him, and he didn't seem to require a response. She thought about all the people she'd lost, starting with her father and finishing with Otis. That night she lay in bed and decided she had no choice but to leave. She crawled out of bed and wrote a brief note under the moonlight spilling from the window. The paper was tucked into the frame that held the bureau mirror. She crept into the kitchen and bundled three biscuits, five jerky sticks, and two apples, tying the knapsack to a broken broomstick. Before dawn, she had walked several miles to the east with the loneliest catch in her chest a girl had ever known.

Chapter 14

AT THE SIDE OF THE road, Belle sat crosslegged and chewed a dry biscuit. Despondent, she'd walked a good share of the night and been caught unaware by the pale light of dawn. By the angle of the sun, it looked to be around 7:30. Sparrows flitted from tree to tree. Sunshine warmed her face. For a moment, she could almost believe everything was going to be okay.

A car rumbled up the road. She hoped it wasn't another stranger who would press her for a ride. A girl had to be careful. The shiny car passed and then braked. Slowly, the vehicle moved in reverse, a beautiful Ford Roadster with whitewall tires. Headlights rose like giant eyes on either side of a wide grill. The top was down, and a lady sat in the driver's seat.

"Good day, there." The woman wore a jaunty cloche hat, white with a black band. "Need a ride?"

Belle dusted the back of her dress. Between the Oklahoma sun and frequent washing of the garment, the cornflower print had faded. "I'd be much obliged."

The woman stepped from the car, clad in a tailored dress that fell six inches above her ankles. She headed for the rear of the Roadster where she opened the rumble seat and attached a strap to maintain the seat's upright position. It was clear that Belle was expected to sit there, though the front passenger side of the Ford remained empty. Servants would be seated in the back—or Indian girls.

"Here you go." The woman smiled broadly and pointed to the step plate on the rear fender.

Belle hopped into the rumble seat. The scent of new leather surrounded her.

"It's a grand day, isn't it?" The slim woman lifted her face to the sun. "A fine day for a drive."

"Yes, ma'am," she said. "New car?"

"Isn't it a beaut?" The woman made eye contact. "I'm sorry. I'm Bridgette Fairlane." She extended her gloved hand like a man. "And you might be?"

"Belle. Belle Tahsuda." She shook the woman's hand heartily as she'd seen her father and grandfather do with other men.

"That's an Indian surname, is it not?" The woman raised an eyebrow as if she didn't already know that Belle was Indian.

"Comanche, ma'am." Since the woman seemed interested in her Indian blood, she played along. "Related to Chief Tahsuda and Quanah Parker on my grandmother's side."

"Oh, do tell." Bridgette's eyes sparkled. "Let's get started and you can tell me more."

Belle wondered how they'd carry on a conversation over the roar of the motor. Bridgette held the steering wheel with both hands opposite each other. "I heard the Comanche were fierce fighters on the plains," the woman shouted back.

Belle leaned forward and cupped her mouth with both hands. "We're famous for that."

"You don't live in teepees anymore, am I correct?"

"The men sometimes hold their sweat lodges there." She refrained from laughing.

"Pray tell, what is a sweat lodge?"

What would it be like to be wealthy and not have a care in the world except where a person might drive and sightsee? Belle began to explain about the lodges when the car backfired.

"What's that again?" Bridgette said.

"It's a place," she shouted, "where they pray to the spirits and wait for visions. They pour water over hot rocks and make steam for the ceremony."

"Visions? What kind of visions?" Bridgette shouted back. "Like a dream or more like a premonition?"

"Some of each, I suppose." Her throat grew raw from strained vocal cords.

"What's that, you say?" The car braked and swerved to the side of the road. "Oh, drat. I can't hear you back there. Crawl on up here, dearie." She complied in a clumsy motion and tumbled into the front seat.

"I wanted to try out the dickie seat." Bridgette furrowed her brows, sheepishly. "Haven't had a chance to use it yet. Maybe on my next adventure. Please continue."

Up close, Bridgette's oval face held flawless skin, a light tan Belle assumed came from riding in the open car. Her wide hazel eyes were as expansive as her questions. A woman open to new ideas and adventures, Bridgette apparently had the luxury of money to pursue both. Belle figured the woman would inquire about her destination, so she beat her to it.

"Where are you traveling to?" Belle asked.

"Back to Shawnee," Bridgette said. "I live there, along with my parents and a married brother." She glanced over. "Where are you headed?"

"What a coincidence." Belle produced what she hoped was a look of surprise. "I'm seeking a job in Shawnee."

Bridgette swerved for a rock in the road. "What type of job?"

"I have domestic training." She strained to employ the language used at Chilocco. "I've worked in kitchens, done laundry and general household work." Inwardly, she cringed. All the things she didn't enjoy at Chilocco were coming back to haunt her. But what choice did she have?

"My, that covers a lot, doesn't it?" Bridgette winked.

She watched the road ahead, unsure if the woman was sarcastic or sincere.

"You know, my brother may be looking for live-in help," Bridgette said. "His wife, Margaret, is expecting their first child. She's going to need more than a housekeeper that comes in once a week." She glanced at Belle. "I'll check with him as soon as we arrive. They live in a big two-story house off Main Street. It's more house than I'd prefer to run, and I can't imagine caring for a newborn and worrying about cooking. We may have an opportunity for you."

"What does your brother do for a living?"

"He works at the State National Bank," Bridgette said. "His home is only blocks from the bank, so he enjoys walking to work. My father, Franklin Fairlane, is bank president."

That answered a lot of questions about Bridgette and her carefree life.

Bridgette reached over and patted her hand. "We'll find you a job."

She felt like a new pet. The rich woman must enjoy serving as benefactor for a poor dark-skinned Indian. Though grateful for the opportunity, Belle ached for her old life on the farm. She blinked away tears at the thought of trees swaying in the wind, the simple luxury of dipping her toes in the creek, and the gentle touch of Otis's hand. Why was life always changing? Against her will, Belle was fulfilling Chilocco's goal for young women and headed toward dreaded domestic service. She recalled her grandfather's tales of warriors holding slaves. Maybe life hadn't changed all that much, after all. Slumped in the car seat, she fell asleep.

Shrouded in shade from three-story buildings, Shawnee's Main Street stretched wide and welcoming. Trolley tracks ran down the middle of the street.

"Looks like a prosperous town," Belle said. "Have they discovered oil?"

"Not close by," Bridgette said. "But we're perfectly located for the many developers and investors in the region. You might say Shawnee is the hub for the outlying area."

Bridgette turned onto a side street. Belle studied the passing houses, ranging from modest bungalows to imposing two-story buildings. Impressive porches held pillars and double doors. At the end of the street, Bridgette pulled alongside the curb and peered up at a three-story house. An enormous porch wrapped two sides of the looming structure.

"This is it," Bridgette said. "It's always good to get back home, isn't it?"

The woman was oblivious to any home Belle may have left. A stately brick tower emerged at one side. Belle had never seen a house with so many windows—oval, round, leaded, and multi-paned. Bridgette engaged the car and pulled into the semicircular driveway.

"Wait here." Bridgette stepped lightly from the roadster. "I'll be right back." Bridgette couldn't walk into her parents' home with a stranger, least of all an Indian.

Belle glanced down at her faded housedress, fully aware she wasn't presentable. There was nothing to be done for it. She sighed and stared at the elegant house.

Minutes later, Bridgette skipped back with a smile on her face. "It's all settled. You'll stay in the servants' quarters in the back. Tomorrow morning, we'll go shopping so you can make a good impression on my brother." She winked. "We'll have a position for you by the end of the day."

Bridgette escorted her to a low building attached to the Queen Anne. She rapped on the door. Footsteps shuffled in the distance, and a black woman appeared. "Corabelle, how are you?"

"Fine, missy. Just fine." The heavy woman darted her eyes toward Belle. "And who do you have with you?" Corabelle smiled.

"My friend, Belle, here is looking for work. I believe my brother and his wife might welcome help now that Margaret is expecting her first child." "Oh, that she will."

"Would you be a dear and let her spend the night?" Bridgette gave an imploring look to the servant, an exaggerated expression theater actors might produce on stage.

"Yessum, we can certainly do that." Corabelle swept her arm toward the interior. "We'll fix you up with somethin' to eat and then git you settled for the night."

"Thank you, Corabelle." Bridgette flitted up the walkway to the main house. "See you in the morning, Belle."

Belle waved and stepped inside the cottage.

"How does hot soup sound?" Corabelle ladled broth into a bowl and sliced a fresh loaf of bread. She brought out a block of cheese. "You look mighty tired."

She yawned. "I walked half the night."

Corabelle narrowed her eyes. "Runaway?"

"Most of my kin have passed away. Don't want to live with the ones remaining."

Corabelle placed her hands at her wide hips and laughed. "Can understand that all right. Yes, I can. Do you have experience as a domestic servant?"

"I attended a school that drilled cooking and cleaning into us girls." She blew over the steaming bowl. "After my grandmother became poorly, I did all the cooking and cleaning. Grandfather raved about my meals."

"That's a good sign." Corabelle sat opposite from her at the table. "If you need any help, I'll be more than glad to give you some tips. Lord knows, I've been doing this all my life."

"Thank you." The bread was delicious, but she was more tired than hungry.

"Girl, your eyes are droopin'. Let me show you where you can sleep."

Expecting a pallet on the floor and a thin blanket, she was surprised at the bed wedged in the narrow room.

"Sorry, it's such a tiny room," Corabelle said.

"This is wonderful," she said. "I was expecting to sleep on the floor."

"Suppose that makes me a grand hostess." Laughter rose from deep in her throat. "Make yourself at home."

Fourteen-year-old Belle crawled under the down comforter and within moments, dreamed she lived with the kind black woman.

Chapter 15

BELLE SAT ERECT IN THE wooden chair. The vice president of the State National Bank appraised her from across the massive desk as Bridgette rambled about her trip. Belle averted her eyes and fingered the buttons on her jacket. The matching dress was purchased earlier that morning.

Like a dress-up doll, she had tried on every outfit Bridgette whisked to the fitting room. Not once did Bridgette ask what she liked. Bridgette stood back and assessed each of the five dresses before she purchased the straightcut navy dress. Before they left, she drew Belle's hair up into a bun. Belle studied her pinched face in the mirror and assessed the severe hairstyle. Was that how a good household servant should appear? Bridgette claimed she looked sophisticated. Belle thought she looked like an old matron.

"Frank Jr., this is Belle." Bridgette's hand swept through the air. "She's trained in domestic work from Chilocco Agricultural School."

"Training, that's a plus." Frank Jr. peered over his wire-rimmed glasses. "We're expecting our firstborn in a few months."

Belle nodded, her tongue thick and unresponsive.

A handsome man, Frank Jr. had broad shoulders, a square jaw, and a full head of light brown hair. But there was a manner about him that she didn't fancy. Was it the airs that wealthy people possessed, or did the tension around his lips reveal a difficult man to work for?

"We will require cooking and cleaning services," he continued. "You'd have your own room, of course."

"Of course," Belle echoed.

"Don't forget serving, brother," Bridgette added.

"You'd be expected to serve food for our personal dining needs and on occasion, for dinner parties."

"How fun! You'll cook for our family dinner at Frank Jr.'s house." Bridgette acted as if the event was a child's tea party. "We all get together once a week with Frank Jr. and his wife. Papa, Mother, and me."

"We'll give you a trial run," Frank Jr. said. "Your service will be evaluated in two weeks. If everything's found satisfactory, we'll discuss a raise."

"She'll be great, Frank," Bridgette said. "I just know it." She winked at Belle and turned back to her brother. "I nearly forgot. I have to tell you what else I saw on my trip."

The confines of the office pressed in on Belle, and she pushed away thoughts of home. Frank Jr. extended his hand, and she shook the cool, smooth palm. Unlike her father and grandfather, he was a man unaccustomed to physical labor. As she stood to follow Bridgette out the door, Vice President Fairlane of State National Bank studied Belle's figure in a long sweep from head to toe. She didn't like the man. Belle glanced at Bridgette, who was too busy talking about herself to notice. Finally, the woman had exhausted all news about her trip. Belle traipsed after Bridgette, who strode across the bank lobby like she was off on another adventure.

The weak light of early morning draped the apron-front sink. At the counter Belle kneaded dough with forced exuberance. She was sick and tired of making bread. The Fairlanes expected two loaves of fresh bread each morning, despite the daily leftovers. There was only so much bread pudding a person could eat. Unable to tolerate waste, she fed the birds in the backyard.

She turned up the volume on the radio. One perk of working for wealthy people included her own radio in the kitchen.

"This is Jimmie Wilson broadcasting from Andrew Jackson Johnson's farm down on the banks of old Polecat Creek."

She loved listening to KVOO, the Tulsa radio station. Jimmie Wilson and His Catfish String Band was her favorite program. A humorist, Wilson exaggerated backwoods attitude. The rural music and homespun humor made her feel she was back on the farm.

Sound effects of fish frying in a skillet came over the airwaves.

"How does he do that?" Margaret had slipped into the kitchen without notice.

"He probably puts water on a hot skillet," she said.

"That would do it, wouldn't it?"

Footsteps marched from the radio. "I know that one," Margaret said. "Boots over a board."

Mrs. Fairlane's elegant face possessed high cheekbones and the bluest eyes Belle had ever seen. Margaret's fair skin appeared almost sickly perhaps because she rarely went outside. She was slimmer than Belle, who was beginning to fill out in the bosom. Margaret's thin body disguised the progress of her eight-month pregnancy. Though always kind, the lady of the house seldom spoke other than with brief requests for the weekly menu. Belle was always taken off guard on the few occasions that Margaret carried on conversation.

Thunder pealed from the radio. Wilson made a joke about fishing in a rainstorm.

"What about that sound?" Margaret lifted her eyebrows.

"I'd guess he's shaking a sheet of metal."

The band played a song, and Margaret swayed to the rhythm. Belle wondered if the thin woman would have a hard labor when her time came. Thank goodness, her family could afford a doctor.

On the radio, the storm had cleared and crickets chirped.

"And that?" Margaret raised her eyebrows with childish delight.

Belle thought for a moment. "Someone ran a fingernail along the edge of a comb."

"You're good at this." Margaret flashed a rare smile. "Did you remember tonight is the family dinner party?"

"Yes, ma'am." How could she forget all the extra work ahead of her that day?

"We want to make a good impression on Franklin Sr."

"Of course." Belle had never prepared a three-course meal, but failure might be a good thing, forcing her to move on to something besides domestic work. Who was she kidding? She didn't have the advantage of a higher education to become a nurse or teacher. Few did. Belle had no clue what other work a Comanche girl could obtain.

Belle stood in the corner of the dining room as instructed by Margaret. She yearned to sit and rest her weary feet after the grueling day spent cooking. Rest would not come until long after the guests had left and dishes were returned to the cupboard.

Soup dishes had been cleared, salad served and removed for the third course. A platter of prime rib circulated. Steaming bowls of mashed potatoes, glazed carrots, and green beans with bacon were passed around the long oak table.

Franklin Sr.'s booming voice bounced off the rosewood paneled walls. "Despite the market crash, the bank has held fast." The portly man filled out his suit. The wealthy always ate well. "We've added several new accounts."

Frank Jr. frowned at his fine-china plate teemed with food. "Yet rural banks are closing left and right."

"We'll be fine, son." Frank Sr. heaped more potatoes on his plate.

Bridgette caught Belle's attention and winked. Belle flashed a smile before she resumed a stoic face. She wore a frilly white apron over her dress and a white maid's cap. Belle was officially Bridgette's odd pet, surely a passing interest.

Margaret motioned her over and whispered, "Bring more mashed potatoes. These men like their potatoes."

In the kitchen, she scooped mounds of potatoes into a new serving bowl. She'd been instructed to use fresh bowls for seconds. Fortunately, she'd made double of everything, knowing it would be disgraceful if they ran out of any of the entrees, as Margaret called them. In the Fairlane household, it was considered better to waste food than to turn up short.

At nine o'clock that night, she finished drying the last of the dishes and replaced them in the cupboards. She felt a tug at her apron ties and whirled around.

"Mr. Fairlane!"

He stood above her smiling. "You did well tonight, Belle. It's time for a break." He stepped closer.

She backed up to the counter. "Th-thank you, Mr. Fairlane."

He placed an arm on each side of her, his hands on the counter. "You're a very pretty girl."

"Thank you, sir." She ducked beneath his left arm and scooted to the garbage pail. "Time to take out the garbage before it smells. Mrs. Fairlane wouldn't want that, now would she?"

She slipped out the door, her employer's laughter spilling from the kitchen. She glanced back, relieved he didn't follow. At the burn barrel, she pulled a match from her pocket and set the garbage on fire, remaining there until the flames turned to embers and the upstairs lights were extinguished.

Chapter 16

SUNLIGHT STREAMED THROUGH THE WINDOW as Belle dried dishes. Earlier, Margaret informed her she wanted sue flay for tomorrow's breakfast.

"Yes, ma'am," she'd answered. Truth was, she had no idea what the woman was talking about. Her job would be at stake if she didn't prepare the food her employers requested. With her thoughts tossing about, she reached for the last plate when a large body pressed against her back.

She squeezed to the side of the sink, but Frank Jr.'s long arms formed rigid fence posts on each side of her body. "Such an industrious maid." His lips pressed against the back of her neck. In panic, she slammed the plate against the sink. Amid the clatter of breaking china, Frank Jr. stepped back.

"Grocer. Need potatoes." She fled the kitchen and headed straight to Frank Sr.'s house. She pounded on the back door. At her feet, empty milk bottles awaited pickup for the next day.

"Come on in." Corabelle waved her heavy arm. "You're just in time for my warm caramel rolls fresh from the oven."

The kitchen smelled delicious, a mix of cinnamon and bubbling caramel. Belle flopped on a stool and joined her hands in a gesture of prayer. "Tell me you know what a sue flay is and how I can make one." Dare she reveal Frank Jr.'s actions? She had no clue how deep Corabelle's loyalty ran.

"'Course, child. Come sit at the table." Humming permeated the kitchen as Corabelle filled the cast-iron teakettle. She winked. "I'll make tea to go with your roll." She set a cup and saucer on the table, and placed a fork and spoon over a linen napkin.

Belle's eyes watered at the thought of being served as if she were one of the Fairlanes.

"Soufflé." Corabelle laughed. "People get themselves some money and the next thing you know, they think they're wealthy Europeans." She resumed humming and placed a warm roll on a plate. The teakettle steamed. She poured water into a china teapot and dunked a metal ball of tea leaves into the hot water.

A gold rim circled the floral teapot. Certainly this china served the elder Fairlanes.

"Now we can talk." With an umph, Corabelle sat on the Windsor chair. "Feels good to get off these old feet of mine." She reached across the table and patted Belle's hand. "A soufflé is a French dish. It's made with egg yolks, beaten egg whites, and I always add asparagus or broccoli in mine. You bake the concoction until it puffs up good. Gotta serve it right away before it falls. Pre-sen-ta-tion." She winked one brown eye. "It's all about presentation with the Fairlanes."

"I need to write down the instructions," she said. "May I have a paper and pencil?"

"Girl, you enjoy your tea and sweet roll first." Corabelle winked. "I overheard you're a hard worker. Frank Jr. and his wife are pleased with your work."

"Frank Jr.," she began. "He's kinda…" She wrung her hands. Maybe it was best kept to herself.

"That no good man," Corabelle muttered. "So he's up to it again. Tell me, child, what's going on in that house?"

"The other day in the kitchen, he made me uncomfortable. Didn't actually do anything. I was too quick, I guess. This morning, he tried…he kissed my neck."

"Oh, my. Poor child." Corabelle shook her head. "A few years ago, Frank Jr. hired a gal to help around the house. Within six months, she came up pregnant and gone."

Belle stared at the big black woman.

"The girl wasn't too bright," Corabelle said. "Pretty, but timid. A girl like that don't have no chance. But you—you're smart, strong. You can outwit him." She sipped her tea. "Keep out of his reach."

She wished she had Corabelle's confidence. One thing was sure. It would always be his word against hers.

With recipe in hand, Belle strolled home. Pregnant. The girl before her had gotten pregnant with Frank Jr.'s baby. Her stomach turned. A sour taste settled in her mouth. She walked around to the servant's door. Clouds covered the sun and threw the house in grim shadow. Her footsteps echoed in the empty kitchen. An impressive house, all the luxuries of the well-todo, yet dark secrets spun in eddies through the banker's house.

"Wonderful soufflé, Belle," Margaret commented the next morning. "Isn't it tasty, Frank Jr.?"

Mr. Fairlane looked up from his newspaper and glanced at his wife. "Very acceptable. Good job." His eyes returned to the newsprint.

Chilocco prepared young girls to become domestic help, but their teachers were definitely untrained in French cuisine. Belle sighed with relief as she cleared the table of dirty dishes. Thanks to Corabelle, the Fairlanes considered her a highly trained chef.

That evening she sank into the down mattress, exhausted and ready for a good night's sleep. Her mornings began early, even earlier than on the farm. She rose before dawn to mix bread dough, grind the coffee, and boil eggs for breakfast. The Fairlanes didn't believe in fried eggs. She was half asleep when a thought pierced her drowsiness.

Under the cover of darkness, wild tomcats crouch and attack. Frank Jr. must have violated the previous maid at night. Without a lock mechanism, Belle's closed door provided little security. Her room was off the kitchen. The Fairlanes's master bedroom was located at the front of the house on the second floor. If he had held his hand over the poor girl's mouth, or if she was as simple as Corabelle suggested, he may have only needed to threaten the girl to get her to comply with his wishes.

She threw off her covers, and goosebumps rose on her bare arms. She tiptoed to the door and slowly—quietly—slid the heavy oak dresser in front of the door. That would do. She vowed this would be her new nightly routine.

Belle slipped back into bed, but sleep proved elusive. When she did sleep, Frank Jr.'s menacing face invaded her dreams.

The next few days passed uneventfully. Like Corabelle stated, Belle was smart enough to outwit him if she stayed alert.

One morning, Margaret slipped into the kitchen. "I have a dastardly headache today." She rubbed her temple. "Set the table for one. Please fix Frank Jr. his usual breakfast. I'm going back to bed."

"Yes, ma'am." She didn't look forward to serving Frank Jr. without his wife present. A few minutes later she heard him enter the dining room. Belle moved to the doorway adjoining the kitchen. "I'll bring your coffee, sir."

Frank Jr. sat at his usual place at the head of the table. He nodded without looking at her, his attention diverted to the outspread newspaper.

The silver coffee urn was placed on a side table. Belle filled his cup and darted back to the kitchen. She prepared a tray of fresh bread, salted butter, jam, hard-boiled eggs, and a bowl of canned peaches and delivered it to the dining room. She flew back to the kitchen. From the deep drawer of the Hoosier cabinet, she dipped her tin cup into the flour bin and mixed egg, baking soda, cinnamon, and sugar to make a sweet batter for freshly sliced apples. No sooner was one meal served, but work for the next began. She stirred the batter. Satisfied with its consistency, she turned toward the table where her sliced apples awaited in a baking tin and came face to face with Frank Jr., who grinned like a Cheshire cat.

"Excuse me, sir," she said. "I didn't know you were there."

Frank Jr. grabbed the heavy yellow-ware bowl Belle held. "Let me help you with that."

She held fast. Margaret was on the second floor, perhaps asleep.

"That's a weighty bowl. Let me help you," he repeated.

The bowl tugged back and forth. She was no match for a full-grown man. She let go at once, ready to flee. The bowl of gooey batter spread down Frank Jr.'s suit pants. Belle ran outside, not waiting for the startled look on the man's face to turn to rage. Behind her, the screen door slammed and curses rang from the kitchen.

Further down the street, she slowed to a walk. Belle smoothed the loose tendrils around her cheeks. She'd go shopping at the grocery. That would be her excuse if asked later where she had disappeared. If she still maintained her job. She stretched her shopping trip to an hour to ensure Frank Jr. had time to change clothes and walk to the bank.

"Keep out of his reach," Corabelle had warned.

That might be more difficult than either of them had imagined.

The New Year rang in with the birth of Jonathan Robert Fairlane. Belle hoped the baby's father would finally recognize his family responsibilities and turn from his philandering ways. Unfortunately, the first few weeks of 1930 proved otherwise. If she wasn't quick enough, Frank Jr. would tug at her dress hem. Sometimes he gave a dinner request with his face too close to hers—a lecherous attempt at brushing against her chest. Too many times, a tap on the rear came as she walked away. The man was incorrigible. In the first few weeks after giving birth, Mrs. Fairlane preferred to have her meals delivered to her room, which meant Belle had to ward off Frank Jr.'s increasing advances.

One evening, she served dinner for Frank Jr. and his parents, who had come to visit the baby.

"The Oklahoma Panhandle is a mess," Frank Sr. said. "People go days without seeing the sky. The dust is so thick it fills a man's lungs. Can't keep it out of their houses. Wind drives dirt through every nook and cranny." "The drought is pretty bad there, that's for sure," his son added.

Belle recalled her grandfather talking about the Panhandle. He swore they should never have plowed the prairie. Native grass was the only thing that kept the soil from blowing away.

The economy worsened by the day. Every week, the radio reported more bank closures. People distrusted banks, held onto their money, and spent less. Employers sold less product and were forced to lay off employees, putting more people out of work. The downward spiral twisted out of control. It made her nervous. What if she wanted to leave the Fairlane house and find another job? Under the present circumstances, employment might be impossible to obtain.

In April, Margaret announced an upcoming trip to New York. She longed to show her family back East their new grandchild.

Belle's heart leapt. She'd have the house to herself and no meals to prepare. It would be heaven. That hope was quickly doused with the news that her husband would not be accompanying her. Unseen by his wife, Frank Jr.

brazenly winked at Belle. She'd be alone in the house with that deplorable man. A wave of terror rolled over her.

Chapter 17

ONCE MRS. FAIRLANE DEPARTED, THERE'D be no one to hear Belle's shouts of protest. No one would know what went on between the walls of the Fairlane house. What was to stop Frank Jr. from breaking down her bedroom door? He could well afford to replace it.

Without a word to anyone, she made plans to leave the day Margaret boarded the train. She considered buying a ticket herself. Not wise, she argued. The small amount of money she'd managed to save needed to be kept for an uncertain future. Belle couldn't remain in town. The family was too influential. Out of desperation, she would head for McAlester and visit Flora. The truth was she didn't know where else to go. Maybe her friend had some contacts and could help her find a job. Regardless of the outcome, it would be good to see Flora again.

On a late April afternoon, Frank Jr. drove Margaret and the baby to the train station. As soon as the car rounded the corner, Belle ran upstairs and retrieved her satchel. She hurried to the edge of town, the sun beating down on her face. Belle pressed a handkerchief to her forehead and again debated about whether she should purchase a train ticket. She pursed her lips. Be practical. Foregoing the highway, she followed a dirt road. For the moment, she traveled free from traffic and inquiries from well-meaning strangers.

A dog barked in the distance where a farmhouse stood amid freshly plowed fields. Drawn to the serene image, she perched on a downed tree in a nearby grove. A breeze fluttered hair at her temples and cooled her skin.

The faint crow of a rooster erupted. A cow bawled for her calf. Belle closed her eyes. For a moment, she was back home, Grandfather in the barn milking, her father mucking stalls, his strong arms swinging in rhythm with the rake. Grandma worked in the kitchen, her bread dough rising, supple and fragrant with yeast.

A deep burst of aaarrrrrOOO broke the quiet. A coonhound. Belle dusted herself off and headed to the crossroads, continuing the road east. Railroad ties rose to the side of the road. She preferred navigating the tracks to a random vehicle stopping on the shoulder. Her foot met every third creosote tie and became a mind-numbing march towards tomorrow. And the next day. And the day after that.

She had walked for over two hours when she sought the shade of a lone black walnut. With her coat spread over the ground, she curled up for a short rest. Sparrows chirped overhead, and an occasional breeze swept across her skin.

"Train don't come by for another two hours." The intrusive voice came from behind.

She jumped to her feet and spun around. A black boy lay in the grass a few feet away, hands behind his head.

"Didn't mean to startle you." He worked a long blade of grass between his lips. "Thought you seen me." With a languid motion, he propped himself on an elbow. The "boy" was actually a young man, probably six-foot tall when he stood. "Name's Freddy. And yours?"

"B-Belle." His clothes were a bit ragged, but his face was clean, the chocolate skin smooth and flawless.

"Ain't gonna hurt ya, if that's what yer thinkin'."

Her instincts affirmed his words. She'd seen men with lewd looks and behaviors. Freddy's face didn't have that. "The train, you say?"

"The train to McAlester. Goes right through here." Freddy chewed on his stalk of grass.

She straightened her dress. "Hopping a freight?"

"Sure. You plan on walking for days?" He looked at her with humor in his dark eyes.

"It's my only recourse."

"Where you headed?"

"McAlester. Got a friend there." She smiled.

"Gal, you gotta flip a fast freight. Be there in no time."

Belle shook her head. "I don't know about that." There was no way she could run with her satchel in tow.

"Two miles down the tracks, the train stops for a lumber load." Freddy glanced at her traveling bag. "When the train starts back up, you toss your stuff on board and hop up."

"You make it sound easy."

"Out here, the trains don't expect freeloaders. Too far from town."

"You've done it before, I take?"

"Yes, ma'am." Freddy smiled broadly. "This is my favorite place. No bulls. No beatings. It's a cinch, all right."

"Bulls?" She glanced from side to side. "There's a pasture of bulls?"

"Not that kind of bull. The railroad man who keeps people from hopping freights. They can be outright mean."

"But they're not on this train?" she asked.

"Oh, he is, but he's not looking for us way out here in nowhere land. He'll take a quick glance and go back inside." He threw the stem in the grass. "Are you in?"

"Do you think I can do it?"

"You look strong enough. And I'll help you, girl."

"All right, then." Looked like she was going to ride a train after all. Freddy proceeded to instruct her on the procedures for hopping a train. But what if she slipped? She'd heard of misfortunate hoboes who'd fallen beneath train wheels. What had she gotten herself into?

"The train will be by about eight tonight." Freddy reclined with his hands behind his head.

She followed suit and reserved her energy for the questionable adventure to come.

Freddy lay with his eyes closed and sang a song she had heard on the radio. Though the title of the song was carefree, the lyrics to "Life is Just a Bowl of Cherries" reflected the hard times. The song joked about making out a will after a person struggled to pay for his grocery bill.

Times were hard for so many people. Her self-pity vanished into the warm breeze. Freddy's song ended. It was her turn to sing, and she repeated the lyrics.

Freddy rose on one elbow, smiled, and joined in.

After the joint stanza, she lay on the grass and hummed the melody until she fell asleep in the warm Oklahoma shade.

Belle flipped the cover of her grandmother's pocket watch. Grandma's initials were engraved on the front, nearly lost in the scroll design. The timepiece showed seven fifty-five. The sun dropped in the rose-tinted sky while a bullfrog croaked a love song to the females. Jog-a-rum, he groaned. Jog-a-rum. She had changed into a pair of boy's overalls she'd purchased expressly for her trip into the unknown. Another frog joined in the competition. Belle's stomach quivered as her fear built in time to the bullfrog symphony.

The sun sank below the horizon as Freddy pressed his hand to the rail. "It's comin'. Get ready." A distant train whistle moaned through the dim light.

They crouched behind bushes near the rails and waited. The ground vibrated beneath Belle's feet, and the roar of the train swelled. The train whistle bellowed a long note and slowed as it passed, the great wheels clacking over the rails. The lumber freight awaited less than an eighth of a mile down the track.

"We'll wait," Freddy whispered. "Give 'em time to load the lumber. When I tell you, grab your bag and run."

The delay stretched forever. Her thighs ached as she crouched. Sweat dripped from her forehead, her nerves testy in the evening chill.

Freddy pointed at an open freight car. "They won't be using that one. Too far back." He slowly rose, hunkered down to half his height. "Now!"

She ran beside him and tried to keep pace with his long legs. They tossed their bags into the open freight car. Slightly behind Freddy, she pushed herself to catch up. Belle placed her hands on the bed of the car and pressed her stomach against the metal. Freddy's arm brushed hers. He was up and standing on the edge of the car.

"Shinny up!" he commanded.

She struggled to lift herself onto the freight car, but her arms wouldn't cooperate. She hung with her feet dangling off the ground. The train picked up speed. One hand slipped. The clacking of wheels resounded faster, louder. Oh, God, help me. She slipped lower, the clang of wheels building over the rails.

Her upper arm burned as she was yanked into the car. They both plunged to the straw-littered floor.

"Oh, Lordy," Freddy said. "I thought you were stronger."

Belle lay in the dark, panting. Her fingertips registered dust and grime. Her eyes slowly adjusted to the shadows. "I tried with all my might." "I know, girl. I know." Freddy draped a hand over his eyes.

Faster and faster, the train trembled in its rolling cant over the rails. So close had she come to falling. Freddy pointed to the side of the car. He took her hand, and they scooted their backs against the rigid metal. The boxcar was like a dark cave.

"Shoot," he said. Freddy crept to the middle of the car and retrieved his bindle and Belle's satchel. The silhouette of his body crept backwards. His profile remained focused straight ahead as he stared at the opposite side of the car.

"What is it?" she whispered.

"We have company," he murmured. "A hobo. Only one from what I can tell."

She worried about the money buried at the bottom of her satchel. Everything she had in the world. She was a young lady and Freddy, only a young man. Far worse things could happen in the dark than losing her money. As if he read her thoughts, he spoke.

"I smelled corn whiskey," Freddy whispered. "With any luck he'll be sleeping it off until McAlester."

The moonless night wrapped around them like a dark wool cloak. Starlight filtered through the open door. Belle brushed against Freddy's shoulder, needing the reassurance of his presence in the deep recess of the car. The occasional glow of a distant farmhouse served as a poignant reminder of the life she'd lost, a life she hungered for like a drifter going from house to house, begging for a piece of bread, hungry but never satisfied.

Chapter 18

A DEAFENING WHISTLE BLARED IN the dark. Cold radiated through her stiff back, and the smell of iron and rust intensified. Where was she? Belle clutched her chest and struggled to catch her breath.

"It's okay, girl," a voice said. "It's me, Freddy. We're almost to McAlester."

Her heart raced.

"We'll wait until the train slows," Freddy whispered. "I'll count the rhythm of rails. When I say—jump, tuck, and roll."

"In the dark?" She sat and fumbled for her satchel.

"You'll see lights from the station by that time."

"I can't do it. I'll break a leg." Worse, she'd break her neck.

"That's why you tuck and roll," he said. "Can't break a leg that way."

Why hadn't she kept walking? Even if it had taken a week, she could have made it to McAlester in one piece. Why did she let this foolish boy talk her into this? But one thing Belle had learned in life was to accept the inevitable.

She peered into the back of the train car, trying to glimpse the shadowy form of the hobo. The pitch-black car revealed nothing.

"Trust me," Freddy said. "I know the best place to get off. The ditch is shallow and thick with grass. You'll be fine. I promise." A rustling sounded from the far side of the car.

The train slowed—still too swift—and the pair perched on the edge of the open door, bags at their sides. The night outside was dark and formless.

"Damn it," a gruff voice broke the quiet. "Didn't know I was sharin' a ride with a nigger and a redskin." A Goliath of a man staggered toward Freddy.

Freddy motioned, and they flung their bags. He shouted. "On the count of three…"

"One."

"Two."

"Three!" they yelled together.

Belle forced herself into a ball. Cool air swept against her face as she spun to her death, the clacking of iron wheels announcing her demise. The hard ground pummeled her spine and tossed her like a ball. Darkness twirled around her. Belle Tahsuda, dead at age fifteen.

She sprang to her feet and ran from the iron beast that heaved her up and retched her out. Dizzy, she stumbled toward a low band of light in the distance and collided into Freddy's arms. Whoops of delight tore the quiet prairie as his voice and hers joined in celebration. He grabbed her hands, and together they waltzed before a golden dawn breaking on the horizon.

With Freddy's back turned, she exchanged her pants for a skirt, and they were on their way, the sky still holding back the day. They followed the tracks. After an initial stumble, Belle fell into a measured pattern, her feet hitting the next railroad tie.

"Is your family in McAlester?" she asked.

"Nope, further south." Freddy swung his bindle over one shoulder. "I'm looking up a buddy who owes me a favor."

Belle wouldn't pry. Better she didn't know.

"And you? What will you do after you find your friend?"

She forced a smile. "Can't think that far ahead." The damp air came in sweet relief after the freight car's fusty atmosphere. She paused, dug through her satchel, and offered a cornmeal muffin to her companion.

"Mighty thankful." He stuffed half the muffin in his mouth, cheek bulging.

On an empty stomach, even dry cornmeal proved satisfying. In the distance, the sun ascended above the town of McAlester. In the low light, a formidable building rose on a hill. "What's that?" she asked.

"Big Mac."

"Pardon me?"

"Oklahoma State Penitentiary." His jaw tightened as he narrowed his eyes. "Sure don't wanna go there."

Had Freddy been there? Her heart jumped at the thought of traveling with an ex-convict. Belle stole a sideways glance at his youthful face. Freddy wasn't a hardened man. He was too young.

On the outskirts of town, Freddy paused and held out his hand. "Nice to make your acquaintance, Miss Belle."

"And yours, Mr. Freddy." She giggled. "Thanks for the unforgettable adventure of hopping a freight. Can't say I'll do it again anytime soon." "You know what folks say." He grinned. "Practice makes perfect."

"Then I prefer imperfection."

They parted ways, Freddy moving to the north with a quick long-legged gait. Belle unfolded an envelope from her pocket. 353 Coal Avenue. Her heartbeat quickened at the thought of seeing Flora. The chit and chirp of sparrows overhead and the warm sun on her cheeks hastened her steps along the streets of McAlester. The town had long been considered the capital of the coal industry in Oklahoma. Freddy told her the population had dropped slightly since locomotives had converted to oil. And of course, there was the Depression.

She was starving. It had been twenty-four hours since her last meal. Belle paused in front of a storefront window and caught her reflection. She straightened her crumpled skirt and patted down wisps of hair. A sign across the street beckoned a breakfast special of biscuits and gravy.

She found a table near the window. Outside the café, businessmen strolled past in pressed suits in contrast to farmers talking in overalls and fedoras. She sipped at the last of the strong coffee and left her money on the table. The waitress gave her directions to North 2nd Street and told her to follow 2nd until she came to Coal Avenue. Reenergized, Belle hurried down the street, stopping occasionally to drop her satchel and stretch her arm.

Upon arrival at the corner of Choctaw Avenue and 2nd Street, she smiled. Flora was Choctaw. She imagined her friend's reaction upon Belle's appearance on her doorstep. The memory of Flora's familiar laugh rang almost audibly.

Further down the street, she spotted a new Montgomery Ward building, but another structure captured her attention. Craning her neck, she studied a brick building that rose eleven stories in the air. The construction looked near completion. A sign out front announced the Hotel Aldridge.

On the next block, the red-brick Busby Theater stood three-stories high with an arched stained-glass window in prominent position. How exciting it would be to see a vaudeville act. Crossing the street, she paused before the Scottish Rite Masonic Temple, currently under construction. Workers added on to the existing building, covering the original red-brick exterior with beige brick. As she passed, the accents of Scots, Italians, Germans, Poles, and Russians echoed off the walls. As a child, she recalled her grandfather speaking of the many immigrants who flocked to Indian Territory to work in the coal mines. Belle could see herself living in McAlester. There were so many opportunities, and she could visit the sights arm in arm with Flora.

After several more blocks, the backs of her heels grew sore. She didn't care and whistled a merry tune, blisters a small price to pay to see Flora again. Upon viewing the Coal Avenue street sign, her steps sprang lighter.

She had to backtrack after realizing the house numbers moved in the opposite direction. Silly girl. At the placard of 353, she skipped up the wooden steps to the one-story house. The building wasn't fancy, but the white paint was intact and the yard tidy. The open porch held a swinging bench. She pictured the two of them, talking in dizzy circles as they caught up with each other's life.

An older woman answered the door. "May I help you?"

This had to be Flora's mother. She looked healthy and robust. "I met Flora at Chilocco Indian School." She leaned and peered around the woman. "We're good friends—"

"Flora who?" The woman frowned. "I don't know any Flora."

Belle dug for the envelope. "But I'm sure…it's right here." She held up the creased envelope. "Flora Stone, 353 Coal Avenue, McAlester, Oklahoma."

"Dear, this is surely 353 Coal Avenue," the woman said, "but Stone was the name of the previous owners." She shook her head, a strand of gray hair falling over her eye. "I'm afraid the woman passed on."

"You must mean Flora's mother. She was ill." Belle's voice stretched thin. "Where did Flora and the children go? She had two younger brothers."

"I do recall that. The last I heard one of the boys had died from TB. Whole family had the dreaded disease. I washed down the walls in vinegar when I heard and—"

"She didn't." Belle's voice broke. "I mean, they couldn't all have died."

"I heard the entire family went to the sanatorium."

Belle's stomach sunk. "Where?"

"The Eastern Oklahoma Tuberculosis Sanatorium." The woman slid the door closed.

Belle shoved her shoe in the doorway. "Please, Ma'am. Please tell me how to find the sanatorium." Tears ran down her cheeks, warm and salty in the cool breeze.

The woman frowned at Belle's foot. "How rude!" She cast a withering look before she answered. "It's in Talihina. Now, leave before I call the police."

Belle stumbled down the walk, her vision blurred with tears. Halfway down the block, she slumped on the curb, head between her knees.

A passing motorist rolled down his window and inquired whether she was okay. Belle nodded, choking back sobs. She dusted herself off and proceeded along the sidewalk to avoid further questions. Clouds passed over the sun. The April chill slid down her open coat and without bothering to work the buttons, she drew the lapels together.

Maybe she had the wrong address. She studied each house as she passed, hoping the woman was wrong. On a corner lot, posts set in stone bases braced an expansive porch. Belle sniffled and crossed the street where an arched door and three gables adorned the front of a brick house. Numb with disappointment, she wandered through the neighborhood, envisioning warm kitchens where families gathered around dinner tables and shared the day's events.

There was nothing worse than the empty feeling of having no compass. Her initial excitement for the city of McAlester dissipated. She no longer saw a reason to stay. In fact, she would forego McAlester out of spite. It had robbed her of her friend. Poor Flora. Was she dreadfully ill, perhaps even dead?

Belle couldn't move on without knowing how Flora fared. Her stride quickened as she headed toward Talihina, the decision bringing a small measure of relief. It gave a direction, be it only temporary. She drew in a deep breath and refused to think about the fact that she belonged nowhere.

At intervals throughout the day, she found places to stop and read Agatha Christie's book, The Mystery of the Blue Train. She'd packed it in her satchel, a Christmas gift from Mrs. Fairlane. The truth was she was paralyzed with fear. Fear of what had happened to Flora. Fear of having to travel even farther. Fear she was becoming a hobo or a gypsy with no place to set her shoes at night.

By early evening. she located a small cafe and ordered a bowl of chili with crackers and a glass of water. Afterward, she wandered to the edge of town, wondering where she'd spend the night. She considered paying for a room, but it seemed foolish to spend her savings. The sun sank on the horizon and the chill of early spring rose from the earth.

In the distance, a fenced enclosure held three horses and farther back, a lone outbuilding. She waited for dark before she approached the shed. Looking around first, she opened the hinged door and darted into the building. Her eyes slowly adjusted to the dark. In the shadows, she made out angular shapes. She reached out, and her fingertips confirmed dusty bales of stacked hay. Like the holy family, Belle would sleep that night on hay amid the shuffle of hooves.

Belle slept poorly. The cold slid deep into her bones, and despite her fear of mice, she burrowed into the musty hay. The next morning, she brushed herself off. A stray stem fell from her hair, and she leaned over and shook her head like a dry mop. She walked out her stiff muscles as she headed for the road.

Located next to a feed store, a rural café emerged as the last resort for food. Although she sat in the corner, she was as conspicuous as a single brown egg in a basket of whites. On every side, farmers in overalls discussed crops and cattle. Her meager breakfast consisted of toast and a cup of coffee flooded with cream. The aroma of bacon and fried eggs filled the room until the tempting smell forced her to leave. Outside, she hurried down the road, keeping to the gravel shoulder.

Fields stretched out endlessly before her. She considered how long her journey to Talihina might take when a tan Packard with black top and trim rolled to the shoulder. A man motioned her over with a smile and a wink. His thin moustache lifted to one side as his eyes raked her from head to toe. Belle shook her head and waved him on. The car veered back onto the road.

Maybe it was unwise for a young woman to take to the highway. Or was an Indian woman seen as easy prey? At least her early start meant reduced traffic on the road. The solitude of the countryside renewed her spirits. Hope blossomed. Flora was fine, sure as another dawn would wake the world. Belle hummed as she took long strides down the shoulder of the highway. She congratulated herself on a wise decision when a gray automobile appeared out of nowhere like a spectre rising from the early morning fog. The driver leaned over and rolled down the window.

"Need a lift, Miss?" The man's wide jowls and shaggy hair reminded her of a lion.

"No, thank you." His leer reminded her of Frank, Jr. "My brother will be along in a few minutes." She'd say anything to deter the man. Her swinging arms matched her rapid stride. The man growled something under his breath, but instead of an accelerating motor, she heard a car door unlatch. She glanced over her shoulder and saw the man followed on foot. Belle ran down the road with the sickening slaps of footsteps in pursuit, the heavyset stranger moving faster than she would have imagined. She darted down the ditch and headed for the field. Cursing rolled on the air, and then the boot steps ceased. Belle looked back. The man had returned to his car. Once the vehicle was out of sight, she made her way back to the road, prepared to run again upon the least provocation. She'd walk all the way to Talihina, if that's what it took.

She stepped back to allow passage of a car before she crossed the road. If she walked facing traffic, they'd realize she didn't want a ride. The vehicle stopped, and a gray-haired woman opened the passenger-side door. "Need a ride?" she shouted. "We're headed to Wilburton."

This looked like a safe bet. Belle ran up to the Tin Lizzie. "Much obliged."

"I'm Mable. This is my husband, Andy."

Gray sideburns framed the man's friendly face. "Nice to meet you, Miss."

Mable motioned toward the backseat. "You'll find a wool blanket back there."

"Thank you, Ma'am."

"Call me Mable."

"Where you headed?" Andy pulled the car back on the road.

"Talihina."

A worried look passed between the couple.

"I'm not sick," Belle blurted. "I'm visiting a friend at the sanatorium."

"Thank goodness." A look of relief softened Mable's face. "You be careful. You don't wanna be coming down with consumption."

"It's a terrible disease," Andy said. "My brother died from it. A horrible wasting away of a once strong man." He shook his head.

"Let's talk about more pleasant things, Andy." Mable aimed her smile toward the backseat. "Aren't you glad spring is finally here?"

"Yes, ma'am. On the farm, I was thrilled when buds popped out on the trees. And I couldn't wait for my grandma to cook pokeweed with onions and bacon."

"Nothing like fresh bitter greens after a long winter. Wild leeks cooked in bacon grease—mm hmm—that's my favorite." Mable glanced back and licked her lip.

Andy pointed out the windshield. "Robber's Cave lies northwest of Wilburton. Jesse James and his gang hid out there. Belle Starr, too."

Mable shook her head. "There's so many tales out there, it's hard to know what's fact or fiction."

"I hunted there." Andy threw his wife a look. "I seen the cave with my own eyes." He glanced over his shoulder. "Bluffs and ravines make perfect hideouts. I can picture those outlaws hunkered down in narrow crevices and poking their gun barrels from the rocks."

"My grandfather," Belle said, "often spoke about the outlaws in Indian Territory. After the Civil War, he said there was a lot of horse rustling, bootlegging, robberies, and murder. Grandpa loved to talk about renegades." "Where do you live, child?" Mable asked.

Obviously, Mable wanted to switch subjects. "I worked in Shawnee. Guess I haven't decided where to land next." Mable twisted back and assessed Belle. "No family?" Belle shook her head and stared at the floorboard.

"I lost my parents when I was young," Andy said. "I was raised by a Quaker family. Ran away when I was eleven. Best thing I ever did."

Mable rested a hand on Andy's shoulder. "I was fortunate to grow up in a loving family. Ma refused to leave the old farm until the day she died. She loved feeding her chickens and tending the garden." Belle thought of her grandmother. "She died happy then."

"You're right there," Mable said. "Though it's hard to make a living on the farm these days. Prices are low. Hay is scarce. Crops are poor. We couldn't make it. The bank's taking our farm. We're headed to my sister's place. At least we'll have a roof over our heads."

Belle nodded. "Times are hard."

"People out of work," Andy said. "Banks closing. Don't know where all this will end. Folks are in for some hard times."

"No sense talking about troubles now, Andy." Mable shook her head and frowned. "No sense, at all."

Belle had to agree with Mable. What good did complaining do? Couldn't fix a thing. Relieved when Mable finally gave up talking, Belle succumbed to the warmth of the blanket and the vibration beneath her feet.

She woke when the car decelerated and turned onto Wilburton's Main Street. They parted company under a heavy sky as gray as lead. Mable hugged her. "Stay strong, girl."

Andy shook her hand. "Wish you the best."

Belle sought the warmth of a nearby restaurant. All the booths were filled and most of the tables occupied. She slid onto an empty stool along the counter and ordered vegetable soup, a biscuit, and a cup of hot joe. Outside the window, a downpour threatened. Stay strong. Was there any other choice?

Over her coffee mug, she studied the diner two stools down. A young woman, maybe nineteen or twenty, flirted with the bus boy. The girl had spunk from the red strapped shoes below her gray skirt to her cherry-red sweater and beret. She said she was from Texas. The boy disappeared behind the swinging kitchen door.

"Cold out there, ain't it?" the stylish stranger said.

"Wish the sun would come out." Belle blew at her coffee. "Are you traveling alone, too?"

"Sure am, but that doesn't bother me. I like the time to think about things."

"Where are you headed?" The waitress delivered Belle's soup. She was glad to see the soup came with a slice of bread. She was starving and could easily eat the biscuit and the bread.

"Going east to visit my cousin." The young woman extended a hand. "I'm Bonnie."

"Belle." She shook her hand. "Glad to meet you. I'm headed to Talihina to see a friend."

"Might that be a boy?" Bonnie raised her eyebrows.

Belle shook her head. "My best friend, Flora."

"A pretty girl like you should have a boyfriend." Bonnie spooned sugar into her coffee.

"That's the least of my worries." Fretting over a boy or wondering where she'd lay her head at night—those were two different worlds. She rooted in her pocket. It was empty. She stood and frantically checked the other pocket.

Bonnie's eyes widened. "Honey, do you need help paying for your meal?"

Her left pocket jingled. "Thanks, but I can cover it."

"Sorry, force of habit. I worked as a waitress for years in Dallas," Bonnie said. "Out back of the restaurant, there'd always be people begging for leftovers. They even took food we'd toss out at the end of the day. Can you imagine?" She shook her head. "I couldn't stand to see people hungry, so I made it a habit to buy one person a bowl of soup every day."

The girl was not only spunky but generous. "So you never miss someone to talk with on your travels?" Belle asked. How bold she'd become, but she guessed that was part of being strong like Mable said.

"Sometimes," Bonnie said. "My boyfriend is currently indisposed, so I've gotten used to traveling solo. But I'm getting bored with my own company." She laughed. "In need of a ride?"

Bonnie had seen straight through her not-so-subtle questions. "I'd be grateful for a ride as close to Talihina as you're traveling."

"Heck, I'll take you all the way. I'm in no hurry." Bonnie threw her napkin on the counter. "I'm going to pay a visit to the lady's room. We leave in ten minutes."

Thrilled to have obtained a ride with someone so young and savvy, Belle relaxed. Against all good manners, she brought the bowl to her mouth and guzzled the soup. Things were looking up despite the gloomy weather.

She followed Bonnie outside where the young woman opened the door of a shiny cream Nash Cabriolet. Bonnie was a waitress? Her boyfriend must be rich. Belle opened the passenger-side door to a seat littered with issues of romance and confession magazines.

"Toss them on the floor. I've already read them."

Bonnie lit a cigarette and pulled the car smoothly onto the highway. Belle had never been around anyone so modern and carefree. Bonnie was pretty.

Petite, she might weigh ninety pounds with clothes on. Freckles sprinkled the strawberry blonde's nose, and when she smiled, deep dimples appeared. In contrast, Belle's dark skin and plain clothes were so unglamorous compared to the suave young woman. She couldn't believe Bonnie thought she was pretty.

"Northwest of town is Robber's Cave," Belle blurted. She couldn't compete with Bonnie, but she could share something of interest. Belle sat straighter. "Jesse James hid out there when he was on the run. It's said Belle Starr was there, too."

Bonnie blew smoke toward the windshield. "Belle Starr, you say? The Bandit Queen herself." She glanced over. "She liked bad boys. Heard that horse rustler, Tom Starr, was Cherokee. What kind of Indian are you, Belle?"

"Comanche, related to Quanah Parker, no less." Belle figured Bonnie would be interested in that piece of news.

"Tell me it ain't so." Bonnie whistled. "I'm riding here next to a bona fide relative of Quanah Parker. I'm impressed."

Bonnie's left hand bore a gold band. But Bonnie had mentioned a boyfriend. "Are you...married?"

"I just like jewelry. Anything gold. 'Course diamonds would be better." Bonnie passed another car. She apparently liked to drive fast. "Tell me again why a pretty Indian maiden like you doesn't have a beau?"

Belle's face grew warm. "Too busy working, I guess." Bonnie had said it again, said she was pretty.

"I've met the love of my life," Bonnie said wistfully as she stared at the road ahead. "Met him this past January. I knew it was love at first sight."

"What's his name?"

"Clyde." Bonnie sighed. "Clyde Barrow."

Chapter 19

BONNIE'S TALES OF WAITRESSING KEPT Belle riveted on the young woman's encounters with belligerent customers and boyfriends met across a menu. Before she knew it, they had made it to Talihina. The sanatorium lay three and a half miles from town. As they drove across the hilly terrain on narrow roads, Belle took in the heavily wooded mountains covered in pine, southern red oak, and dogwood. Her eyes teared up.

"Are you okay?" Bonnie asked, driving too fast over the one-lane road.

"It's so beautiful." Belle glanced out the window. The Winding Stair Mountains tumbled down in a chain of steps. A few miles later, a sign announced the Eastern Oklahoma Tuberculosis Sanatorium. Belle's stomach twisted at what might lie ahead.

A glimpse of a roof appeared on the ridgeline, poking through the pines. Bonnie pulled into the entrance to the institution where a pair of stately buildings stood adjacent to each other with signs proclaiming one as the administration building and the other as the hospital. Nearby open-air porches lined a long one-story building. Altogether, the complex included six brick buildings, two barns, and four small cottages.

Bonnie parked the car and stretched her legs. She gazed over the grounds. "Who would have thought?"

A network of sidewalks crossed the groomed lawn and behind the buildings, dense woods bordered the campus. Belle's heart pounded. How could death exist in such a lovely place?

"I'll wait in the car." Bonnie applied a coat of lipstick. "If your friend's…uh…not here, I'll give you a ride back to Talihina."

Belle couldn't blame her. No one wanted to be exposed to tuberculosis. People were sent to the sanatorium and some were cured, but some died. There weren't any guarantees. With heavy steps, she walked up the sidewalk toward two women standing on the lawn. One aimed a camera at the other who posed with a hand at her hip. The camera subject wore a lemon-colored dress that fell mid-calf. The young woman's hair coiffed in short, dark waves. Matching pumps completed her ensemble, the light dress setting off her dark skin.

After the camera clicked, Belle stepped forward. "Excuse me." Both women spun around.

"Do you happen to know of a patient by the name of Flora Stone?"

The white woman turned to the woman in the yellow dress. The Native woman shielded her face from the sunlight. "Belle?"

"Flora? I didn't recognize you…your hair."

Flora wrapped her arms around Belle, pressing face to cheek. When she pulled back, she held Belle's shoulders. "Belle, are you sick?"

How like Flora to first embrace and then inquire about whether Belle had TB. "I was told you were sick. I was so worried." Belle's words rattled nonstop. "I didn't know if you were still alive. I'm not sick. Not at all. Oh, Flora, how are you?" Tears rolled down her cheeks. Flora was fine, more than fine from looking at her.

Two short honks drew their attention to the cream-colored Nash. Bonnie extended an arm out the window, cigarette in hand. Belle raised her hand in return as the Nash sped up and roared out the gate. Belle's satchel sat on the edge of the lawn.

Flora's eyebrows drew together. "Do you need a place to stay?"

Belle fell silent. It took a moment to find the right words. "I came to find you, Flora. I needed to see that you were okay. I'm just passing through."

Flora narrowed her eyes. "Little sister, everything's going to be okay." She pressed her chin on top of Belle's head. "Don't worry."

The white woman walked ahead with Belle's satchel in hand. A warm smile spanned Flora's face, and the two strolled arm in arm toward the parking area.

At the car, Flora introduced her to Anne Johnson.

"Glad to meet you." The top of the woman's head came to Belle's shoulder. Her round, friendly face somehow reminded Belle of her grandmother.

Anne drove them to town.

"What are the odds we'd meet here." Flora leaned over the front seat and smiled. "Anne needed to deliver some supplies today. The grounds are so beautiful that she insisted we had to take a photograph of me in my new dress."

"When I heard you were here," Belle said, "I figured you were sick."

Anne and Flora exchanged a look. Flora glanced back at Belle. "Honey, they don't allow Indians at Eastern Oklahoma Sanatorium. That's only for white folks."

"They don't help us skins?"

Flora's musical laughter rang out. "Natives go to the Choctaw-Chickasaw Sanatorium. It's not far from here."

"That makes sense." Belle didn't want Flora to think she was dull. "You...you look so beautiful, Flora." Her friend was obviously doing well for herself.

"It's amazing what a little makeup will do." Flora framed her face with both hands and laughed.

Belle had missed that laughter.

"I work at the hospital." Flora glanced at Anne. "The Indian hospital, that is. I'm in charge of ordering supplies for Anne, here, who is the head nurse. I also help Mr. Otto on occasion when he's overwhelmed with recordkeeping for the state."

"Which is more often than not," Anne quipped.

Belle studied every storefront and sign on Main Street. The town didn't look like it had much more than a few hundred souls. "What does Talihina mean?"

"It's from two Choctaw words. Tully and hena mean iron road," Flora said. "The name came about because Talihina was built around a railroad."

"Reuniting with a good friend calls for taking the rest of the day off," Anne announced.

"Do you mean it?" Flora's face lit up.

"Don't worry about losing pay," Anne said. "We'll call it a little bonus for my best employee."

143

Anne navigated a right hand turn off Main Street and hung a left onto an alley. Midway down the block, the car stopped and idled. Why were they stopping there? Belle glanced at barrels overflowing with garbage and wooden crates stacked six feet high.

Flora leaned over the seat and hugged Anne. "Go on now," her supervisor said. "You have a lot of catching up to do."

"You're a jewel. See you tomorrow."

Belle followed Flora to the back door of the brick building. A ceiling light flashed on and revealed a dingy one-room apartment.

"This used to be the office for the grocery store, but Mr. Wilson wanted his office centrally located." Flora tossed her purse onto a ladder-back chair. "It's not much, but it works for my brother and me." Flora pointed to the woodstove in the corner. "And it's warm. That stove will run you right out of the building, it gets so hot."

A sinking feeling grew in Belle's stomach as she surveyed the apartment. There was barely enough room for Flora and her brother. A diminutive table with folding leaves made for a dining area. A hotplate on the counter stood in for a stove, and a dented icebox wedged into a corner. A narrow bed hugged the far wall, and a cot near the door served dual purpose of sofa and bed. A window the size of a cracker box looked out onto the dismal alley.

Flora hugged Belle tightly. "I can't tell you how glad I am to see you. What a treat this is. Let me change out of this thing before I get it soiled."

"It's beautiful." Belle watched Flora change into a plain cotton dress.

"A patient's family gave it to me." Flora's face disappeared as she lifted the dress over her head. "Never dreamed I'd have a dress so nice. It was a thank you gift for keeping their daughter company until…until they arrived at the hospital."

With a screech, the door swung open and daylight flooded into the room. A boy hobbled into the apartment with a crutch under each arm. The door slammed shut. Flora's brother stood before her with wide eyes.

"Jeremy, this is my good friend, Belle."

The boy beamed. "The girl you always talk about." Jeremy leaned on one crutch and extended his arm.

Belle shook his hand. "Nice to meet you."

"I've heard all the stories." He looked mischievously at his sister.

"Excuse me while I start a fire and warm a pot of stew." Flora opened the door to the woodstove.

Jeremy hopped toward the cot and set his crutches in the corner. He sat, his alert eyes following Belle's every move.

She felt transported into Mr. Dicken's Christmas tale with Tiny Tim's crutch propped against the wall. By the looks of the few canned goods in the open cupboard, Flora's little family didn't fare much better than the Cratchits. She started to ask about Flora's other brother, but thought better of it.

While fire caught in the woodstove and a cast-iron pot warmed on top, Flora chattered cheerfully. "I was fortunate to get my job at the hospital. And working for Anne, well, I couldn't ask for a better supervisor. She's the best. The woman has a solid-gold heart."

Flora added another log to the stove and shut the hinged door. "Jeremy attends the school provided for the employees' families. He's doing well. He's such a bright lad."

Jeremy looked down and grinned.

"Remember the honey bear episode?" Flora giggled.

"A bear? A real bear?" Jeremy asked.

"Not quite."

Belle chimed in at various points of Flora's story. Jeremy insisted on hearing another boarding-school exploit.

"What about the matron tea?" Belle said. "That was quite a salty affair."

"Tell it," Jeremy begged. "Tell the story, please."

Belle happily complied. After she finished the trixing tale, she remembered another escapade. "We can't forget the vanilla."

Flora shook her head at Belle and glanced meaningfully at her brother. Belle understood an older sister wouldn't want to encourage that behavior.

"Vanilla?" Jeremy looked perplexed. "Tell me about that one."

Belle thought quickly. "I was speaking about the wonderful vanilla cakes we used to bake in the kitchen." Jeremy's shoulders slumped.

"Time for dinner," Flora announced.

The pot of reheated stew was half-full. Belle counted one chunk of meat in her bowl, snippets of carrots, and an abundance of chopped potatoes. Though she was still hungry, she declined a second serving. Jeremy needed nourishment more than she did.

After dinner, Flora helped her brother with his sums. Later while Jeremy read a schoolbook, Belle relayed her escape from Chilocco. She held her emotions in as she briefly mentioned the death of her grandparents but described in length her sister-in-law.

"What a dreadful woman," Flora said.

"After that experience, I left home," Belle said, "with no idea of where I was going or what I would do."

Flora cooed sympathetically. In the back of Belle's mind, she considered what Flora's story might entail. "I met a banker's daughter on the road," Belle continued, "and ended up working for her brother and his wife."

"What was your job?" Flora added another log in the stove, and the smell of smoke spewed out.

"Cooking and cleaning and pressing," Belle said. "All the things we were taught at Chilocco."

"All the things, you swore you'd never do." Flora laughed. "Jeremy, time for bed."

"Yes, ma'am." He closed the book, picked up his crutches, and carried his pajamas into the small commode in the back.

Once Flora tucked Jeremy in, she motioned Belle to the kitchen table. "We'll have to talk quietly." They pulled their chairs close together.

Flora folded her hands and stared at the oak table. "I wrote that Mother was sick," she whispered. "It proved to be consumption. Months later, it was obvious my brothers had contracted tuberculosis, too." Belle sucked in her breath.

"Mother passed away three months after my return. As soon as she passed, I brought the boys here. I was blessed by meeting Anne. She found me a job so I could stay in Talihina near my brothers." Flora clamped her eyes shut. "Despite all the doctor's attempts, even surgery at one point,
Thomas died six months later."

Belle reached for her arm. "Flora, I'm so sorry."

Flora's head rose and she smiled through her tears. "He's in a better place. I remind myself of that every day." Belle nodded.

Flora glanced at the sleeping form curled over her bed. "Jeremy survived, thank heaven. But children are susceptible to spinal tuberculosis. The disease went into his leg. He'll be crippled for the rest of his life." Her eyes shone with tears.

"Oh, Flora." It was all she could manage.

"But he's alive, Belle," she said. "He's a delightful boy, isn't he?"

Her thick throat wouldn't allow speech, and Belle worked at holding her tears back for Flora's sake. She bobbed her head.

"I'm so glad to see you again." Flora flung her arms around Belle's neck.

"Me, too," she mumbled.

Belle slept that night on the cot while Jeremy shared Flora's bed. She had trouble getting comfortable. Long after Flora's breathing grew deep, Belle lay awake. Her hopes of finding a job in the little town had vanished. She refused to be a burden to Flora.

She thought of the pitiful shantytowns cropping up on the outskirts of towns, people living in makeshift shacks of cardboard and tin, begging for food at backdoors, snatching milk bottles from porches, uprooting farmers' gardens, and slipping through unlocked kitchen doors. She shivered at the image of warming her hands over a campfire, smoke burning her eyes. As if in concurrence, her stomach growled.

Chapter 20

THE NEXT MORNING FLORA STIRRED a pot of oatmeal on the stove while Belle poured water into a teapot. She dunked a tea ball and replaced the lid. All three sat at the table with Jeremy perched on a wooden box. The oatmeal tasted odd with the powdered milk Flora used, but Belle ate without complaining.

"I'm headed back to McAlester today," Belle announced.

Flora gaped. "But you just got here."

"McAlester's a great town," she said. "I plan on getting a job there."

"Can't you stay a few more days, at least?"

"Please, stay." Jeremy tugged at her sleeve.

"I need to find work." Belle forced a smile.

Flora shoved her half-eaten bowl of oatmeal to the center of the table. "How will you get back?"

"I've, uh, arranged a ride with someone." She searched for an excuse. "A friend of Bonnie's, that girl you saw drive away." She hated to lie.

Flora studied her. "What time will you be leaving?"

"At noon." Belle cleared her dish. She poured hot water into a basin and stirred soap flakes into the steaming water. The narrow window revealed an overcast sky. Hopefully, the temperature would rise by midday since she'd be hitching a ride.

"Off to school now." Flora fastened the top button of Jeremy's coat.

He shuffled up to Belle on his crutch. "It was nice to meet you."

Belle wrapped her arms around the sweet boy. "I'm glad Flora has such a great brother to keep her company."

A horn honked in the alleyway. Flora grabbed her purse and coat. "I'll be back and we'll have an early lunch together." She grabbed Belle's shoulders. "Don't you leave before we have lunch."

Belle glanced down and nodded. Another honk blared from the alley, and the door slammed. Flora was gone. The last thing she wanted to do was leave Flora after they'd just been reunited. She slumped in the chair and cried silently.

Alone in the apartment, Belle opened the cupboards. It was just as she expected. A tin of baking soda and salt. A nearly empty box of oats. Two cans of beans. She shook the box of powdered milk. Flora had used the last of it on her account.

Belle had sewn her small savings into the lining of her wool jacket. She pulled at the basting stitches and left most of the money on the table for Flora and Jeremy. Just enough remained for toast and a cup of coffee. She'd leave it up to Providence to make a way.

Outside, a breeze slid down the neck of her thin coat. Belle tucked a scarf into the collar and trudged down Main Street in the direction of the highway. She'd been fortunate to get rides in the past and hoped her luck would hold. At the edge of town, she stood on the side of the gravel road and stared at the long, empty highway. The wind built in strength. Threatening clouds hung low, and the smell of rain rode the air. She flung the strap of her satchel over one shoulder. Belle strode down the road, arms swinging to keep herself warm. There was no turning back.

Wooded hillsides flanked the road on both sides as the charcoal sky closed in. In the distance, something dark lumbered across the highway and disappeared into the trees—too fast for a cow, too bulky for a dog. The mountains probably held bear like stagnant water held skeeters.

Grandma Tahsuda once told a story about Belle's great-grandmother. Along with Grandma, then six-years-old, and her sister, Faye, Greatgrandmother Rose gathered berries one afternoon in the mountains. Faye shrieked. Rose looked up at a huge black bear that lumbered a few yards away. The bear pursued berries, but perhaps human flesh would make a richer feast. Rose formed a stirrup with her hands and helped her daughters scale a rock outcropping. She climbed after them, her fingers clutching depressions in the rock, her fingertips bleeding. Faye wouldn't stop crying, and the bear charged. At the bottom of the outcropping, the bruin stood on its hind legs, its great claws swiping at the trio huddled on the rocks. Rose stabbed at the bear's paws with her knife. Furious, the bear roared and swung its deadly claws. Rose slashed another paw. The bear bellowed and dropped to the ground. The rogue bear had loped through the brush, leaving a trail of blood.

Belle glanced at the dark woods crouching at the side of the highway. Every few yards, she turned and checked behind her. On this lonely road, she'd be at a bear's mercy. Only two vehicles had passed. One whizzed by, the other slowed briefly only to continue on. Gusts of wind whipped up dirt, and she walked face down to keep grit from her eyes. When a motor rumbled behind her, she didn't lift her head.

"Belle!" The wind muffled a woman's voice. "Belle, stop!"

She looked back at a black Ford. The driver's arm waved—Anne, Flora's supervisor. Belle hurried to the car.

"Get in." She motioned to the backseat. Heavy drops of water splashed on the car.

"What are you doing?" Flora twisted around, her face strained in anger.

"I…I needed to get going."

"You make a horrible liar." Flora swung around to face the road.

Anne wore a smirk. She pulled onto a dirt road, placed the car in reverse, and turned back in the direction of town.

"We returned to the apartment, and you weren't there." Flora's voice grew cold.

Belle stared at the back of her head.

"I found the money you left," she said. "I have a job, you know."

"You need the money more than me," Belle said. "With Jeremy and all. I know you're short of food."

"We're in the process of vacating the back room," Flora said. "That's why the cupboards are bare. We're moving."

"Wh-where," Belle stammered. "Where are you going?"

"One of the staff bungalows is opening up," Anne said. "Flora will have a lot more room."

"Good," Belle said. "Good for you and Jeremy."

"Enough room," Flora said, "for you, too."

"That's kind of you, but I need to find a job. I can't impose on—"

"I need another nurse's aide." Anne glanced back. "Do you happen to know anyone who might be interested, Belle?"

Flora swiveled her head back, her eyes misty.

"I just happen to know a gal who's dying for a job," Belle said.

"That's what I thought." Anne glanced over at the passenger side and smiled.

Flora reached back and Belle took her hand. "We'll be roommates, again," Flora said. "We'll be family."

Belle nodded, her eyes welling with tears. She pulled an embroidered handkerchief from her pocket—her grandmother's handiwork—and dried her eyes.

The following morning, Belle sat across from Anne's wide desk on the first floor of the Choctaw-Chickasaw Sanatorium. The hospital was located on a hill a few miles from town. Outside the window, the sun blazed in bright opposition to the previous day. A nurse's cap stood at attention on the desk. A starched white uniform hung over the door, and a pair of soft-sole shoes lay on the floor as if an invisible person stood waiting.

"Belle, I'm glad to have you on board," Anne said. "Anyone who sacrifices their last earnings for her friend and little brother has the character to make a dedicated nurse's aide." She smiled warmly. "You have a lot to learn, but that's why you'll spend the first month under Nurse Braxton's supervision. After your initial training, feel free to ask me or any of the nurses for assistance."

Belle couldn't believe she was about to work at a hospital. She was excited, but she would have slopped hogs for a living if it meant staying with Flora.

"But there's something you must understand," Anne said.

That sounded like a warning.

"There is an inherent risk involved working with tuberculosis patients." Anne's face grew solemn. "There's a chance you could contract TB."

Consumption was a horrible disease: fever, coughing up blood, and a body growing weaker by the day. Even at the sanatorium, some never recovered. Belle drew her shoulders back. "Being out of work. Living in a shantytown. Starving," she said. "None of that's too good for a person's health, either."

Anne gazed out the window. "These are hard times, that's for sure. So many people suffering one way or another." She pushed back her chair and rose. Anne extended her hand across the walnut desk. "You're a survivor; you have the right attitude. Welcome to the Choctaw-Chickasaw Sanitorium."

"Thank you for the opportunity." Belle pumped her hand. "I won't take it for granted." She grabbed her hat along with the rest of her uniform and hurried down the hall, her reflection shining in the waxed linoleum.

She considered Anne's words. A survivor. Was there another option? The boy hopping a freight train was a survivor. She could only guess at Freddy's story. The couple who'd lost their farm—Mable and Andy—were surviving the best they could. Without complaint, Flora took on the role of guardian for her brother. And those poor souls in shantytowns, she couldn't even imagine it. As she headed to the restroom to change into her uniform, Belle mused on the reason for her good fortune. She wasn't anyone special. Why did some get a break but not others? Why did one die from tuberculosis and another lived?

Chapter 21

NURSE RUTH BRAXTON WAS A woman of contradictions. Her serious green eyes could see straight through a person, and she had a way of squinting when disappointed. The towering nurse's uniform did little to hide her bony shoulders, and her angular face produced a stern look. Ruth Braxton was all business with her narrowed eyes and pursed lips. But when she smiled, her face made a dramatic transformation, and most people would be inclined to do about anything for the woman.

The first time Belle heard Ruth laugh, she scooted to the hall to witness the commotion. When Nurse Braxton laughed, everyone in hearing distance joined in. Her infectious laughter made a person believe the world was going to turn out right after all.

The black stripe on Braxton's hat designated a registered nurse and differentiated the professional uniform from the plain white hat of a nurse's aide. But when it came to patients, everyone in uniform was a nurse, an "angel of mercy," though in the tuberculosis ward, Nurse Braxton remained their favorite.

Belle soon discovered the hard work required of a nurse's aide. Her duties included scrubbing floors, changing linens, disinfecting chairs and bedposts, and serving meals. Around severely ill patients, she was required to wear a mask. Two weeks into her new job, she learned how to fire up the furnace in case Joe Little Hawk couldn't make it into town. Her days were busy. After a long shift at the sanatorium, falling asleep never proved to be a problem.

The tuberculosis epidemic would not be reined in easily, and it wasn't uncommon that patients who recovered hired on as hospital employees. Jobs were hard to find in the Dirty Thirties, as people had started to call the times, and people felt fortunate to find any employment. Government funding made work at the sanatorium a stable job.

Nurse Braxton introduced Belle to another nurse's aide, a woman in her mid-forties. "Belle, this is Betty Brown, one of my best aides."

Belle tried not to stare at the woman's misshapen body. Betty's chest sank in a deep depression.

"Glad to meet you, Belle." Betty tilted her head toward Nurse Braxton. "As long as you smile and don't slack, you'll be her favorite, too." She winked.

Once the aide walked away, Ruth Braxton pulled Belle aside. "Betty underwent surgery a year ago and had one lung removed." Braxton smiled and her expression lightened. "I've never seen anyone with such a positive outlook on life. She never complains and always has a smile for everyone." "I imagine she's glad to be alive," Belle said.

"And savoring every minute." Braxton pointed to the linen closet. Belle complied with the unspoken request for a set of fresh linens.

Two months after Belle arrived, the expansive screened windows were opened to allow patients to breathe fresh mountain air. Wheeling patients onto the manicured grounds for sunbaths became Belle's favorite part of her job. She inhaled sweet pine-scented air as greedily as her patients. Summer had arrived, and the sun shone with bright promises as if meant for Belle alone.

The best part of her new life was living with Flora and her brother. The bungalow had two bedrooms, one of which was allotted to Belle. Jeremy slept on a cot in the larger bedroom he shared with Flora. Though he was eight, the boy requested stories every evening before falling asleep.

"Belle, I can't think of a single new story," Flora said. "Can you be a dear and give me a break?"

Belle would talk about life on the farm, which Jeremy never seemed to grow tired of hearing. She recounted the chores she used to do.

"Tell me more about the cows," Jeremy asked. "Weren't you afraid they'd stomp your feet with their hooves?"

"You learn to be careful around them, but once you gain their trust, there's not much to worry about."

"Tell me about that crazy cow again," he begged.

Belle told the tale of the Holstein cow who attacked a pair of coyotes when the wild dogs had come too close to her newborn calf. Clara raked the ground with her front hoof and charged the coyotes with her head down, horns protruding.

"So you see, Crazy Clara wasn't really crazy. She was only keeping watch over her calf. Just like Flora would do anything to protect you." "And you, too?" Jeremy's brown eyes fastened on hers.

Belle smothered the boy in a hug. "I'd fight for you, too." She smoothed the boy's dark hair from his forehead and pulled the blanket to his neck.

Even with paying half of the rent, Belle managed to save a percentage of each paycheck. She might have spent it on new dresses or shoes—Lord knew she needed them—but with the country in a depression and so many people out of work, her better sense hounded her to save what she could. Other than an occasional Sunday service, she had no reason to dress up. After several months, Belle was able to purchase gold bullion. She hid the coins in a box under her bed. Her grandfather had never trusted banks and with newspaper headlines of soup lines and bank runs in New York City, she preferred to keep her savings close at hand.

Flora and Belle took turns cooking meals. With their two salaries, their cupboards remained stocked, though they still had to stretch their meat with egg and noodle dishes. They planned short hikes in the hills when their days off corresponded. If they could catch a ride with someone who worked at the hospital, they'd spend a day at one of the man-made lakes near Talihina. After cooling off in the water, they'd enjoy a picnic lunch. Jeremy often brought a friend from school, and a blown-up inner tube helped him participate in water games with his buddy.

For weeks they saved up so they could attend a movie at the local theater. The long-anticipated day arrived, and the three of them stood outside the theater, gazing up at the marquee. Flora approached the ticket window.

"Three tickets, please."

"Here's three additional tickets for our door prize." The window attendant chomped her gum. "Next please."

Flora glanced back at the line of people. "Come on, Jeremy. Let's buy some popcorn."

Belle held the door for Jeremy, the boy's face flush with excitement. Inside, the smell of hot buttered popcorn pervaded the lobby. The clerk at the refreshment station took Flora's money and asked for her ticket. The sharp-nosed young man shook his head. "Sorry, maybe next time."

Jeremy waved his ticket. The clerk checked a list of numbers posted on the counter. "Sorry, kid."

Jeremy's bottom lip protruded.

"Honey, it's just a gimmick. But we're here, aren't we?" Flora ruffled his hair. "Give me a smile, and let's go find a good seat."

Belle gave her door-prize ticket to the clerk, sure it was just a ploy to pull in more customers. The young man smiled cockeyed and his voice boomed out. "Ladies and gentleman, we have a winner of tonight's door prize. One free movie ticket."

The customers behind Belle clapped. She rushed to the entrance of the theater where Flora and Jeremy waited. She waved the ticket. "I won." Belle glanced down at Jeremy. "I believe you have an important date coming up. Happy Birthday."

Jeremy glanced at Flora, and she nodded.

He beamed. "Thank you, Belle."

They paused for a moment in the dim theater and searched for the best seats. Flora led them down the aisle until they reached the fifth row from the front.

A third of the popcorn was gone by the time the lights dimmed. Music rose from the front speakers, and the curtains parted. The projector lit up the screen.

Jeremy sat between them and squirmed in his seat, unable to stop laughing at Groucho Marx's antics in Animal Crackers. Belle and Flora exchanged looks and laughed. Flora was right. They had become a little family.

Juice cans clinked and thermometers jingled in a metal cup as Belle pushed a cart down the hall. She paused to adjust her mask before entering the patients' room.

"I'm going to run away," a girl's voice came from within.

Belle froze. She'd have to inform Nurse Braxton.

"I'm not going anywhere," another voice said. "I want to get better, and this is the only place where that can happen." There was silence.

"Then I'll stay," the first girl said. "Sisters have to stay together."

Belle wheeled the cart into the room. "Good morning, girls. How are you today?"

The older girl, ten-year-old Gwen, glanced at the cart and grimaced. "When I get out, I'll never take a spoonful of castor oil ever again."

Her eight-year-old sister nodded, but a smile lit up her face. In contrast to Gwen, Amy was a compliant patient.

"I can understand that," Belle said, "but think how healthy you'll be by then. There won't be a reason to even consider castor oil."

Gwen crinkled her nose and muttered, "That doesn't help me now."

Belle mixed the oil with tomato juice for Gwen and with pineapple juice for Amy. Belle rolled up the brown tarp that covered the window, and a warm breeze blew into the room. "Did your mother visit yesterday, girls?" "She always comes on Sunday afternoon," Amy said.

"I hate having to talk to her from the second floor." Gwen pouted. "It's like we don't even have a real mother."

"Don't say that, Sis."

"I know it's hard." Belle handed the tomato juice to Gwen. "But we can't have your baby brother exposed, can we?"

Gwen scowled. Amy smiled at Belle. "I can't wait to hold him."

"I know he'll love his sisters." Belle glanced at Gwen, who refused to meet her eyes. "Have a good day, girls."

Belle continued her rounds. She couldn't imagine having to be relegated to a hospital room at such a young age. To wake up to the smell of bleach and the taste of castor oil every morning would be horrible for any child. Belle refrained from pity. Their very lives were at stake. Hopefully, the girls would move on to live full lives, and their current experiences would all be just fuzzy memories.

After her shift, Belle headed to the bungalow where Jeremy waited for her to make good on her promise. She'd offered to take Jeremy to the park in Talihina. Daylight stretched long this time of the year, and as a special treat, she would pack a picnic basket. Flora had to work late that night on a supply inventory required by the state. Arlene, a friendly kitchen employee, had agreed to give them a ride to town, and Anne would bring them back to the bungalow later that evening.

Outside, Jeremy waited on a bench, wearing shorts, oxford-style shoes, and a beanie. "Can we go now?"

Belle propped her hands at her hips. "Do you plan on walking? Besides, I need to change out of my uniform."

"I'll wait here." Jeremy sighed and tapped his foot.

She changed into a cotton print dress and prepared chicken sandwiches. Belle spooned the last of the potato salad into a glass jar and wrapped two dill pickles in butcher paper and tied them with string. She wrapped sugar cookies next, grabbed a blanket, and was out the door. Arlene waved from her parked car.

"No more daydreaming. Let's go, boy."

She walked ahead, knowing even with crutches he'd catch up with her.

"I brought my marbles, Belle." He drew up to her side.

Belle removed a drawstring bag from her pocket and shook it. "Hope you plan on losing a few."

His eyes sparkled. "Naw. It'll be your loss, girl."

Arlene dropped them off at the town park. Jeremy had grown quite adept at using crutches and could keep up with Belle's gait. The public park was awash in sunlight, and a soft breeze made the heat bearable. Ahead, three young men approached and when they were ten feet away, stopped. The middle boy held out his hand and glared at Belle.

"Don't go no further." The boy's brown hair had a cowlick at the crown, and he looked to be about fifteen or sixteen.

Belle guessed the boys were from the nearby sawmill town. A soiled fedora with a hole near the brim capped the adolescent to the left. They all wore bib overalls and shirts. The tallest boy's hat was comical, the flatcrown straw incongruent with the rest of his attire. If not for the threatening look on his face, she might have laughed out loud.

Sawmill employees and their families lived in the company town called Pine Valley. They often came to town to attend a movie. Talihina's theater had talking pictures. The company town showed only silent movies.

The stocky boy with the cowlick smirked. "Go back to your teepee." On his right, the tall, wiry boy jutted his jaw in derision.

"This is a public park." Belle kept her voice level but firm. "You can see this boy is on crutches, and we'd appreciate if you'd make way, gentlemen." In reality, she figured they didn't possess an ounce of chivalry, but she hoped to appeal to their budding manhood.

"Not another step," the cowlick barked. "Damn Indians givin' decent people consumption."

Belle glared at the boy.

"Bet that boy's on crutches 'cause he has consumption. Dirty injun." The cowlick spit on the sidewalk, mucous landing midway between the two races of people.

She glanced at Jeremy, whose wide eyes stared at the leader in the middle. His crutch shook.

"Step aside." The cowlick narrowed his eyes.

Belle slid one hand in her dress pocket. With a flick, she opened her switchblade and held it out. "Like I said this is a public park."

The cowlick's eyes widened in surprise. Then he frowned, reddening with rage. "Damn redskins."

She'd brought the knife to carve branch skewers for a marshmallow roast.

The husky boy stepped back. "They always carry a damn knife. Can't trust 'em."

"We don't want to be in this lousy park anyway. Come on, guys. Let's find someplace cleaner. We don't want to catch tu-ber-q-lo-cus." The three boys crossed the lawn to the street. The tall, thin boy looked back once, but the trio kept walking.

"We're not dirty." Jeremy's voice wavered.

"No, we're not." Belle knelt in front of the boy. "But those boys have filthy hearts."

"Why?" Jeremy asked. "Why were they so mean?"

"Honey, there's bad people of all colors. Let's find a park bench. I'm famished." They continued down the sidewalk and located a bench. Belle removed the food from the picnic basket and set it between them on the seat. The scent of freshly cut grass hung on the air.

"Belle, why did they think Indians would give them tuberculosis?" His brown eyes looked out from between furrowed brows. For once, Jeremy didn't dig immediately into his food.

"Unfortunately, a lot of whites think they'll catch it from Indian people. But you want to know the truth?" He

nodded vigorously.

"It was the whites that brought the disease to this country."

"Then why—"

"People get funny ideas about diseases. They get scared and want to blame it on someone." She unwrapped the chicken sandwiches. "Do you want to know something else?"

"Sure." Jeremy eyed the sandwiches.

"There's another tuberculosis sanatorium up the hill for white people, and it's just as full of sick white people as the Choctow-Chickasaw hospital is full of Natives."

"That makes sense," Jeremy mumbled between bites.

Belle smiled. "It does, doesn't it?"

"You wanna know something, Belle?"

"Sure thing."

"Their blood's the same color as ours."

She laughed. "Right you are. The Creator made us all the same inside, didn't he?" Belle spooned potato salad onto two small plates. "Eat up. I'm going to win all your marbles today."

"Huh-uh. I'm gonna clean you out."

Their marble game turned out to be an uneven match. Jeremy played marbles every day after school with his friends. His skill had increased since the last time they played.

"I give," Belle said. "Better quit before you take all my marbles." Her real reason was more ominous. For the last five minutes, she'd kept an eye on the lanky boy across the street watching them. He wore the unmistakable straw hat. Something was up. "Let's check out the other end of the park."

She wondered where the sawmill boy's buddies had disappeared to. Were they planning on retribution for her courage to stand up to them? She didn't worry about herself as much as Jeremy. A sick feeling worked at her stomach. They neared the opposite side of the park when a black Ford with police insignia parked along the street. The policeman stepped out of the vehicle, and another man exited the passenger side. The Cowlick!

Belle kept walking and once parallel to a thick pine, tossed her switchblade into the grass. Jeremy and Belle came out on the other side of the tree in full view of the officer. The sawmill boy pointed. "There she is, officer. There's the trouble-making squaw!" "Belle?" Jeremy looked worried.

"It's okay. Keep walking. Look straight ahead as if nothing's the matter." The officer marched towards them. "Hold up."

Belle looked straight ahead and acted as if she hadn't heard. She smiled down at Jeremy as if they were enjoying a simple summer day at the park.

"Stop right there injun!" The policeman pulled out his club.

Chapter 22

BEADS OF SWEAT FORMED ON Belle's forehead. The smell of pinesap and needles swirled lazily under the warm Oklahoma sun. The heavy officer patted her down, his crude inspection performed in front of strolling couples and children who stopped to gawk. She averted her face from the rancid tobacco on his breath.

"Instead of a walk through the park, you'll pay a little visit to my holding cell."

The officer clutched her upper arm, and Belle's head swung toward Jeremy. Cowlick mimicked the officer's hold on the boy's arm, and Jeremy's eyes brimmed with fear. "The boy," she blurted, "he's innocent. He's the brother of a woman who works at the hospital."

The officer caught sight of Jeremy's crutches. "Let him go, fella."

Cowlick narrowed his eyes at Belle and reluctantly released his hold.

"Go home, Jeremy," Belle said in a firm voice. "Go home, now!" She cast a stern look at the boy. The long walk would be hard on him, but he had to reach the safety of home as soon as possible. She was relieved when Cowlick followed the officer to the patrol car. At the curb, the officer bound her wrists with handcuffs. He looked over at Cowlick. "You need to come to the office and fill out a report."

"'Course, Officer Hagar." Cowlick straightened his shoulders. "Be happy to assist."

Hagar pushed Belle's head down and shoved her into the backseat. Cowlick sat in the front of the patrol car, his back straight and chin held high.

As the key was placed in the ignition, the young man glanced over his shoulder with an evil grin.

The vehicle rounded the corner, and Belle spotted the tall "straw-hat" standing at the far side of the park. Her stomach clenched. Would Jeremy see him in time and avoid the troublemaker or hobble right into the trap?

A brief drive brought them to the Talihina jail located on Main Street. A sign on the adobe structure stated the building served as both city hall and jail, a gabled portal providing entry to the jail. Officer Hagar jerked her from the backseat and whisked her into the building.

Hagar motioned to Cowlick with his chin. "Take a seat." He dragged Belle back to a holding cell. The iron door swung shut with a clank. "I'll deal with you in a minute." Heavy eyebrows drew together, and his ruddy face dipped in a scowl.

Belle withdrew to the far end where daylight leaked through a narrow window. She shivered. The stark enclosure held a cement bench and a toilet. A sour smell rose from the dingy cell, the cement walls exuding cold.

Belle moved near the iron door as voices rose and fell from the office. Drew knife...just walking...park...dirty squaw. Papers shuffled. Thanks...be in touch, boy. A door shut. Heavy footsteps approached, and Belle retreated to the back corner where she stood in the shadows.

A set of keys jingled on a metal ring. Officer Hagar opened the door, locked his hand around her arm, and escorted her to his office. "Sit." Belle obeyed and sat in a chair in the corner.

His clasped hands fell over the oak desk. The portly man frowned at her for a few moments.

"Causing trouble in the park, huh?" he said at last. One eye narrowed while the other remained wide open.

She shook her head and twisted her wrist against the metal cuff biting into her skin.

"Speak up," he barked.

"We were having a picnic."

"Not what I hear. You Indians sure like your knives, don't ya?"

"What knife, sir?"

Hagar frowned and his lower lip protruded. "You best be respecting the white people in this town." He squinted. "You're not from around here, are you?"

"I moved here recently. Came from McAlester, sir." She hated saying sir, but she was in no position to stand up for herself, and she knew it.

"Here in Talihina, we expect our Indians to show some respect." He narrowed both eyes. "You get my meaning?"

"Yes, sir."

"Stand up, girl."

She stood before the desk as he brushed his eyes over her body. She was repulsed by his thick hands and large knuckled fingers.

He came around the desk. "Think we need to let you sit and stew about your behavior for a few days." With his fingers digging into her arm, he escorted her toward a cell that contained a cot. He removed her handcuffs and nudged her inside. The door clanged shut. "Gets pretty cold here at night." He leered at her breasts. "You'll be begging for body heat before the night's over, if you get my meaning." With a low chuckle, he stomped back to his office.

Oh, God. Her stomach cramped. Belle knew exactly what she was in for. She leaned over and heaved.

Hours later, Officer Hagar unlocked the cell, and a young boy delivered a bowl of watery soup. Their footsteps retreated down the hall. Belle stirred the broth. No meat. No bread. She refused to eat. The light outside the window dimmed, and soon it would be dark.

She'd be alone with Officer Hagar. She fought off the dark image. Her thoughts turned to Jeremy. Had he avoided the sawmill boys? She hated to think what they would do if they caught him. Flora would never know where to look for either of them. Belle's stomach churned, but there was nothing left to purge.

The window framed a slice of the night sky. A dim light leaked from the office. A few minutes later, a bright light flicked on at the end of the hall, and boots stomped down the corridor. Her stomach twisted in on itself. Belle slid into the corner of the cell as Hagar stared through the bars.

"A few more hours and the good citizens of Talihina will retire for the night."

Though his face was shadowed from the light behind him, she could make out a smug grin.

"I'll be back to check on you, girl. Don't you worry."

Her breath slowly returned as his boot steps faded. She cowered at the back of the cell. After several minutes, she took a deep breath, and sat hunched over on the lumpy cot. Physically, she was no match for the large man. And what was Jeremy's fate? Boys could be so cruel, and these were white boys steeped in hate and scorn. Completely powerless, her head dropped to her hands.

A door slammed. Female voices rose on the air. She caught only part of the conversation. How dare you…state director…immediately! Hagar's voice rolled low in apology, Ma'am…didn't know…of course. The hall light hummed on, and footsteps marched towards her cell. Hagar unlocked the door. For once, he didn't clutch her arm. Two silhouettes stood against the light at the end of the hall.

"Go on, now," he growled under his breath. Then he spoke louder for the benefit of the indignant citizens out front. "Don't want to see you back here again."

Belle hurried down the hall and into the arms of Anne Johnson. A few feet away, Ruth Braxton addressed Hagar, her eyes ablaze. "The director of the hospital has connections in this state. He knows people with great influence with the governor."

Anne wrapped her arm around Belle's shoulder and escorted her to the car. Ruth Braxton joined her in the backseat and patted Belle's hand. "Are you okay? Did that swine hurt you?"

"I'm fine." Belle rubbed her arm. "Jeremy—is he all right?"

"He's going to be fine," Anne said. "Let's get you home."

Ruth held Belle's hand as they drove up the hill. Outside Flora's bungalow, the pair of women framed Belle as they walked her to the front door. They entered without knocking. Flora sat smoothing Jeremy's hair as he lay on the sofa. She placed a finger to her lips, slipped from beneath his sleeping form, and motioned to the back bedroom. Jeremy's head slipped sideways, revealing a bruised cheek and several scrapes. Belle's hand swept to her mouth.

Flora clicked on the bedside lamp and rushed toward Belle. She embraced her—too tightly.

Anne stepped forward. "Is there anything you need, Flora?" Flora shook her head.

Ruth filled the doorway with her statuesque height. "We're going to take care of this. That's a promise."

"We'll be going now." Anne wrapped a pale arm around each woman. "We'll talk more tomorrow."

"Thank you," Flora whispered.

Flora and Belle sat on the edge of the mattress, their cotton dresses joining in a bouquet of floral prints. The bedside lamp cast an amber glow over their knees. "Jeremy," Belle whispered. "What happened?"

Flora's voice shook. "That boy from Pine Valley harassed Jeremy in the park." She covered her face and wept.

Belle leaned her forehead against Flora's temple. Tears streamed down Belle's cheeks as they sat without talking.

Flora pulled a handkerchief from her pocket and blew her nose. "For a while, he kept Jeremy from leaving the park. Scared the boy to death. Threatened him. Swore at him and said foul things. Once he let him go, he badgered him, following him halfway home. He pelted him with pinecones and pebbles. Jeremy tried to hurry, but he fell on the way up the hill to the sanatorium. When I returned home, I found him cringing in the corner. He could barely talk. Finally, I got it out of him what had happened. I ran for Anne. I knew it would take a white person to handle Officer Hagar."

Belle stared at the floor. Sweet Jeremy. Didn't he have enough to deal with? A simple outing at the park had turned into a nightmare. Her bravado had put Jeremy in danger. She blamed herself.

After the incident in the park, Jeremy withdrew. The disappearance of his usual sunny disposition was more disturbing than had he cried. Flora could be heard whispering to Jeremy in the middle of the night, reassuring him his nightmare was only a bad dream. But it was more than a nightmare, evil had pierced the boy's safe little world.

Chapter 23

ONE AFTERNOON, BELLE RETURNED HOME before Flora. Jeremy sat in the wicker rocker in the corner, reading a book.

"How are you doing, Jeremy?" The boy nodded without lifting his head. She changed out of her uniform and returned to the front room. That was when she noticed. The crutches in the corner held bright red and blue paint.

She walked over and inspected the intricately painted design. Jeremy cast a quick glance from the corner of his eye before returning to his book. A blue arrow shaft ran the length of the crutch with an arrowhead drawn at the end. Fat drops of blood radiated from the tip as if the arrow had just pierced its prey. "This is beautiful," Belle said.

Jeremy worked to keep a straight face.

His artistic talent didn't come as a complete surprise. Jeremy liked to doodle, and his drawings were well crafted for someone so young. She wondered how Flora would respond.

Belle said nothing more and set about soaking pinto beans for tomorrow's meal. That night after Jeremy had gone to bed, the two women discussed Jeremy's latest creation.

"Maybe he's expressing his Native heritage," Flora said. "It's harmless, right?"

"It could be his way of showing strength," Belle said. "After what happened, he needs to feel a sense of power."

"But I'm still worried about the fact he's so glum. He's not himself."

"I know." She hugged Flora. "It worries me, too."

"Maybe he just needs time to adjust."

"We need to be patient."

The next day, Jeremy's teacher contacted Flora. Miss Finch insisted the bloody design on the crutch was distracting and inappropriate.

"She agreed to allow the arrow design," Flora told Belle, "but she insisted the drops of blood had to be removed."

"That's something at least."

"You know, I've never seen that woman smile," Flora said.

"That can't be a good thing for someone who works with children. Remember the matrons at Chilocco?"

Flora laughed. "How could I forget?"

That night Flora instructed Jeremy to scrub off the red drops or paint over them. Jeremy spent several hours sanding the crutches, his face scrunched in anger. He never said a word.

Two days later, Flora was called in again. Miss Finch accused Jeremy of bullying two older boys in class. She had called in the students, who insisted they had walked away from Jeremy and refused to fight with a younger boy on crutches. They didn't understand why he was egging them on for a fight. They were much bigger than Jeremy.

Flora had a talk with Jeremy that evening. She ordered him to behave but received little response.

She confided in Belle. "I can't get him to talk. He won't explain why he's picking on the older boys. He's never been a problem at school. It's like he's another person."

Though Belle had little experience with children, she knew it all went back to that day in the park. "What happened with the sawmill boys and the police has had an impact on him. It must have been terrifying." It was terrifying for her, too, but she didn't mention that.

Flora was on the verge of tears. "What can we do?"

"I wish I knew." She felt compelled to say something positive. "Despite everything, we need to keep loving him and hope for the best."

The following day, Jeremy was suspended from school for harassing another boy, a younger student this time. For the next week, Flora would pick up daily assignments for Jeremy to complete at home.

One evening, Belle sat at the table as Jeremy doodled on a piece of paper. The aroma of that night's meatloaf hung on the air. "It must have been frightening to see the police take me away." He kept his eyes down as his hand spun over the paper.

"But it turned out okay, didn't it? I came home that night." He kept doodling. "Are you listening, Jeremy?"

He shot a look and dropped his head.

Belle drew in a deep breath. Nothing seemed to make a difference.

Jeremy returned to school a week later. Within two days, Flora was called in again to the teacher's office, and she asked Belle to accompany her. The two sat in hard chairs across from Miss Finch. The stoic teacher frowned, silent for a few moments as if she considered what to say.

"Today Jeremy pushed me." Miss Finch cleared her throat. "He shoved me up against the chalk board."

Belle and Flora exchanged shocked looks.

"I cannot have him in my class until he can control himself and act appropriately." As if in final judgment, Miss Finch folded her hands over the desk. "This is a drastic departure from the quiet, sweet boy who used to be in my class." She cleared her throat again. "I know you explained he had an unfortunate experience a while back, and I agree he's probably acting out the trauma, but you need to understand that I can't have other students penalized for his behavior. What he did today jeopardizes my authority in the classroom and sets an unprecedented lack of respect. Surely, you understand this."

Speechless, Flora nodded. Belle had to agree with the teacher.

"I believe it would be best for everyone if Jeremy does not return to school for six months."

Flora's mouth flew open. "That's too long! He's just a little boy."

"Let's go." Belle gently took her arm as Flora glared at Miss Finch. "Come on, Flora." Belle escorted her out the door, where her friend erupted in sobs. With wide eyes, Jeremy watched his sister cry.

"Come on, Jeremy," Belle took his hand. "Let's go home."

Later that evening, the three sat around the table after dinner. Flora turned to Jeremy. "Why did you push Miss Finch today?" Jeremy narrowed his eyes and thrust his jaw.

"We're not leaving this table until you explain." Jeremy stared at the tabletop.

"Silence is not an option. We'll stay here all night if we have to." Belle had never seen Flora so forceful.

Mumbles rose from Jeremy's downturned face.

"I can't hear you," Flora said.

"She said men should never go to war," Jeremy said louder. "We were discussing the Great War, and Miss Finch insisted war was wrong and men should never go off to war."

Belle and Flora exchanged looks.

"Wars happen," Flora said quietly. "Even if we don't want them, sometimes men have to defend their country."

"That's what I tried to tell her, but she wouldn't listen. Said I'd never be able to be a soldier anyway."

Belle gritted her teeth. How dare the woman say that to a young boy?

"That's when I shoved her." Jeremy straightened. "I'm going to learn how to shoot a rifle. My arms are strong, and I can take care of myself." The defenseless kitten had grown into a bobcat.

"You're right about that," Belle came to Jeremy's defense. "You're going to grow into a strong young man, and you'll be able to defend yourself."

Flora narrowed her eyes. "But that doesn't make it right that you shoved your teacher."

"No, ma'am, it doesn't," Jeremy said. "A man should never shove a woman. A man needs to know when to pick his fights."

"That doesn't include picking fights at school," Flora said.

"You're right." Jeremy nodded and glanced between the two women.

"It's time to work on your homework," Flora said. "Just because you're working at home, don't think it'll be easy."

"Maybe, we'll be even tougher than Miss Finch," Belle said with a straight face.

Jeremy grabbed his crutches and headed for his stack of books.

Over the next several months, Belle and Flora took turns helping Jeremy with his homework. He slowly became more animated, and his familiar laughter rang out in the bungalow once again.

On Saturday evening they stayed up late listening to the radio. At 10 PM, they tuned into WKY out of Oklahoma City for the Lucky Strike Radio Hour.

"And so begins this hour of dance music, presented for your pleasure by the manufacturers of Lucky Strike Cigarettes. The Lucky Strike Dance Orchestra will be heard in these lively tunes."

The three sat close together on chairs arranged around the radio.

"Here's a real dancing combination," the announcer continued, "a good one from George White's Scandals—Pickin' Cotton, and another old friend, Bambalina."

Flora tapped her feet to the music, while Belle sashayed back and forth in her chair. Jeremy struck one crutch in time to the beat.

"Now for a waltz. The Lucky Strike Orchestra will play the famous classic from The Merry Widow."

Belle and Flora moved chairs out of the way and shoved the kitchen table against the wall. Flora taught Belle how to waltz, demonstrating the steps in slow motion. "Now let's try it as a couple."

Belle's feet faltered, her feet like lead weights. "I'm no good at this."

"Let's try again. Move on the balls of your feet. Watch me." Flora patiently showed her the steps again. "You can do this. It just takes practice."

After repeated attempts, Belle finally got the concept. It helped to lift her heels. They flew across the room in a smooth, quick gait.

"Your turn to be the gentleman," Flora said. She laughed at Belle's imitation of a male dancer: shoulders back, chin lifted, and lips comically pursed.

Belle arranged her hands in the proper position. They danced around the small room, from the sitting area to the kitchen and back again. After the music ended, they dropped to the sofa laughing. Jeremy applauded their performance.

That night, Belle discovered she loved to dance. Flora dreamed of attending a community dance with live music and handsome partners. Belle, on the other hand, hoped their lives would never change.

Chapter 24

-1931-

NIGHT SHIFT EMPLOYEES PACKED INTO Nurse Braxton's office as President Hoover gave a radio address to the nation. Everyone listened somberly that October evening as the president called for a six-week campaign to raise local relief funds to help the unemployed. Towards the end of the address, Ruth clicked off the radio.

"It's like an evil spirit spreading over the country," an older nurse declared.

The deepening Depression weighed on everybody, including Belle.

"Some good that campaign will do," Nurse Braxton said. "Where's he expect to find money to feed all the poor souls living in Hoovervilles." Ruth explained to a young aide that a Hooverville was another name for a shantytown, the term obviously used in reproach of the president. "Hoover blankets," Belle blurted. "Do you know what those are?" Ruth Braxton looked at her blankly.

"I'll give you a hint. They're black and white and read all over."

Furrowed brows appeared. Some shook their heads and shrugged.

Belle smiled at her captive audience. "Newspapers."

"That would be funny," Ruth said, "except I can picture all those poor souls shivering beneath layers of newspapers." She shook her head. "What a pitiful situation."

"Do you think..." Dare Belle ask? "...our jobs are in danger?" Sometimes at night while waiting for sleep, Belle worried about losing her position. People lost jobs every day, a sad fact that made the newspaper headlines and radio reports.

"Don't worry your pretty head," Ruth said. "Fighting tuberculosis is a top priority for the state."

That came as a relief. Belle couldn't imagine where she'd go next. Even worse, she couldn't bear the thought of Flora and Jeremy out in the cold. They were all so blessed. Every day the radio continued to report dismal statistics. Upon hearing how many others went hungry and homeless, Belle thought how easily it could have been her.

Flora had a new beau, a nice young Choctaw man named Charlie Stilwell. Once a month, he took her out for a movie or dinner. Sometimes they went for walks in the city park or stopped for a cup of coffee and slice of pie at Fern's Cafe. Belle considered what would happen if they married. She'd be left alone again. But to her relief, Flora seemed content with the occasional date.

One Saturday evening, Charlie came calling on Flora accompanied by another man. Flora invited them in, and Charlie introduced the stranger.

"This is my cousin, Luke Stilwell," Charlie said. "Luke, this pretty lady is my girl, Flora, and her roommate, Belle Tahsuda." He tousled Jeremy's hair. "And we can't forget Flora's brother, Jeremy." The boy looked up and smiled.

"Glad to meet you, Flora." Luke's hat slanted at a jaunty angle, and he hurried to remove his hat. "I've heard great things about you. Made me quite jealous, truth be told."

Flora glanced shyly at Charlie, pleased at the remark.

Luke was striking—the most handsome Native man Belle had ever seen. His broad shoulders tapered to a trim waist and long legs. And his smile, any girl would swoon over that.

"Nice to meet you, too, Belle," Luke said. "Charlie didn't warn me Flora's roommate was so gorgeous."

Not knowing what to say, she turned to Jeremy. "I baked some cookies today. Let's find you one." Jeremy hesitated, caught between sweets and Charlie's attention.

"Go ahead," Charlie said. "A man can't turn down a cookie."

Belle stole another glance at Luke. High cheekbones chiseled his handsome face. Charlie's cousin was beautiful—if one could say that about a man. She wouldn't like to have such a boyfriend. He was the kind of man that drew women's attention and that type of thing went straight to a man's head.

Luke turned to Charlie, and his eyebrows lifted in a question.

"We were wondering," Charlie said, "if you'd like to come out with us, Belle."

Belle glanced at Flora. She hadn't expected this.

"Belle, we'd love for you to come." Flora softly touched Belle's arm. "We're going out for coffee and pie."

"Well, I…I," she stuttered, "I think I should stay with Jeremy."

"Oh, fiddlesticks," Flora said. "Joan is home next door. She'll gladly check on him. You'd be okay with that wouldn't you, Jeremy?"

"I don't need a sitter." Jeremy's chin protruded. "I'm not a baby."

"You're certainly not." Charlie playfully slugged Jeremy's arm. The two got along well. They had an ongoing match with marbles, and Jeremy often went with the couple on their walks through the park.

"Come on, girl," Flora begged. "You need to get out once in a while."

And so it was that Belle had her first double date. Had he really called her gorgeous?

To Belle's relief, Flora sat with her in the backseat of Charlie's car. The men talked between themselves on the short drive to town. Charlie parked outside Fern's Cafe, known for their homemade pies. After studying the menu, they ordered mincemeat, Dutch apple, and cherry pie. Belle requested blueberry ala mode.

"They have the best pie here," Flora said. "The crust is perfect. Fern told me her secret—lard makes the crust nice and flaky."

Belle carefully crossed her legs and uncrossed them. Her neck tightened and radiated into a fiery knot in her back. Other than boarding school and Otis Harwood, she'd never been around young men. Chilocco didn't count as boys and girls were separated for most activities. Otis didn't count because she considered him just a friend.

The waitress arrived balancing a tray. Charlie rubbed his hands together. "You're in for a treat, cuz."

"Looks good to me." Luke smiled at Belle.

Once served, the guys dug into their dessert with gusto. Belle glanced over at Flora, who winked.

"Luke is from Dry Run," Flora said. "He's Comanche, too, Belle." "Part Choctaw," Luke added.

"Where's Dry Run?" Belle kept her eyes on Flora. Was Luke's Comanche background supposed to impress her?

"A ways northwest of McAlester," Luke spoke from the side of his mouth, his opposite cheek bulging with pie.

"I came through McAlester," Belle said, glancing at Luke. "It's a nice town."

"We shop there occasionally," he said.

Belle didn't know what to say to that and swiftly forked a second bite of dessert. She barely tasted the pie with her mind so distracted.

"Luke's a farmer," Charlie said, "He farms with his family just outside Dry Run."

"Belle grew up on a farm." Flora raised her eyebrows. "Didn't you, Belle?"

She nodded, her mouth full of warm blueberries and flaky crust.

"At school, I remember how homesick she was for the farm." Flora rolled her bottom lip. "I was really worried about her. Figured she'd try to run away."

Luke's head drew up at that.

"I did run away," Belle said, "after you left school."

"That's right." Flora laughed. "You did." She glanced at Luke. "But she's a good girl."

"She's a great gal," Charlie added.

Belle cringed at their all too obvious attempts at pairing her up with Luke. "Bet you keep busy on the farm," she said, desperate to change their tactics. She rambled on. "Farming leaves little time for traveling." She threw Flora a pointed look. Why set her up with a guy who didn't live here?

"Pa lets me have time off now and then." Luke grinned at Charlie. "He unlocks the cellar door every once in a while and lets me out." With his confident manner and mature face, Luke appeared to be in his early twenties.

The waitress approached. "Anything else I can get you?" Her question was directed at everyone, but she stared at Luke.

He winked at Belle, acting unaware of the waitress's attention. Belle reassessed her initial opinion of Charlie's cousin as a lady's man.

"This pie is so good, think I'll have another piece," Luke said.

How extravagant, Belle thought. He must not be responsible with money.

"Make that a piece of cherry pie this time with two scoops of ice cream." Luke turned to Belle. "How about you? Would you like another slice? I'm buying."

"No, thank you," she said. "Still working on this one." "Guess that's how you keep your figure. Anyone else?" Charlie ordered another mincemeat, his favorite.

Flora shook her head. "You boys are gonna need that new product, Alka-Seltzer."

"Plop, plop, fizz, fizz, oh, what a relief it is," chimed Charlie.

"They created it for the Depression," Luke said.

"How's that?" Charlie winked at Flora.

"For all the headaches and ulcers this Depression is giving people. Alka-Seltzer's a regular Hoover beer."

"That's a good one, Luke." Charlie thumped his cousin's shoulder.

Belle joined in with Flora's infectious laughter. She had survived her first date, after all.

The following morning, Belle placed a stack of pancakes on the table. Flora poured tea and pulled up her chair. "I think Luke likes you."

Belle felt her face flush. "He was friendly to everyone."

"Don't you think he's handsome?"

"Sure, he's nice looking. But he probably doesn't make it to Talihina too often."

"We'll see." Flora gave a conspiratorial smile.

"Besides," Belle said, "we have fun just the three of us. Don't we?"

"Of course, we do." Flora raised her eyebrows. "But it was nice to go out with the guys for a change." Belle shrugged.

All through her rounds, Belle shoved aside thoughts of Luke. Who needed a man? She was perfectly happy with Flora and Jeremy. But her thoughts drifted to the farm where Luke lived, and she wondered how it compared to her grandparents' place. She missed the smell of alfalfa and hay, the baying of dogs, and the bawling of cows waiting to be milked. At the sanatorium, the sharp scent of bleach and cod liver oil pervaded the halls. Moaning exuded from hospital beds. She longed for country life.

Belle shook her head. She didn't really know Luke. Knew nothing about him other than he farmed with his family. What was it Grandpa used to say? Until you've worked beside a man you don't really know him. The real character of a person was revealed in day-to-day living, not eating pie.

"Got nothing to do there, girl?" Nurse Braxton stared at Belle with stern eyes. "I've never seen you daydream. Get back to work. There are several patients waiting on you."

"Sorry, ma'am." Belle rolled her cart to the next doorway and withdrew a can of juice and a bottle of cod liver oil from the tray. She vowed never to be caught in a silly trance again.

A month later, Flora relayed news of a letter Charlie had received from his cousin. Luke was coming to visit the following week, and could they all four go to the movies? Outwardly, Belle displayed no emotion, but inside, her stomach dipped in excitement. Luke wanted to see her again.

Flora finished curling Belle's long hair and insisted on applying eyeshadow.

"You don't think that will be too much?"

"A little emphasis won't hurt." Flora applied brown grease paint in the crease of Belle's eye and smudged the color. Satisfied, she held up a hand mirror.

Belle looked like a movie star, with darker skin of course. She hoped her new hairdo and eyelids weren't too dramatic. The last thing she wanted was the appearance of fawning over Luke. She slipped on a blouse with a tiny blue print and a crossover neckline. She zipped a blue skirt that reached mid-calf. Next came black pumps, her all-purpose shoes. Unlike illustrations in fashion magazines, she couldn't afford a variety of shoes to match her outfits.

"How do I look?" she said.

"Like a million bucks." Flora twirled to showcase her own skirt with its fluctuating hem. "How about me?" The pink blouse with gray collar stood out against her dark complexion.

"Like a million bucks," Belle echoed. "Guess that makes us the two million-dollar babes."

Flora giggled. A knock came at the door, Charlie's signature announcement of two raps, a pause, followed by two final knocks. "They're here." Flora checked her hair in the mirror one last time.

Charlie looked dapper in his shirt and argyle vest. He whistled at the sight of the girls. "It's our lucky day, Luke. We have the privilege of taking two beautiful dames to the movies."

Belle stood back, her confidence all but evaporated. Just because Luke returned to visit Charlie didn't mean he was interested in her. She may have spun a sugar-syrup dream out of nothing.

Luke stepped alongside Charlie and grinned. "We're two lucky guys, that's for sure." He winked at Belle, and her face warmed. She couldn't help smiling.

Charlie boxed playfully with Jeremy as Luke looked on. The stripes on Luke's shirt emphasized his shoulders. Dark trousers were belted at his trim waist. One thing for certain, Belle hadn't imagined his good looks. She turned to Flora to avoid staring at Luke.

"Charlie would you mind walking Jeremy to Joan's bungalow?" Flora glanced at her brother. "I heard she baked a spice cake this afternoon." "That's my favorite!" Jeremy said.

Flora winked. "What a coincidence."

Upon Charlie's return, they headed for town in Luke's late-model Ford. Belle was glad he drove. It would be uncomfortable to sit in the backseat with a guy she barely knew.

Luke glanced over at Belle. "So, how's work at the hospital?"

"Today was a good day." She stared out the windshield. "Two young girls—sisters—were discharged from the hospital. I've never seen such happy kids."

"Is it hard to work around sick folks?"

Belle stole a look at Luke. "I wondered about that myself before I took the job. But it feels good to help people." They passed the park as they drove into town, and Belle recalled that horrible day with the sawmill boys. But since then, there had been new developments. Under pressure from the community, Officer Hagar had been dismissed from his position. The city council fired him after several charges of harassment had been filed by local women. A younger officer had been hired to replace him.

"Bet it helps to have such a pretty aide dispensing medicine." Luke winked.

Belle turned from his smile and looked out the side window. She didn't consider herself pretty, just a normal-looking girl.

"Hey, Casanova," Charlie shouted from the backseat. "You just passed the theater. Where'd ya get your license? In a box of Cracker Jacks?"

"Naw, in a box of Quaker Oats." Luke grinned and turned the car around.

Flora giggled. "You guys act more like brothers than cousins."

"We spent a lot of time together on our grandparents' farm," Charlie said. "My folks sent me to Dry Run every summer. They didn't want me growing up soft, so I had to work for Grandpa." "So that's where you got your muscles," Flora said.

Belle glanced back and saw Flora squeeze his bicep.

"Naw, it's genetics," Charlie said. "Choctaw braves are naturally strong."

Luke laughed. "That's laying it on thick, but I'll go along with that." He flexed his arm.

"Park there." Charlie pointed to a parking space in front of the theater.

Luke turned off the engine. "So, Belle, you're Comanche?" "That's right," she said.

"We're fierce warriors."

"The last to come into Indian Territory," Belle added. "Our people held out to the end."

"Should I be worried about a full-blooded Comanche gal?" He feigned a worried look.

"Only if you give me any trouble." Luke and Charlie howled with laughter.

"That's my girl," Flora said.

At the theater, the guys purchased popcorn and soda while the girls chatted in the lobby. The rare treat of a movie was made even more special because they both had dates. The featured movie that night was Frankenstein.

"Let's find a good seat before they're all taken." Charlie grabbed Flora's hand and dashed ahead.

They sat in the center section three rows from the front. Flora entered the row followed by Charlie, which left Belle stuck between the two men. She would have been more comfortable sitting beside Flora, but a change couldn't be made without making a fuss.

The screen lit up and the movie began playing. When it came to the scene where Dr. Frankenstein and his assistant steal away to a graveyard and dig up a freshly buried corpse, the moviegoers slunk in their seats, anticipating the worst. The good doctor's mind was deluded. Next the physician created a creature from body parts collected from graveyards and gallows. Belle thought of all the surgeries at the hospital. The last resort for the gravest of TB patients was surgery and removal of part of their lungs. Reality didn't travel too far behind the tale of Dr. Frankenstein.

She thought of Betty Brown with her sunken chest. Betty had undergone a thoracoplasty, an operation performed in three stages in which the surgeon removed rib bones to collapse the underlying lung. She shuddered. That was almost as gruesome as stitching together body parts of corpses. And yet the woman seemed incredibly grateful for her life. Nurse Braxton claimed it was done to snatch the patient from the grave after everything humanly possible had been tried.

The smell of buttered popcorn pervaded the theater. Belle shook her head when Luke offered her some of the salty snack. Though they'd come for entertainment, she'd been caught in dismal thoughts of the sanatorium.

Belle had read Mary Shelley's novel, Frankenstein, in school, but the story was more frightening in film. Boris Karloff played a terrific monster, truly hideous with his neck bolts, scarred face, and dark shadows beneath his eyes.

Universal Studios had taken a lot of artistic license with the original story. In the novel, the monster learns to be kind, but the movie portrayed him as an unrepentant murderer. Townspeople killed the creature in the movie, but in the novel, Dr. Frankenstein pursued his creation to the North Pole but never killed him. The movie ended, and the lights came on.

Luke turned to Belle. "Didn't you like the movie?"

"To tell the truth," she said, "I liked the novel better. In the book, the monster has a human side."

"Aw, my little Florence Nightingale," Luke said. "Looking out for the monster."

"How about some of that good pie at Fern's?" Charlie suggested.

"You read my mind." Luke glanced at the women. "Are you ladies up for a slice of pie and brilliant conversation with two debonair gentlemen?"

"Sure," Belle said, "where exactly might we find these gentlemen?"

"Aw, Belle," Luke said. "You're breaking my heart." "Good one, Belle." Flora jabbed her ribs.

She hadn't expected to be quick-witted or able to banter with a young man. Belle felt more confident. Maybe she wasn't such a wallflower, after all.

After a round of Fern's pies, the boys drove them home. As they neared the hill leading to the Choctaw Sanatorium, Flora leaned over the front seat. "Hey, drive around the back of the hospital."

"Yes, ma'am." Luke rounded the corner.

"I have something to show you," Flora said. They all piled out of the black Ford. "Shh, we have to be quiet."

Belle couldn't imagine where Flora was leading them, but she was caught up in the adventure. A half moon lit their way as Flora directed them halfway up the hillside behind the hospital. Belle slipped once, but Luke grabbed her arm and saved her from rolling down the slope.

"Careful," Charlie whispered. "Don't need anyone getting hurt even if there is a hospital handy."

"Everyone sit." Flora gestured to the ground. The damp grass soaked through Belle's dress. "See that tall smokestack?" Flora pointed at the brick chimney that rose above the hospital.

Luke peered at the long neck of brick. "That chimney is higher than a heating furnace requires."

Flora whispered, "That's no ordinary smokestack." Under the moonlight, she slowly scanned their faces. "What is it?" Luke asked.

"What do you think they do with all the poor patients who die of tuberculosis?" Flora's eyebrows lifted.

"Oh, no," Charlie moaned.

"Tell us," Luke said.

"They need a long chimney for the incinerator," Flora whispered, "when they burn up…" she paused dramatically, "the diseased bodies."

"Jeez, Flora," Charlie said. "That's kind of gruesome, isn't it?"

"We just watched a horror film." Flora pouted. "I thought it would be fun to come here. You know, kinda scary like the movie."

Belle looked away from Flora. She agreed with Charlie. Tuberculosis was reality. How could Flora compare tragedy to the fun of watching a horror film?

"Are you okay?" Luke whispered.

"Yeah," Belle said. She thought of the kindly man who had died that week and Rose, the young mother, the week before that. "Kind of creepy, don't you think?"

"I agree."

"I was just trying to have fun." Flora sniffled and lowered her head. "I wasn't trying to be mean, but I guess it was tasteless." Charlie offered her his handkerchief.

"I love you, anyway," Charlie said. "I know you were just trying to entertain us."

"I'm sorry, everyone." Flora whimpered.

"We all love you," Belle said. "But next time you want to scare us, take us into the woods on a dark night."

"Not me," Luke declared. "There's too many bears and panthers out there for my comfort."

"Yeah, not unless we got a rifle with us," Charlie said.

"Maybe we'll just stick with a movie," Flora offered.

"Sounds good." Charlie rose. "Let's get you girls back home before Joan thinks we've kidnapped you."

Flora sat beside Charlie in the backseat, and Belle slid in front with Luke. He drove around to the front of the hospital and up the road toward the bungalows. In the dark interior of the car, Luke reached for Belle's hand. She was too bashful to make eye contact. But after the grisly revelation of the incinerator, his warm touch was comforting. As the car neared the bungalow, she withdrew her hand and shuffled through her purse for the key. She still held reservations about the good-looking man who turned heads, even those of white girls.

"I'll let Charlie walk you ladies to your door," Luke said. "I'll keep the car running in case we need a fast getaway, like Pretty Boy Floyd." Belle opened her door as Charlie and Flora exited the backseat.

"Heard he's hiding out in the backwoods of Oklahoma," Charlie said. The car door slammed. "God knows we have plenty of rough country around here for a man to hide."

Luke leaned over the seat and glanced up at Belle. "You'll be okay with us around." In the dark, the men's laughter broke the stillness. "Goodnight, Belle."

"Have a safe drive home," she said.

"Thank you, pretty lady." He tapped the front of his hat.

Belle darted ahead of Flora and Charlie in order to give the couple privacy as they said their goodbyes. The warm touch of Luke's hand remained on her palm. She'd have to work double time at keeping those crazy daydreams away. Besides, she didn't know much about him other than the fact he was Charlie's cousin.

Charlie was a good guy. Maybe that was testimony enough. She entered the bungalow and tossed her purse on the kitchen table. A deep sigh escaped. A wise woman would give it time before coming to any conclusion.

Chapter 25

WITH AUTUMN CAME SOME OF Belle's favorite things: the crunch of leaves beneath her feet, their fermented bouquet swirling through the air; brushstrokes of mahogany, crimson, and gold erupting in every backyard and hilly woods. Fall unfurled like a banquet for a queen and with the season also came Talihina's Harvest Dance.

"Luke's coming!" Flora grabbed Belle's hands and waltzed across the kitchen. Charlie had written his cousin and asked Luke to come for the community dance at the end of the month. "We'll find you a beautiful dress. The dance will be so much fun."

"I don't know." Belle's sigh blew like a sudden gust of wind. "I've never been to a dance."

"But you dance beautifully," Flora said. "You picked up everything I taught you. Pretend you're dancing in front of the radio. You'll do fine."

"You really think so?"

"Remember, the secret is to let the gentleman lead."

Two weeks later, the girls primped in front of the mirror, perfume drifting across Flora's bedroom. Belle had finally spent some of her savings on a dress with soft, fluttery sleeves and an empire waistline. The V-neckline was perfect, revealing a little skin but no cleavage. The back had a slide fastener, the new invention that replaced buttons, which had become too expensive. Flora sported the yellow dress she'd worn on the lawn of the sanatorium the day Belle arrived.

Flora stood back and tilted her head. "Your hair shines like onyx against that dress. Cobalt-blue is definitely your color. Now for the final touch." She held a tube of lipstick. "Stand still." She applied color over Belle's lips. "Take a look."

Belle gazed in the mirror. She pivoted in her new sling-back shoes and studied herself from different angles. With her long curled hair and bright red lips, she looked like a different person. "You don't think it's too much?"

"Quit scowling! It's all the fashion and you look beautiful." Flora held out a tissue usually reserved for removing cold cream. "Blot your lips with this. You don't want red all over your pearly whites."

Belle pressed the tissue between her lips as rapping sounded at the front of the bungalow.

"They're here," Jeremy yelled, his crutches clomping to the door.

All painted up and swathed in fine fabric, Belle followed Flora to the front room, her carriage stiff and nerves jittery.

Luke's jaw dropped, and his air of self-assurance vanished. He reminded her of Jeremy on his birthday, opening presents with wide eyes and open mouth.

"Say something, boy." Charlie nudged Luke's arm. "You've got one of the two prettiest women in the county. Better tell her how good she looks."

Luke took a deep breath. "You're wrong, Charlie. The most beautiful gals in the state. Heck, the whole country, I bet." He winked at Belle, his self-confidence returning.

Flora slipped into the outstretched coat in Charlie's hands. Belle rushed to put hers on. They all said goodbye to Jeremy, and Charlie walked him next door to Joan's bungalow.

Driving to town, Charlie and Luke reminisced about hunting when they were boys. Flora chattered about a new dress she'd seen in a store window. Before long, they were in Talihina. They entered the community hall, abuzz with people waiting for the music to start. On stage, the band warmed up their instruments, and the air pulsed with excitement.

"Good evening, ladies and gentlemen," a man announced center stage. "We hope you'll all have a grand time tonight. We'll start out the evening with Fats Waller's song, "Ain't Misbehavin'.""

The crowd applauded, and the pianist broke into a lively jazz tune. Luke grabbed Belle and led her to the dance floor. She loved swing dancing and caught up in the music, forgot her nervousness. Not to her surprise, Luke turned out to be light on his feet.

That night she did the Lindy Hop and the one-step, both of which she had learned from Flora. Luke was, in fact, an exceptional dancer, which he proved with the Carolina Shag. He taught her the basic steps to the dance and explained the guy did the fancy moves. Luke's footsteps swept as feathers lifting on a breeze.

Dancing to the radio had been fun, but to hear live music and actually see the performers play their instruments was magical. She'd never tire of hearing the deep-throated trumpet, trombone, and saxophone accompanied by a light-fingered pianist.

Luke slid a hand over her shoulder as the band played a slow tune. It was the closest they'd danced all evening, so close she could smell his cologne and feel the warm rhythm of his breathing. Toward the end of the song, Luke pressed his face against her cheek. Belle wasn't prepared for how she felt.

The band took a break and the dream dissipated. They joined Charlie and Flora at the side of the dance floor.

"Great band, huh?" Charlie's arm hung over Flora's shoulder.

"Best I've ever heard," Belle quipped.

Flora nudged her arm. "It's the only band she's heard."

"They're good as gold." Luke glanced around the room. His next words disappeared in the mounting drone of conversation and laughter around them.

"What did you say?" Flora asked.

Luke pointed toward the stage. "I said that man could really play the saxophone. Charlie, let's go outside for a smoke. We'll be back by the time the band starts up again." He pointed at Belle. "Don't dance with anyone else."

"Go on, get out of here," Flora said. "We've got girl talk to do."

The guys crossed the crowded dancehall. Through the open door, flickers of light danced like fireflies as smokers lit up cigarettes.

"Isn't the band glorious?" Belle said.

"Told you we'd have a great time." Flora finished her cup of punch. "Let's go find the little girls room and freshen up."

In the restroom, Flora reapplied her lipstick. "Luke couldn't take his eyes off you at the bungalow." In the reflection of the mirror, Flora's eyes darted toward Belle.

"Maybe I had lipstick on my teeth." Belle laughed as she smoothed her hair.

"I hear the music. Let's get back out there."

The guys waited for them on the sidelines, laughing at something Luke said.

With only occasional breaks, Luke and Belle danced most of the songs that night. As they danced the final song of the evening, Luke swept her across the dance floor in the quick step. Belle decided that "Puttin on the Ritz" was her favorite song of the evening.

Days grew shorter, and the year drew to a close. Flora, Belle, and Jeremy celebrated the New Year in their little bungalow. They popped popcorn and listened to the radio announcer declare the beginning of 1932. Brimming with optimism, the man's voice held hope for the coming year, wishing the audience prosperity and better days ahead.

Months passed. Once winter set in, Luke needed to feed cattle every day. Though she enjoyed their double dates, Belle remained content in the little bungalow that proved a warm refuge from the Oklahoma winter. On long, cold nights, they played board games and cards. Made hot chocolate or apple cider. Flora purchased a game called Criss-Cross Words where wooden tiles, each printed with a letter, were placed on a board to make words. The initial word formed at the center, and subsequent words were added in perpendicular fashion. Flora was a natural at the game.

At first, Belle thought of Luke frequently. But as time went by, the memory of their dates faded like a bloom pressed between pages of a book.

Chapter 26

WINTER STRETCHED ITS LONG ARMS around Talihina until finally it drew back and conceded to a new season. Belle welcomed the return of ruby-throated hummingbirds, sunny days, and tulips poking through the stiff ground. The scent of spring on the air taunted, but then temperatures plummeted again. By April, the change of seasons was assured despite occasional throwbacks.

Belle stretched the length of the sofa, bare feet hanging over the armrest. The song on the radio rose and fell, rolling over her like a warm lullaby. Flora was attending a movie with Charlie. Jeremy had fallen asleep an hour ago. Though not as head-turning as his cousin, Charlie held a respected job as the hospital's bookkeeper. Charlie's parents were welleducated Choctaws, who had encouraged their son to go to business college. Belle appreciated the qualities in Charlie that Flora had fallen for—respect for other people and a kind heart.

Flora confessed she loved Charlie, but knowing how her mother had struggled with her marriage, Flora preferred to keep company with Charlie on Saturday nights or an occasional lunch in the hospital cafeteria when schedules permitted. That was fine with Belle. She liked things the way they were. Her eyelids grew heavy, and she nestled her head into the sofa pillow.

The door latch clicked and Flora flew through the door. Her bias-cut dress hugged her waist and slid over slim hips, the turquoise fabric playing off her dark complexion. Belle raised herself on her elbow.

"You won't believe it!"

Belle rubbed her eyes and tried to focus. Flora had a habit of painstakingly replaying the movie plot. Belle prepared to listen to a long, drawn-out story and covered her mouth to hide a yawn.

Flora reached for her hands and the scent of Lily of the Valley wafted from her wrists. "Charlie asked me to marry him." Had she heard right?

"Charlie," Flora said. "He asked me to marry him tonight."

Belle was wide-awake. "I thought—"

"I know. I didn't want to end up like my mother, wondering where the next meal was coming from." Flora's eyes lit up, and she wrapped her arms around herself. "But Charlie got a raise last week, and he's leased a house in town. And he loves Jeremy."

Belle had to admit Charlie was good for Flora…and Jeremy. "I'm happy for you."

"I knew you would be." Flora hugged Belle and headed for the kitchen. "And Charlie says you can live with us. It's a big house, big enough for all of us. Let's celebrate and have some of that carrot cake I baked this morning."

Belle retrieved two plates from the cupboard. With her back turned, she worked to compose herself. She would never live with Flora and Charlie. Even at seventeen, Belle knew newlyweds required time alone to start their life together. Flora, Charlie, and Jeremy needed to bond as a family. Belle would remain at the bungalow, alone. A bushel of carrots plunged to the pit of her stomach. With no appetite for cake, she went through the motions and struggled to swallow the first bite.

"We'll invite all the employees from the hospital. Charlie said we might even rent the dance hall for a reception. Wouldn't that be great?" Flora lifted an eyebrow. "You know of course, Luke will be there."

Belle managed a weak smile. Luke was the last person on her mind. Her world had just hit bottom.

"I need to check on Jeremy," Flora said. The boy had a habit of kicking off his covers.

"I'll go." The scoot of the chair squeaked over the linoleum, and Belle rushed from the kitchen. In the bedroom, she pulled the blanket over the boy's shoulders. Her stomach twisted like it did after her father died.

A few minutes later, she returned and found Flora still wound up with excitement. Belle could take no more that night. "I'm so tired, Flo. I need to go to bed."

"We'll talk tomorrow," Flora said. "There's so much to plan, and I need your help."

Belle lay in bed unable to sleep. She tried to reason. Flora and Charlie weren't moving out of town. She'd still be able to visit them, still have marble matches with Jeremy. She'd help Flora organize her new house. But deep down, she knew it wouldn't be the same. She would have to make arrangements to visit. Belle would return every night to an empty bungalow. Jeremy's smile would no longer greet her at the end of the day. Flora's face would no longer brighten at something Belle said at the dinner table. But Jeremy would have a father figure and Flora a husband. Belle rolled onto her side. The glass window pane reflected a deep wedge of darkness.

By the end of April, wedding dresses consumed Flora's thoughts. The scheduled ceremony fell in the middle of June.

"Won't shopping for a gown be fun?" Flora was as giddy as a young schoolgirl.

"We'll find you a beautiful dress." Belle smiled broadly, something she learned to perform on command. But inside, she felt lifeless. Shopping for a wedding dress brought her life one step closer to ruin. She had finally convinced Flora that she looked forward to having the bungalow to herself. Belle had become such a good actress that she was ready for an audition on the big screen. In reality, she was a big, fat liar.

The afternoon sun polished an aquamarine sky as Charlie's car pulled up outside the bungalow. Belle and Flora piled into the Ford. He'd drop them off in Talihina for Flora's long awaited shopping day.

"Flora's been all atwitter about looking for a dress." Charlie leaned over the seat. "Bet that's no secret to you, Belle."

She rolled her eyes heavenward. "That's all she talks about."

"Since this is a special day, I'm treating you girls to lunch." He handed three bills to Flora. "I'll pick you up at five."

They drove down Main Street where sunlight dappled the sidewalk and sifted through budding trees. The smell of morning rain lifted on the air. Flora deserved a man like Charlie. Jeremy adored him. On that beautiful spring day, Belle's heart grew heavy with dread of the future. Her future.

The first dress shop gave Flora some ideas, but she wasn't taken with what they saw.

"Don't look so down in the mouth," Belle said. "Let's try the other shop." They crossed the street, and Flora studied a dress on display in the shop window. Her face lit up. "I like this shop better already."

They strolled through the store and studied several gowns displayed on dress forms. Flora carefully considered each one, pausing at the third dress. She circled the mannequin to examine the garment's details, and Belle followed suit. The ankle-length dress buttoned on the side. Short puffed sleeves and velvet bows at the bust line created a fashionable gown.

"What do you think, Belle?"

"It's very pretty."

The salesclerk approached. "Isn't that a beauty? The dress is silky nylon with an overlay of dreamy tulle." The clerk tucked a strand of red hair behind her ear. "I like the cream color, don't you?"

"It's beautiful," Flora said. "I love the ruffles at the bodice." She turned to Belle. "Gives the dress a shapely fit, doesn't it?"

Belle admired the band of ruffle above the hemline. At the bottom, four inches of tulle extended beyond the nylon, giving the gown a delicate look. "The dress has so many pretty details."

"You must try it on to get the full effect, Miss," the clerk said.

Five minutes later, Flora stepped from the fitting room. Belle couldn't believe how the dress transformed Flora's body.

"Say something, silly." Flora turned first to one side then the other in front of the long mirror. "What do you think?"

"It's beautiful." The bodice accentuated Flora's narrow waist, and the brief puffy sleeves revealed her lovely arms.

"It was made for you," the clerk said. "But if you'd like to try on another, you're most welcome to."

"I love it." Flora beamed. "This is the dress." After a few minutes of admiring the gown, she returned to the fitting room. Moments later, she returned with the dress folded over one arm. "Wrap it up, and my fiancé will pick it up tomorrow."

"Certainly." The clerk gently took the dress from Flora.

"Oh, Belle," Flora whispered. "Didn't I look beautiful in it?"

Belle grinned. "Like a bride in the movies."

"I'm so excited to begin my new life as Mrs. Charlie Stilwell." Belle produced a smile for the friend she loved so much.

"We'll always be the best of friends, won't we?" Flora whispered.

She nodded, her throat tight.

"You're like the sister I never had." Flora hugged Belle's neck. "No, you are my sister."

Belle's eyes burned as she fought tears.

On the day of the wedding, the humidity reached even to the Methodist Church basement. Flora had been wise to avoid the hotter temperatures of July and August for the ceremony. Belle's face needed a break from smiles and well wishes and the wedding celebration in general, so she stepped into the restroom. She dabbed her forehead with an embroidered handkerchief. The mirror above the sink reflected the flat expression on Belle's face.

She straightened the mint-green bow at the waist of her chiffon dress. Belle was maid of honor, and Anne Johnson was the other bridesmaid. The wedding party might be small, but the church pews would overflow today. Flora and Charlie had invited every employee from the Choctaw-Chickasaw Sanatorium. The restroom door swung open.

"Come quickly," Anne said. "Flora's beside herself."

Dashing from the restroom, she followed Anne to the end of the hall where Belle had just assisted Flora in putting on her wedding dress. Almost on Anne's heels, Belle asked, "What happened?"

"I have no idea." Breathless, Anne swung her arms to the pace of her short, thick legs. "I can't imagine what she's thinking."

Their footsteps clattered over the linoleum floor. A moment later, they entered the bridal room and were met with the sight of Flora's bare shoulders and exposed white brassiere. Flora slipped the wedding gown to her feet.

"Flora! What are you doing?" Belle rushed over. Flora's face was flushed, and her wild eyes flashed like a frightened animal.

"I can't do it," Flora said. "I just can't do it."

Anne patted Flora's shoulder, but Flora shook her off. "Leave me alone!"

Anne's face registered shock but even worse, terrible hurt. "I'll leave you two alone." She fled the room. Flora shuddered and sobbed. This was so uncharacteristic of Flora that for a moment, Belle wondered if an evil spirit had overtaken her friend. She placed her hands at her hips. "What is the matter with you?"

Flora sank into a nearby chair. "What was I thinking?"

Flora's timing was lousy, but there it was. Belle envisioned their life continuing as it had. Just the three of them, happy as larks, as the saying went. A warm glow of hope filled her chest for the first time in months. She pulled up a straight-back chair and faced Flora.

"But you love Charlie." Belle was surprised at her own words.

"Of course, I do, but people change."

"Charlie's a good man, you know that," Belle said. "And he loves Jeremy."

"But what if he changes after we have our own children?" Flora's brows knitted together. "I've heard of husbands mistreating a woman's stepchildren. Well, in this case, he's my brother, but you know what I'm saying." Flora wrung her hands.

"I can't imagine that. I've never seen a man so calm and even-tempered," Belle said. "And how many young men volunteer at the church? No, he's a rare catch. If you don't marry him, I will."

Flora's eyes swept up at that. A smile twitched at the corners of her mouth and then faded. She lowered her voice, "What if he changes how he feels about me?"

"Flora," Belle said. "Where is all this coming from?"

"I didn't tell you," she said, "but when hard times came upon my parents, my father started drinking. My mother had to clean for well-to-do women in town, and she had to take on sewing at night. On her day off, she dragged the little kids to the orchard with her and picked fruit to make up for the money Father wasn't bringing in."

Belle took Flora's hands. "I'm so sorry."

"He…he…" Flora dropped her head. "He'd come home drunk and beat her in front of us kids." She broke down and sobbed.

"Oh, Flora." Belle placed a hand on her shoulder and waited. After a few moments, Flora dried her eyes.

"Honey, Charlie's not like that." Belle moved a strand of hair from Flora's temple. "He wouldn't even take a swig of Luke's moonshine that night of the dance. Remember?"

Flora nodded and accepted Belle's outstretched hankie. "I was so mean to Anne. Will she ever forgive me?"

"You make yourself presentable, and I'll go find her." Belle winked. "You can beg her forgiveness."

Flora stood, and Belle helped draw the dress up to her shoulders. Belle kissed her lightly on the cheek.

Out in the hall, Anne paced back and forth, her eyes rimmed in red. She stopped upon seeing Belle. "Is the wedding still on?" "Still on." She explained Flora's fears.

"Poor dear," Anne said. "I knew it had to be something awful. I've never seen that woman anything but kind and gentle." "She feels horrible about how she spoke to you."

"Oh, gnats and chiggers." Anne charged back to the room. "I talk worse to myself than that at times."

Belle laughed, relieved the wedding would proceed. There was no one who deserved happiness more than Flora.

The scent of roses filled the sanctuary as Flora and Charlie exchanged rings. Charlie had shown Belle Flora's wedding ring months ago. The band was engraved with a filigree design, and a small ruby nestled in the center like a rose bud. A miniscule diamond chip framed each side of the ruby. Due to hard economic times, few in eastern Oklahoma could afford such luxuries. Most couples felt fortunate if they sealed their vows with a thin gold band.

Standing between Flora and Anne, Belle anticipated the ceremony's traditional kiss, but instead Charlie waved to someone in the audience. Charlie's older sisters approached the wedding couple, each holding a corner of a Pendleton blanket. They draped the red blanket with a banded-arrow pattern over Flora's head, kissed the bride, and stepped back.

Charlie addressed the audience. "This blanket is a symbol of protection over my wife." He turned to Flora. "My family and I will protect you for the rest of your days." He leaned in and kissed his bride, sealing the deal in the traditional fashion. People stood and applauded.

Belle's tears threatened to ruin the eye makeup Flora had insisted on. Conscious that she was in full view of the crowded church, she blinked away the moisture and focused on her smile.

The minister announced the reception would immediately follow at the community hall. Charlie and Flora marched down the aisle and waited at the door to accept a constant stream of congratulations. Anne and Belle drove ahead to the reception hall where they'd check on the refreshments and ensure everything was set out properly.

"Who's that young man waving at you?" Anne asked as she turned onto Main Street.

"That's Charlie's cousin, Luke, from Dry Run."

"What a good-looking man." Anne turned to Belle. "He seems to like you."

"It's nothing. We know each other through Charlie and Flora."

"Hmm, I see."

Belle glanced over and caught Anne's knowing smile. "It's not what you think." She looked straight ahead. Why did everyone want to pair up a single gal? This wasn't Noah's ark.

In the reception hall, Anne instructed the women who would serve cake to wait until the wedded couple cut the first piece. She rearranged the punch bowl and requested a dish to catch drips from the coffee urn. The first arrivals settled in a row of chairs that lined the hall. At the rear of the room, band members set up their instruments.

Belle looked forward to hearing the band. Several young men from the hospital had asked her to reserve a dance. Although she wasn't interested in any of them, she couldn't wait to dance again. People continued to drift in and soon the hall was filled with voices and laughter. A few moments later, applause erupted, announcing the happy couple had arrived. Belle stood on her tiptoes and caught sight of Flora's smiling face. The couple made their way to the table with the wedding cake.

Charlie cupped his hand over Flora's as they sliced a piece of cake. The crowd clapped as the couple exchanged bites. Lively notes lifted from the piano, and Charlie led Flora in a waltz around the hall.

"They make quite the pair, don't they?"

Belle turned to find Luke beside her. "They're a beautiful couple."

"Bet you'll miss your friend."

She lifted her chin. "They're not leaving town, you know."

"I come to visit Charlie every now and then." Luke watched the couple spin around the floor for the second time. "I'd like to take you out when I'm in town."

"If you can talk the happy couple into going with us," she said, "I guess that would be all right."

"Oh, sure, sure," he said.

Had he really thought she'd go out with him—just the two of them? George Mender from the hospital ambulance crew stepped up at that most opportune moment. His deep-set eyes stared at her, eyes like pinto beans. "Have you saved me the next dance, Belle?" George's pale skin blushed as his face registered doubt, and his wiry frame seemed to shrink.

"Of course, George," Belle said. "I'd love to dance with you." The wedding couple's song ended, and the crowd applauded. Charlie gestured for the crowd to join in dancing. Belle took George's hand and led him to the dance floor. As they stepped to the rhythm of the music, she glanced back and saw Luke's startled face. She smiled. He was too sure of himself.

George was not a good dancer. He couldn't keep time to the music and stepped on her foot several times. She steeled herself against the pain and with much effort, avoided a grimace. Luke might be watching.

"Sorry." He blushed. "Afraid it's been awhile."

"Don't worry," she said. "You're doing great." George smiled gratefully. Would this song never end? A couple breezed past them in graceful steps. Belle looked again. It was Luke with an attractive girl on his arm. The light-skinned girl stared at Luke adoringly.

After a break for punch, Belle danced with bald Abe Johnson from the cafeteria, stocky Ben White Horse from the janitorial staff, graying but graceful Dr. Haberkorn, painfully shy Thomas Eagle from the second floor, and Jimmy White from pharmacy. If anyone wanted to pair her up, Jimmy would have made the best choice. Known as a true gentleman, Jimmy was a trained pharmacist with a good career ahead of him. But Belle was not attracted to the awkward young man with droopy eyes. She sneezed at the sweet, oily scent of Brylcreem that clung to his thinning hair.

Afterward, she kept a wary watch against another approach by George. She couldn't handle another stumble across the dance floor. Upon his repeated advancements, Belle escaped into the crowd. From the corner of her eye, she saw Luke approaching and decided a spin around the dance floor with him wouldn't hurt. But another gentleman stepped up first.

"Will you dance with me, Belle?" Jeremy grinned.

"I would be honored." She offered her arm, and he set his crutches between two chairs. From the sidelines, Luke winked. They walked slowly as Jeremy leaned on Belle.

"Save me a dance, butterfly," Luke said.

She smiled, appreciating the handsome face that kept Luke in high demand on the dance floor.

After the song ended, Jeremy asked, "Do you think Flora will dance with me?" A glimpse over her shoulder revealed Luke waited on her.

"Of course," Belle said. "I bet she's been waiting for you to ask."

"Even though it's her wedding day?" Jeremy's brows furrowed. "Do you think Charlie will care?"

Belle leaned down, her hands on her chiffon-draped knees. "A gentleman should always ask if he can dance with a man's wife." She winked. "Charlie will definitely say yes."

Jeremy's face brightened, and he led her back to the punch table. Before they reached the sidelines, Luke stepped up and held out his hand. "May I have the honor of the next dance?" His spicy cologne surrounded her, masculine and inviting.

"See ya, Belle." Jeremy disappeared into the crowd.

"I'll be watching." Belle placed her hand in Luke's palm as they moved to the dance floor.

She recognized his cologne as Spanish Leather. Everyone on staff at the hospital knew of Jimmy White's obsession with the fragrance. Belle once caught Jimmy dabbing on cologne behind the pharmacy counter. He quickly replaced the cork stopper on the clear glass bottle and pretended he hadn't been observed. But on Luke, the smoky leather scent rose warm and alluring. The woodsy aroma reminded her of the outdoors with its musk and patchouli.

Luke directed her across the floor, stepping effortlessly in perfect rhythm with the music. She had to admit Luke was the best dancer in the crowd. He was also the easiest on the eyes. Lost in the lively music, she danced the way it was meant to be performed. Envious eyes darted their way as they danced five songs in a row.

Tomorrow would come soon enough. Her new life without Flora and Jeremy would arrive on schedule, but for the moment she lived in a world of flowers, graceful gowns, handsome men, and smooth music. One step forward, spin, step back—and begin again. Dancing wasn't all that different from life.

Chapter 27

THE SANATORIUM NESTLED IN THE Winding Stair Mountains with
its healing gifts of pure air, sunshine, and rain-cleansed hills. Along with
patients, those hills also blessed Belle. There she escaped her loneliness. The
song of the goldfinch and the rustle of a breeze transported her back to her
days on the farm. Sometimes she'd speak the names of her family and swore
they whispered in return.

When their schedules permitted, Flora and Belle shared lunch in the
hospital cafeteria. Flora repeatedly said she'd have her over for dinner once
she was settled, but evidently married life took some settling. Belle didn't
blame her. Her friend needed time to adjust to running a household, and as
newlyweds, Flora and Charlie deserved their privacy.

"How's Jeremy?" Belle always asked.

"Charlie and Jeremy are inseparable," Flora said. "Jeremy really needed
a man in his life."

"Every boy needs that," Belle said.

Flora's eyes sparkled. "And Charlie's so good to him."

"I knew he would be. To you, too?"

Flora blushed. "He's a loving husband."

Belle's evenings stretched long and uneventful. She missed Saturday
nights and popping corn before their favorite radio shows came on the air. The
lively music didn't have the same effect it once had. Many nights, she turned
down the volume and immersed herself in a book.

On her days off, she hiked into the mountains and wandered through the woods, taking deep breaths of pine-pitch and green undergrowth, content to watch for an occasional deer or a coyote slinking into the shadows. For the first time in her life, she treasured the luxury of breathing—many patients were unable to inhale deeply or to breathe without blood in their phlegm.

According to Nurse Braxton, the Great White Plague took its greatest toll on those in the bloom of life, patients between the ages of fifteen and forty-five. The disease afflicted more women than men. Belle guessed that a woman's role of caretaker played into that sad fact since physicians had confirmed the bacteria spread through close contact.

The day before at the sanatorium, a woman delivered a baby but was immediately isolated from the infant. After witnessing the mother's sobs, Belle raced to a supply closet and wept. A few moments later, the door opened and Nurse Braxton switched on the light. Ruth's eyes widened for a moment, then she stepped in, and closed the door. Belle relayed what had happened.

"You'll see many tragic things here." Ruth placed a hand on her shoulder. "But remember, our job is to save lives. We do everything humanly possible to make that happen." She looked sternly into Belle's eyes. "Do you understand?"

"Yes, ma'am."

"Good." Ruth turned to go, paused, and looked back. "I'm thankful I have compassionate people on my staff, but ultimately emotion has to take a backseat to a patient's wellbeing."

As time went on, Belle's emotions grew armor against ravaged throats no longer able to swallow food and emaciated bodies that needed assistance to move. She saved her tears for her pillow at night.

The mother that sent her fleeing to the supply closet had to wait six months to hold her own baby. Nurse Braxton made sure Belle was present the day the happy mother reunited with her infant and beaming husband.

Another young woman in her early thirties, Clara White Hawk, was separated from her three children for two years. The doctors collapsed her infected lung—a procedure many didn't survive—only to find the lung refilled with air. Stories like that made Belle happy she wasn't a surgical nurse.

At a staff meeting, Nurse Braxton had explained the procedure. "The doctor inserts a long needle under the arm to puncture the lung and draw air back out."

Belle gasped and everyone turned in her direction. Her hand flew to her mouth.

"This is standard hospital procedure." Ruth had tossed her a critical look. "Doctors take all measures necessary in order to heal their patients."

Belle prayed the woman would survive and be reunited with her young children. When that day came, the youngest child, a little chubby girl, cried and pulled back from her mother. The mother broke into tears at the fact that her own daughter had forgotten her.

Though many left the facility healthy, thankful for their care and their recovery, not all stories ended happily. On isolated wings, patients diagnosed as "Pul. TB. Far advanced, active unimproved" proved a fatal diagnosis for the dreaded White Death. In public, coughing for any reason, drew heads up in alarm. Low-grade fevers and weight loss were viewed suspiciously. Rumors of TB infection spread like wildfire and sometimes innocent people were shunned. Even though the odds for survival had greatly improved since their great-grandparents era, people remained fearful.

On days when Flora didn't join her for lunch, Belle avoided conversation with other staff members. She didn't want to hear about a patient's turn for the worse, an unsuccessful surgery, or an untimely death. Instead she'd climb the wooded hill above the hospital where she pretended all was right with the world and disease did not exist. Before Flora married, life with just the three of them acted as a buffer to what they dealt with at work. That shock absorber had been dissolved upon Flora and Jeremy's move to town.

Out of boredom, Belle accepted Abe Johnson's invitation to a movie. Flora joked he polished his bald head just for Belle. Painfully shy, Abe never tried to kiss her. Thank goodness, she'd hate to hurt the poor man's feelings.

The following weekend, she went to dinner with Ben White Horse. Not bad looking, he had a good sense of humor, but when he tried to steal a kiss at the end of the evening, she made up her mind. She wouldn't wait to discover if he was desperate or worse, had a tendency to wield a strong arm.

On Monday afternoon, Belle rounded a corner and glimpsed Ben approaching with a mop and bucket.

"Just the person I wanted to see." His lips curved up on one side of his face, dipped on the other.

"Ben." She spun around. "Sorry. Forgot something for a patient."

* * *

Belle had not been to Flora's house since late July. At that time, only the kitchen and bedrooms had been furnished. They sat in the kitchen and poured over Sears and Roebuck catalogs for drapery and furniture ideas.

Summer's oppressive heat came to an end, and autumn ushered in cooler weather. On a sunny Saturday in mid-September, Flora invited Belle for lunch. Belle managed to hitch a ride with a staff member headed to town. With a lively gait, she climbed the porch steps. It was only the second time she'd been invited to the house. Flora had purposely waited until both the upstairs and downstairs had been decorated before inviting her to view the final result.

The front door swung open, and the women hugged. Flora waved her in, wearing a dress with a double-breasted bodice and a skirt that ended in pleated flares. Red beads at her neck contrasted with the gray fabric.

"Aren't you looking sharp?" Belle glanced down. "Ooh, I love the red pumps."

"Thank you." Flora pivoted her right foot in emphasis. "A gift from Charlie."

Belle looked around. "Where's Jeremy?"

"Down the block playing with a friend," Flora said. "Charlie's out bird hunting so we hens have the place to ourselves. I have to show you the entire house. You won't believe how nice everything looks."

Belle hid her disappointment and trailed Flora throughout the house. She made appropriate comments on each room, which Flora had so meticulously decorated. Her friend definitely had a knack for design and for being a homemaker. After the tour, Flora served fruit cobbler on china plates.

"I've missed you," Flora said.

"Me, too." Belle knew she far outweighed the scale on missing. She recalled Flora's fears on her wedding day. "How are things between you and Charlie?"

"Wonderful. He's such a sweet husband." Flora filled their cups with coffee. "Charlie suggested that I quit my job."

"How do you feel about that?"

"He makes enough money, so it wouldn't be a hardship, and I've had a chance to get everything I wanted for the house."

"So you wouldn't miss work?" Her stomach flipped. She'd never see Flora.

"Oh, I'd miss everyone," Flora said, "but there's another reason." She smiled coyly.

"You're—"

"I'm pregnant!" Over the table, Flora reached for Belle's hands. "Can you believe it? I'm going to be a mother."

"I'd been wondering about that." Another thing to take her friend away. "Congratulations."

"I'm only four months along, but I'm so excited."

"You should be, silly."

That old saying that change was the only constant in life proved true.

Two weeks later, Belle met Flora in the cafeteria on her last day of work. Halfway through their chicken sandwiches, Flora began coughing. Heads turned their way.

"Just a little cold, people," Flora said. "Jeez."

"Everyone who works here gets a little paranoid about a cough or sniffle," Belle said.

"That's so true. Another reason Charlie doesn't want me to work here."

"At least you don't work directly with patients."

"Regardless, he thinks it's for the best," she looked around and lowered her voice, "since I'm in a family way."

Belle smiled at that. City people talked about a woman's pregnancy like it was something embarrassing. But country folk viewed the condition as natural as breathing.

"Don't think I've forgotten your birthday," Flora said. "A girl doesn't turn eighteen but once in her life. It's next month on the fifteenth, right?"

"There's no need to fuss."

"Of course, there is. You're my best friend, and I plan on having you over for a little celebration."

The sad day had been salvaged by something to look forward to.

Charlie was due any minute to pick up Belle for her birthday dinner. In the bedroom, she posed before the dresser mirror. She had splurged and purchased a dress the color of ripe pumpkins, the light-wool dress appropriate for an October dinner. A matching fabric belt and buckle cinched her waist.

The collar dropped to the bodice in two wide triangles. But the bottom of the dress proved the most fashionable. Pleats bordered either side of the six-inch flat hem at the center.

Belle reached for the cloche hat on the dresser. The back of the hat conformed to her head while the brim angled over her forehead. The mirror confirmed she looked quite fashionable. No sooner had she adjusted the hat when a knock came at the door. "Coming!" She waltzed to the front room.

She opened the door and froze.

"Surprise!" The man before her wasn't Charlie.

"Luke?" Belle peered around his shoulder. He was alone.

His cropped hair was parted off center, and the scent of pomade drifted over. Luke's smile drooped. "I guess it wasn't such a great surprise."

"I'm sorry. I don't understand."

"Flora's idea. She thought you'd be pleased."

"Of course I am." She hooked her elbow in the crook of his arm. Belle hated to see his feelings hurt. "I was so surprised," she improvised, "that I didn't know what to say." She smiled up at him. "Let's go. We have a party to attend."

His smile returned. "You look beautiful. A regular fashion plate."

Why not have a handsome man on her arm? It was her birthday, after all.

Flora embraced her at the door. "I've prepared several courses of food. But first, we must have hors d'oeuvres over a glass of white wine." She winked. "All recipes compliments of Better Homes and Gardens." Flora placed a hand-inked menu in her hand.

Hors d'oeuvres and wine
Iceberg salad with radish tops and red onion
Roast beef and mashed potatoes
Ginger-glazed carrots and asparagus topped with mint butter
Surprise Dessert

"I feel like royalty," Belle said. She was glad she had worn a new dress for the unexpected formal dinner.

Flora wore the dress Charlie had given her a few months ago though it seemed to hang on her frame. Wasn't she supposed to grow plumper in pregnancy? Now in her fifth month, Flora needed to eat well for the baby's sake.

The men were dressed sharply. Charlie sported a button-down sweater with a wide round collar, his shirt and tie visible at the V-neck. Luke wore a dress shirt and trim sweater vest. Belle smiled at the picture they made. Stylish dinner partners, lit candles, and a formal table setting fit for a queen—it was like being in a motion picture.

After dinner, Charlie poured coffee while Flora retrieved the dessert. A birthday cake, no doubt. Belle stood to help her.

"Sit back," Flora said. "Relax, birthday girl."

The men discussed hunting and a decrease in the deer population. Luke claimed poaching had increased, no thanks to the Depression. Twenty minutes passed. Belle rose to check on Flora and help carry dessert plates. She opened the kitchen door to the sound of rasping coughs and found Flora leaning over the sink.

Belle rushed over. Flora turned her head, her wild eyes beseeching heaven itself as bloody phlegm pooled in the sink.

Chapter 28

AT FIRST, CHARLIE REFUSED TO believe Flora had tuberculosis, so Belle enlisted the help of Nurse Braxton and Anne Johnson.

"You have to consider Jeremy," Anne pleaded, "and yourself."

Charlie's eyes were wide with fear. "I won't leave her!"

"I promise she'll get the best care in the world," Nurse Braxton said. "I guarantee it personally."

Flora realized the sanatorium provided her best chance for survival. The week following Belle's birthday, Flora admitted herself to the hospital.

Belle swore she'd never watch another person she loved waste away. But Flora had always been there for her. At the hospital, Belle visited her several times a day, wearing the mandatory mask over her nose and mouth.

"I have to live," Flora said. "For the baby's sake."

"You will, dear," Belle whispered. "I know you will." Nurse Braxton had emphasized the importance of bolstering a patient's morale.

But as weeks passed, Flora lost weight, and her sunken cheeks turned gray. One day Flora suffered a grueling coughing spell, and Belle ran for a nurse, unable to watch her best friend suffer.

Late November was a difficult time of the year for tuberculosis patients. The summer benefits of fresh air and sunshine, a treatment advocated by the sanatorium, vanished. Flora went through a regiment of bed rest, high protein diet, and heliotherapy—sunlamps that aimed to replicate sunlight. But her condition only deteriorated.

On the onset of 1933, what Belle feared came to be. The doctor deflated one of Flora's lungs. Could any of this be good for the baby? Belle wouldn't even consider asking the doctor for fear of the answer. Neither Charlie nor Jeremy were allowed to visit. Occasionally, Flora made it to the window with the help of an attendant and waved.

Belle prayed constantly for Flora's recovery, but instead of gaining weight with her pregnancy, Flora continued to lose pounds. Her face was gaunt, her skin pallid. Belle arrived at work one morning and was called into Nurse Braxton's office.

Ruth sat still, composed except for her hands. Her fingers kneaded together repeatedly. "I wanted to let you know that Flora miscarried last night."

Belle crossed her arms and squeezed. "How is she taking it?"

"She doesn't have the energy to mourn. She's fighting for her life."

"Does Charlie know?" Ruth nodded sadly.

The moment Belle entered Flora's room, she saw the sorrow lining her face. Flora might not have the strength to mourn, but a new emptiness filled her friend's eyes.

One night, long after most of the staff had left for the evening, she stole into Flora's room and lit a bundle of sage. She blew out the flame and waved the stick. Pungent smoke spiraled throughout the room, sliding into high corners, under the metal bed, and across Flora's fragile form beneath a starched white sheet. Belle chanted Comanche words her grandmother once sang over a sick child. A physician would have been enraged, insisting smoke would only further injure a lung-damaged patient, but Flora had gone downhill in the past week and her chances were slim. The situation called for the ancient traditions of her people.

Belle wasn't caught in the act that evening and spent the rest of the night by Flora's side. She told her she loved her. Told her everything would be all right, but deep inside, she knew it wouldn't.

Like a ghost, Charlie sat lifeless on the front pew of the church next to his parents. Jeremy sat limply between Charlie and Belle. Next to Belle, Luke wore a stiff black suit. The entire front pew looked like the living dead: breathing but not alive, thinking but not comprehending, seeing but blinded by tragedy.

Belle would have taken custody of Jeremy without a moment's thought, but a young boy needed a male role model, and she knew no one better for Jeremy than Charlie. And Charlie needed the love of the sweet little boy to make it through the hardest time of his life. She focused on the pine knot near her shoe. The dark swirl in the wood held her gaze, slowly tightening before her eyes. She had to keep herself together for Jeremy's sake. And for Charlie's.

Oh, Flora, why did you have to leave us?

She dabbed her eyes with a handkerchief. Looking straight ahead, Luke slid his arm around her shoulders. It was tough for men to see women cry, harder yet for Charlie to watch helplessly as his beautiful young bride had grown worse by the day. Men had a hard time with tragedy because their natural desire to make things right proved impotent.

During the funeral reception, Belle remained close to Charlie. At moments, he would stare into space. Other times, he would graciously accept condolences. Jeremy slid between the two of them as if unsure who represented the most security. Despite his grief, Charlie hugged Jeremy or held his hand whenever the boy came near. Once, he even picked him up in his arms as if he were a young child. That reaffirmed her belief that the two should stay together.

She didn't recall much more about the day. After the reception room cleared, she said goodbye to Charlie and Jeremy. Belle was halfway to Anne's car when Luke called out. "Belle, wait!" She
paused at the curb.

"I'll be back in a few weeks to check on Charlie." He looked different somehow without his characteristic smile. She supposed they all did. Luke took her hand. "I'll check on you, too." She nodded.

He kissed her cheek and she slid into the car.

They drove away, two women with nothing to say. The vehicle droned down the road that led from the little town into the wooded hills. Belle half expected the car to lift at any moment and fly above the treetops, over the high smokestack of the hospital, far above the Winding Stair Mountains, and into the slow-moving, hazy clouds of eastern Oklahoma to where they would all meet in the sky, happy and free forever.

Chapter 29

EVERY WEDNESDAY, BELLE BROUGHT A hot meal to Charlie's house. She caught a ride with anyone headed into town. Charlie's family took the other days, the dinners delivered as much for moral support as for sustenance. It broke Belle's heart to see Jeremy without his characteristic smile. After dinner, he would sit next to Belle on the sofa and lean his head against her shoulder. She elicited only a nod or mumble at her questions about his classes, teachers, or friends. Charlie took to reading as if he had no words left to say. As the weeks passed, he put on a show of managing, but his eyes told another story. Belle ached at the depth of pain revealed in the man's face. If it wasn't for Jeremy, she couldn't have continued the visits.

"I have lots of cousins, now," Jeremy told her one evening. "Two are my age, but only one is a boy. I like him best."

"That's because you have more in common," Belle said.

"Charlie's going to help us build a treehouse out back this spring."

"Will you show me when it's finished?"

"Clint—that's my cousin—says girls aren't allowed." Jeremy straightened his shoulders. "But I'll make an exception for you. I'll take you up when he's not around."

"I'll never tell." Belle crossed her heart. "I'll even share a special story in the treehouse."

"A story?" Jeremy said. "I'd like to hear it now."

"You're sure you wouldn't rather wait?" She smiled, knowing the answer.

"Please, Belle. Tell me the story."

"It's the story of the creek." She spread her hands. "Life begins at the waters of the creek. The deer come to drink and coyotes, too. Birds build nests in the blackjack oak along the banks, and copperheads slither through the grass." Belle paused and looked into his eyes. "Did you know the creek talks?"

Sprawled across the floor, Jeremy leaned on his elbows, chin cupped in his hands. Charlie sat in the upholstered chair that Flora had carefully chosen to match the rest of the furniture. He glanced over the top of the newspaper.

"The creek babbles and chimes as it flows along its course. Have you ever heard its voice?" Belle asked.

Jeremy nodded.

"The creek isn't just babbling; it's talking to the creatures: the birds, the serpents, the frogs, and most of all, to us Native people." "What does it say?" Jeremy asked.

"It whispers to the birds when it's time to build nests and when to migrate. It shouts to the bear, 'Find a den for the winter.' But it has a special message for man. You'll hear it only when you're quiet. You must sit by the riverbank and listen very carefully. The creek won't speak to those who are impatient or cynical."

"Cynical?" He frowned.

"Who don't believe," she explained. "It helps to close your eyes. You have to tune out the birdsong and the rustle of grass and the breeze rushing through the trees."

She whispered, "Then it will speak. Very quietly, it will talk to you." Belle looked into Jeremy's upturned face.

"And you heard it?"

She closed her eyes. "The creek told me we are all part of the stream, ever flowing. It's the only thing that continues—the moving, the changing. And when a man realizes this, he knows the Creator made it so. Only the Creator stays the same, but all his creation is fluid like the creek. One day flowing softly and slowly, the next day roaring like a flood after a storm, but we are always changing." She paused and opened her eyes.

"That's when you listen for the Creator," she continued, "who never speaks with a man's voice. Instead, He talks through his creation, teaching lessons, showing his concern for us like He takes care of the animals, plants, and birds. Man has to be still to know that He is just over the hill or above us in the sky, watching and waiting for us to listen." In Jeremy's rapt face, she saw Flora's eyes looking up at her. Belle quickly glanced away and took a deep breath. "He never leaves us, though it might appear He has." She turned to Jeremy. "So, how can you hear what the creek says?"

His mouth pressed in concentration. "Listen very quietly."

Belle smiled at the boy's thoughtfulness. The newspaper rustled and hid Charlie's face. He had been listening, too.

Loud rapping drew all eyes to the front door. Without waiting for an invitation, Luke stepped into the living room.

"Who started the party without me?" He grinned at Belle. Charlie rose from his chair, and Jeremy jumped up from the floor.

"What are you doing here?" Charlie removed his glasses.

Luke clapped him on the back "I'm here to help build a snow fort." He unwound the long knitted scarf at his neck.

"A snow fort?" Jeremy's eyes widened in excitement. "Real snow?"

Luke swung the door open to the dusky light. To their amazement, flakes of snow spun like cotton. More likely to experience ice storms in Eastern Oklahoma, they celebrated the event. Everyone wrapped up in coats and headed outdoors.

Jeremy dashed outside. It was unlikely that enough snow would accumulate for a snow fort as Luke had suggested. Belle laughed as powdered-sugar flakes dusted their crowns. Lights from the surrounding houses cast a pewter glow over the snow. Under the fairy flight of snowflakes, the four of them joined hands and danced.

Cold and soaking wet, they returned indoors and Belle heated hot chocolate. The unexpected snowfall had brought a brief respite from all that had happened.

Belle glanced at the clock. "Afraid it's time for me to go. My workday comes early whether I want it to or not." She hugged first Jeremy and then Charlie.

Charlie walked to the coat rack. Their weekly routine included Charlie driving her back up the mountain.

"I'll take her home." Luke grabbed Belle's coat from Charlie. "You take it easy, old man, and I'll be back shortly."

The unblemished snow sparkled under the car's headlights as the muffled sound of tires rolled down the road. Luke turned to her as he drove through town. "How is he really doing?"

"Charlie?" She stared at the darkness outside the window. The snow had stopped. "He tries to put on a good face, but he's tormented with grief." "And Jeremy?" Luke focused ahead on the road.

"Charlie says he wakes up crying in the night. He has to sit with him until he goes back to sleep."

"Poor little guy," Luke said. "I have nephews that age. Sure hate to see him suffer."

"It breaks my heart." Her voice caught on the last word.

"And Belle?" he asked. "How is she doing?"

She didn't care to discuss her feelings. "I'm fine."

"Flora was your best friend." He glanced across the car seat.

"I miss her so much." Belle looked straight ahead. "Some days it's a struggle to get out of bed."

Luke reached for her hand, and tears trickled down her face. Why did he have to go and do that?

They continued up the hill in silence. Outside the bungalow, Luke parked the car.

"Thanks for the ride," she said, her palm on the door handle.

"Hold on," he said. "A guy's gotta walk a girl to the door."

The snow had resumed and turned to sleet. She unlocked the bungalow. "Thanks for taking me home."

"Belle," he said. "I'm sorry about Flora."

She nodded and lowered her gaze. A warm kiss brushed her check. She drew her head up in surprise and looked straight into his brown eyes. Before she could back away, he leaned in for a kiss, his lips warm and searching as his cologne swirled around her. Her body tingled at the nearness of him, his shoulders so close, his hand on her back.

"Good night, Belle." He returned to his car.

Inside, Belle leaned against the door. She'd been kissed for the first time, and she couldn't share it with Flora. Belle slumped to the sofa and buried her head in her hands. She didn't care if her sobs carried through the walls.

Preoccupied with thoughts of Luke's kiss, she sat on the couch and stared into space. What would Flora have said? She could almost hear the ring of her laughter. Belle turned on the radio and listened to gospel music. The hymns helped at those times when she missed Flora so much she ached. After a few minutes, she worried about the music disturbing the neighbors and turned off the radio. She unfolded a newspaper, the pages rustling in the silence of the room. A large black and white photograph plastered the front page: a man held a young woman in his arms, her shoes dangling in the air. The headlines read—Trail of Violence Left as Lovers Crisscross the Countryside.

Belle examined the photo and gasped. Bonnie! There was no mistaking the vibrant young woman who offered her a ride to Talihina. Bonnie's smiling face stared out at her from yesterday's paper.

She browsed the article. Bonnie Parker and Clyde Barrow leave havoc stealing cars and robbing gas stations and grocery stores. Several shop owners and law enforcement have been murdered in their wake.

Renewed tears streamed down Belle's cheeks. "Oh, Bonnie, what have you done?"

A grieving widower, a boy too young to experience deep loss, and Belle, a lost orphan in a grown body. Now Bonnie. The whole world had come undone.

The next week, Charlie relayed unexpected news over their weekly dinner. "I've been offered a job."

"Here in town?" What would pay better than the hospital?

"In Oklahoma City." He placed his napkin down. "It's more money, and it's a great career opportunity."

Despite her best efforts, tears formed in her eyes. "But I'll never see you and Jeremy."

Jeremy's sullen face dropped to his chest.

Charlie tipped his head and rolled his eyes pointedly in the boy's direction. "That's not true."

She glanced at Jeremy's red eyes and caught Charlie's meaning.

"You can always visit," Charlie continued, "and we'll be back since my family lives here."

She remained speechless.

"Jeremy, let's get out that textbook," Charlie said. "You need to review for your test tomorrow."

"Yes, sir." With slumped shoulders, he shuffled to his bedroom.

Charlie helped clear the table. In the kitchen, he placed a hand on her shoulder. "I know you don't want us to leave." He squeezed his eyes shut and sighed. After a moment, he said, "I can't stay in this house any longer, Belle. I see her everywhere."

"You could find—"

"It's everything. The house, the town, the hospital." His voice broke. "I can't be here."

She stacked the dishes in the sink. "I understand." But she didn't. She couldn't comprehend any of it.

Flora's death had changed Belle's life and somehow started an odd domino effect. Some people thought she was rushing into it. Anne warned Belle that her head might not be clear enough to make a life-changing decision. Nurse Braxton regretted losing her as an employee but wished her well.

Thrilled to see Belle and Luke get hitched, Charlie officially welcomed Belle into the family. She took comfort in the fact she'd see them again at family events. Part of her worried about so much change. Another part of her melted under Luke's admiring eyes. As in her Native American story, Belle lay in the stream and let the current carry her down the creek—its waters ever changing, ever moving.

Chapter 30

THE FORD ROLLED DOWN THE highway, leaving behind her life in Talihina. Luke reached for her hand and turned his attention back to the road. Nervous about meeting his family, she worried that they hadn't invited them to the wedding. Only Charlie and Jeremy had stood with them before the Justice of the Peace. Though Luke's mother had died years ago, his father and siblings lived in the area. They might be resentful. Luke insisted it wasn't a problem, but what did a man know about family affairs?

Eager to replace the hospital's stark walls for open sky, she looked forward to living on a farm again. No more peering through a window to catch a glimpse outside. She took one last glance back. Nothing would replace the beautiful Quachita Mountains, but Luke insisted she'd like the wooded hills.

That late March day, they drove out of the piney woods and traveled into farm country. Leafless trees along the road made supplication to the sky as if they ached for the return of spring. She yawned. Sunlight warmed the interior of the car, and she closed her eyes.

She woke to Luke humming an unfamiliar tune.

"We're almost home," he announced. "You're officially in Dry Run proper."

Belle gazed at the three-block Main Street. Brick facades housed a grocery store, drug store, and dry goods.

"Quite a bit of farming here, but there's also oil fields," Luke said. "Back in 1914, Frank Hendrickson discovered natural gas on his farm. That was a game changer for the entire region. Many of our men work in the Dry Run

Smelter where they process zinc ore." He pointed west. "The home place is only a few miles out of town."

Belle gazed up at her handsome husband. He smiled and patted her knee. Reassured, she watched the passing scenery with interest. They left the main road and turned south on a dirt road that twisted and curved. On each side, bodark and redbud covered the rolling hills.

"Here it is," Luke said. "Home sweet home, as they say."

Her stomach dropped. The peeling white paint of the clapboard house revealed weathered wood. Out front, chickens scratched the bare ground. Belle spotted a chicken coop behind the house and further back, a corrugated-tin silo. A tractor stood idle near an outbuilding, but there wasn't a barn. Luke said they raised beef cattle and corn. An old mare lifted its head as they drove up. She hoped to find the interior of the home in better shape.

An elderly man blocked the doorway. "What took you so long? I need my car to go to town." He scowled, one thumb hooked behind the strap of his overalls.

Luke narrowed his eyes and clenched his jaw. Belle's face grew warm. Luke's mother had passed fifteen years earlier from consumption. In lieu of a mother-in-law, Belle had hoped for a kindhearted father-in-law versus the man who stood before them.

"Pa, this is Belle," Luke said. "My new wife."

He swept his eyes in brutal inspection and humphed. "Hope you can cook."

"Yes, sir," she managed to say.

"Come on in then," he mumbled.

Coats hung over chairs, and soiled overalls draped the back of the sofa. Near the door, boots and work gloves were scattered over a plank floor. Wallpaper, faded and dingy, lined the living room; one section curled halfway down the wall. The sofa was threadbare at several points.

Luke showed her the kitchen. Pots and pans piled high in the sink with more pans stacked on the stovetop. The table looked like it hadn't been wiped in years and dirty dishes nearly obscured the oilcloth. She wanted to turn and leave. Run, a voice inside screamed. Run back to your job in Talihina.

"I'm sorry it's such a mess, Belle," Luke said. "'Fraid it's been just us bachelors living here." He looked truly repentant.

He showed her to their bedroom on the other side of the kitchen. They passed a smaller room across the hall. Belle's skin crawled to think the old man would be so close to their room. Thankfully, their bedroom didn't share the ramshackle appearance of the rest of the house. An iron-rail bed was centered against the far wall. A walnut dresser with an oval mirror stood in the corner. The bed was neatly made, the floor uncluttered.

She found her voice at last. "What a pretty quilt." The patchwork quilt had been painstakingly sewn with blue and violet fabric.

"My mother sewed that, God rest her soul." Luke set Belle's bags at the foot of the bed. She stood, arms at her sides, without a thought of what to do or think. Luke stepped up and took her in his arms. He nuzzled her neck and kissed it.

"I need to go into town with Pa and pick up some seed," he said. "That'll give you time to unpack." He kissed her on the lips and left.

She sat on the edge of the bed. The front door slammed, and the car engine chortled for a few moments before it changed to a steady thrum. When she could no longer hear the engine, she released her held back tears.
Foolish, foolish girl.

Belle's hands were deep in sudsy water when Luke and his father returned. As much as she was resentful that Luke had brought her to the rundown house, she couldn't abide living in such filth. Soon clean pots and pans covered the oak table, turned upside down to dry on the oilcloth.

"'Bout time we had a woman around this place," the old man said. The furrow above his brows appeared permanently engraved.

"Oh, sweetie," Luke said. "I didn't expect you to start in right away."

She forced a smile but didn't believe for a minute he hadn't expected it.

"Pa said there's a roast thawed out on the counter," Luke said. "Would you like me to fix it?"

She studied him for a moment. The men had been living alone, so surely he knew how to cook. "Thank you. That will give me time to clean the cupboards. By the way, I put the meat in the icebox." She'd seen crumbs and signs of mouse droppings in two of the cabinets. She was beginning to wonder if Luke had only married her to clean house.

Luke stared dumbfounded before he regained his composure and grabbed logs from a stack in the corner. He banged a fry pan around and stomped to the icebox. She was on the verge of telling him she'd do it herself, but she reconsidered. He'd brought her to this dirty rat trap. He could help.

"There, it's cooking," he said. "It'll be done in an hour. I'll put the potatoes in, peeling and all." He paused and glanced her way. "Unless you want to peel them."

She glanced up from on her knees and shook her head, dipped the cloth in the wash bucket, and wrung it out. Luke plopped whole potatoes into the roasting pan and stomped from the room. A moment later, the screen door slammed.

As she cleaned the rest of the cupboards and placed items back, she thought hard about the misconceptions she'd had about Luke. He always appeared so clean looking and dapper when he came to Talihina, driving that Ford she thought was his own. She had assumed he took after his cousin. Charlie had a good job and did well for himself. He'd purchased the beautiful house that Flora had spent so much time decorating. She'd been naive to think that Charlie's handsome cousin was well situated, too.

A stew pot slipped from her hands and smacked her foot. She hopped around the kitchen. It hurt like hell, and the pain burst a dam of held-back emotions. She yelled and cried. Belle found herself wishing her foot had broken. Make them wait on her. But no, these men would expect her to continue on with her duties despite an injury. With the house to herself, she swore like a sailor on leave, cursing everything and everybody, but most all, Arabella Morning Glory Tahsuda.

How could she have been so stupid?

A day later, Bernie Stilwell, her father-in-law, paid a visit to his brother in the next county. Belle had no idea if the trip was calculated to give the newlyweds time alone or mere coincidence. For all she knew, Luke might have encouraged the visit for that very purpose. Whatever the reason, she was grateful. The wide bed earned its keep, and she relished their warm embraces at all times of the day and night. Mid-afternoon became her favorite time, such a scandalous, sweet time of the day.

She was determined to adapt to her new situation. After all, what had she owned in Talihina? She had a comfortable cottage, a good job, but she would never have owned a house or land. Even her gold bullion was worthless now. President Roosevelt had signed an order making it illegal to possess gold. But like many people, she wasn't going to turn it in anytime soon. Someday the order might be overturned, and gold would be valuable once again.

Buds formed on trees around the farmhouse, and grass greened in the ditches. Belle lived on the land again, and that made up for the dilapidated house. Once clean and tidy, both the house and her morale greatly improved. Barely a week passed when Bernie returned, and that same day Luke announced it was time to meet the rest of the family.

"The whole family's coming for dinner on Sunday. They'll bring pies, cakes, and bread. We'll make the main meal."

What he meant was she'd do the cooking. "How many people?"

"Thirteen," he said. "Make that sixteen with the three of us."

"What should we serve?"

"Fried chicken, potatoes, and gravy."

"You kill 'em. I'll cook 'em."

He laughed and kissed her cheek.

Two days later her attitude turned sour when Luke tossed dead birds on the front steps and walked away. She fumed as she plucked five fat hens by herself while Luke and his father drove to the neighbors to collect a load of fertilizer.

"I'd rather shovel manure," she mumbled as she butchered chickens on the wooden chopping block. The face of her Chilocco teacher appeared in the whorls of the wood. She stabbed the pale face who'd taught them cooking skills.

Sunday arrived. Belle was exhausted from preparations made early that morning. In the days preceding, she'd done a thorough cleaning of the living room. She'd found some pretty red and white calico in the bedroom closet and made pillows from the feathers of the recently deceased chickens. At least, the pillows added a touch of color to the drab room.

Her three sisters-in-law appeared in the kitchen. With her forearm, Belle wiped the sweat from her forehead. Luke introduced her to Anna, Lilith, and May and promptly disappeared. Children cavorted outside, and men smoked on the front stoop. Belle smiled at the silent sisters and stirred a pot. She looked over her shoulder and caught curious eyes darting away. Like a bull being examined at the stock barn, she half expected to be prodded, poked, and deemed unworthy.

She wiped her hands on her apron, wondering what she should say to these quiet women. A sudden eruption of conversation hummed behind her. The women talked among themselves as if she wasn't in the room. They spoke in Choctaw. Belle was convinced they talked about her.

She went about her cooking. Obviously, the jury was out on their new sister-in-law. Belle might be as Indian as they were, but she wasn't family. She instinctively knew only time would make a difference with these women. The sweet face of Flora appeared before her in the steam of boiling potatoes. An eddy of loneliness and the memory of being loved by her best friend rolled in the hot, steamy kitchen.

"Looks like we're ready to eat," Belle announced.

Two of the women went to call the men and round up the children. The remaining sister, Lilith, helped her spoon food onto serving platters and into bowls. Lilith never once looked at her or spoke.

Luke's older brother, Leon, was a quiet man. He nodded politely when he met Belle, but that was it. He filled his plate and took his food to the living room. His two young sons, Amos and Sam, made up for the man's silence. Leon's wife had been admitted to the hospital nine months before Belle arrived. She died from heart complications due to diabetes.

With loud, clipped speech, the three women prepared plates for the younger children now seated at the table. That left no room for the women, who traipsed to the living room to eat. Belle found herself left in the kitchen with the chattering children. She leaned against the counter and ate her food.

One of the children laughed.

"Pasawi'oo," a little boy said in Comanche. He pointed at Belle.

Belle continued eating. The family was a mix of Choctaw and Comanche. At least, she knew some of this language.

"Pasawi'oo," Bobbie pointed again at Belle. He placed two fingers, one at each eye and pointed at Belle again. The girl next to him giggled.

Belle knew enough of the Comanche language to know that he called her a frog. He was making a joke of her supervising the children.

"Wakarée." Belle said, catching the attention of the little girl called Rose. Belle pointed at the boy, and the girl giggled. "I'm faster than that wakarée," Belle said.

Bobbie, who looked to be around nine, frowned at being called a turtle.

"Tell him," Belle said. "I can beat him at a race. Even a frog is faster than a turtle."

Rose laughed and mashed potatoes spurted from her mouth. She repeated what Belle said though everyone in the room had heard.

Bobbie rose from the table and drew back his shoulders. "Tell her to prove it."

Rose repeated the boy's challenge. Belle put down her plate and untied her apron. She stooped slightly, pressing her hands to her thighs, ready to run.

Rose raised her arm, paused, and dropped her hand. "Go!" Bobbie ran through the doorway to the living room where all heads turned. One of the sisters-in-law frowned. She probably thought Belle was trying to reprimand her son. The woman stood abruptly as Belle raced behind him and allowed the boy to exit the front door before she did.

"Belle!" Luke's stern voice came from behind.

Belle ignored him and ran down the dirt road after Bobby, who thought he'd already made his point. She pumped her arms, gaining on him. He turned his head, and his eyes widened in disbelief.

Belle ran behind the boy and challenged him. "First to the piney woods!"

He nodded and spurted ahead, his mouth agape with puffing breaths.

She caught up with him, and with lungs burning, she kept pace. The woods loomed twenty feet ahead. Bobby matched her gait, and they raced neck and neck. At the last few feet, she slackened her pace and allowed the boy to win.

They stood panting, unable to talk. In the distance, the family gathered and watched from halfway down the drive.

"Not bad for a pasawi'oo." Bobby smiled up at her.

"Even better for a wakarée." She patted him on the back, and they returned to the house. The family laughed at the two walking up the road. Luke tapped her on the rear as she passed. He looked pleased.

Back at the house, Belle heated water on the stove and cleared dishes from the table. The women gathered in the kitchen.

"We'll call you deer from now on," Grace Little Hawk said. The pretty woman, Luke's adult niece, took the dish cloth from Belle's hand and wiped the oilcloth.

"Maybe kwihnai would be better," Lilith said. "She flew out of the house like an eagle."

Belle joined in their laughter. They looked in her eyes now. Indian people enjoyed a good joke, and Belle was no longer the invisible stranger.

But one person had not been impressed. Later that night, Bernie Stilwell glanced at her and shook his head. "Chasing after little children."

Unfortunately, the heart of the oldest relative proved to be impenetrable.

Chapter 31

BELLE DRAINED THE KITCHEN SINK, dried her hands, and let the screen door slam behind her. The men were in the fields planting corn. Now that the weather had warmed, she often stole a little time for herself and walked in the woods after breakfast. She drew her sweater close. Blackjack oak belted the ridge behind the house, air lifting from the ground in rich, fertile currents. She glanced back—the house out of sight—and twirled in the late-April sunshine.

A month had passed since her arrival as a new bride, and yet she still found the fact surprising. Had she made the right choice? Cooking and cleaning dominated her days and for what—a crotchety old man and a husband who grew more distant by the day.

She crouched and examined a purple locoweed, the plant poisonous to cattle. The locoweed contained selenium, a toxic chemical, but farmers grew concerned only when the plant became weedy. Cattle wouldn't eat locoweed unless it was the only food available. She plucked a few leaves and tucked them in her pocket. Dried locoweed would be good to have on hand. An infusion of its leaves could be applied to sores, speeding the healing process.

At the bottom of the hill, Belle wove through black gum trees and delicate columbine blossoms that dangled in the breeze. She picked her way through white flowers of toothwort growing in the shade. By summer, the flowers would be gone. Her grandmother had used toothwort in cooking, giving the food a peppery, slightly horseradish flavor. A few feet away, rusty fronds of cinnamon ferns spread at the base of trees. Spring made her happy.

Begrudgingly, she started for the house. Bread dough needed to be mixed and allowed time to rise in the midday heat. But first she'd fix a cup of tea. In the kitchen, she crushed dried mint with a wooden pestle and lit the burner under the teakettle. The scent of sulfur lifted.

Footsteps sounded on the front stoop. Bernie entered the kitchen with that characteristic hitch to his step. "Luke went to town for supplies."

"I'm making tea," she said. "Would you like a cup?"

"I'll consider it," he said. "Shouldn't ya get that bread going?"

She refused to give credence to his bossy remark and measured yeast into a cup. From the corner of her eye, she saw Bernie pull out a chair. Belle retrieved two cups from the cupboard.

"Luke's mother made the best bread," he said.

She retrieved a yellow-ware bowl for the flour. "I wish I had her recipe," she said to be polite.

"She didn't use no recipe," he bragged. "Knew it in her head."

"Learned it from her mother, I'm sure." She measured flour into the bowl and added a bit of sugar to the yeast.

He nodded. "I'm glad Luke settled down. He needed to."

She glanced up but didn't say anything. The teakettle steamed. She poured water into a small bowl and waited until it cooled to the right temperature, not too hot or it would kill the rising property of the yeast, not too cool or the yeast wouldn't activate.

"You're a good cook," he said.

"Thank you." She laughed. "That means a lot to me since it's not my favorite thing to do."

His head lifted. Surprise etched his face, but he didn't make the smart remark she expected. Maybe he understood. Surely men grew tired of planting fields year after year and harvesting at the end of each season.

Belle dissolved the yeast in tepid water and stirred it into the flour. Bernie watched her knead the dough and cover the soft mound with a dishtowel. She filled a tea ball with the muddled leaves and placed it in a ceramic teapot. The blue-floral pot had belonged to Luke's mother. Belle joined Bernie at the table and waited for the tea to steep.

"Heard you worked at the TB hospital there in Talihina."

"I did."

"Luke probably told you that's how we lost his mother." Bernie looked down at the oilcloth.

"Mm hmm."

"Terrible disease."

"I lost my best...guess you know. Charlie's wife." It was Belle's turn to stare at the tablecloth.

"Good to have a nurse in the family," he said at last.

"I wasn't exactly a nurse." She poured tea into their cups. "I was a nurse's aide."

"I'm sure you must've learned a thing or two."

She learned sometimes there's healing, and sometimes, despite the best efforts and a heart full of prayers, a loved one died.

Bernie slurped his drink. "Good tea."

"Thanks, Bernie." Two compliments in one day. The old man's heart must be thawing.

He smirked. "You'll get better as time passes."

She couldn't help but smile. They finished their tea in silence, both glancing out the window on occasion.

Bernie stood at last. "Gonna check on that old tractor. Tune it up a bit."

"See you later, Bernie." He

harrumphed.

Belle stared after the old man. Bernie Stilwell had softened towards her. Who would have guessed?

May arrived hot and dry. The Farmer's Almanac predicted the driest summer on record. Bernie and Luke worried about the amount of hay and corn they'd be able to harvest. Belle could see the underlying tension behind their words. She focused on her garden out back. Despite the backbreaking work to haul water from the well, she intended to can vegetables for the coming year when a low harvest would be felt in the wallet.

Belle had just hauled her tenth bucket of water that afternoon for a seedling crop of beans. Dizzy in the midday heat, her hand pressed against the small of her back. She dropped to her knees, leaned over, and lost her breakfast.

"Belle!" a woman's voice rang. "Are you all right?"

231

She looked back to see Lilith's black hair swinging at her waist as she ran.

Embarrassed, Belle wiped her mouth with the hem of her apron. Red Oklahoma soil clung to her hands. "Heat got to me."

"Let's get you inside." Lilith offered a hand and pulled Belle to her feet. They linked elbows and walked to the house. Lilith settled Belle at the kitchen table. "Let me get you a drink." She drew water from the porch cistern and handed Belle a glass of cool water.

Lilith studied her with wide brown eyes. "How long has it been since your last monthly visit?"

Belle laughed. "It's not what you think. I hauled too many buckets from the well."

"Uh huh." Lilith removed two canning jars from a canvas bag. "I brought some canned apples. Thought you might want to make some pies."

"How wonderful. It's been a long time since I've had a good apple pie." Belle finished the glass of water and realized she couldn't recall her last female cycle. She'd been so preoccupied with moving and settling in. She glanced at Lilith. "Do you think it's possible?" "The pie or the baby?" Lilith laughed.

Belle shook her head and smiled.

"Only you know the answer to that," Lilith said, "but I rather doubt you and Luke have separate beds."

She blushed. "Two days ago, I felt a little indigestion but I blamed it on the chili I made for dinner."

"What time of the day did your stomach bother you?"

"About this time, I guess." She worked at the oilcloth with her finger. "But I thought it was supposed to be morning sickness."

"Every woman's different," Lilith said. "Just like some women tend to give birth to all their babies in the morning, others midday, and some at night."

"I've been so busy," she said, "I haven't given much thought to cycles and babies."

"Your baby will have lots of cousins." Lilith smiled mischievously.

Between running a household and her lingering grief for Flora, Belle hadn't considered the consequences of the marriage bed. How silly of her. She took a deep breath.

Lilith smiled and patted her hand. "Let me know if I can help with anything." She draped the long strap of her bag over her shoulder. "Time to get back and make a few pies myself."

"I feel better. I'll walk you to the road." Lilith and her husband lived on a farm a half mile down the road.

"No, no," she said. "Rest up while you can. I'll check on you next week."

Belle watched Lilith from the screen door. Her sister-in-law could be wrong. Too much hot sun and exertion could make a person sick. Lilith marched down the road, her arms swinging in time to her determined gait. Something told her, the woman was right.

Weeks later, her stomach formed a small pouch. With Belle's tall, slim frame, her figure didn't look out of the ordinary, but she knew. She had to tell Luke.

She waited until after dinner. Belle sat beside him on the front stoop and studied the bank of trees across the road. "Have you given any thought to a family?"

Luke leaned back on his arms, gazing into the distance. A stem of grass twisted between his teeth. "Not really." After a moment, he turned and stared. He lifted an eyebrow. "Are you...?" She nodded.

He grabbed her hands and drew her to her feet. Like on the dance floor, Luke spun her with one arm, the dry ground turning to dust. "I'm going to be a father!"

He flew into the house. A moment later, her father-in-law appeared wearing a big grin. "Good news. Just what we needed." Bernie winked and joined them on the stoop. He patted his son's shoulder and offered him a cigarette. No further words were spoken, but something had changed. Belle was officially part of the family.

Upon greeting anyone, Luke would blurt, "Did you know we're having a baby?" He joked that he expected a son, but he'd accept a little girl, too. Luke's family rejoiced with them. Even the children grew excited. They could never have enough cousins. Choctaw or Comanche, it didn't matter. Family dominated the lives of Native people.

One afternoon she walked to the end of the lane to retrieve the mail. She turned back to the house, shuffling through the few bills and advertisements.

One letter was addressed to Mr. and Mrs. Luke Stilwell with a return address of Oklahoma City. Belle tore open the envelope and started reading.

Dear Luke and Belle,

How are the newlyweds doing? I miss you both. Jeremy has made several friends at school and is looking forward to classes ending for the summer. We live close to a park, which Jeremy takes full advantage of after school and on weekends.

My job is going well, and I have a smart assistant who works under me. That's very helpful since this is a much larger hospital than in Talihina. Jeremy says to say hello and that he misses you, Belle. I swear that boy is growing stronger every day. Luke, old fellow, hope you're doing well and make sure you take care of that fine lady you married.

Yours,

Charlie

P.S. In regard to your question about my welfare, Belle, I'm grateful to have such a busy job. But evenings are tough. Don't know what I'd do if I didn't have Jeremy. He lights up the dark corners of my life, and I do my best to reciprocate.

As months passed and her middle increased, Luke became sullen and moody. The scarce rainfall and low cattle prices dictated conversation over the dinner table. She wondered if Luke's change in mood came from the pressure he felt as a prospective father. Didn't he know that they'd fare all right? The one cow they maintained for milk supplied the needs of the small household. They could barter a quarter beef for flour, sugar, and yeast. With her canned vegetables and cold-storage potatoes, they'd get by.

"We won't starve," she remarked one evening in August. "I put up ninety-five quarts of vegetables this summer, and there's more to harvest.
And with old Bessie, we'll always have milk and butter."

"That old milk cow won't buy gas for the car, now will it?" Anger flashed in Luke's eyes. "Or clothes. Never mind a movie ticket." He stormed out of the house. The screen door slammed.

Belle stood in the doorway. Bronze dust rippled in the sunlight as he drove away. She closed her eyes and sighed. When she looked again, a shadow swept over the road as clouds obliterated the sun.

Chapter 32

BELLE CARRIED A TEAPOT INTO the front room. A cup of wild-mint tea typically followed the evening meal. Luke had kicked off his boots and leaned back in the upholstered chair. Bernie's face was concealed behind an open newspaper.

After the tea had steeped, she poured three cups. The newspaper lowered and revealed her father-in-law's somber face. Bernie reached for his tea. "Roosevelt is offering payments to cotton and wheat farmers if they reduce their acreage." He snapped the paper up again. "Says farmers are plowing under part of their growing cotton." The top of Bernie's head shook. "Drought hurt most of the wheat crop, but farmers will receive payments if they promise to reduce acreage next year." He humphed.

"Some 'New Deal.'" Luke blew at the steaming tea. "That helps the big operations but won't help the small farmer."

"Government's trying to balance supply and demand, but I agree," Bernie said. "It won't help the little guy. Glad it doesn't affect us." The newspaper rustled and spread its wings.

Belle sipped her tea. She stayed away from agricultural topics after Luke's last rebuff over the cow.

The paper crackled. "You ain't gonna believe this one." The newspaper fell to Bernie's lap. "The darn government bought 40,000 cattle in Nebraska."

"Nebraska?" Belle asked.

"They're one of the states with the highest concentration of cattle," Luke said, gazing out the window. Belle appreciated the handsome profile of her husband's face. She only wished that his once characteristic smile appeared more often.

"Don't forget Texas," Bernie said.

In the spring, she had helped move their cattle from one pasture to another. She enjoyed watching the calves jump and frolic, so full of life and energy. She never grew tired of laughing at their antics.

"But that's not the half of it." Bernie folded the paper and set it aside. With a grim expression, he stared at Luke. "Thousands of cattle were shot and buried in pits. Paper said the farmers hated to lose their herds, but the buy-out saved many of 'em from bankruptcy."

Belle's stomach twisted at the thought of healthy cattle killed and dumped in trenches.

"Damn government." Luke's face darkened. "They couldn't even put the meat to good use? There's starvin' people all over this country!" He stood and, without another word, stormed out the door. The engine of the Ford started up, and the sound faded as Luke drove down the road.

Heavy silence hung in the room. Bernie stared out the window. "All those healthy cattle wasted. They didn't even spare the calves."

Belle rolled restlessly in bed. She held the windup clock to the moonlight shining through the window. It was well after midnight when she heard the Ford rumble up the road. She turned on her side and pretended to be asleep.

Luke must have removed his shoes on the stoop because the only sound she heard was the door creak. Clothes landed onto the floor, and the springs sunk as he climbed into bed. He reeked of liquor. Hard liquor. In another few moments, raspy snoring engulfed the room.

Moonshine.

Belle slid to the edge of the bed. Careful to listen for her husband's breathing, she crept from the bedroom. In the front room, she grabbed a light blanket and tiptoed out to the front stoop. She was seething.

The still night air drifted, moist and cool, carrying the scent of water from low-lying creeks. She bundled the blanket around her shoulders and twisted her hands. He dared to complain about the low market price of cattle and corn yet blew their precious money on liquor. The man rebuked her attempts at encouragement. What kind of man did that? Belle worried about the type of father Luke would make if he had no more sense than to become inebriated.

Without regard for her bare feet, she strolled down the lane to the county road. Under the illumination of a gibbous moon, the distant woods looked like inky blockades. Anger raged through her body, her stinging soles a minor irritation compared to the situation in which she found herself. Something shuffled in the brush, and she flinched. The nearby cry of coyotes rang out. She turned and fled. Returning to the dark-paned house on tender feet, she sat on the stoop and drew the blanket around her neck. The yip of coyotes shifted and shimmied as the wild dogs hunted prey in the wooded hills.

There in the middle of the night, she compared the debonair, reassuring Luke she'd known in Talihina to the discontented, angry husband he'd become. The drumbeats of her ancestors resounded in her head. She tapped her foot in time to the somber Native beat. The coyotes' shrill cry rose again. A vision emerged of Luke as a shape shifter, moving between one kind of creature and another. Her hand slid to her belly. She and her baby were caught in the middle.

Late September, Belle surveyed the plump pumpkins in her garden. She cradled her swollen belly with one hand, feeling as ripe as her produce. For the past month, she'd kept busy canning food for the winter. Jars of green beans, corn, tomatoes, apples, and beef lined the wooden shelves in the cellar. The food could be rationed well into the following spring. She swept loose strands of hair from her face and caught sight of someone walking up the road. She shaded her eyes. Lilith carried something in her arms. Belle went to meet her.

"I brought you baby clothes." Lilith had the same high cheekbones and dark expansive eyes of her brother. She was as pretty as Luke was handsome.

Belle always looked forward to her sister-in-law's visits. She grew tired of having only men around. "Come in, and I'll put the tea kettle on."

Lilith placed blankets and clothes on the kitchen table. "How are you feeling?"

"Like a fat toad." They both laughed.

"You're a skinny mouse compared to what you'll be two months from now." A small smile tugged at Lilith's face.

"How are the kids?"

"Busy as a swarm of bees," Lilith said, "flitting around the place. Always up to something."

Lilith usually left her oldest child in charge and came alone. Belle figured her sister-in-law needed a break from her boisterous household. She placed the teapot on the table along with two cups and sat across the table from her. "Luke seems unhappy." That was the mildest way of saying it. "Is the Depression upsetting your husband, too?"

"James is an owl," Lilith said. "He watches and waits. As long as we have food, he doesn't worry. Worry does no one any good."

"That's so true." How she'd tried to convey that to Luke. "But sometimes it's hard not to be anxious." Belle rubbed a spot on the oilcloth. "Does James drink?"

"He's a man," Lilith said. "They do what they're going to do."

Belle burned at her comment. That didn't make it right. Luke was throwing away good money on moonshine. Coming home drunk. She glanced at Lilith who folded baby clothes in tidy stacks. His sister's allegiance would always be to her brother. No good would come of saying more. "Thank you for the clothes." She picked up a soft yellow sleeper. "Whose was this?"

"Ah, that was Jimmy's." Lilith proceeded to talk about her youngest child. "He was my best baby. Hardly ever cried."

Later, Belle accompanied Lilith to the main road. They hugged.

"Luke will be happier when the baby's here." The corners of Lilith's mouth curved into a quiet smile. "Men have to see the child to appreciate it."

Belle walked back to the house. A raven flew overhead, landed on the wood pile, and watched her progress. She hoped Lilith was right.

As her body swelled, Belle found Luke more attentive. A new routine developed. In the mornings, he rose before her. He woke her with a kiss and a cup of tea on the bedside table. Had her growing form brought fresh realization of the baby to come? But on Friday nights, her husband would leave like clockwork. After dinner, two hours to the minute, the Ford would start up and disappear down the drive.

On the last day of December 1933, Belle abandoned her bed in the middle of the night. She made it to the doorway of the bedroom and leaned against the doorframe, waiting for the contraction to cease. A full moon filtered through the window. She reached the next bedroom door before another pain seared through her middle. It was Friday night.

The sound of snoring rippled through the wall. After the pain passed, she rapped on the door. Knocked again. The snoring ceased. Bedsprings squeaked. "Bernie." The start of another contraction corded around her middle. "Bernie, wake up!"

The door opened. Bernie's eyes and mouth widened in imitation of the moon.

"Get Lilith," she managed to say between clenched teeth.

Bernie retreated into the bedroom and reappeared buttoning his shirt. He lit a kerosene lantern in the kitchen. "Where's the damn keys? Where's Luke?"

"He's gone." She leaned over the table, propped on one arm. "There's no car."

"Irresponsible son of a bitch." Bernie grabbed a heavy coat from a hook near the door.

Lilith lived a half mile down the county road. Belle feared she'd be left alone to deliver her child and reconsidered. "Don't leave me, Bernie."

"Have to," he said in the open doorway. "The truck isn't working, and I don't know a damn thing about birthing." The door slammed.

Tears ran down her cheeks. "I don't either, Bernie. I don't know a damn thing, either." She moaned as another contraction took control of her body.

Better to be an old maid than a wife left alone when she needed her husband. Even her father-in-law had abandoned her. Belle returned to bed drenched in the rupture of the embryotic sack. The baby was coming, waiting for nothing and no one. She didn't care if the sheets and mattress would be ruined. She didn't care if Luke never came back.

She roared in pain and desperation and anger. The contractions came harder and closer together. Belle squeezed the metal rung of the headboard and yelled as the baby wrenched her insides in a violent attempt to free itself. Sweat trickled down her face, salt burning her eyes. The contractions became so severe she feared she'd be ripped apart. The pain blazed nonstop and unmerciful. Would she die alone in this dark room? Die in the middle of the night in the darkest season of the year?

She couldn't take the excruciating pains much longer. If only she'd die so the pain would end. One roiling stab stole all thoughts, and the baby slid from her body. She leaned over and reached for the slippery infant still attached by the life-giving cord. She grabbed the end of the sheet and wiped the infant's face, clearing the nostrils and mouth. The baby wailed and permeated the empty house with his presence.

Nineteen-year-old Belle cradled her newborn son to her breast. "Sh-sh, child."

A car engine announced a vehicle outside. The door opened, and footfalls beat their way into the bedroom. Belle turned from the blinding light of a lantern as Lilith approached the bedside and cooed at the child. A moment later, her sister-in-law withdrew a sharp knife and severed the cord. Lilith swabbed the infant with a damp cloth and swaddled the baby tightly in a blanket. She placed him in Belle's arms. A warm, wet cloth was drawn against Belle's legs. Afterward Lilith slipped the wet sheets from beneath her and drew a blanket over her shoulders. Another vehicle spun up outside the house. Loud drunken shouts sounded.

"In here," Lilith yelled.

Luke stumbled into the bedroom with a stupid grin on his face.

"You have a son." Lilith smiled

He started to fall but caught himself by grabbing the bedpost.

Luke approached Belle, grinning. "Are you okay?"

Belle nodded and looked away. At once, Lilith removed the baby from her arms and offered her son to his drunken father. "No," Belle shouted. "He's drunk. He'll drop him."

Lilith silenced her with a frown. She left the room and accompanied Luke and his new son into the front room. Belle would have raged or cried, but weariness overtook her.

She dreamt of the stream back home. The clear water flowed slowly as if in regret. The chatter of birds ceased, and the stillness was disquieting. Then the creek rumbled, brown with silt, and overflowed the bank, tearing at tree roots along the stream. The roaring grew louder until it changed to nature's cries of protest. She tossed to the side of the bed.

"Belle, wake up." A dim light shone from the hall. "The baby's hungry." Lilith placed the crying infant at her breast.

"Where's Luke?"

"Sleeping. Don't worry about him."

She wouldn't. Her thoughts focused on her child. He was her priority now.

In the morning, Lilith was still there. She brought a tray with scrambled eggs, bacon, toast, and a cup of tea. To her credit, she had not left Belle and the baby alone with an elderly man and his worthless son passed out on the sofa.

"Nursing the baby helps your body recover." Lilith sat at the foot of the bed. "Teddy is a strong infant. Lusty cries, that one." She smiled.

"Teddy?" She set her cup down.

"Luke named him Theodore after his grandfather."

So it was done—without as much as a nod from her. Belle kept her silence. "He does have hearty lungs. Impatient too. He was in a hurry to arrive in this world."

"That's the sign of a healthy baby." Lilith smiled at the infant. "I gave orders that the men are to cook for the next two days." She winked. "They know how."

Belle would gladly let them take over for the next few days—the next few weeks—but that would never happen. Lilith removed the empty tray and took it to the kitchen. The baby fell asleep in Belle's arms.

The night before she heard a coyote call in the dark. A cry had echoed in return—a loud, hair-raising call close to the house. Teddy's sign would be the coyote. Strong, agile. He'd be one who would work well with others, as coyotes work in a pack. Be there for his wife one day. He wouldn't forget his mother in her old age. She leaned over and whispered a soft, quiet howl. A tiny smile formed on the fat cheeks of her little boy.

For two weeks, Luke handed out cigars to everyone he knew and many he didn't. He was elated with the birth of his son, and Belle welcomed back the light-hearted, handsome man she'd married. An attentive husband, he helped with the baby while she cooked dinner and even dried dishes afterwards. Fatherhood agreed with him, and she was convinced that with little Teddy's arrival, Luke had finally awoken to his responsibilities.

But a few weeks later, she once again watched the back bumper of the Ford charge down the road on Friday night. Soon Saturday nights became part of the routine. When he left after dinner midweek, Belle knew there was no help for it.

Charlie and Jeremy made a surprise visit in late February. Belle made so much commotion upon seeing them on her doorstep, she woke the baby.

"He's so little," Jeremy said as she placed the baby in his arms. "And you've grown so big," Belle said. "You're almost a man now." Jeremy beamed upon the compliment.

"Had to see this new little guy," Charlie said. "And my folks kept begging us to visit."

"You need to visit more often. Luke will be home for dinner soon. I made plenty so I expect you to stay and join us."

"Sure, we'd like that."

They all turned as the front door opened. "Well, look what the cat dragged in," Luke said. He threw his arm around Charlie and the two shadowboxed. Bernie walked up and shook hands with both Charlie and Jeremy. Over the dinner table, the chatter was non-stop as they all tried to catch up on what was new with everyone. Bernie asked questions about Charlie's new job. The two cousins reminisced about childhood adventures on the farm. The evening ended far too soon, but Charlie's parents deserved time with their son.

"Will we see you tomorrow?" Belle jiggled the fussy baby up and down.

"Afraid, we have to head back to the city," Charlie said. "I need to be at work Monday morning."

Belle controlled her emotions until goodbyes were exchanged, and the rear lights of Charlie's car faded into the distance. She handed the baby to his father and withdrew to the bedroom. Saying goodbye to Jeremy was like saying goodbye to one of her own children.

In March, Belle accompanied Bernie to town. She cradled three-monthold Teddy in her arms as the car navigated the rough road.

"Can't wait till the county blades the road," her father-in-law muttered.

They entered Dry Run city limits. Belle used the excuse of needing to buy needles and thread. In truth, she had plenty at home, but she welcomed an escape from her sullen husband and the four walls in which she'd been captive all winter.

Bernie parked in front of the five and dime along Main Street.

"Bernie, look at that man." Belle pointed.

A gaunt man walked down the sidewalk in a high-stepping, footslapping manner.

"He's got the Jake leg," Bernie said. "Damn fool."

"What's that?" It wasn't polite to stare, but she couldn't help herself.

"Damn moonshine. Something they're puttin' in the ginger jake is making it poison. It causes paralysis."

"How horrible." She turned her face away as the man neared their car.

"Sometimes it's temporary. Sometimes permanent." Bernie opened his door. "Meet you back here in half an hour."

Belle nodded, unable to speak. She remained in the car for a few minutes. Luke was not only frittering away good money, abandoning his wife and child, but also risking his life. Her anger smoldered.

Three months later, anger turned to despair when Belle discovered she was pregnant again. Lilith had claimed nursing a child kept pregnancy at bay, but in Belle's case, the old wives' tale proved false. They had trouble making ends meet, and despite all her attempts at being frugal, their clothes were faded and patched. The hard times stretched everyone's nerves. Too many beans, soup, and stew filled the menu. The thought of another child to provide for became more than she could bear. If it wasn't for Teddy, she'd leave the farm without a moment's thought. That was when she took up knitting. The act of working needles kept her sanity—and her hands from choking her husband.

Chapter 33

A YEAR LATER SHE WAS home alone with the children when wind shook the house and gusted down the stovepipe. Outside the window, treetops swayed violently and something thudded against the clapboard. Belle pried the door open and spotted an empty bucket rolling on the stoop. She wrestled the door shut against the dust storm as a single bass note blew in the chimney like the sound from her grandfather's bone pipe. Not one drop of rain fell.

The next morning, she changed into a fresh housedress and rode with Bernie into town. Her days of fashion seemed far away. She purchased a newspaper for her father-in-law while Bernie shopped at the hardware store. With baby Jacob in one arm and Teddy clasping her hand, she settled on a park bench outside the grocery. She placed the sleeping baby on her lap and read the headlines: Black Sunday hits Panhandle on April 14th. The newspaper reported a storm had struck the Panhandle of Oklahoma when a bank of clouds rolled in from the northeast and plunged everything into an inky darkness. The article claimed a person couldn't see his hand two inches from his face. Many feared it was the end of the world.

Belle gazed at Jacob's little face. Dust would be dangerous to a baby's delicate lungs. The spring sun warmed her face and carried memories of running along the creek, her father's smile, and her grandparents' faces—all things from the past. Across the street, Bernie exited the hardware store. She tucked the newspaper into a bag filled with yeast, baking soda and Ivory soap flakes, gathered the children, and strolled down the sidewalk to meet him. Ahead, a young woman rested on a park bench with her eyes closed. She wore a plain blue dress with moccasins that brushed her knees. Long black hair draped her lowered face.

Intent on meeting Bernie, Belle hurried past the woman.

"Osage orange," the stranger muttered.

Belle glanced back.

The woman sat with her hands on her lap. One eyelid opened, that eye directed at Belle like an owl.

"Pardon me?" Belle shifted the baby in her arms.

The stranger opened both eyes, and her voice rolled soft and level. "Nothing like the smell of an Osage orange, is there?"

Caught off guard, Belle was speechless. The woman closed her eyes again as if she didn't expect a response. Belle continued down the sidewalk to Bernie's car. She looked back. Strange, but as Belle had reminisced about her family, the tart scent of a crushed Osage orange had come to mind.

Spring flew into summer. Summer brought constant—nearly futile—work in the garden. The hot, dry summer finally waned, and Belle welcomed the cooler temperatures of autumn. Consumed with caring for two young children, time passed quickly, but she relished each new stage of her children's growth. They were the light of her life, dispelling the shadows of a less than desirable marriage.

The following washday changed her dull acceptance of their marriage. As red as the northern cardinal she spotted on walks around the house, a glaring smear on the collar of Luke's shirt captured her attention. Luke's handsome face transformed into the pileated head of the pompous songbird as her blood pressure soared.

Belle was ready when Friday night came again. Luke left as usual after dinner. Teddy fell asleep in his grandpa's bed, the old man snoring like an angry bear. After the sun set, she wrapped the baby on her back with cotton duck. She saddled the old mare and rode three miles down the road. Rumors circulated of a crowd that gathered by the creek to drink moonshine on the weekends, and she planned a surprise visit.

A harvest moon lit the night like breaking dawn. Shadows from trees and fence posts stretched across the road, the air spinning cool but not yet cold. Belle drank in the scent of horseflesh and damp undergrowth mixed with moldering leaves. The night was so beautiful she nearly forgot her mission. She felt like a girl again, off on adventures on her grandparents' farm. If only…but so much had transpired in the last few years, and there was no going back. In life, forward was the only direction allotted.

The clopping of hooves rang over the night air as critters scurried in the underbrush and an occasional coyote yipped in the distance. Then the muted sound of revelry rose from down the road. A light flickered through the trees. She came upon a grass field packed with a medley of cars. Someone had tied two horses to the bumper of a truck. As she grew closer, a bonfire illuminated figures milling about the flames. A few people sat on stumps. Belle dismounted and tethered the horse to a tree at the edge of the field. Satisfied that the baby slept, she approached the campfire, wood smoke mixing with the tang of alcohol. She scanned the crowd for her husband.

There were Indian people, white people, and even a few black revelers. At last, she spotted Luke near the bonfire, a woman on each side vying for his attention. Her jaw tightened. He was a gamey buck in rut. He laughed at something one of the women said and took a swig from a bottle. Belle stepped softly, not wishing to announce herself too soon. She was curious about which woman left the lipstick. Fool. Who said there was only one Jezebel? She slipped five feet behind Luke. A slim woman—a white gal— sidled close to Belle's husband and brushed his neck with her lips. Red painted lips. Belle froze.

"Luke, there's a wasápe breathing down your neck." A tall Indian man stared Belle straight in the eyes, a wiseacre grin on his face. She recognized the Comanche word for bear and realized that with the papoose on her back, her silhouette resembled the broad back of a bruin.

Luke spun around, and his mouth dropped. The two women pivoted towards Belle. The thin one glared. The chubby one ducked behind Luke.

"What are you doing here, woman?"

Belle narrowed her eyes. "Same thing you're up to, I suppose." His jaw clenched. "This is no place for a mother of young children."

Luke's low voice held an edge she'd never heard.

"No place for a father of two sons," she retorted, "who need to be clothed and fed."

At that, Luke lunged. He clutched her upper arm and dragged her into the shadows. Alcohol oozed from his breath. She trembled, afraid he would beat her.

He lowered his voice, but his tone stretched bitter and angry. "How did you get here?" He squeezed her arm until tears rose in her eyes.

"Come home," she choked out the words, "to your wife and children."

"No woman will tell me what to do." Luke pushed her towards the Ford. The baby whimpered.

Clearly, her husband would not be reasoned with tonight. "I rode the horse." She jerked from his grip. "I'll find my way back."

He released her arm and spit in her direction. "Go home, woman."

She hurried toward the horse, untied the reins, and mounted. Luke watched from a distance. For a moment, she stared, her anger threatening to explode. He ran towards her, arms spread high in the air. "Git!"

The mare reared, and Belle struggled to remain on the horse's back. "Whoa, girl." She turned the nervous horse toward the road. The mare strained against the bit. A sudden uproar of shouting along the river nearly made the horse bolt. Belle's heart beat fast, but her thoughts remained frozen. Not until the firelight vanished and the drunken voices died out did her body loosen. Had she embarrassed him enough to stop his drinking? Only time would tell.

She'd heard of men who beat their women, and tonight she saw how easily it could happen. A man's rage. A woman of little value. The bright moon illuminated her despair.

Dark twisted limbs hung over the road, their thin branches clawing overhead. A woman alone could leave. She'd left Chilocco. She'd left her uncle, the farm, and everything familiar. She'd fled the employment of the Fairlanes. She'd given up the security of her job in Talihina. But a woman with two young babes, no money, and no way to work had nowhere to go.

The following Friday night, Luke stayed home. Belle worked hard to act normal, knowing too much cheerfulness would only rub his face in the concession. Teddy climbed over his father's shoulder and curled around to peer into his laughing face. She asked Luke to hold the baby while she heated homemade apple cider. Cooing came from the front room. When she returned, Jacob smiled at his father's silly faces. Her heart was so full it threatened to burst.

At breakfast the next morning, Luke was churlish, even with his father, whom he usually treated with respect. Belle hoped a good day's work would improve his mood, but at dinner that night, he complained about the food. The meat wasn't tender enough, the mashed potatoes lukewarm. She served their after-dinner tea in the living room, the baby asleep in the crib. Teddy played at his grandfather's feet. Luke jiggled his foot and tapped his fingers on the arm of the sofa. Belle's stomach twisted. Nerves shot to the surface of her skin. Please, God. Please, no.

"What's in this tea?" Luke frowned at Belle. "Tastes like crap." She wanted to run.

Teddy bumped the end table, and the lamp shook.

"Theodore!" Luke roared. "To your bedroom."

The boy took one look at his father's contorted face and sobbed.

"Now!"

Teddy ran to his bedroom. The look of hurt on her son's face was the proverbial last straw. Belle made for the door. She raced down the dusty drive, running under the waning sunlight. Belle pumped her arms and pushed her speed. Her lungs heaved. Though her chest burned, her throat stung, and her calf muscles blazed with pain, she kept running.

She didn't pause to admire a doe staring from the edge of the trees or listen to the songbirds announcing the day's end. Half a mile down the road, her unfit body rebelled. Stooped over, she braced her arms against her thighs. After she caught her breath, she walked the remaining half mile to the junction in the road. The sky spun a violet hue into the clouds, and moments later, the color bled to shades of gray. She brushed sweat from her face with the end of her apron and inhaled deeply. Belle turned back. At last, she headed up the drive where the farmhouse stood in silhouette against fading light at the horizon. Lamplight glowed from the front windows like eyes scrutinizing her approach. Belle checked the side of the house. The Ford was gone.

"Make sure," Bernie said, "the spark advance lever is all the way out before you start the engine. Here's your throttle lever." He tapped the throttle arm. "Give it a little gas. Always place it in neutral. Hit the starter button with your right foot, and keep your left on the clutch."

Belle concentrated on his instructions but worried she wouldn't remember the correct order. Teddy bounced on the back seat. Inside the house, the baby slept in his crib, his father snoring across from him in bed. Luke had arrived home minutes before dawn. It was Sunday. After two nights of carousing and drinking, Luke wouldn't wake up any time soon.

"Let the clutch out easy," her father-in-law said. "That's it."

The car stalled. "Sorry, Bernie."

"You let out the clutch too fast," he said. "Try again."

This time she managed the right synchronization, and the Ford puttered down the drive. Teddy clapped his hands. "Mama drive."

Belle gripped the wheel as if it might fly away. She straightened her shoulders.

"Now, you're going to brake before you get to the county road," Bernie said. "Make sure you press the clutch in or the engine will die."

"I don't know if I'm ready for that." Belle panicked. He wanted her to drive on the main road. What if another car approached?

"Do what I say and you'll be okay."

Belle shot a quick glance at Bernie. He had more confidence in her than she did. She pressed the clutch and the brake at the same time, a little too quickly. Bernie reached for the dash, and Teddy fell to the floor.

Belle anticipated peals of crying. "Honey, are you okay?"

Teddy pulled himself upright. "Go, Mama. Go."

Belle and Bernie laughed at the little guy, whose wide eyes begged for the adventure to continue.

"Repeat everything you did before," Bernie said. "Let off the brake and let the clutch out slowly. Except turn right this time."

Belle sucked in her breath and repeated the maneuvers. She slowly steered right and the car eased down the dirt road. "I'm doing it! I'm driving."

Her father-in-law grinned. "Guess I make a good instructor."

"Thank you, Bernie." Being able to drive would give her a small measure of freedom. It would be nice to drive to town when she needed a few supplies. Lately, Bernie's rheumatism had flared up and on those days, he barely moved from the rocking chair.

Belle congratulated herself for making a wise decision. What if one of the kids got sick, and Luke was hungover? They slept in the same bed, but that was it. Between the booze, the hangovers, and his cheating, Luke probably had no more desire for her than she did for him. That was one way to prevent another pregnancy, the last thing she needed under the circumstances.

* * *

Belle feared she might explode. She refused to wash any more shirts with lipstick and cheap perfume. That Sunday, she put on a fresh dress and cleaned up the kids.

"Bernie, would you like to go to church with us today?"

"No, no," he said. "You go ahead."

Luke stumbled to the doorway. "Where the hell are you going?" His eyes drooped. His head was probably killing him. Good.

"We're going to a better place." With that, she headed to the Ford with Teddy and the babe. She inched down the drive. Luke probably thought she was leaving him, seeing her dressed up and with both kids in tow. A smile slowly built across her face.

She'd passed the little country church a million times without a thought, the building a mile and a half from the farmhouse. Belle needed some hope in her life and figured church would be a good place to start. She parked the Ford at the back of a dozen cars and gathered the kids. Above the church steeple, two red-tailed hawks circled. That was a good sign.

"Teddy, you be good for Mama. You have to sit still and be quiet."

Teddy nodded, eager for another new experience. She'd packed paper and pencils, wrapped cookies, and brought one of Teddy's favorite toys, a small wooden tractor. She found a seat in the back pew nearest the door. On the opposite side of the aisle, a family with five kids filled the pew. A young woman sat down the pew from Teddy with bowed head, apparently in prayer. On the drive over, the baby had fallen asleep. Belle settled Teddy with paper and pencil, but he preferred gawking at the congregation. The woman next to Teddy opened her eyes and smiled. Belle recognized the strange woman from Main Street.

The woman picked up the pencil and paper meant for Teddy and started drawing. Rude and strange. At the front of the church, three women began to sing as the paper was passed back to Teddy.

"Look Mama. A house." Teddy handed her the drawing.

"Shh," Belle whispered. She examined the picture, a good rendition with graphic detail. It could easily have been a drawing of her grandparents' house. Tears formed at the memory of the farmhouse the tornado had totally obliterated. She glanced again at the paper. On the front porch, a bucket had been drawn with what appeared to be sudsy water. Thoughts returned of the

251

day she came home with chiggers, and her grandmother washed her from head to toe. Belle stared across the pew. The woman stood with eyes closed, swaying back and forth as if there wasn't another person in church but her and Jesus himself.

By the end of the service, Belle was glad she'd come. The preacher had spoken on God's love, how He knows everything we're going through and hears our cries for help. The message was the most comforting thing Belle had heard in a long while. As she made her way from the church, she noticed the strange woman had disappeared. Belle stood in the bright sunlight, shading her eyes with her hand. The woman had vanished like a vision.

"Come on, Teddy," she said. "Let's go home, and Mama will fry us some chicken for dinner."

Teddy surveyed the crowd with wide eyes, excited to see so many people. He stared at a boy around his age. Belle took his hand, and they wove through the mingling parishioners. Two women glanced in her direction; one drew a hand to her mouth and whispered to the other. Belle thought she heard Luke's name. She refused to be cowed by their gossip and smiled. One woman smiled back. The other made a sad face and shook her head.

Belle pulled Teddy to the car and slammed the door. So, I'm the object of pity. That meant everyone knew about Luke's philandering. She hated the idea of rumors almost as much as her husband's despicable ways. Belle slipped into the driver's seat, the baby nestled on the seat next to her. She accelerated, dust swirling behind the car like a funnel cloud.

In front of the farmhouse, she hit the brakes a little too hard and the tires skidded. She opened the door for Teddy, who ran ahead. In the kitchen, Belle dipped the chicken in flour. She slammed the pots and pans.

"Must have been some service." Bernie couldn't mask his smile. "Did he preach hell and brimstone today?"

Belle ignored him and slapped the fry pan on the stove.

"Keep it down in there," Luke shouted from the bedroom.

She deliberately drew two more pots out and clanged them together.

"Good god, woman!" Luke dragged himself from bed and headed for the back door. From the window, she watched him trudge to the outhouse.

The baby! Belle flew from the kitchen. She ran to the car where the infant slept peacefully in the warming sun and drew the baby into her arms. That was the day Belle promised herself no one would ever make her feel inferior again.

She'd hold her head high and never apologize to anyone, not even in her thoughts.

Chapter 34

DURING THE SUMMER OF 1936, a dome of heat locked in place over Oklahoma. Belle blotted her forehead with her grandmother's embroidered handkerchief as the Stilwells gathered at the family plot. Newspapers reported a record of 120° the day before in Alva, Oklahoma, though temperatures in Dry Run hadn't reached that high. The Choctaw elder's deep voice broke the silence at the graveside service for Bernie Stilwell.

"Our brother has passed over to the other side and joined our ancestors."

Over time, her father-in-law had shed his thorns, and they had become good friends. The death of the kind man she'd come to know had left a void in her heart. Teddy had adored his grandfather, and Belle felt her son's loss as an added burden. Beside her, Luke held Jacob while she held Teddy's hand. They stood united for the funeral, but that's where the solidarity ended. The family held a wake for twenty-four hours after Bernie's death. Belle tried to help Teddy understand what was happening, but his confused expression broke her heart. Death was difficult for adults to deal with but harder yet for a child. Whether Teddy comprehended the concept of death or not, the blank face of his grandfather and the horrible stillness of his body registered a dreadful reality.

The Choctaw held a custom of keeping a fire burning for four days after a death. The men had stacked logs at the side of the house in preparation for the event that night. After the service, everyone brought food to the house and gathered for a reception.

"A living person," an elder explained, "has 'shilombish' or spirit, and a 'shilup' or shadow. At night, we dream because our shilombish has left our body and traveled to another place. Our spirits return before we awake.

"When we die, both our shilup and shilombish leave our body. The shilup may remain on earth as a ghost for a long time while the shilombish stays only for a few days or months. The shilombish makes a long westward journey to the Land of Ghost, to where all our People gather."

For the next two evenings, Luke's family took turns tending the fire throughout the night. By the third night, a fresh stack of logs were left by the fire pit. Belle realized the family assumed Luke would keep the fire going. Not to her surprise, her husband bolted after supper. Once the children fell asleep, Belle returned to the smoldering fire and fanned the flames, adding wood until the fire blazed three feet into the air. Though Bernie's own son had abandoned him, she stationed herself by the fire and honored her fatherin-law with the mourning ritual.

Singing the few Comanche songs she learned as a child, she interlaced them with English and sang for the man who had loved her children, who taught her to drive a car, and who thanked her for every meal she ever prepared for him. She cried for losing another person she loved.

As she tended the fire on the fourth night, a peculiar sadness enveloped her. Darkness encircled her, encroaching with a deep sense of desertion. Bernie had been a light in her home, a candle that burned amid the darkness of her marriage. He had left her all alone.

In the distance, an owl hooted. The sad who-hooing reached into the shadows, and minutes later three coyotes yipped somewhere in the hills. Then the night was still. The fire crackled and embers spit. A coolness settled on her forehead. Strange because the temperature remained in the nineties, refusing to cool after the heat of the day.

Exhausted from two nights of keeping the fire manned, Belle forced herself to stand. She sang a sad Comanche song and danced slowly around the campfire. Again a stroke of cold brushed her forehead. The odd sensation vanished as quickly as it had come. She returned to the chair, leaned back, and gazed at the stars. A galaxy of lights sparkled across the heavens.

A chill swept across her skin again, a cool ribbon the width of a finger. An owl hooted from the woods. The day of the funeral reception, Lilith had leaned into Belle as they washed dishes. "Many believe," she whispered, "a person's spirit returns to say goodbye to loved ones before it journeys to the next world."

Whoo hoo hoo. That was it—Bernie had stroked her forehead. With her head arched to the heavens, she thanked him for every kindness he had shown her.

Belle grew tired of worrying about the dreadful heat taxing the fields of corn, about how many times she must mend their clothes, and whether Luke was tending to the cattle as he should. She ached to escape the house and the never-ending chores of cooking and cleaning. When Lilith showed up one morning with a bag of hand-me-downs for Teddy, Belle saw her opportunity. "Teddy loves riding the horse. Would you mind taking the baby?"

"I'd love to watch this little guy." Lilith loved babies, and Jacob had been an easy baby from the start.

She kissed Lilith's cheek. "Teddy, we're going riding."

"Yippee!" He tugged at her hand. "Let's go."

Belle dragged the blanket and saddle from the shed. Teddy watched her brush the mare's back with the currycomb.

"See how I ease the bit into her mouth?" Though he was too young to bridle the horse, her instructions would make Teddy feel important. "Then loop the bridle gently over the ears. Never be rough with a horse's ears."

Teddy nodded. She positioned him at the front of the saddle and placed her foot in the stirrup. She hitched herself up, and they headed down the road. The high wispy clouds held little promise of rain, but they would prevent the triple-digit temperatures Oklahomans had suffered lately.

Teddy gestured toward cows, sheep, and dogs as they passed neighboring farms. She pointed out a deer that studied their slow passing. To Teddy, riding a horse was a grand adventure. They trotted toward town where a promised treat awaited at the drugstore soda fountain. Belle's egg money came in handy.

On Dry Run's Main Street, Belle spotted her sister-in-law, Anna, and her two daughters. She reined the horse to the side of the street where they dismounted and tied the mare to a post.

"Why it's the Pony Express." Anna stooped to Teddy's eye level and smoothed the wild hair at his crown. "Did you like riding the horse?" Teddy nodded double time, a grin on his face. His cousins, Amber and Joy, each took a hand, eager to mother the little boy.

"I'm going to treat Teddy—" Belle froze at the look on her sister-inlaw's face and followed her gaze to Luke's car. Her husband drove down Main Street in animated conversation with someone on the passenger side. A blonde stretched her arm across the seat between them.

"Watch Teddy." Belle untied the horse and mounted. She kicked the horse's sides and caught up with the car, glaring at the harlot. The white woman startled at the sight of Belle only arms-length from the car. With a smile still on his face, Luke glanced over and saw Belle astride the trotting horse. Anger flashed in his eyes.

"Go home, Belle!" He accelerated the car.

Belle spurred the horse into a run and matched the car's speed. Luke gunned the engine but realized too late he was gaining on the bumper of a slow-moving truck. Another car approached on the opposite side of the street. He jerked the steering wheel and careened in front of the horse. In a split second, she imagined her motherless children. The horse reared, and Belle plunged to the ground. Luke's car accelerated as her breath was wrenched away. Lying on the ground, she struggled to breathe.

Brown moccasins appeared near her head, and a woman helped her to a sitting position. Belle clutched her ribs and moaned. The odd woman from church knelt beside her.

"Let me check." The woman's fingers rolled over her ribcage on each side. "Good news, they're not broken." The woman pursed her lips. "Bad news, they'll feel like the blazes for a day or two." She helped Belle to her feet.

About to thank her, she saw the stranger's gaze drift toward the horse in the distance.

"That's only trouble. Digging a hole." The woman shook her head.

Despite her pain, Belle's jaw stiffened. Who was she to tell her what to do when it came to her husband?

A farmer in bib overalls appeared leading the horse by the reins. "Is she all right?"

"I'm fine." Belle dusted herself off and groaned mid-gesture.

Footsteps thudded from behind. Her nieces ran up wide-eyed, and Anna lagged behind with Teddy in hand.

"Are you hurt?" Anna took Belle's arm and escorted her to the sidewalk. Belle grimaced upon sitting on an iron bench. "Mama, are you broken?" Teddy asked.

"A little bit, Teddy, but I'll be okay."

The helpful stranger crossed the street and retreated. "Who is that woman?"

"That's Shikoba, Choctaw for feather." Anna said. "Her birth name is Shirley Hanks. Lives west of town, about a mile from your place."

That's only trouble. Reluctantly, Belle had to admit the only thing she'd gained from chasing her husband was a bruised ribcage.

"I'll take you home," Anna said. "I'll send Carl back for the horse."

"First, we have to go to the drugstore. I promised Teddy a treat. Help me up." She groaned. "Let's go get that soda, Teddy."

Anna never mentioned the other woman with her brother. Belle knew enough not to say a word. She'd found the old saying, blood ran thicker than water, to be true.

At the drugstore counter, Teddy slurped a pink frothy drink through a straw. Her son was happy and carefree, but Belle was not. If Luke flaunted his whore in broad daylight, what was next? Would he move in with the woman? With Bernie gone, he might kick Belle out of the farmhouse. Surely, he wouldn't take the children. But anything might happen with a man so brazen as to be seen in town with his hussy.

Teddy blew bubbles with his straw, and the girls giggled. Something inside Belle screamed for action, but what?

Days passed in tense repetition. Days became weeks. Belle prepared breakfast for the man she abhorred. Luke spoke only to the children. Her husband's handsome profile was like the rosary pea that adorned twisting vines, the bright red pods attractive but toxic. The black spot on the end of each pea warned of the vine's poisonous seed.

Luke kissed the boys goodbye before he checked on the cattle. He never came home for lunch. Seldom did he come home for dinner. When he did, she relinquished the bed and slept on the lumpy sofa.

One morning, Teddy came up to her. "Mama mad at Daddy?"

"Oh, honey." What could she say to her little boy? "Daddy's sad since Grandpa Bernie passed."

"I miss Grandpa." Teddy looked up, his little face cocked. "I miss Daddy, too, but he hasn't passed to the other side."

Belle's heart dropped. Not only had she lost a husband, but her sons had lost a father.

Behind the house, moonlight lit the bedposts of an old iron bed and turned rusty rails bronze. The August heat drove Belle outside, dragging a feather-tick mattress. Indoors she had tossed in bed, the still, hot air unbearable. Without a breeze to cool the interior, the open windows brought no relief. The children slept fitfully, their little heads damp with sweat.

Teddy hopped on the mattress. The novelty of sleeping outside had only energized him.

"Honey, lay down," she whispered. "If we stay very quiet, we might hear a coyote. Look up and you can see the stars." The baby drifted off, the slight decrease in temperature enough to soothe him to sleep.

Lying on her back, she pointed to the North Star and the Big Dipper. "See how that makes a big dipper like the one in the cistern? See the long handle?"

"I'm thirsty, Mama."

Belle had come prepared. She leaned over the bed for the enamel pitcher and poured water into a tin cup. She lay back. If she remained still, an occasional current of air flowed across her body, so slight it might have otherwise gone undetected. Bernie had said he and his wife had used the bed many times on hot Oklahoma nights. Belle wished she had known Luke's mother. From the little Bernie told her, she gathered they had a good marriage. The kind she assumed she'd have with Luke. But she was beyond wishing and dreaming. Most days, even beyond hurting. She had her boys, and they filled her heart.

"Tell me a story," Teddy pleaded. "Please, Mama."

"I'll tell you a tale about Comanche warriors. You're three-quarters Comanche, you know."

"I know, Mama. Chok-ta too."

"That's right, Teddy. Quarter Choctaw from Daddy." She settled Teddy on the downy mattress. "A long time ago, long before Oklahoma was considered Indian Territory, the Comanche people traveled long distances. Famous for their skills on horseback, Comanche warriors had no match. They could hang over the side of a horse, shoot their arrows, and slip back on." She paused. "Wouldn't you like to see that?" Teddy nodded vigorously.

"The fierce warriors protected their people and guarded their—"

A motor rumbled in the distance. Probably someone out looking for moonshine or a party down by the creek. Belle prayed it wasn't Luke. He'd wonder where they were. She'd have to get out of bed and explain. The vehicle's lights appeared on the main road. After a moment, the headlights turned up the drive. Shoot. She turned to tell Teddy to stay put, but he had fallen asleep. She threw her bare legs over the mattress, the soles of her feet drawing in the warm earth. Belle rounded the corner of the house and saw a car in place of the old Ford. She slipped back behind the house. Inside, the shotgun was propped behind the front door. Outside, Belle was defenseless. The front door creaked.

"Belle!" A man's voice shouted from the house. "Belle, where are you?"

The screen door slammed, and it took a moment before she recognized Leon's voice. She met him on the front stoop. In the moonlight, dread etched across Leon's face.

"Leon?"

His loud sigh escaped on the still air. "Where are the kids?"

"We're sleeping on the old iron bed outside. Why are you here at this hour?"

"Sit down, Belle."

"Tell me, Leon."

"I'm afraid that..." Leon's voice caught, and he cleared his throat. "It's Luke, Belle. He's had an accident."

"What are you saying?" The haunting call of an owl rose behind the house. Whoo ooo.

"He was in a car accident on the other side of town. Two miles out."

"Let me put something on." She headed for the door, aiming to drape one of her husband's shirts over her nightgown.

Leon grabbed her wrist. She glared, and he released her.

"Belle...he's gone."

"Help me get the children," she ordered, "and take me to him."

"He's dead, Belle."

"Take me now, Leon!"

He clutched her upper arm. "Belle, there was a fire. The car's ablaze." Her legs buckled.

Leon guided her to the stoop. He sat beside her, shoulders slumped. "I can stay the night."

Belle refused. Relief crossed his face when she asked him to return in the morning.

"See you tomorrow then." He stood and paused a moment before he headed to his car.

She watched the rear lights of the Plymouth slowly fade. The vehicle turned, lit up the trees for a moment, and vanished. Belle moaned, rocking back and forth like a child.

Duty cut her grief short. Her children needed watching. With a child snuggled on each side, she spent the night in the old bed, staring at the heavens.

Chapter 35

LEON ARRIVED THE NEXT MORNING with bloodshot eyes and matted hair. Obviously, he hadn't slept either. They dropped the children off with Leon's neighbor because she didn't want the children around relatives until she could break the news to Teddy. From there Leon drove her to the site of the accident.

The night before, Leon told her the car had flown off the road on a blind curve and settled in a ditch. But neither of them was prepared for the sight they encountered in the light of day. A gaping hole had swallowed the road and the ditch. Only the back bumper of the Ford protruded from the smoking pit.

Leon's face registered astonishment. "What in the world?" "God in heaven!" Belle held a hand to her chest.

Leon exited the car. Belle flung the door open and ran behind him. They stood speechless as they stared into the cavernous hole. Moments later, a patrol car pulled to the side of the road. Gravel crunched beneath the sheriff's boots as he crossed the road and joined them in mute observation.

"It's a damn sinkhole," Sheriff Mason said at last.

Leon gaped. "A sinkhole?"

The sun warmed Belle's arms. A fly buzzed near her face. Was this all a strange dream? But the morning light was too bright, the scene too real.

Luke had never liked Mason. Moonshine surely had something to do with that. The sheriff's ruddy face turned and met Belle's gaze. He quickly shifted to Leon. "My brother's a geologist for the oilfield. He says sinkholes can appear in saturated or dry soil." He turned his back to Belle and lowered his voice. "Witnesses say he was chasing another car driven by Betts Johnson. They'd been seen drinking along the river."

"I'm sure jugs of moonshine packed in the backseat didn't help any," Leon said with bitterness.

A lit cigarette always hung from Luke's lips when he drove. Belle imagined the car bursting into flames from the ignited moonshine. Shikoba's words returned—That's only trouble. Digging a hole. Belle had taken offense, figuring the statement was aimed at her. She stared into the sinkhole, smoke drifting up from the charred automobile. All along, the woman had been talking about Luke. She felt herself sway. It was the last thing she remembered.

Charlie and Jeremy arrived the day before the funeral. Jeremy had grown so tall she wouldn't have recognized him on the street. He used a cane, but his arms and shoulders were muscular. She cried when he hugged her without prompting. "How I've missed you," she said.

"We'll stay at Leon's place," Charlie said. "We don't want to burden you at a time like this."

Belle squeezed Charlie's hand. "Please, I want you to stay here."

"Okay then. We'd be happy to help with the boys." Charlie's eyes misted up. "I'm sorry, Belle. I know what you're going through."

Evidently Leon had not told Charlie about the woman in the other car or the moonshine in the backseat. Her fury rose. She was expected to play the part of the dutiful widow.

"Momma." Teddy tugged at her skirt, his little eyes brimming with tears. "Are you gonna leave, too?"

Belle kneeled in front of him. "Honey, I'll never leave you." She wrapped her arms around him and glanced at Charlie. "First, his grandfather. Then Luke. It's too much for a poor child."

The evening spent with Charlie and Jeremy brought a lift to Belle's spirits. Her heart warmed at the sight of Jeremy playing with her boys. She made cookies and served hot apple cider. Charlie looked puzzled when she suggested they play a game of cards at the kitchen table. He must have thought she was in shock or some strange denial of Luke's death. To Belle, it was a night of reunion and celebration, a night when she didn't have to consider her future.

At the funeral, people stole glances at Belle and whispered behind their hands. Were they gossiping about her lack of tears? Or maybe they were saying Belle had every right not to grieve a husband who died chasing another woman.

Walking back to Leon's car, a hand settled on her shoulder, a touch that both warmed and drew shivers at the same time. She turned and found Shikoba at her side. The woman's eyes glazed with tears, but Belle didn't feel resentment as she might have at someone else's pity. The woman peered into her soul, something no one else could do. Belle handed Jacob to Leon. She hugged Shikoba, and they rocked back and forth together. The woman sang in Choctaw, low and sad, before she released Belle and walked into the trees. Leon nudged Belle's elbow and escorted her to the car. She glanced back as the woman disappeared into the woods like a spirit.

Leon took Belle and the children home where once again a fire would blaze day and night in front of the house.

Charlie had to return to work the next day. Relatives came and went, keeping the traditional fire going. On the third night, Luke's relatives stopped coming. On the fourth evening at dusk, Belle found herself staring at embers in the fire pit. After a few moments of deliberation, she added kindling to the coals. She entered the nearby woods with a lantern and searched for dead limbs to drag back to the fire. Teddy ran ahead and scouted for branches. With the baby strapped to her back, she gathered enough wood to keep the fire burning through the night.

How ironic that the woman Luke had scorned and cheated on was the only one left to mourn his passing. She concentrated on the Luke she'd known in Talihina—light-hearted and handsome. But Luke couldn't deal with the bleakness of life. Some weren't strong enough to struggle against hard times. He didn't have eyes to see the beauty all around him. Teddy looked up at her with his round cheeks and wide eyes, waving a fallen branch. Luke had missed so much of his precious children. Why couldn't they have been enough for him? Why wasn't she?

With the children tucked in bed and the windows open so she could hear their cries, Belle stoked the fire, the snap and crackle of flames the only sound in the gloomy night. Around midnight, the clopping of hooves announced a rider in the pitch-black darkness. She grabbed a sturdy branch from the stack of wood.

A dark form dismounted and approached the fire. A woman's voice drifted in the dark. "Halito."

Belle welcomed her sister-in-law. She was tired of being alone.

"Chim achukma?"

Are you well—Belle had learned that much of Choctaw. The fire lit up a different face altogether, and she gasped. Shikoba!

"Chim achukma?" the woman repeated. Shikoba crouched by the fire and stared into the flames.

"Sa yoshoba," Belle answered. I am lost. The honesty of her answer came as a surprise.

Shikoba rooted for something in her pocket, reached into the fire, and lit the end of a sage stick. The end burned for a moment before she blew out the flame. She rose and began chanting words Belle didn't understand. Shikoba waved the smoke over Belle's head and traced her shoulders and back.

Belle guessed that words of protection were being said over her. After a few moments, Shikoba sat cross-legged beside her.

"You'll be okay." Shikoba smiled. "You and your children."

Belle wished she could find comfort in that, but she couldn't.

Shikoba pulled a cloth bundle from her pocket and offered it to Belle. "Herbs for tea. Healing herbs. Comforting."

At once, everything made sense. "You're a medicine woman."

The corners of Shikoba's mouth turned up slightly. "Some call me that."

"What do you say?" Belle couldn't help but smile.

"Some call me crazy." Shikoba drew in the dirt with a stick. She looked up and smiled broadly. The young woman's plain face transformed into a thing of beauty. "Suppose both are true."

"Some call me the Scorned Wasápe," Belle said. "That's Comanche for bear."

"Aw, we're a good pair, then." Firelight flickered in her eyes.

Belle reached for Shikoba's hand and squeezed. Embarrassed, she pulled her hand away. Why did she feel so familiar with this strange woman?

It was as if she were a sister or a long-lost friend.

"You're a strong woman."

"I don't know about that." Belle stared into the fire. The land and the farmhouse turned back to Leon now. He was the eldest son. Though the family might allow her to stay in the house, Belle worried they would send her away. That wouldn't be the Indian way, but still she worried. With two small children, she could contribute little to the workings of the farm.

"You're a strong lost woman then." Shikoba folded her hands and made a show of tossing them over her lap. She turned and looked at Belle with upraised brows.

They burst out laughing.

"I have an idea," Belle said. "You sing a song. Then I'll sing one." Shikoba nodded.

"Nothing sad. I can't take one more sad thing. You begin."

Shikoba rolled her lips for a moment then jumped to her feet and sang. "Everyone's goin' down to the river, to the river of love." She shuffled her feet and waved her hands. "Goin' down to the river to see all the People baptized." Belle joined in with clapping.

"Little Jessie's kissin' Jimmy back in the woods. Another baby's gonna need baptizin' down at the river. Six months later, Jimmy's disappeared. Jessie's singing, my baby's done gone and left me. Done left me with a little bitty baby.

"But Jessie finds work for a woman on the hill. Now Jessie's singing, Me and my baby, we're okay. We go to church on Sunday and head down the hill to dance with all the People.

"Everyone's goin' down to the river," Shikoba waved Belle to join in, "to the river of love." The two women clapped and danced around the fire. "Goin' down to the river to see all the People baptized. Little Jessie's kissin' Jimmy back in the woods. Another baby's gonna need baptizin'…"

Even as Belle sang the lyrics, she recognized the potion the young Medicine Woman served up for her benefit. Her message was obvious. Through the good and the bad, the cycle of life continued. It was up to Belle to keep dancing.

Chapter 36

FROM THE TOP OF THE cellar stairs, a shaft of light lit the blue Mason jars like jewels in a pirate ship's belly. The canned food was precious to Belle. The jars represented hours of work in the garden and sweat-soaked days processing food in the kitchen, but most of all, they provided security. Her family would have food for the following year: canned beef, applesauce, green beans, pickles, tomatoes, and corn. Belle grabbed a jar of applesauce and ascended the stairs. She was halfway up when something blocked the light. The silhouette of a man loomed overhead, barring the doorway.

Belle's heart pounded. By now, everyone knew she lived alone in the farmhouse with two young children. Hoboes and drifters abounded. The homeless begged for handouts and even had their own system of communication: marks on a fencepost, symbols on the side of a barn. She glanced at the jar in her hand. Shards of smashed glass would serve as a knife.

"Belle?" A deep voice broke the quiet.

She didn't move.

"Are you down there?" he said. "It's me, Leon."

She took a deep breath. "Be right there." She stepped into the bright September light and shaded her eyes.

"Mornin', Belle."

Her eyes slowly focused. "Hello, Leon." She forced a smile. "Just getting a jar of applesauce for the boys. Would you like a cup of coffee?"

"That sounds good."

Leon walked beside her without talking. It had been six weeks since Luke's funeral. Belle hoped this visit revolved around cattle or harvesting hay.

The boys were down for their naps. She prepared coffee and set two cups on the table. Belle removed a stoneware pitcher from the icebox and set the cream next to the sugar bowl. She glanced at her lean brother-in-law. His muscular arms revealed he was a hard worker. Leon hadn't inherited his brother's good looks, but he possessed a strong, masculine face. An easygoing man by nature, he'd never shown himself to be angry or for that matter, even disgruntled.

There was an uncomfortable silence as they waited for the coffee to perk.

"How are your boys, Leon?" Her brother-in-law's two boys were ages six and eight.

"Doing well." Leon cleared his throat. "And yours?"

"They're good." She poured coffee in each cup and sat across the table. "Healthy as a pair of oxen." What was the reason for his visit?

"That's good to hear." He blew at the steam rising from his cup.

"Would you like some carrot cake?" She glanced at him and looked away. "Made it yesterday, but it stays moist for days." "That sounds good," he said. "I like carrot cake." She served him a slice on a dessert plate.

Leon forked a mouthful. "Mmm, you're a good cook, Belle."

"Thank you." She wished he'd get on to what brought him. Within minutes, only crumbs were left.

Leon placed the fork down and pushed the plate back. "Belle, I want to talk to you about something."

She set her cup down and held her breath. Her future was at stake. The pit of her stomach confirmed it.

Leon gazed at the oilcloth. "After my wife died, I didn't know how I was going to make it with two boys and all. I know it can't be easy for you, either."

"I'm making do." She straightened and lifted her chin. "We're getting by fine." Belle turned from his piercing look.

"I was thinking," he said. "I'm alone with my two boys, and you're alone with your two little ones."

Belle stood abruptly and the plates clattered. She cleared the dishes.

Leon shoved in his chair. "We could combine our families. It'd be good for everyone, don't you think?"

Belle swung around. "Or what? You'll kick me off the place?"

"I didn't say that." His face registered hurt and something else— offense? His voice lowered. "I'd never do that to a relative."

Belle swung a dishtowel over one shoulder. "I'm sorry, Leon. I've been…" She stopped. Why admit she'd been worrying about her situation? Best not to give him any ideas.

Leon brushed her hand lightly, his touch warm. She struggled to keep from shaking off his hand.

He stepped back. "Think about it, Belle. That's all I ask." He turned toward the door and adjusted his cap. "If you need anything, let me know." The door closed softly.

Belle slumped in the kitchen chair. Before she had time to think, Jacob began crying. Teddy wandered into the room, rubbing his eyes.

"I'm hungry." Teddy crawled onto her lap. "Mama, why you crying?"

Teddy helped her make sandwiches. She wrapped them along with cookies in a bandana, tied it to a stick, and handed it to him. They walked to the creek. Teddy pretended he was a hobo, traveling to places unknown. In the ditch, sunflowers drooped, heads heavy with seed. Chalky dust powdered grass and weeds. Belle carried Jacob in one arm and carted a jug of lemonade. Their footsteps stirred up dust from the road.

Under the shade of blackjack oak, they enjoyed their picnic. Teddy dug in the sand, building roads and what looked like a farmstead. Jacob sat nearby and picked small rocks from the dirt. Belle mulled over Leon's suggestion. The man needed a housekeeper, cook, and overseer of his children. A marriage of convenience would be more his convenience than hers. What would she gain? Two more children to care for and three more mouths to feed. A shiver shimmied down her back. She couldn't imagine sharing the marriage bed with her brother-in-law. For months she hadn't even shared it with Luke.

What did a man bring to a marriage anyway? More work for a woman. More babies. Her stomach twisted at the thought. She couldn't imagine more children, not with a man she didn't love. Hell's bells. Why couldn't Leon have left them alone? All she wanted was to live in peace with her two boys. Why did he have to complicate everything? She pitched a rock across the stream. The boys raised their heads and stared at their mother.

"How about a contest, boys?" She held up a two-inch stone. "Let's make a pile of rocks this size, no bigger. Then we'll see how far we can throw them."

Teddy stood with a glint in his eyes. Within minutes, he stacked half a dozen rocks. Jacob toddled along the creek side and searched for smaller stones. While the boys gathered rocks, Belle slung more stones across the creek, pitching them with all her might.

"Momma, wait for us!" Teddy frowned.

"Momma's just warming up," she said. She aimed at Leon's face transposed on a boulder across the creek. The rock hit its target and pinged under the canopy of trees. She pitched another stone. And another. Her tension burned away.

She allowed Teddy to win the rock-throwing contest and announced Jacob as runner up. On their return home, Belle warned the boys away from a row of short, black trunks. She explained the bodark trees produced horse apples or, as others called them, hedge apples or Osage oranges. "Be careful. There's lots of thorns." She found three on the ground, one for each to carry home. Her grandmother had used them to ward off pests, but Belle merely liked their novelty.

Delighted at their unusual gifts, the boys examined the globes that resembled green brains. Bernie had told her the trees were planted in hedgerows by early settlers, who used them as prickly fences across the prairie. Over the years, they had spread across the state.

"Bumpy balls," Teddy said. Jacob's eyes grew wide as he held the grapefruit-size sphere.

"You can call them monkey balls if you want." She stooped. "Jacob, smell the Osage orange." Belle demonstrated by drawing the globe to her nose.

"Ooh." Jacob stretched out his tongue.

"Monkey balls, Mama," Teddy frowned.

"Sorry, the monkey ball." She laughed. "Doesn't it smell like an orange?"

Teddy nodded and Jacob giggled.

Further down the road, they passed the entrance to a farmhouse.

"Mama, look!"

Three limp snakes dangled from an overhanging limb. Belle recognized the superstition. Desperate for moisture, some people believed hanging snakes upside down would draw rain.

On Leon's unexpected visit, he had mentioned the poor hay crop and the need for selling half the cattle. He wouldn't be able to feed the animals through the winter. Belle was grateful for the surplus canned food from last year. This year's garden had not done as well.

His proposal took over her thoughts. In her imagination, she saw herself running away, racing down the road as a young girl, but this time with a child under each arm. Running to somewhere, anywhere. Would the Talihina hospital rehire her? Unlikely, her position easily filled. And who would watch the boys if she worked? She couldn't bear the thought of another woman watching her children.

What were her options? Before Leon's proposal, there was a good chance the family would have allowed her to stay in the farmhouse. Out of charity, they might donate a cow every year. But now that Leon had provided an offer that would take care of her children's needs and her own, her refusal would be seen as an affront to the family. That could lead nowhere but to everyone's disapproval. Leon might marry someone else, and that wife might insist Belle be put off the family farm. Perhaps, one of the sisters-inlaw would be gracious enough to take her in. Belle dreaded that idea. She didn't want to live under another woman's jurisdiction.

There was only one option. Her shoulders slumped. She'd have to marry her brother-in-law.

Chapter 37

BELLE INSISTED ON NOT MAKING a fuss about the wedding. She suggested the justice of the peace, and Leon agreed.

She wore the lace-trimmed dress from her first wedding. The dress had no sentimental value, not after what she'd gone through with Luke. Leon surprised her in a dress suit and tie, looking quite smart and dignified. Afterward, the justice's wife smiled and remarked they made a handsome couple. As they turned to leave, Belle caught their reflection in the windowpane. Alongside Leon's broad shoulders and thick hair, her dark hair cascaded down her shoulders in soft waves, her figure still intact after two children. Their image gave credence to the matron's remarks. If the woman only knew.

They arrived at Leon's farm along the creek, his house surrounded by a swarm of trucks and wagons. Belle swung her head toward Leon.

"Honest, I didn't know anything about this," he said. "I told Lilith we didn't want a reception."

Belle gritted her teeth and studied the house. At least the exterior donned a fresh coat of paint, and the shutters hung straight.

Leon opened the front door for her and applause exploded. All at once, they were caught in a huddle of embraces, handshakes, and congratulations. Belle forced a smile and carried on. At the first opportunity, she retreated to the kitchen.

Pots of food steamed on the stove. Cakes and pies filled the table.

Lilith rushed to Belle and embraced her. "I'm so glad you're remaining part of the family."

That confirmed it. Belle would have been viewed as an unwanted burden if she'd refused Leon's offer of marriage. It brought a small degree of satisfaction in knowing she'd made the right decision, but most of all, her boys would benefit. Teddy ran up and hugged her legs. Jacob toddled close behind, giggling.

After several hours of family, food, and socializing, people drifted from the house. Lilith held Teddy's hand and winked. "I'll take the boys until tomorrow."

"No, no, that's not necessary." Belle struggled for an excuse. "I think it might be too much for the boys." She stood on her tiptoes as Lilith wove through the crowd of women in the kitchen. "You know, too much change at once."

But Lilith was halfway through the living room, ignoring her plea.

After everyone left, Belle replaced all the clean dishes in their rightful places and swept the previously cleaned floor. The scritch of the broom sharpened in the stillness. Leon sat in the living room, reading a newspaper. She wiped down cupboard doors and rewiped the spotless counters. Belle slumped onto a kitchen chair with nothing left to do.

"Belle." Leon leaned against the doorway. "Let's go for a walk."

Relief rolled over her. "Let me grab a sweater." The sun fell low in the sky, color amassing in thin, worthless clouds. She was glad he didn't reach for her hand.

"We can ride horses some evening, if you'd like." He slowed his gait to keep time with her pace.

An idea gleaned from Lilith, she was sure. "That would be nice."

"The boys should get along fine. They've always liked each other." Leon left her side and dropped into the ditch. He pulled at some plants and returned with stalks of dried coneflowers. "They'll make good dried arrangements for the house."

Belle sighed. He was trying too hard. She accepted the stalks, and they continued on. After several minutes of silence, he spoke again.

"I know this isn't what you wanted," he said. "But I'll do my best to make a good life for you and the boys."

Belle stared straight ahead. "I know, Leon. I know you will." She felt like crying, but she didn't. Her decision was made, the ink already dry on the marriage certificate.

On the way back, they walked without talking as the sun painted magenta clouds on the horizon. Under other circumstances, she would have appreciated the scene. Leon talked about selling some cattle before winter arrived and told her she could get any supplies needed for the house. Belle made short, polite replies.

Later, Leon came to bed after she'd extinguished the lantern. She held her breath as the mattress dipped with his weight. After a few minutes, he touched her arm. Belle drew her arms in and stiffened. Leon lay beside her for a long time before he finally mumbled goodnight and rolled on his side.

Belle lay awake long after his snoring filled the bedroom. What had she been thinking when she accepted his proposal? She concentrated on what was best for her boys. What was done, was done.

The boys got along well, but Sam, the eight-year-old, flaunted his resentment of Belle's invasion into his life.

"I hate this food." He shoved the sandwich to the middle of the table. Leon was out rounding up cattle with his brother-in-law.

"It's a long time until dinner," Belle said.

Sam spit on the floor.

"Young man, you clean that up." Belle held a rag in her outstretched hand.

"That's your job." The insolent boy glared in an official standoff.

"It's your job now." She stood with hands at her hips.

"Naw, it's your job," Sam said. "That's the only reason my dad married you."

"Go to your room, immediately!"

The boy walked out with a smirk on his face. Belle narrowed her eyes at Leon's six-year-old, but the younger boy's eyes were cast down. A gentle boy, Amos wouldn't give her any problems. Teddy stared with wide eyes at the foreign scene that had played out before him.

Belle softened her voice. "Boys, as soon as you finish lunch, we'll go on a little expedition to the creek. How does that sound?"

Their faces lit up, and they devoured mouthfuls in their rush to begin the adventure.

The next several nights replayed as they had on their wedding night. Leon would reach for her, his warm breath inches away. She would stiffen and roll over, pretending to be exhausted. Another week passed. Belle returned from tucking the boys in and met Leon in the doorway to the bedroom, a pillow tucked under his arm and a blanket in the other.

"Get your boys, Belle." His face registered all business. "I'll sleep with mine. You sleep with yours."

Her throat caught, and it took a moment to respond. His tall form stood in the darkened living room as she returned to the back bedroom where the boys slept. She cradled Jacob in her arms and nudged Teddy's shoulder. "You're going to sleep with Mama." Teddy groggily followed her to the bedroom. Leon's back was to her as he waited for the transfer.

"Good night," she managed to whisper.

Silence.

That night began their new arrangement. Belle was the official live-in help.

After that, they refrained from conversation unless absolutely necessary. Leon became reclusive, retreating to the living room immediately after meals. She received a thank you after every meal, but Belle figured that was more for an example to the boys. Leon read his newspaper front to back and probably knew every advertisement by heart. With kitchen chores finished, she'd join him in the living room. She became an avid reader of books borrowed from family and neighbors.

Once she looked up from her book to catch Leon's eyes darting away. Belle began to feel sorry for the quiet man. He probably thought he'd made a wise decision—a mother for his children, a father for hers, a spouse for them both. She turned back to her reading. Life wasn't that easy.

After the change in sleeping arrangements, Sam became more unruly. It seemed with the change, he knew he'd won. He didn't give her much trouble after Leon arrived home at the end of the day, but it proved a different story when his father was absent.

Sam would track in mud despite her instructions to leave his boots at the door. He'd drop school books in the middle of the floor. And the same week Teddy found two frogs in her bedroom. The next day a snake slithered from under Belle's bed. She didn't think for a minute it was a coincidence. One night before Leon had returned from helping a neighbor, she coaxed Sam to do his homework.

"Don't have to," he said. "You're not my mother."

"I realize that, but you still have to do your schoolwork."

"Nope." He jutted his chin out. "Don't have to."

Later as she reheated Leon's dinner, she approached him with the matter.

"I'll talk to him," he said. After chewing a mouthful, he placed his fork down. "You wouldn't be picking on the boy because he's mine, would you?"

She stared at him from across the table. "I expect no more than I do from my own boys." She set her jaw.

"I'll talk to him."

After he was done eating, Leon strode to the back bedroom where his boys had retreated after dinner. She slipped into the hall and listened.

"Belle says you refused to do your homework, Sam."

"She ain't my mother."

"She isn't your mother, but you'll do as she says. I don't want to hear that you're not doing your homework again. Understand?"

"Yes, sir."

"I don't want to hear that kind of talk either." Leon's voice rolled stern and low.

"What's that?"

"Don't ever say 'she isn't my mother' again. We all know she isn't, but it's disrespectful to say it."

"Yes, Pa."

Belle dashed to the kitchen and grabbed the dishcloth. Leon's footsteps echoed down the hall and a moment later, he paused in the doorway.

"I talked to the boy. Let me know if he doesn't do his homework again."

She glanced up from the sink. "Thank you, Leon. I appreciate it." He returned to the living room. At least she had that much.

The late October sun warmed the air, ignoring the inevitable shift of seasons. By the time Leon's boys walked up the drive after school, she had a bonfire going.

"Hungry, boys?" They approached the fire.

"Starvin'." Amos watched with wide eyes.

"We're makin' treats," Teddy informed them.

Sam stood slightly back with a frown on his face.

"Look, Sam!" Amos said. "Hershey bars!"

He stood back, but his eyes betrayed the fact his belly was empty.

Belle handed each boy a stick and demonstrated how to spear the marshmallow on the end. "Keep turning the stick, so they don't burn. Like this." She demonstrated. "Then after it's roasted, we'll make a sandwich with chocolate tucked between two graham crackers."

Teddy and Amos held their sticks over the fire. Sam held back.

"Do you want me to fix it for you?" she asked.

"I'll do it myself." He grabbed the stick and skewered a marshmallow.

After two or three s'mores, the younger boys watched the flames, their little bellies satisfied. In the act of placing his blackened marshmallow between the crackers, Sam's marshmallow slid to the ground. He threw an angry look at her. "I hate you." He ran into the house.

Belle had been about to tell him it was okay. He could make another. But his resentment against her ran deep. Amos walked over and touched her arm. "It's okay, Belle. He'll get over it." But she wasn't so sure.

After a few weeks, Leon talked more, discussing the price of cattle, plans he had for building a chicken coop for Belle next spring, and how bad the black blizzards had been in the Oklahoma Panhandle. Belle assumed he had finally accepted their arrangement and decided it best to be civil to each other. She appreciated how he took time in the evening for the boys, hers included. He'd play a card game or roughhouse with the children. She kept an eye on her boys and found he wasn't as rough with them.

One day he returned from town with a package under his arm. Belle was frying chicken in the kitchen. Leon placed the brown paper parcel on the kitchen table.

"Got something for you."

"Oh?" She wiped her hands on her apron and untied the string. It felt like a book. "Oh, my. Gone with the Wind!" Belle glanced at Leon. New books weren't cheap.

"I know you like to read," he said. "The paper's been talking about this one since June."

"Thank you, Leon." She ran her hand over the dust jacket, the title in all capital letters with an illustration of Scarlett in a Southern-belle hoop dress. It was the first new book she'd ever owned. She fought tears. "It's too expensive. You shouldn't have."

"Call it a late wedding present." He turned and left the kitchen.

Was he expecting something in return for the gift? She was watchful for the next few weeks, but Leon never approached her. Belle felt ashamed. Leon was simply a kind man.

One cool morning in November, Belle and the boys accompanied Leon to town. She needed a few supplies from the grocery and the dry-goods store. An hour later, she waited in the Plymouth with the boys. Leon said he purchased the four-door sedan in 1930 before he knew how bad a turn the Depression would take. She pointed out how well the car worked with their four boys.

Anxious to get home, she glanced across the street at the hardware store and spotted Leon talking with an attractive woman. Whatever the conversation, he sure was laughing. The white woman smiled a lot. Leon's physique was not altogether unattractive—tall, wide shouldered with a trim waist and hips. The pretty woman's cheeks held a touch of rouge or was it the chill? It seemed forever before Leon finally crossed the street to their car.

"All set?" Leon slid into the driver's seat.

"We've been waiting for you." She hoped he got her meaning.

The ignition fired, and Leon pulled away from the curb. The boys giggled in the backseat at something one of them had said.

"Good friend?" she asked.

"Who?"

Was he serious? "The woman you were talking with in front of the hardware store."

"Oh, Francis. Francis Walker." Leon steered the Plymouth west toward home. "We went to school together."

Belle noted the leafless trees as they drove down the county road. She glanced over her shoulder and found her boys asleep. Amos looked droopy eyed, but Sam stared glumly out the side window.

"Why didn't you marry her?" Belle glanced at the profile of Leon's face. She supposed some women would think he was just fine enough.

Leon pulled into their drive and turned to Belle. "You wouldn't be jealous now, would you, Belle?" His right eyebrow lifted.

Belle turned and stared straight ahead. "I've no reason to be."

Leon parked the car at the side of the house. The boys awoke and piled out of the vehicle. Belle went for the door handle, but Leon's hand stopped her. She looked down at his arm and flashed a look at him.

"I'm not Luke." He stared into her eyes. "I'm not my brother."

She nodded, speechless. He moved his hand and cupped her face. Despite her best intentions, warm tears filled her eyes. "Thank you." She fumbled for the door.

Leon joined the boys. "Hey guys, wanna play catch?"

Belle hurried into the house and started dinner. Had she been jealous? That didn't make sense. Theirs was just a sorry marriage of convenience.

The next afternoon, a knock came at the front door. To Belle's surprise, Shikoba stood on her front porch.

"Come in." Belle swept her arm towards the living room.

Shikoba wore a plain blue housedress, a yellow sweater, and moccasins. With outstretched arms, she offered a jar of canned peaches and beamed. "Welcome to the neighborhood."

"Thank you." Belle peered behind her, but the drive was empty.

"Peppermint and chamomile for tea." Shikoba dangled a drawstring bag.

"That would go good with the apple pie I baked this morning." She motioned toward the kitchen.

Belle poured hot water. "You had a long walk."

"Good for the legs. Would have come sooner, but I wanted you to settle in first."

"We should get together more often," Belle said.

"My Jed and Leon are good buddies," Shikoba said. "'Spect we'll get together more often than you might like."

"Jed?"

"My husband." Shikoba caught her eye. "Ah, you thought the strange medicine woman was a recluse."

"Oh, no, no." Belle flushed. "Well, actually…yes." Shikoba laughed and Belle joined in.

"Where are the boys?" Shikoba glanced around.

"They're napping. It's my favorite time of day."

Shikoba sipped at her tea. "How are the newlyweds?"

"Oh, dear." Tea leaves settled at the bottom of her cup. "I'm afraid it's a marriage of convenience. Leon needed a woman to help with his boys and I…I had to think of my own children. They're so young."

"I see." Shikoba glanced out the window. "The scorned Wasápe won't mate again."

"How…" Belle stared. "How did you know?"

"It's obvious." She stirred a teaspoon of sugar into her tea. "It's written on your face." She glanced up shyly. "And I also had a dream the day you married."

"A dream?" Belle shivered at the earlier prophecy of Luke's death. Did she want to hear about Shikoba's dreams and visions?

Shikoba closed her eyes. "The bear won't lie down with a buck, but a doe will lie down with a lion."

The cryptic saying sounded like a Bible passage. "What does that mean?" Belle's stomach knotted.

"How do I know?" Shikoba laughed. "I receive the visions. Don't always know what they mean. Thank the Lord, for that."

Belle had never considered that having Shikoba's gift might not be something a person necessarily embraced. Who would want to know the future? No one could change it anyway.

"Maybe it was just an ordinary dream," Belle said. "You do have ordinary dreams, right?"

"Could be, I suppose."

They discussed uses of herbs. Shikoba was familiar with the healing properties of many local plants. She'd be a good resource.

Shikoba stood to leave. "Next time, come and see me. You told me you learned how to drive."

Belle escorted her to the door, Shikoba's dream niggling at her thoughts. They hugged on the porch.

Shikoba narrowed her eyes. "Do I make you nervous?"

"Of course not." Belle smiled, full of confidence. "You're my friend."

Shikoba's eyes brightened, and she looked relieved. "See you soon." She waved and ran down the road.

Another runner! Belle smiled at the connection. She went to check on her sons. They would be waking soon, and the older boys were due home at any moment. She sighed. Belle hadn't been honest. Shikoba's visions scared the hell out of her.

Chapter 38

Sam became more cunning in his rebellion. He did as he was told but with the weakest of intentions. If she asked the older boys to fetch wood for the cast-iron stove, Amos would fill his arms while Sam brought two scrawny pieces. If she asked Sam to retrieve the mail, he'd bring half. Belle figured that out one afternoon. On a hunch, she walked down the lane and opened the mailbox where she found the remaining letters. Despite how hard Belle worked to treat him kindly, Sam wasn't about to warm up to her.

Trees held color like a quilt, maroon, rust, and gold patches ablaze along every road and shelterbelt. Albert Hawkins' invitation to his barn dance that Saturday added a festive note to the season. Albert's barn had a potbelly stove for heating, and the Hawkins figured since the crops were in and the cattle off to market, they were all due for a party. The old grandmothers would watch younger children in the house. Everyone brought a dish to share. Belle made four pies: two Dutch apple, a pumpkin, and a tart cherry. She looked forward to getting out of the house and visiting with other women.

Late that afternoon, Leon hummed as he drove the family to the dance. It appeared he needed a break, too. Upon arrival, the boys raced ahead to the barn, excited to play with other children. Leon helped her cart pies to tables set up outside the barn.

"These will be the first to go," he said. "You're the best pie maker around these parts."

Belle smiled. "Thanks for helping." At least he was appreciative of her cooking. Heaven knew she did enough of it.

Belle left Leon with the men gathered at the side of the barn. Some smoked and others chewed a stem of grass while they discussed the price of seed and cattle. She caught up with Amos and took him aside. "Keep an eye on the younger boys. If you want to go off and play, come and get me. Okay?"

He smiled up at her. "Sure, Belle."

Belle kissed his cheek and patted him on the shoulder. Unlike his brother, Amos enjoyed having her around, and she was growing attached to the sweet boy.

Belle visited with Lilith and caught up on family news. Minnie Hawkins asked for Belle's recipe for her Dutch apple pie as her husband had raved about it ever since stopping by to see Leon last week. A wrought-iron triangle clanged, effectively ending all conversation. Albert shouted, "Time to eat. Gather the young 'uns and fill your plates." Belle gathered the four boys, and Leon joined them in line. The assortment of food spread over the tables was incredible. In such hard times, a feast blessed the spirit.

Once they filled their plates, she spread a blanket on the barn floor, knowing there wouldn't be enough chairs and stools for everyone. Dust motes spun in the air, and a lingering smell of manure arose on occasion.

Leon playfully tugged at Sam's ear. "Did you get some of Belle's pie?"

The boy shook his head vehemently. "Don't want any." He flashed his eyes at her and back at his plate.

Belle ignored the look. What had she done to incur the boy's anger? She couldn't come up with a single thing.

After everyone had eaten, the musicians shuffled back to the rear of the barn. Teddy and Jacob swayed to the rhythm of fiddles, banjos, and a jug. Belle surveyed the crowd. She hadn't seen that many carefree faces for a long time. The gathering was a rare treat for everyone, and the music took troubled minds off the hardscrabble times.

At seven o'clock, she led Teddy and Jacob to the Hawkin's house.

"Aw, Mama," Teddy said. "Do we have to?"

"There'll be other kids your age there, and I know for a fact the grandmas will tell you stories."

"Better be stories about panthers and bears."

"I bet if you ask them, they'll tell those stories, too."

She kissed them and returned to the barn. Belle leaned against the doorway as the band embarked on a new song.

"Whiskey, rye whiskey, I cry," an elderly man sang. "If I don't get my whiskey, surely I'll die. If hard times don't get me, I'll live till I die." It could have been a song about Luke. She gritted her teeth at the thought of how moonshine had ruined their marriage.

An arm settled around her shoulders. "Got the boys settled down?"

She gazed up at Leon and nodded. "I was just about to look for Sam and Amos."

He pointed to the south end of the barn where the boys drank punch and laughed with their cousins. His arm remained in place. "This is a good thing, isn't it Belle? Folks don't get enough time to laugh and enjoy themselves."

She'd seen a few men drinking from flasks at the side of the barn, but Belle didn't detect the smell of alcohol on Leon's breath. That was a good thing. The band moved on to another song with a lively tune called "Cripple Creek."

"Let's dance." Leon grabbed her hand, and they joined couples dancing in the middle of the barn. He twirled her, and they high-stepped around the floor.

"Going up to Cripple Creek to have a little fun," the musician sang. Belle's long hair swung as around they went. She'd forgotten how much she loved to dance. The song ended, and they moved to the edge of the dance floor. Flushed, Belle fanned her face.

"I'll get you some punch." Leon headed toward makeshift tables formed from boards and sawhorses where older women served refreshments.

Belle couldn't help but smile at all the happy faces. She'd almost forgotten what is was like to have a good time.

Leon held out a cup of punch.

"Thank you." She emptied the cup in a few gulps.

Leon laughed and handed her his cup. "I'll get another."

Belle tapped her foot to the beat. Albert's son, Jordan, strutted up and asked her to dance. The young man was quite attractive. "Why, sure," she said.

She could dance all night if her legs held up. The song ended, and Jordan thanked her for the dance. Leon watched from the sidelines where he drank punch. No sooner had she joined him than he set down his cup and pulled her back on the dance floor.

Grateful for the slow tempo, she welcomed a break from the rollicking beat of bluegrass. Unaccustomed to so much dancing, her legs ached. Leon's arm pressed her close, and his warm breath rolled against her neck. Cologne lifted from his collar. The hardness of his shoulders and strong arms beneath her hands came as a surprise. He was her husband. He was a stranger. Her emotions jumped like a banjo player's fingers across metal strings.

Leon kissed the side of her neck, and the sensation shot through her body. She wanted to run but ached to kiss him in return. The song ended, and she backed out of his embrace.

"I'll check on the boys," she said. Before he could respond, Belle was halfway to the dessert table. Leon was right. Only crumbs remained in her pie tins.

Amos strolled up to her. "Belle, I saw you and Pa dancing. It looked like fun."

"Dancing is great fun, Amos." She tweaked his round cheeks.

"You were smiling at each other."

She studied his face. It must be obvious to the children that their marriage was a sham. Did that have something to do with Sam's cold treatment?

Leon returned to her side. "S'pose we should be getting home." He tousled Amos's hair.

"Do we have to, Pa?"

"It's getting cold, and its time for young boys to be in bed."

Belle didn't want the night to end either, but Leon had made a decision. He gestured to Sam across the room, and the boy joined them.

"Darn, I'm not ready to go." The boy pouted.

"Ready or not, we're going," Leon said.

Belle threaded her hand into the crook of Leon's arm. He turned to Belle. "I'll pull the car up to the house." A sense of disappointment arose that they wouldn't be walking together. Still confused about what had transpired on the dance floor, she avoided his eyes.

The ride back was quiet. By the time they arrived home, the children had fallen asleep. Leon offered to carry the little guys into the house. Belle woke the older boys and escorted them inside. Sam and Amos shuffled off to their bedroom. Would Leon suggest the boys all sleep together tonight? Did she want him in her bedroom?

Behind her, the front door opened, and Leon crossed the room, cradling Jacob in his arms. Without a word, he carried him into Belle's bed. Well, that was that. She put away a pan left to dry in the sink. The thud of the door alerted her to Leon's return. Teddy's droopy eyes opened for a moment before he fell asleep again. Without a look in her direction, Leon carried the second boy into her bedroom. She leaned back against the sink.

Leon walked out of the kitchen. "Night, Belle."

"Goodnight." The man she had married retreated to his own room. Belle sighed and dimmed the lantern. The weak glow of light pierced her bedroom and fell over the curled forms of her boys beneath the quilt. As she put on her nightgown, the jaunty music of the fiddle and banjo spun in her head. She extinguished the flame and crawled into bed.

The soft wings of her children's breath fluttered on either side. Tonight was the best night she'd had since moving to Dry Run. The memory of Leon's lips against her neck made her skin tingle again.

She counted sheep. She tried cows. It wasn't until Belle had planned next year's garden and inventoried from memory all the canned goods remaining in the cellar that she finally fell asleep.

The door slammed and footfalls raced through the front room. The heady smell of yeast spun through the kitchen as Belle punched the dough with her fist. Amos skidded into the kitchen, his face blanched with fear.

"What's the matter?"

"It's—it's—" He huffed, struggling to catch his breath. "Jacob. We can't—find him."

Belle abandoned the mound of dough, her hand still sticky, and rushed to Amos. She knelt in front of him, grasping his shoulders. "Tell me everything."

"We were playing down by the creek—"

Her fingers dug into Amos's shoulder. "Teddy and Jacob aren't allowed down there without your father or me."

"It was Sam's idea." Tears trickled down the boy's face. "I told him you wouldn't like us down there with the boys."

Sam. "Show me where you went." Belle's jaw set. "Now!"

Outside a gust whipped around the house. The wind lifted her hair and wrapped her dress around her legs like a flag around a pole. Dirt saturated the air. Belle's stomach flipped, contorted like the cow with a prolapsed uterus.

289

Her grandfather had to push it back inside the heifer. Her father had waited with a needle to sew the cow shut.

Halfway down the drive, Sam and Teddy appeared on the road. Belle ran to meet them. Teddy was crying and Sam avoided her eyes. Belle grabbed his shoulders and shook.

"What have you done? Where's Jacob?"

"Dunno. We were playing in the trees, and the next thing I knew he was gone."

"We lost 'im, Mama." Teddy sobbed into her skirt.

Amos caught up with her.

"Amos, you go to the Hanks. Tell them to get your father. He's at the hardware store in town. Tell Shikoba to meet us at the creek. Hurry!" Amos took off, kicking up dust as he ran.

"Sam, take me where you were last playing." Belle picked up Teddy. "Hurry. I'll catch up."

Two bare trees towered along the ditch, their twisted arms and jointed fingers waving through a cloud of dirt. Sediment thickened the air and muted their footsteps. Farther down the road, the wind lessened and cattle could be seen browsing in the corn stubble of a harvested field. Teddy bounced in her arms, her lungs burned, but still she ran. Oh God, help me find him.

By the time they reached the creek, they were both out of breath. "Where was the last place you saw him? Think, Sam!"

Sam's expression went blank. He looked oddly about. "There, I think I saw him there." He pointed at a fallen tree near the bank.

The wind relinquished its bellowing breath. For a moment, gusts whimpered to a breeze. She set Teddy down. "Don't move, do you hear me?" She pivoted to Sam. "What were you doing? Tell me."

Sam stared at his feet. "Playin' hide 'n' seek."

"How dare you!" Belle slapped the boy. "Just because you hate me." A tear rolled down Sam's cheek. Teddy began sobbing.

"Jacob," she shouted and spun in a circle. The thick woods closed in around them. "It's Mommy! Jacob, where are you?" She took a step and faltered, not knowing where to begin. Panic overtook her, and she thought she'd suffocate. At last, she gasped and sucked in air. Her hands encircled her mouth. "Ja-cob!"

A firm hand settled on her shoulder. "Shikoba, thank God." Amos stood close behind. Belle rattled off the situation as she understood it. "How will we find him in all these trees?"

"You look to the west, I'll look to the north," Shikoba said. "Sam, you stay with me. Keep up, you hear?" She looked at Belle. "You keep Teddy with you at all times. Amos will stay and show the men where we went. They'll be here soon." She squeezed Belle's hand. "Don't panic. If we're going to find him, you have to keep your head."

Belle nodded at the outrageous request. She shouted for Jacob, tugging on Teddy's hand, waiting for him to navigate fallen branches and trunks. That proved too slow, so she scooped him into her arms. "Momma needs you to be a big boy and not cry. Can you do that?" Teddy nodded and stuck his thumb in his mouth.

"Jacob! It's Mommy. Yell if you can hear me."

Shikoba's shouts echoed in the distance. Time was against them. They needed the men to help search. From the corner of her eye, she caught a coyote running through the trees, its bushy tail flowing in retreat. In a moment, the wild creature vanished. Oh, God. Black bears, panthers, or coyotes would find a little boy easy prey. Oh God, please, no.

Still carrying Teddy, Belle's arms burned as she scrambled up the riverbank and continued for a quarter of a mile. The trees opened into a meadow with stiff grasses shivering in the breeze. To her horror, a pond rippled in the center despite the dry season. Tall amber grasses bordered the water like a compound fence.

A horrible image came to mind. An illustration in a book in the Fairlane's parlor held a copy of the painting, Ophelia, based on Shakespeare's Hamlet. Ophelia floated in the stream, singing before she drowned, flowers in hand, her hair afloat like seaweed, and eyes staring as if she were already dead. A sob erupted in Belle's throat.

Despite the threat of deadly water moccasins, Belle waded through the marshy mud. Water bugs stippled the water's surface as they lighted on stagnant water. She guessed the pond was no deeper than a foot, yet twelve inches was sufficient for a two-year-old to drown. At the far end of the pond, something skimmed the water, weaving side to side. Not knowing what kind of snake swam there, Belle turned back to solid ground.

Her mind muddied as murky as the swamp. Where should she look next? North of the swamp, the bodark grew so thick that only bear and other wild creatures dared its thorny acres. Should she search the road? Jacob may have come out onto the road and followed it. The more she calculated the more uncertain she was where to look. Unable to think clearly, she retraced her steps, hoping the men had arrived.

Halfway back to the creek, Shikoba met her. "They found him! They found Jacob."

"Is he okay?" Belle set Teddy down. "Is he hurt?"

"He's fine. A little dirty but fine. The men found him sitting on a rock farther east from where we started." Belle fell to her knees and buried her face in her hands. Shikoba knelt and wrapped her arms around her.

They walked back to meet the men. Cigarette smoke drifted on the air, and the cab of a truck came into sight through the trees. The men leaned against Leon's car, smoking cigarettes. Sam stood farther back, kicking rocks. There was no sign of Jacob.

Belle ran up to them. "Where is he?"

Leon held her shoulders and looked into her eyes. "He's fine, Belle. He's sleeping in the backseat."

She broke away, swung the door open, and reached for her baby. Jacob's eyes opened and he smiled. Belle rocked him back and forth, silent tears drenching her face. Shikoba leaned in and stroked Jacob's hair. "Thank you, Shikoba. Thank your husband."

Belle stomped up to Leon. "Let's go home."

He turned from talking to Jed, still smiling about something the man had said.

"Now."

Leon's smile faded. His jaw clenched as he turned to Jed and Shikoba. "Thanks for your help, folks."

Belle sat in the front and stared straight ahead. A small hand reached from the backseat and patted her shoulder. She said nothing to Amos. After a moment, he withdrew his hand. They drove home in silence.

Belle ushered her boys into the bedroom and shut the door. Her mind was made up. She'd pack tomorrow.

Chapter 39

FROM THE OPEN DOOR, BELLE waved down Leon. He braked and unrolled the window. A silent week had passed since the frantic search for Jacob.

"Sam forgot his lunch." She hurried to the Plymouth and handed the paper sack to Leon. "I suppose this is it." She looked into his brown eyes and shoved hands into her apron pockets.

Leon stared over the car hood, his face rigid, jaw clenched. "Hope you find what you're looking for."

She struggled for the right words. "I wish the best for you and your boys."

Leon looked over his shoulder and shoved the car in reverse. She stood on the stoop and watched a raven land on a fencepost. It was over.

Shikoba would arrive soon and drive them to the bus station in McAlester. Five days earlier, Belle informed Leon of her decision. All the children had been told. She prided herself on the civil way she handled the situation.

A job as kitchen help awaited her at the Choctaw-Chickasaw Sanatorium in Talihina, a lesser job than before but a job nevertheless. They would survive by the "skin of her teeth" as the saying went. She hated the fact that another woman would be hired to watch her boys, but Belle wouldn't risk her children's lives any longer. The terrifying incident with Jacob had decided it.

Shikoba pulled up in her old Buick, sadness stretched over her face. Did Belle detect a hint of criticism, or was it her imagination? Shikoba didn't have children. She didn't know what it was like to protect your children at all costs.

They hugged on the front stoop.

"I'm going to miss you," Belle said.

Shikoba followed her inside the farmhouse. The odor of that morning's bacon and eggs hung on the air. In the middle of the front room, the boys played with wooden animals Leon had carved for them last month.

"Time to go, boys."

Teddy glanced up. The look in his eyes confirmed his reluctance to leave.

A vehicle engine rumbled outside. She opened the door, surprised to see Lilith and her husband step from their truck. Leon's car raced close behind, dust flying up the lane. Her first thought was the family had come to persuade her to stay, but their faces told another story.

"Lilith, what's wrong?"

"Sam," she said. "He never made it to class."

Leon rushed up to Belle. "Have you seen Sam?" Amos trailed behind, his shoulders drooping. His chin trembled.

"Not since this morning," she said. "I saw the boys walking down the lane to meet the Fultons' car as usual."

"Amos last saw Sam outside on the playground talking to friends."

"I thought he went inside when the bell rang," Amos said. "I never saw him leave."

"Bill, you and Lilith search along the creek," Leon ordered. "Amos, you remain inside. Don't take one step from this building. Stay here in case Sam returns to the house."

Shikoba glanced at Belle.

"We'll help, Leon," Belle said. "Amos, you watch the boys. Don't let them leave the house." She trusted the boy unlike his errant brother.

Leon narrowed his eyes. "What about your bus?"

"It can wait. I'll catch another one," she said. "Where should we start?"

"I'll comb the bodarks to the north," Shikoba piped up. "I know the game trails. You go with Leon."

Belle saw through her thinly veiled plan, but she couldn't worry about that now. Sam was their first priority. Though he had made her life miserable, he was still a young boy.

Leon frowned but didn't argue. "We'll look to the south. Lilith sent word for a family search to the east." He turned towards the car. Everyone took off,

Shikoba on foot, Lilith and her husband by truck, and Leon and Belle in the Plymouth headed to town.

Belle glanced at Leon. She understood the fear etched on his face.

"If Sam ditched school, there're two directions he might take—west following the creek that leads to our place or south of town where his cousins live."

Belle nodded, avoiding conversation. Leon's head must be on fire, grasping for routes Sam might have taken. Poor Leon. Despite everything that transpired between them, he was a good father.

They drove down Main Street, turned onto a side street, and headed south from the school. A half mile from town, Leon parked the Plymouth by the side of the road. He flew from the car, and Belle slammed the car door in her hurry to catch up with him. He crossed the ditch and looked back. "You're not dressed for this."

"Clothes can be replaced," she said, curtly. Her long coat was the only one she owned, the dress one of two garments fit for church, but a child's life was at stake.

He shrugged. "It's your call." He headed for the woods, and she followed, weeds snagging her thick stockings. Good thing she knew Anne Johnson and Nurse Braxton because she'd look like a hobo by the time she made it to Talihina.

"Sam!" Leon's deep voice resounded over the field. "Shout if you can hear me."

Tears welled in Belle's eyes. Nothing was worse than the fear of losing a child. Leon's stomach must be in knots, his heart beating in his throat. Men were good at holding in emotion, but she saw the fear in Leon's clenched jaw and the panic in his eyes.

They followed a cattle path that wound through a bank of trees and came out onto an empty pasture. Leon shaded his eyes and scouted the opening. Belle turned up the collar of her coat against the breeze. Leon had left his coat in the car. She thought of going back to retrieve it but knew she'd never catch up with him again.

"S-a-m! Come out where I can see you." Leon paused. They waited a moment, greeted only by the wind, and resumed walking. A thick grove of hedge apple bordered the far side of the field.

Leon pointed. "The creek flows behind those woods." He glanced at her clothes again.

"Never mind. I grew up around those thorny trees." Belle trudged ahead without another word.

Leon passed her in a few strides. "We're close to Anna's place. I remember a tree fort somewhere around here that they built for the kids. Maybe he's holed up there."

Once in the trees, Leon motioned Belle to the left, and he searched to the right. "The tree fort is about nine feet high." He gestured with his arm above his head. "Whistle or shout out if you locate it."

The dense trees broke the wind. Clouds covered the sun, and the woods became gloomy. She looked back but there was no sign of Leon. Belle continued searching. Thoughts of panthers lurking in the woods made her heart race. She shook her head. She couldn't afford to think about wild creatures at a time like this. The moldy scent of autumn lifted from the woods, the crunch of dry leaves exploding beneath her feet.

She paused and cupped her hands around her mouth. "Sam! Are you out here?" The swish of treetops murmured in return. That was when she spotted something ahead high in the leafless canopy.

"Oh, God."

A dark form swung from a limb outside the crude tree house. A figure the size of a young boy. "Oh please, God, no."

Leon didn't deserve this. He'd been nothing but good to her and her boys. He'd treated her fairly even when he realized theirs would never be a true marriage.

Stumbling through the underbrush, Belle covered her mouth and moaned. As she drew near, she forced herself to look up at the body swaying in the wind. Her hand flew to her stomach.

A soiled canvas tarp flapped in the wind. Belle closed her eyes in relief, her hands trembling.

"Sam! Are you up there?" There was no reply. She had to look inside the tree fort and check for any sign of recent occupation. Leon would want to know that much. Belle placed her shoe on the bottom rung and climbed the boards nailed to the trunk. She propped her elbows on the platform of the fort and peered inside. A wooden stool. Curled yellow papers. An empty Mason jar. Spider webs. A heap of tattered cloth. Prepared to descend the tree, she measured the distance to the nearest rung when a scuffle sounded in the corner. Belle screamed.

She scampered down the ladder. Halfway down, a voice called, "It's me, Belle." She froze with one foot midair as Sam's dirty face peered down.

"We've been searching all over for you," she said. "Your father's worried sick about you."

Sam's eyebrows crinkled together. "You're still here?"

"I'm here, aren't I?" Belle descended the last few rungs. "Git down here, young man."

Sam pressed his lips into a pout. "Not if you're gonna give me a lickin'."

"I'll leave that to your father." She stood with feet apart, elbows flared at her waist.

He turned around and descended the crude ladder. Sam stood before her and hung his head.

"What do you have to say for yourself young man?"

Tears rolled down his cheeks, carving streams through a film of dirt. "I made you leave. It's my fault."

What could she say to that? It was the truth. Belle stood silent for a few seconds. "I'm sorry you never liked me. I tried my best."

"I knew you'd never stay. You're leavin' just like my ma."

Of course. Why hadn't she seen it earlier? He was afraid she was a temporary situation. She couldn't blame him. Even a child could see the marriage wasn't what it should be. Belle stooped to one knee and wiped his cheeks. All at once, his arms wrapped around her neck, and he sobbed.

"Oh, Sam," she whispered. "Hush, child. It's my fault, too." She cried along with the wayward boy. "It's okay." She kissed his cheek. "Everything's going to be all right." Belle rocked the boy as she held him.

Leaves crunched behind them. Leon stood twenty feet away, his head tilted as if he glimpsed a doe with a newborn fawn. "Pa," Sam said. "Belle found me." She released the boy.

"I see that, son."

Sam ran into his father's arms. Leon closed his eyes and clutched his son to his chest.

The wind picked up, and dark clouds scuttled across the heavens.

Leon studied the sky. "We best be getting home." Belle followed as they picked their way through the thick underbrush. Once in the open field, Leon paused and looked back. He held out his hand and Belle took it. The three hurried through the barren field, their heads lowered against the wind.

In the car, Sam fell asleep between them, exhausted after his daring escape. Leon glanced at Belle and returned his eyes to the road. In her mind, she had already arranged the little staff cottage in Talihina for the three of them, just her and her two boys. The Ford bounced over a pothole, and Sam rolled against her shoulder. Belle pictured herself arriving at the cottage at the end of the day with Teddy and Jacob. In the summer, they'd picnic in the Quachita Mountains. She'd share stories about their Comanche roots. Let her boys know there were still medicine women who saw things the rest of them couldn't possibly know. Belle looked forward to the chance to be in charge of her life once again.

The car crested a rise. A white-tail doe leaped from the ditch and bounded across the road. Leon braked hard. He stretched his arm across Sam and Belle to restrain them from impact with the windshield. As the car idled, the deer soared over a barbwire fence.

Belle watched the beautiful creature, so wild and wary, traits that kept the animal safe.

Leon reached for Belle's hand, his palm warm, his hand strong.

The bear won't lie down with a buck, but a doe will lie down with a lion.

Leon. Lion.

She swung her head in surprise, and their eyes met. Life was changing again. Belle gazed out the windshield and smiled. Shikoba was right. The doe would lie down with the lion after all.

Acknowledgments

Thanks to Dorothy Tahsuda, who was a gracious early reader of my manuscript. My wonderful critique groups were invaluable as they gave feedback on my later drafts. Thanks to Rebecca Carpenter, Patti Hill, Pam Larson, and Karen McKee for their careful eyes and wise suggestions. I'll always be grateful to Muriel Morley, who opened my eyes to the art and craft of writing. She shared her knowledge with such enthusiasm and taught me to pass it on.

Dear Reader,

I hope you have enjoyed my story. As a writer, creating this unique perspective of the Depression as seen through Belle's eyes proved to be a grand adventure. Historical fiction remains a wonderful way to experience history on a personal level and makes the extensive research required by the author well worth the time and energy. If you liked (4 to 5 stars) Dry Run, Oklahoma, please leave a review on amazon.com or barnesandnoble.com so others will be encouraged to read this story (and the author encouraged to write more!) There you will also find other titles I have written.

Happy reading,
Lucinda Stein

CPSIA information can be obtained
at www.ICGtesting.com
Printed in the USA
LVHW111359021118
595750LV00001B/261/P